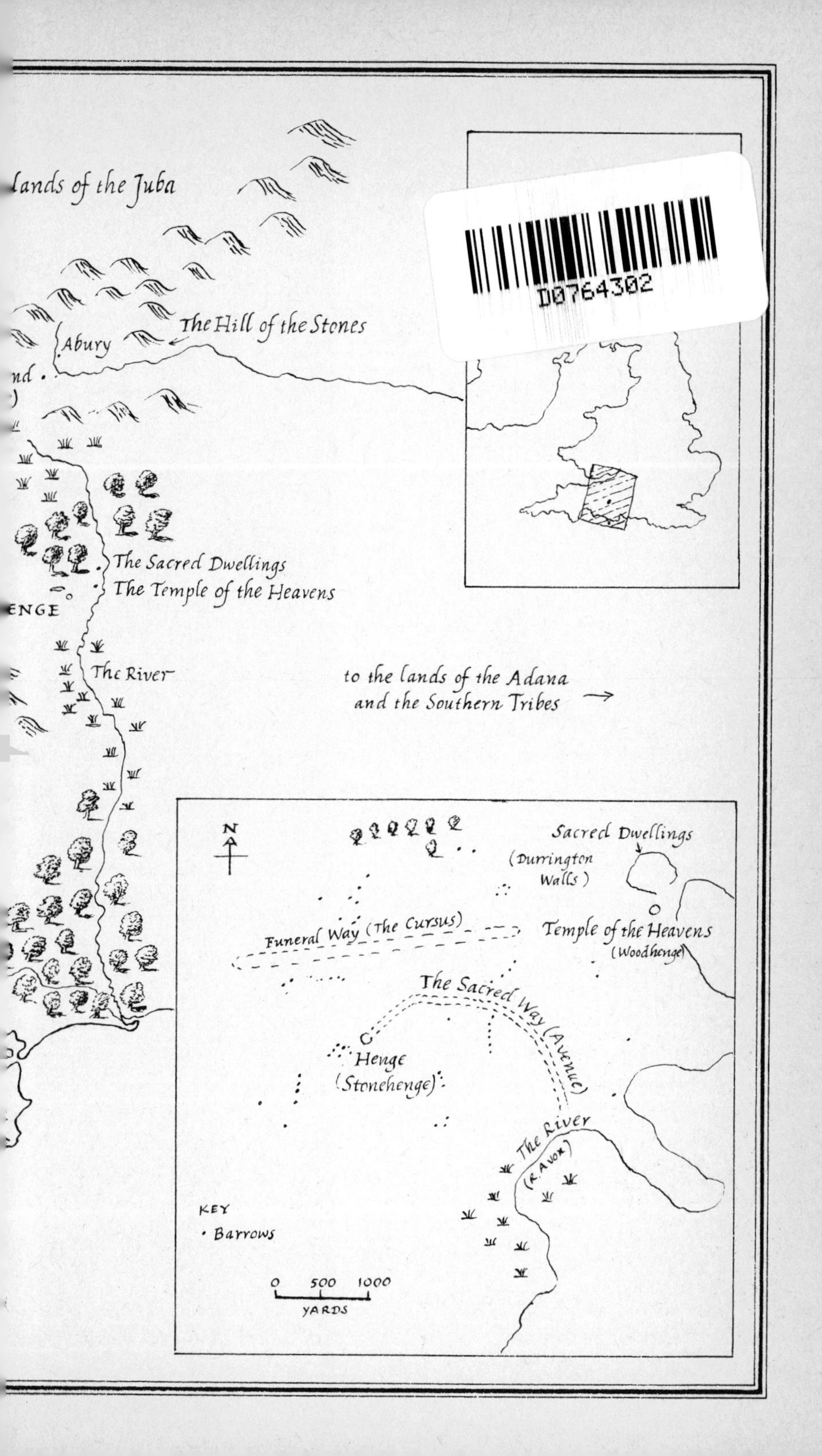
lands of the Juba
The Hill of the Stones
Abury
The Sacred Dwellings
The Temple of the Heavens
ENGE
The River
to the lands of the Adana
and the Southern Tribes
N
Sacred Dwellings
(Durrington Walls)
Temple of the Heavens
(Woodhenge)
Funeral Way (The Cursus)
The Sacred Way (Avenue)
Henge
(Stonehenge)
The River
(R. Avon)
KEY
• Barrows
0 500 1000
YARDS

# THE PRIESTESS OF HENGE

*By the same Author*

THE CRANBORNE CHASE

# THE PRIESTESS OF HENGE

A novel

## David Burnett

'The subject of antiquities must be drawn out with such strong lines of verisimilitude, and represented in so lively colours, that the reader in effect sees them as in their first ages: And either brings them down to modern times, or raises himself, in the scale of time, as if he lived when they were made.'

William Stukeley, *Stonehenge* 1740

HAMISH HAMILTON LONDON

First published in Great Britain 1982
by Hamish Hamilton Ltd
Garden House 57–59 Long Acre London WC2E9JZ



*British Library Cataloguing in Publication Data*

Burnett, David
The priestess of Henge
I. Title
823'.914[F] PR6052.U/
ISBN 0-241-10753-9

Photoset by Rowland Phototypesetting Ltd
Bury St Edmunds, Suffolk
Printed in Great Britain by St. Edmundsbury Press
Bury St Edmunds, Suffolk

# *Contents*

To Sarah

# List of Characters

| | |
|---|---|
| KAI | A healer, or shaman |
| MORRIGEN | Of the Cunei tribe |
| MORRIGEN'S MOTHER | |
| SERAPHA | The Moon Goddess |
| BALA | The Sun God |
| HYRA | Son of a Cunei chieftain |
| CERUDUC | A Cunei warrior |
| RALLA<br>AELINA | Novices in the Temple |
| FRAM | A seer of Bala |
| TEINA | Servant to the novices |
| ATIUS | A merchant |
| UBA | A Cunei village elder |
| TUAH | An old rainmaker |
| CAEDOR | A Cunei villager |
| ISHTAR | The High Priestess, a Dobuni |
| LYLA | Sister of Ceruduc |
| LEOID | A Dobuni seer |
| ZARXUS | A Dobuni chieftain |
| CRONUS | Hyra's father |
| RHIONAN<br>KIRSTEN | Hyra's sisters |
| ORTUS | Lord of the Rites |
| THARAH | A Cunei chieftain |
| TARXIEN | Cronus's steward |
| ELMEK | An old pedlar |
| Young CRONUS | Son of Hyra and Lyla |
| ARTUS | A shaman |
| NAXOS | A young seer |

| | |
|---|---|
| SALLERNO | A widow in Epius (Malta) |
| TYRUS | Son of Morrigen and Ceruduc |
| Young KIRSTEN | Daughter of Hyra and Lyla |
| AEDUM | A chieftain |
| SHAEDON | A villager |
| SHALLON | A mute acrobat |

# PROLOGUE

'. . . to Stonehenge, over the Plain and some great hills, even to fright us. Come thither, and find them as prodigious as any tales I ever heard of them, and worth this journey to see. God knows what their use was! they are hard to tell, but yet may be told.'

SAMUEL PEPY'S, *Diary*, June 1668

# PROLOGUE

The procession moved slowly through the darkness, led by the healer Kai. Only stunted trees and a distant burial tomb broke the emptiness. All else was moonlight and shadow, the rolling wind-swept Plain.

Kai was an old man now, with greying hair and a lugubrious face. Squirrel skins hung from his waist. Above his head rose the forked antlers of the stag that had been driven into the nets during the Harvest Hunt. The men and women from the westernmost villages in the lands of the Cunei walked behind their shaman. Oxen hauling pole-sledges laden with tents and cooking pots surrounded them. Some were chanting the praises of the Goddess Serapha. In their wake, their faces blanched by the dust, were an old woman and her daughter, Morrigen.

The herdsmen's torches streamed sparks as the procession climbed the downland. The wind gusted, chill with autumn. It seemed to steer their steps across the scrub, for wailing and the sound of drums accompanied it. In answer a solitary whistle shrilled its counterpoint from near the front of the procession. Many of the women started swaying in time to its music, their children and the babies strapped to their backs forgotten. Morrigen's heart quickened with fear when she heard the drums. But she did not dance, nor did she draw any closer to her mother. The ties that united them served also to keep them apart.

Human bones hung from the old woman's belt. Age had shrivelled her cheeks and given her body its stoop. Her eyes were bloodshot from the thrust of childbirth. Moonlight pencilled shadows in the lines on her brow and made her toothless mouth seem as dark and deep as a cave. Her voice was without tenderness, and when she spoke it sounded harsh and embittered, like the yap of a dog that barks without reason.

'Stop quaking, child! You're a fifteen-year-old woman now,

not a baby in its cradle. By dawn tomorrow you'll have been sold, married and robbed of your maidenhood.'

Morrigen stumbled at her mother's push, then lifted her gaze to the fires that straddled the horizon. For a moment her green eyes seemed to brighten and become luminescent, supplying the strength to fight back.

'Father made you promise to let me do as I wish,' she answered. 'I don't want to marry. You've no right to go back on your word.'

'Your father's dead. I'll do as I please. I was brought here, and so was my mother. Ever since our forefathers first farmed these hills the Cunei have gone to the Maiden Lines at Henge when old enough to marry. So will you.'

The old woman fell silent. The herdsmen had started binding ivy round the horns of their oxen. Watching them, memory snared her, carrying her back to the day her own parents had brought her to the temple, a virgin worth a flock of milking ewes to any man who hoped to make her his wife. Remembrance made her maudlin. Her eyes misted as she fumbled for one of the smooth weathered bones hanging from her waist.

'Pretty as hawthorn blossom I was then,' she said finally, lifting the bone to her lips. 'But it wasn't enough. Your father wanted sons to help till the fields, daughters who would add to his flocks.' She snorted, mocking her own misfortune. 'And all I bore him were two stillborn sons and a seven-month runt I'm now shamed into selling for offal.'

Morrigen was used to her mother's moods; the self-pity that preceded malice, the admission of failure blamed on the failings of others. Contempt sharpened her answer.

'So must I be branded as well and sold to the first swineherd who can spare a hog?'

The old woman started cackling, enjoying her daughter's anger. 'Stop boasting, child! Only a blind man or a fool would sell a live pig for the pleasure of marrying you. A set of trotters or a basin of tallow is the most I'll get for you.'

'At least you'll be rid of me!'

'And for the pleasure of that I'd take last summer's straw. It would still be a bargain.'

Helpless against such taunts, Morrigen hid her shame behind the copper mane of her hair. It was knotted and thick with mud, and fell tousled and unkempt across her shoulders, hiding the almost imperceptible swell of her breasts. She glanced down at the blood and dung that caked her robes. The hides were torn and beginning to rot. Bare feet and thin, bruised legs poked from beneath the hem.

Her mother must have sensed her thoughts, for suddenly she said, 'What you wear doesn't matter. You're an outcast. We both are. Those who bear no sons have been cursed by the Gods.'

'But I've yet to wed. Father said . . .'

'Your father was a fool.'

Morrigen did not answer. Her earliest memories were of conflict and argument, the incessant abuse that had goaded her father to violence. But he had sheltered her from her mother's temper and his death during the previous winter had seemed final proof of her wretchedness. She was a brooding, reclusive child. Without him she felt robbed of her only ally in the village. Scorned and unloved, ignored by her contemporaries, she had spent the summer plucking fowl and scraping fat from cattlehide outside the hovel to which birth had condemned her.

Before departing for Henge, she had left it and walked the stubble for the final time, halting beside the stream that edged the fields. Its waters had returned her reflection: florid lips, gaunt face grown blemished by sores on a diet of meat leavings and chaff bread, thin arms burnt nut-brown by the sun. Despising what she saw, unable to exorcize the dreams that had fed on her loneliness, she had decided that she bore a taint no waters would wash away; that if cursed, then that curse would always remain part of her and might even shape her future. This knowledge had frightened her, making her toss a stone into the stream and watch the spread of its ripples, drowning her image.

Yet now, as she hurried on through the darkness, her fear gave way to a strange and unfamiliar sense of exhilaration, even excitement. In the last few moments the fires above the horizon had blossomed into colour. Smoke scented the breeze. The drums had grown louder and when the wind shifted their echo lingered on as a dull ache in her heart. On instruction from the elders, the cattle and sheep were herded, dogs snapping at the heels of the stragglers. Oxen lowed as their drovers circled their eyes and nostrils with chalk. New torches were lit from the stumps of the old. In their light Morrigen saw a cluster of humped earthen burial tombs rise above the scrub that stretched away on either side of the procession. Reminded of her father, she reached out towards her mother's waist and the bones that had once held his flesh.

The old woman pushed her aside and spat into the dust. 'Forget him,' she snapped. 'He's dead. He may not have sired sons or been buried in the family tomb, but the Gods will think no less of him for having been laid to rest on the racks.'

Morrigen turned away. The mortuary racks stood on the edge of the village. Even before the last of the snow had finally melted his corpse had been picked clean by carrion. Now all that remained of his gentleness were the few bleached bones clattering one against the next in time to her mother's steps.

She retreated from her memories, glancing up at the moon as its face slid free of cloud. It was full and fat and replete with the harvest. Seeing it now, high over Henge, something of its sanctity seemed to reach down and touch her. For to Morrigen, as to all Cunei, it was not merely a source of light that eternally waxed and waned, but Serapha, the Moon Goddess who rose out of the earth at dusk and returned to it at dawn. Serapha, the source of the fertility she was presumed to lack, the giver of life and guardian of the dead without whom the world would be as barren as her mother's womb.

The procession halted. Kai turned to face it. Moonlight silhouetted his flapping beard and uplifted arms, the antlers sprouting from his head. To Morrigen he seemed to link both sky and earth, becoming the human bridge between the two worlds over which Serapha held dominion.

'We left our homes when the moon was new!' he cried, raising his voice against the din of the cattle. 'Tonight it's full and the sacred stones of Henge will soon be in sight. Try not to forget that we come to them as free-born Cunei who want to celebrate the Harvest Rites, the birth of winter and mourn summer's passing. To our chieftains we bring gifts of the livestock that'll have to be slaughtered before the days shorten and wolves attack the herds. Speak to them of your fears. Consult the shamans and seers – if there are any you trust. Offer sacrifices to Serapha in the hope that your villages will be spared the hardships of winter and the Toil of the Stones. Lament the corn spirits killed by the sickles of the reapers during harvest. But remember, be wary. The Cunei are a subject tribe and those who anger our masters risk never seeing their homes again.' Kai paused and turned gravely to the women. 'It's to you I now speak, the unwed maids who have made this journey to take their place in the Maiden Lines.'

The shaman beckoned them forward. Morrigen hesitated, then joined the others. Those who knew her giggled and moved away, leaving her isolated and friendless. She ignored them. Experience had taught her that if she did not move or attract attention to herself her presence was soon forgotten. At such moments she believed herself to be invisible, much like a hunted animal.

Kai glanced at each of them. Reaching Morrigen the glance became a stare that made her blush and lower her head: the trick had failed her. In one hand he held a stick of charcoal, in the other some small sheaves of corn that had been twisted into spirals.

'Tonight,' he said quietly, 'the men will join you and choose their wives as you stand in the Maiden Lines. Before dawn most of you will be married. You'll have lost your maidenhood and become women. Some of you will be with child. It is then that the Goddess will plant the spirit of the corn in your wombs. For winter approaches and the corn spirits must be cared for and warmed until spring. It is a sacred Rite. Guard it well and the Gods will reward you with the sons and daughters you want.'

The wind slapped at Morrigen's hair and brought a shiver to her cheeks. She felt humbled, chastened. Soon she would be Serapha's servant. Perhaps motherhood would give purpose to her life, help banish the past?

Kai ushered one of the girls forward and brushed her face with a sheaf. 'Here is the Goddess Serapha, mother of all men, which you, when with child, must scatter over the fields when they're next sown.' He gave it to her, then marked her cheeks with the charcoal. The older women circled their daughters and began pounding the turf with their feet.

Morrigen stood motionless whilst Kai branded her face with the black spirals that symbolized her maidenhood.

'You're afraid,' he said.

She shook her head.

He smiled. 'It's not something to be ashamed of.' Abuse and beatings had sucked the youth from her eyes. The irises had the hard translucent green of pieces of jade, so that although they met his gaze he could read no trace of her thoughts. 'We're born alone and die alone,' he said softly. 'But need others whilst we live. It's a lesson you've yet to learn. The Goddess can strengthen you, but only by taking a husband can you bear children and make amends for your mother's barrenness.'

'And if I fail?'

'Doubt won't spawn sons. I've watched you since your father's death. You're a strange child. The unloved yearn for love but find it hard to give. The outcast turns aside from friendship. In some ways we're the same. You want to deny the instincts of your own body. As a shaman, I must leave mine in order to shepherd the dead into the Underworld and pursue the wandering souls of the sick. I'm a healer, you are scarred. We've both known solitude and suffering.'

Until now Morrigen had thought Kai immune to the weaknesses that shaped others. As healer he had always seemed distant and aloof, an austere almost mystical figure who left his dwelling only to gather herbs or consult with the soothsayers for portents of contagion.

'Words won't change me,' she said harshly, still resisting his sympathy. 'We both know that no one will marry me.'

He lifted her chin, his dry spindly fingers rasping against the skin. 'Cattle die, kinsmen die. You and I will die. Only one thing is immortal, the reputation we leave behind us. You alone know what you are. You must learn to live with that knowledge, be it of good or evil. You think yourself blemished, already spurned. But the years may prove you wrong. Even the dog-rose needs time to flower.'

For an instant Morrigen longed to be comforted by his embrace. She would confess her fears, he would assuage them and make her whole again. But she remained silent, fixing him with a gaze so empty of expression that Kai felt the touch of her coldness and knew that his words had been wasted. He ordered the procession to move on. The dancing ceased. The girls rejoined their families. Oxen and sheep flowed past Morrigen as she fought back the impulse to run after Kai. Her mother checked it, brutally jerking her to one side.

'Pay no attention to him!' she cried. 'He once told me I bore a curse only you could lift. You! The daughter who made me cry out at the pain for a night and a day when you were born.'

'At least I lived!' retorted Morrigen.

Suddenly she perceived that it was the memory of that pain, and the travail caused by the miscarriage of two sons, that had caused her mother to hate her. Kai's words returned, bringing with them the understanding that the years of bickering had suppressed. But it was too late for sympathy. She freed herself from her mother's grip, pushing her way between the lines of oxen to where darkness and moonlight married the night . . .

'We're there! Look!'

Morrigen spun as she heard the herdsman's shout. The procession disintegrated. The villagers began running, abandoning both children and livestock. Morrigen's dread of all that lay ahead made her hesitate before giving chase, but when she did so her mind shed its confusion with every step. She began scrambling up a slope. Smoke tasted sharp in her throat. Drums filled her head. She stumbled, straightened, hurried on . . .

A new world opened up in front of her. Awe-struck, half believing she had reached the kingdom of the Gods, she dropped to her haunches and stared blindly about her. For a moment the glare of the fires drowned shape and shadow, even their own dazzle. Tents, Plain and sky, all fused and became one. Then she found focus, glimpsed the swirl of dancers, the circular temple, the immense scarlet eye that had been painted on the stone standing high in its centre. She began crying. The month-long journey through forest and swamp was over. They had reached Henge. She lifted her gaze to it, seeing not stones but an abstraction, the living soul of the Cunei raised by her ancestors for the worship of the Goddess Serapha.

She rose and began walking again, drawn towards it by an instinct she could neither comprehend nor evade. The noise made thought impossible. Images formed, then as quickly faded: the Plain decked in tents, the blurred shape of the herds grazing the surrounding downland, the crowds massed outside the temple.

Kai began chanting the Song of the Dead as the procession reassembled and moved on. Some of the women took off their clothes, daubing their bodies with circles of chalk so that they, like the stones, would become part of the Goddess and enriched by her fertility. The wind scattered their robes and drove them before it with the dust like fallen leaves. The sheep bolted, panic-stricken by the noise, and stood bunched in the darkness, bewildered eyes mirroring fire-light. Dogs howled and children screamed. Oxen had to be whipped into movement. The drums were so loud that it seemed as if their rhythms were emanating from the earth itself.

Morrigen felt their tremor as she quickened pace and pushed her way towards the front of the procession. Henge vanished, reappeared. She glimpsed the Village of the Shamans, their coloured tents encircling the temple as if clamped to it like the limpets she had gathered as a child. Torches lit its precincts, showing her a circular bank, a few stones standing isolated on its perimeter, and an unfinished double circle of stones that had been raised round its centre. The first she had seen dwarfed its neighbours, but even the smallest was as tall as a man; all had been garlanded with branches and many bore red-ochre lips and eyes of chalk.

Kai drew alongside her. Ever since his initiation as a shaman he had come to Henge to attend the Rites. But what once he had accepted as being the will of the Gods now made him angry and ashamed.

'Faith and muscle started what you see,' he shouted. 'Fear completes it.'

Morrigen was too excited to note his bitterness. 'Are those the shamans?' she cried, pointing to the lines of dancers circling the stones.

Kai nodded. 'The women dancing with them are the priestesses of Bala, the Sun God who must be coupled with Serapha before dawn.' Anger deepened his voice. 'Don't forget that Henge isn't ours any more. The Dobuni are our masters now and we Cunei have to worship Bala whether we want to or not.'

'The Dobuni may not rule us for ever.'

Kai laughed at her naivety. 'They crossed the Dark Seas and settled on the Plain before my father's father was born. They won't leave now, and we won't shift them. There may not be many of them, but it's they who forge bronze out of copper and control the trading routes that link the tribes. If they wish to turn Henge into a temple to Bala and appoint themselves seers of the Sacred Rites, then so shall it be. It's the same with the temple of Abury* in the lands of the Tan. They're warriors, bred to fight. You and I may curse them, but it'll take more than curses to drive them from the Plain.'

* Avebury, Wiltshire.

Morrigen grinned ruefully. 'Before beginning this journey I knew nothing of what went on outside the village. There's much to learn.'

'The wise remain ignorant. We praise Serapha now, but one day she'll be forgotten. The Dobuni are powerful, so's Bala. No, take a husband and bear him sons, but don't defy the Dobuni. Those who've done so are dead.'

Morrigen frowned at the resignation in Kai's voice. It was as if, she thought, arrival at Henge had marked both the end of her childhood, and its simplicity. Until now her life had been bounded by the hills that looped the village, making it a backwater into which gossip or merchants rarely ventured. Standing on their summit, she could glimpse the Dark Seas to the south or look down on moorland and forest. It was a hostile and mysterious landscape, peopled by demons, sprites and sea-monsters, and she now realized that its character had caged her mind as well as her body.

Since leaving it she had tasted freedom, and, as she gazed out over the sprawling patchwork of tents that dotted the Plain, she felt a longing to indulge that freedom, not end it in a stranger's bed. She tried to dismiss the thought. Beyond the tents and fires, oxen stood tethered or herded into pens, hidden by drifting smoke. A solitary beacon coloured the distant horizon. Torches stabbed the darkness, revealing small groups of tribesfolk wending their way across the scrub as they slowly converged on the temple. Watching them, aware that one might contain the husband she had yet to meet, the longing returned and doubt's first seed was finally sown. She smiled at her foolishness. Excitement must have made her light-headed. She was fifteen, a dowdy fatherless pauper. It was not for her to question the destiny her mother had mapped for her.

Reaching the outlying tents, Kai marked out the site where their own tents were to be pitched. A fire was lit from the sacred pyre burning near the temple entrance. Water-skins were filled, the livestock driven off to graze and regain the weight lost during the trek. The women started unloading the sledges, spilling bedding, pelts and pots in piles across the turf. Poles were placed in the ground and hauled upright to serve as centre-posts for each of the tents. The men began binding lengths of wattle into frames to support the hide roof canopies. As each tent was raised and pegged, Kai entered it to banish the demons and invoke the protection of the Gods.

The old woman ordered her daughter to follow her. She was weeping, one of her husband's bones lay swaddled in a withered hand. 'It was with this arm that he held his bow and cradled you when you were a babe,' she said.

Remorse and self-pity had sapped her hate, the memory of the blows that same arm had dealt her. Morrigen tried to calm her, but she continued sobbing as they retraced their steps through the darkness. Tears washed the dust from her face, leaving as its silt a swirl of broken veins. Morrigen placed an arm round her waist, supporting her weight as they walked.

Reaching the neat heaps of stones that marked the Place of the Dead, they knelt and together scraped a shallow hole in the turf with pieces of flint. The old woman laid the bone to rest, aligning the knuckle towards the rising of the harvest moon. Beside it she placed the worn shaft of an axe and a handful of corn.

'The dead watch over the living,' she murmured. 'If your womb is as empty as mine you'll need your father's help in guarding the corn given to you by Kai. I can do no more for you. But maybe it'll spare you all that I've suffered.'

'Mother.'

'Yes, child.'

Even now they could not look at each other. Morrigen was very still, her mother's tears pitted the soil as they fell.

'Please don't take me to the Maiden Lines.'

'I've no choice. Serapha's will must be done.'

Mother and daughter stared down at the bone, dark against the white of the chalk, all that was left of the man they had once both loved. For an instant they stood locked in an intimacy that made Morrigen long for that love to become theirs, the one legacy they might inherit. She kissed her mother, who sighed and said, 'It's too late, child. Tonight we part. It'll only be chance if we meet again.'

'Can't we do so as friends?' pleaded Morrigen.

The old woman did not answer as she replaced the turf and marked the grave with a small cairn of stones. On its crest she wedged the shell of a cuttle-fish, its oval shape a memorial to the tomb in which his ancestors had been buried.

The moment for reconciliation had passed. Morrigen's shoulders slumped briefly in defeat, then she swept round, feigning indifference, and strode briskly towards the temple.

Suddenly she saw Kai. Accompanied by the other shamans

he was circling the stones in time to the drums, alternately beating the ground with his fists then stretching splayed fingers towards the moon. Many of the shamans wore bull and wolf-masks and she could only distinguish the soothsayers by the snake skins wrapped round their bodies. The rainmakers carried stone maces, some scattered lime as they danced, others were festooned in the strings of shells they used to make wind. She rose to tiptoe, but caught only a fleeting glimpse of the priestesses. Crowds stood thickly on the rim of the surrounding bank. Fires dazzled, stones obstructed, and all but the glistening mica-flecked summit of the central stone disappeared from view when her mother began leading her through the encampment.

Despite her disappointment, her eyes missed nothing as they passed the lines of pedlars displaying their wares. Some stood amongst the season's fruits, baskets of nuts, berries and crab apples. Others squatted in flint waste, knapping and shaping tools. Women haggled. Children slept oblivious to the noise on mounds of lime bast and flax that had been harvested for rope making. Foreign traders from beyond the Dark Seas mingled with Dobuni merchants, swarthy and stockily built, as they bartered mead and copper for cattle. Huntsmen balanced on piles of skins waved boar tusks and bear teeth at her as she passed. One, seeing the charcoal on her cheeks, offered her a set of freshly shed antlers as a charm against the pain of childbirth. She tried to halt, but soon lost sight of him as her mother tugged impatiently at her wrist.

The crowd engulfed them when they reached the temple ditch and tried to climb its inner bank. Morrigen saw little, but gradually the fevered, delirious behaviour of those round her began to infect her mood. The drums' rhythm had the potency of an intoxicant. The day was sacred. Serapha was full and her light shone down, bathing them in her glory. The shamans' dance was one of propitiation, a language of drums, voices and feet that would be heard by the Gods. The naked drummers, their bodies glistening with sweat and their clay instruments pressed between their knees, squatted in a ring in the heart of the temple. As the beat quickened, those watching joined in the dancing. Women shed their clothes and cried out in their ecstasy, the men waved bows and spears.

The old woman began swaying to and fro on her heels, her daughter forgotten. A flat leathery breast spilled through a rip in her robes. Her mouth gaped open, her eyes started rolling. Morrigen waited for a moment, then slipped forward, forcing her way to the brow of the bank.

The temple precincts stretched circular in front of her, allowing her a clear view of the priestesses as they snaked slow and sinuous round the unfinished ring of stones. She stood motionless, bewitched by their dance. None was much older than her and their braided hair hung down over bodies that gleamed with oils. Their only clothing was the hide round their waists and the ravens' feathers tied to their wrists and ankles. She watched them enviously. She had come to Henge to be sold, they to intercede with Bala on behalf of the tribes, to praise and placate the sun at the birth and death of each day. They knew power and comfort. She wore rags, slept on straw amongst swine, would soon be led away, a woman of no worth unless she bred and drudged until too old to do anything but pick fleas from the beasts that shared her bed.

When the dancing ceased one of the shamans was lifted on to the central stone. He stood, then raised a wooden mace whose shaft had been carved with circles and empty eyes in imitation of winter's darkness. The crowd fell silent as he begged the Gods to watch over the tribes during the months ahead and spoke of the coupling that must now take place if the season's cycle was to be reborn. The other shamans joined in, each taking it in turn to list one of their needs: a winter without snow, tempest or sickness; a spring that brought green pastures, the sun's warmth, rivers filled with fish and woods with game.

Silence returned to Henge. Morrigen felt herself shiver as the shaman began tapping his mace against the stone beneath him. The sound was virtually inaudible, but it frightened her, reminded her that what was about to commence was to be done to her before morning.

The drumming resumed, slowly gathering momentum as one of the rainmakers stepped forward. He was dressed as a stag, a human symbol of the autumn rut. Its mask hid his face, skins draped his legs and strips of coloured hide hung from its antlers. His companions started blowing ox-bone whistles to summon up the spirits of their ancestral guardians from the Northern Star. The priestesses began dancing again. They were stately and graceful and each spun on her toes before weaving between the stones. Suddenly, without warning, one broke ranks, tossed aside the last of her robes and advanced toward the rainmaker, standing motionless in front of him as another smeared her limbs with musk and oils.

Her companion retreated, leaving her alone with the rainmaker. She began swaying, simultaneously spiralling upward from the crouch and rotating her head so that it first faced sky and then the earth. Sweat dripped from her face and breasts. She seemed to be forcing herself into trance. Her eyes grew wide and lifeless, only their whites remaining visible. The shaman moved closer, antlers tilted to simulate menace. Cupping her breasts with her hands, she slowly spread her legs and lowered herself to her haunches. The rainmaker parted the skins round his waist, revealing a distended wooden phallus carved into the shape of a spiral. The crowd wailed. The women round Morrigen began imitating the motions of the priestess. The whistles rose an octave, becoming shrill and cacophonous. Suddenly rainmaker and priestess appeared to merge into one. The music ceased, leaving only the tap of the mace from high above them to maintain the rhythm as they acted out a ritual coupling intended to refertilize the earth, now weak after giving birth to the harvest.

There was no passion to their act, but Morrigen trembled as she witnessed its climax. In ritual, she saw reality; the moment that lay ahead of her. Curiosity, apprehension, a longing to put the experience behind her made her turn and push her way through the crowd to where her mother slumped exhausted near the ditch.

'It was to sell me to a husband that you brought me here,' she said. 'I wish it to be done. Now.'

The old woman sneered. 'Eager as ever to part from me are you? Or did watching the priestess make you think that there's pleasures to be found in the flesh? Come, you'll learn the truth soon enough.'

A clawed hand fastened on Morrigen's wrist, pulling her away from the temple. The ground sloped slightly, allowing the two women their first view of the surrounding Plain. Morrigen gazed out in amazement. Three vertical stones stood in line outside the entrance, beyond which ran a broad avenue flanked by parallel banks. Fires charted its course and in the distance, where it receded into night, she glimpsed human shapes bent low against the chalk of the banks.

'The toilers of the stones. Poor devils,' muttered her mother.

Morrigen shaded her eyes against the glare of the torches. The shapes became gangs of men using antler picks and ox-bone spades to dig the ditches from which the banks were being quarried.

The old woman spat her disgust. 'The Dobuni would like us to believe that building the Sacred Way is a Rite in itself, though what's sacred about treating men like beasts I've yet to be told. It's the same with the stones. Even your own father served at the Toil. You were a baby. The village had drawn the shortest tally straw at the Spring Lottery. We had no choice. The elders in a neighbouring village once refused to send men from the hay fields. The Dobuni visited them. Every dwelling was razed. The women were sold, those who resisted were driven into the sea.'

Morrigen peered into the darkness. Torches bobbed and flickered where the Way vanished into a wood. Two lines of men hauling a timber sledge suddenly emerged from the trees. A stone lay lashed to its baulks. One of the toilers was calling the time and she could hear the answering chant of his companions as they slowly dragged it through the night, backs bent double.

'No task could be better named than the Toil,' muttered her mother. 'The stones come from a temple near Abury and it's a twenty day haul over hills and through bogs before they can be floated down river to the start of the Way. Some break loose and crush those hauling them, but you'll see no Dobuni put his hands to the ropes; only we Cunei are fit for that.'

'Can we watch?'

'And let me be cheated of what little I'll get for you?' The sight of the toilers had made the old woman angry. She grasped her daughter's hair and began pulling her through the maze of tents that surrounded the temple. Only when they reached an open space crowded with merchants and tribesmen did her humour return. She began cackling. 'These are the Maiden Lines. From now on you'll still your tongue and only speak when you're spoken to.'

Tears brimmed in Morrigen's eyes as her mother released her. Pine-root torches scented the air and to awake the maidens' fertility sprigs of wych-elm had been strewn over the grass. Her rivals for the unwed men come in search of a wife stood in ranks on either side of her. Despair made her turn away after scanning their faces. All bore the same circles on their cheeks, but many had coloured their hair with henna or weld and some wore freshly scrubbed robes that had been cut low to display their breasts. Wetting her fingers, she tried scraping the dung from her clothes. It was pointless.

'Was there nothing else I could have worn?' she blurted. 'No man will want a wife who still reeks of the byre.'

'Fine feathers won't win you a husband. Stand straight and put a hand to your mane.'

Morrigen untangled the worst of its knots then allowed herself to be propelled into a gap in the line. 'Let him be young,' she pleaded. 'Not lame or close to the grave, or a man with other wives.'

'You'll take who chooses you, and that's an end to it.'

Morrigen brushed away her tears and gazed out over the tents. In the distance she could hear laughter, the muted drone of the drums, the occasional shout of the toilers. She closed her eyes; willing the night to swallow her, spare her the mocking glances of the men moving solemn and attentive in front of her. A sprinkling of Dobuni merchants come to bid for serving-girls mingled with the unwed. The girls stood demure and silent. A few giggled nervously or acted the coquette. Mothers fussed round them, fathers roared their contempt at offers they thought an insult to the blood of their ancestors.

Morrigen froze. A young Cunei was staring at her. He was one of a group sauntering the length of the Lines. Suddenly he parted from his companions. A copper blade glinted against his waist and he was well-dressed in boots and wolf-skin leggings. She tensed, averting her head. The pounding of her heart sharpened into pain.

He touched his brow in homage to her mother. 'Greetings. I am Hyra, son of Cronus, of the villages in the High Vales.'

Morrigen tried to speak but the words died in her throat. She blushed and met his gaze. Kindly eyes set wide on a bearded face stared back at her. He seemed diffident, even shy. Beneath the courtesy she sensed wariness and disquiet.

He smiled. 'I won't harm you.'

The old woman crossed in front of her daughter. 'Cronus is a chieftain. Are you also his heir?'

'It isn't the father who stands here now.'

Morrigen lowered her head as she detected the obsequiousness in her mother's voice and the disapproval in the stranger's reply. But her mother ignored the rebuke, first introducing her, then telling him of her father's death.

Hyra indicated the charcoal on Morrigen's cheeks. 'I read that in the shaman's marks. Also that she has no brothers or sisters.'

False tears welled from the old woman's eyes. 'The Goddess took them from me when they were still babies. It isn't for us to dispute her wishes. But they say only the strongest live,' she added hurriedly, concerned that Hyra might disregard her excuse and question her more closely.

'Are the strong always so lean?'

'Even the oak was once a sapling. She'll fatten when she has a son to suckle.'

Hyra turned to Morrigen. 'Can't you speak for yourself?'

Her blush deepened as his eyes locked with hers. 'My mother speaks the truth.'

'Truth has many faces.'

'I don't want to boast.'

'Modesty becomes a maiden, but it's no virtue in a woman who wishes to be a mother.'

Something in his manner infuriated Morrigen. Politeness hid condescension, remarks that were too glib to be honest.

'In which case you must be looking for shamelessness in the woman you want to wed,' she said angrily. 'Very well, you shall have it.' She loosened her robes, letting them collapse in a puddle at her feet.

There was silence. Hyra frowned, suddenly uncomfortable and thrown off balance by her behaviour. She was staring at him, and for a moment he sensed an almost enigmatic quality to her that disturbed him still further. Her lips had tightened into a cold expressionless smile, but her eyes portrayed wildness and vitality. The contradiction confused him, so in the end he tried to make amends by laughing and saying, 'You've a quick wit. The robes did you no justice.' But there was no laughter in his gaze as he scanned her body, noticed its lankiness, bruises, bare-boned limbs.

Noting his embarrassment, aware that her gesture had not helped her cause, Morrigen turned beseechingly towards her mother.

The old woman began sobbing. 'There's no better maiden in the Lines,' she wailed, coming to Morrigen's rescue. 'I don't want to part with her. She and I have been as close as any mother and daughter you'll meet, haven't we, child?' She stroked Morrigen's hair. 'Even the shamans have told me that joy and good fortune await the man who makes her his wife. A ram and six ewes are all I'm asking for her. Feel her for yourself.'

Morrigen evaded Hyra's gaze as he circled her. His hands were cold but gentle where they touched her stomach. Already she regretted her nakedness, that sudden urge to shock that was part insecurity and part the need to have someone dispute her ugliness.

Suddenly a new voice broke the silence.

'Leave the wretch alone, Hyra! She's as scrawny as a salmon kelt. Lying with her would be worse than bedding the bones left untouched by the dogs. Anyway, what would Lyla say if she saw you now? It's I who needs a wife, not you.'

Hyra laughed. 'Your sister has yet to snare me. And if mother has her way and I'm sent as a novice to Abury it'll be years before she does so.'

'Yet more reason to stop wasting your time.'

Hyra hesitated, then left Morrigen's side. As he did so, she realized that the stranger's words, uttered carelessly without thought for her, were proof that Hyra's attentions had been no more than an amusement, a means of idling whilst the stranger chose a bride. She looked up at her tormentor.

He was broad-shouldered and dressed in skins. A bow and bronze axe hung down his back. Copper bracelets circled arms bare but for the archer's guard of polished stone tied to one wrist. Sinew had thickened his neck and filled out his cheeks. His eyes suggested recklessness and his black hair had been cropped short to expose the boar's tusk pinned close to his skull. Watching him, she sensed a strength rarely thwarted, an arrogance grown undisciplined by never being questioned.

Hyra grinned at him. 'Is this a trick, Ceruduc? Perhaps you want her for yourself?'

Morrigen reddened as the stranger slapped her buttocks. 'This!' he cried. 'I may not have found a wife, but I'm not so hungry for one that I need to dine on crumbs merely because I'm late for the feast. Come, I've bought a crock of mead and ordered it to be taken to my tent. There's too many Dobuni about; the air's not fit to breathe.' He wrapped an arm round Hyra. They began walking away, laughing as they went.

The old woman gave chase. 'A hog in farrow, that's all I

want for her!' she screeched. Hyra and his companion vanished into the crowd.

Morrigen closed her eyes on her tears and the stares of those round her. She could hear them sniggering at her humiliation and nakedness, at the public display of a mother's eagerness to be rid of a daughter – at any price. Indifferent to her shame, the old woman returned and tugged angrily at her hair.

'Why was I cursed with a raw-boned fool no man will look at?' she screamed. 'Why? I may be barren, but at least I was worth the fondling when your father took me to his bed! You, you could stay here from now until next year's harvest and not be wed.'

'Leave me alone!' cried Morrigen. She pulled her robes up round her shoulders. Suddenly she could listen to her mother's whine no longer. She freed herself from her grip, then turned and ran, stumbling over the wych-elm and forcing her way through the crowds until the Maiden Lines were behind her and her mother's shouts had faded.

The stranger's taunts still shamed and haunted her, and for a while she walked lost and anonymous through the encampment. Gradually its magic consoled her. The pedlars were still crying their wares. Noise and colour surrounded her. The moon drifted above her across a sky shot with stars. She stifled her tears and made her way towards the temple.

The priestesses were still dancing, but their movements had grown languid to match the slower beat of the drums. By contrast, the drumbeats had carried the crowd into the Rite of Delirium, the collective chaos indispensable to any new creation. Some were scourging themselves with nettles; others writhing in the convolutions of the Rite. Yet more had gathered in groups to perform a lewd and carnal dance that only verged on the profane where mead had made them drunk.

As always, the Rite left Morrigen unsettled. She turned away, only forgetting it when she glimpsed the toilers of the stones inching slowly towards Henge, their feet fighting for purchase in the mud as their leader called the time and the sledge jerked forward. Those building the banks had downed tools to help. Ochre daubed their burden and when the wind flamed in the torches it glistened blood-red in their light. When they reached the tallest of the three stones in the entrance, they paused, first prostrating themselves before it, then decorating their bodies with chalk and charcoal before moving on.

The priestesses stopped dancing and formed a line either side of the entrance into the temple. A group of men crossed the causeway. Ashes smeared their faces. Most were Dobuni, but all wore patterned cloaks and an amber head-dress. Morrigen turned to her neighbour and asked him who they were.

'The seers of the Sacred Rites,' he replied. 'Only they can interpret the wishes of the Gods. It's they who laid out the temple to please Bala and know where the stones must stand.'

Morrigen studied them as they took up position. They seemed self-assured and at ease, accustomed to power. Yet there was enough of a child's intuition still left in her to sense the fear behind their pomp, their dread of what might happen if they failed in their task. One stepped forward. He was old, a staff supported him, but his voice rose firm and strong above the noise of the crowd as he offered the new stone to Bala.

Both growls and applause greeted his words, a sudden tension sweeping the crowd as the Rite of Delirium ended. Many of the shamans and older Cunei began murmuring. Others chanted the Sun God's name. Morrigen's neighbour joined in. Noticing her uncertainty, he paused and shouted, 'Some have no liking for Bala and the Dobuni. They're fools. Who melts the snow and warms the soil? Whose motions tell us when to plant, gather the hay and reap the harvest? Great elks once roamed these plains. Times changed. The elks died. And so will our shamans unless they let us worship who we please.'

Morrigen gave a timid smile, then turned to watch the toilers as they cut the lashings round the stone and drove stakes into the ground to lock the sledge in place.

Ropes were lifted, the strain taken up. The stone shifted on its bed, then slid to the ground, furrowing the turf as it was slowly dragged round the rim of the temple to where a deep trench marked its final resting place. The seers assembled round it, each pouring a beaker of mead over it as a libation to Bala. Ochre ran red over the grass, leaving behind it a long grey stone whose rippled surface held a hint of blue where it was still wet with the mead.

'There's no rock like them on the Plain,' explained her neighbour. 'They were found in the mountains on the shores of the Western Sea. The Tan built boats to carry them to Abury.'

'When?'

'No one's certain, not even the seers. It was before the Dobuni came.' The man paused and indicated the largest of the three stones in the entrance. 'Some think it was when the Serapha Stone was raised to appease the Goddess and the tribes were still at peace.'

Morrigen remained silent. Only the present concerned her: the seer standing motionless on the recumbent stone, head raised to where the sun would rise with the dawn. He was so still that he seemed to her to be an extension of the stone. But movement washed round him; the seer using pegs and ropes to check measurements, the shaman sprinkling powdered horn into the base of the trench. Then the seer stepped from his perch and the toilers moved into position. A drum began beating, a second merged with it. As the other drummers picked up the beat the sound seemed to shift from stone to stone, finally becoming a deep boom that embraced all those in the temple.

Morrigen could not stem her excitement. She pressed her hands to her ears and watched spellbound as the toilers manoeuvred the stone until its base rested above the trench and the lip could act as a fulcrum. Ropes were lifted, hands drenched in ash to prevent slipping. The toilers kicked their heels into the turf and began hauling at the ropes, others braced themselves against the poles wedged beneath the stone. The stone tilted and rose sluggishly upward. Suddenly it slid out of control and slammed into the stakes lining the trench, splitting and splintering them with a sudden crack. A rope frayed, then parted, the broken end whipping back into the faces of the men. The stone began swaying. Morrigen turned away, certain it was about to topple and crush the men holding the poles. But the remaining ropes held and the stone gradually steadied. The work continued. The stone rose again, inching upright in time to the drums and the chant of the crowd. The noise became deafening as it swung into the vertical and lumps of chalk were quickly packed round its base to hold it firm. The seers walked forward, each of them pressing his brow to its outer face, the place where the morning sun would first strike it. The ropes were pegged, the Toil was over.

Morrigen did not move when the crowd began to disperse. She began weeping, whether from joy or sorrow she could not be sure. Her tears made a prism of all she saw, so that her surroundings became a kaleidoscope of colour that kept splintering and adopting new forms. Henge! It seemed to course her veins, be the one place that might nourish her dreams.

'Found you.' Hands snarled her hair, brutally jerking her to her feet.

'Let go of me!'

'Thought you'd run from me, did you? I brought you here to stand in the Lines, not watch the Toil.'

Morrigen swung round, leaving a handful of hair still clenched in her mother's fist. 'What about the shame I felt when you chased after Hyra and begged him to take me? I left the Lines because I could bear no more, because you yourself said that no one would marry me.'

Her mother began dragging her through the crowd. 'I was wrong. Whilst you've been skulking, I've been busy at the task that brought us here. Patience pays. I've found a swineherd who'll part with a brace of piglets in exchange for a wife.'

'No!'

'You'll do as I say. No woman could want more in a man. Teeth lengthen, he's not the whelp he once was. But at least you'll be wed.'

'I'd rather whore!'

'Then whore for him. Another word and I'll thrash the skin from your back.'

The Maiden Lines were deserted. The torches smouldered and the fires had dwindled to embers. The old woman halted, stirring one with a stick. A moment later a squat hunched figure spitting phlegm as he walked emerged from the shadows.

Morrigen backed away, crying out in disgust as she saw his eyes prospect her body for a glimpse of flesh. The years spent tending pigs appeared to have moulded his features, for there was something almost porcine in his close-set eyes, long jaw and protruding blackened teeth.

He moved closer. A running scar stitched the diagonal of one cheek. 'She'll do,' he grunted, going on to justify his decision. 'A surfeit of beauty in a wife is wasted pleasure. It keeps a man so busy looking over his shoulder to see who else wants to share her that he doesn't have the time to enjoy what he's got.' He spoke solemnly, as if to suggest that those two sentences encompassed an entire philosophy, not just an observation. He pinched her cheek, his voice softened. 'But you'll keep me company, won't you? It's cold in the forest. A man needs a woman to gossip with by day and keep him warm come dusk.'

Revulsion and despair flooded through Morrigen as she detected the leer in his voice and tried to imagine what it would be like to give herself to his stench, the weight of his unwashed body. She turned to her mother, hoping to see in her some trace of sympathy or regret. She was grinning, cackling to herself. Morrigen shuddered. In exchange for two piglets she was to become the property of a swineherd, an object he could do with as he pleased as she followed his beasts in search of mast.

All round her, a backcloth to the numbness within, she could hear music and laughter and celebration. Gradually the full horror of what lay ahead took root in her thoughts. Here at Henge the Gods would watch over her. Here no one knew of her past or had conspired to plot her future.

She tensed, closing her eyes. The drums echoed inside her, urging her on. Suddenly she lowered her head, bit deep into the swineherd's wrist, and began running. She could taste his blood as behind her she heard an enraged bellow and her mother's screams. But she kept moving, dodging tents and fires until their cries had faded and the night hid her from their search.

She collapsed in the lee of a tent and began crying. Those outside it were preparing for the feast that followed the Rites, the men jointing beef, their wives shaping dough into loaves. A young girl came and stared at her, stood wide-eyed and puzzled as the tears washed away the marks of her maidenhood, proclaiming her a woman. The child's presence calmed her. When she had left, Morrigen gazed up at the moon and called on Serapha to still her fears and guide her steps. Staring into its light, a strange lucidity filled her thoughts, bringing with it a strength she had not known she possessed.

She remained there for much of the night. The moon had begun its descent when she heard singing and saw the priestesses of Bala moving towards her in single-file through the encampment. The crowd parted in front of them. A seer holding aloft the phallus worn during the Rites led the procession and an old woman and some younger girls brought up the rear.

The darkness washed round them as they turned north on to the Plain. Their voices grew fainter. Those watching them returned to the warmth of their fires. Only Morrigen, flitting unseen through the shadows, had followed in their wake. When she next looked back, Henge had vanished.

# BOOK I

# PRIESTESS

# CHAPTER I

'It'll soon be dawn. The fire needs tending. Morrigen, wake Teina and ask her to fetch some wood from the stack. It may be our last day as novices, but no seer would forgive us if it dulled and went out . . .' A pause, then a harsh uneasy silence. 'Didn't you hear what I said, Morrigen? Have you forgotten what happened to Aelina? I've no wish to join her . . .'

The group of young women squatting round the fire smiled nervously amongst themselves. Some, sensing the birth of another argument, peered into the shadows behind them. Green feline eyes parried their glances.

'Aelina is dead. I'm not.'

'Oh, Morrigen. Stop being so silly. We needs logs. Someone must tell Teina.'

'Or leave her to sleep and get them without troubling her.'

'Do as I say.'

'Rouse her yourself, Ralla. I'm not your handmaid now. Anyway, the moon is in no danger tonight.'

No one stirred.

The silence lengthened as each of the women recalled what had happened to Aelina. Nearly two years had passed since her death, but all were still haunted by it. At that time the novices took it in turns to remain awake and stoke the fire. Aelina had fallen asleep, letting it cool and go out. Shortly before dawn the moon's light had been darkened by the awesome and inexplicable passage of shadow across its face. Apocalypse had seemed imminent. At dawn, only bats and owls daring to venture from refuge, the landscape surrounding Abury had echoed to the wail of the doomed.

Remembering that day, many of the novices peered through the gloom of their dwelling to where Aelina now lay buried, a sacrifice to the Sun God Bala, hands crossed over eyes turned sightless towards the sunrise, only the beaker at her knees and some charred animal bones to keep her company on her solitary voyage into the Underworld.

One of the women rose. She had the sharp but perfect teeth

of a predatory pike, crow-black hair and a full, rounded body that vanity insisted be dressed only in robes that pampered its shape. She lifted a burning log from the edge of the fire and said, 'I hope you're going to obey me, Morrigen. A log can scar as well as warm.'

The figure in the shadows smiled. But did not move. 'We last fought in the autumn. What you won then, you may lose today.'

'Stop it, both of you!' demanded another of the novices. 'Whilst you bicker, the fire grows lower.'

Ralla scowled. 'You should blame Morrigen, not me. After all, if Aelina had lived, Morrigen would still be our servant.'

'But I'm not. And by the end of the day I'll be a Priestess of Bala, not the waif you once scorned and made wait on you. Anyway, it's your turn to wake Teina.'

'Yes, that's right. Stop being so stupid, Ralla, and put that log down,' insisted a third of the novices.

Ralla moved cat-like towards Morrigen. For a moment it seemed she might strike her. Then, knowing she had lost and afraid of what might happen if she delay any longer, she tossed the log to the fire, turned and vanished into the temple-dwelling that was the home of the novices.

There was silence as the others waited for her footsteps to recede.

'Why does she hate you?' asked someone, glancing at Morrigen. 'It can't just be because you're a Cunei and the rest of us are Dobuni or Tan.'

'I don't know.' Morrigen shrugged. 'It doesn't matter any more. Tomorrow we'll part. Fram's sure to send us to different temples.'

'But you've made an enemy,' ventured another of the novices. 'Ralla won't forget that.'

'That's nonsense,' said another. 'She can't harm Morrigen. After tonight they'll be equals. Anyway, she's more interested in choosing a lover than bearing a grudge.'

Her companions began giggling. 'Ssh . . . here she comes.'

Still scowling, Ralla swept into the open courtyard that formed the heart of the temple. Behind her walked an old woman carrying a basket of firewood. She emptied it on to the fire, then straightened and patted plump creamy cheeks that bore no evidence of age.

'There, that'll warm you,' she said cheerfully. 'Even old

Teina doesn't mind being shaken from her slumbers on a morning such as this. Think of it, it's nearly three summers since you first came to Abury. And soon you'll be gone, like chicks from the nest. This time tomorrow I'll be packing your robes and bidding you farewell.'

'We'll come back to visit you. I promise you we will,' said Ralla.

Teina shook her head. 'Aye, I've heard that before. But you'll be priestesses, and what with the Rites and serving the seers you'll not have a moment to come gossiping with the likes of me.' She paused, her placid face breaking into a smile as she noticed Morrigen sitting alone in the shadows. 'As for you, it must be the Gods themselves who turned you from Teina's kitchen-help into Bala's servant. What a creature you were when I first clapped eyes on you: all skin, bone and tears.'

'Please, Teina,' said Morrigen softly, hoping to silence her chatter.

The old woman laughed. 'That's right, pretend it isn't true. But I can still see you now, face stained purple with berries, following us homeward from Henge, not speaking, just gazing at us as quiet as any mouse and bedding in leaves when we made camp for the night. Some thought you were a living shadow or a wood sprite you stayed so close to us. Now look at you. You're as pretty as midsummer rain. Aye, and soon you'll be a priestess and you don't like it when I hark back to the months before Aelina's death when we fetched and carried together, cooked for them, flayed skins, threaded their robes and dressed 'em as fine as fancy for the nights of the Rites.'

Guilt and remorse conjured Aelina's image in Morrigen's thoughts. In an attempt to exorcize it she snapped at Teina, 'Stop it! You talk too much. It's dull and wearisome and I've heard it before.'

'Talk!' cried Teina. 'It was you who taught me I had a tongue. You never spoke, not even when we reached Abury and Fram took pity on you and gave you work as a handmaid. I began chattering for both of us for fear I'd go mad in the company of a mute.'

Sensing that Teina was upset, Morrigen stood and helped her stack a second basket of logs. 'I'm sorry,' she said. 'I didn't mean to hurt you.'

'That's all right, lass. A whit of temper won't harm me.' Teina smiled at the memories her help had re-awoken. She kissed both her cheeks, then hobbled back to her bed.

Ralla sneered and began imitating her unhurried asthmatic gait. 'She's a fool and a servant,' she said scornfully. 'It's not right that she should kiss you.'

'I thought you'd promised to visit her?' Morrigen spun and vanished into the temple. Its thatched circular roof rose high overhead, muffling the echo of her steps as she made her way between the lines of posts that supported it. She squeezed past one of the squat upright stones that stood in a ring round its centre. 'Teina,' she whispered.

'Yes.'

'Come outside and talk to me. It'll soon be morning.'

The old woman abandoned her bed again. The two of them moved slowly through the darkness to the entrance and walked out across the turf to where a second line of stones surrounded their dwelling.

Morrigen looked down into the valley that fell away in front of her. The river flashed silver in the moonlight. Geese honked. There was the sudden splash of an otter. In the distance, where the valley rose to the downs, she could see the stone façade of a burial tomb stand like an ox in silhouette against the sky. Above it, a cluster of stars burned brightly between yet more stars shaped like a pair of horns.

'Can you see the sparks above the constellation of the Bull?' she said. 'It seems strange that I may never stand here again and watch them rise. It was you who taught me what they mean.'

'Winter's end.'

'And now they herald our parting.'

'Even mother and daughter must part.'

Morrigen nodded. An involuntary sadness narrowed her eyes. She thought of her own mother as Teina began braiding her hair in readiness for the morning Rites. She leant against her warmth, let the deft touch of her fingers soothe her thoughts. 'I'll miss you.' The words sounded trite.

'I know that, child. There's no need to speak of it.'

'I owe you so much.'

'You owe me nothing. You've made an old woman happy, that's gift enough. Now you must go. It's the things that are the most precious that are often the most easily broken, be it a pot from the furnace or the knots that bind us. You'll learn that as you grow older.'

Morrigen smiled and gazed out into the night. 'Abury. After three years it feels as much a part of me as my own heart beat.' Glimpsing the immense chalk-white dome that rose from the valley floor, she grinned and added, 'Do you remember when we first climbed the Goddess Mound* ?'

Teina laughed. 'And I slipped and slid from summit to base.'

Morrigen fell silent as she looked eastward to where the sun would soon rise and begin arching the sky. Even with her eyes closed she could chart the first flash of its light on the surrounding countryside. First it would strike the boulder-strewn downland behind her and the track that followed its crest. Then the Goddess Mound, her own dwelling and the stone-flanked avenue that linked it to the temple of Abury. Finally it would warm the second avenue that joined the temple to a lonely coombe and the tombs that marked the place where the souls of the dead descended into the Underworld.

Near the coombe lay an abandoned temple. Many of its stones had been removed and dragged south to Henge, and once, when still friendless and a handmaid, she had often gone there to watch the toilers at work and be reminded of the world she had fled. But time had dulled her homesickness. Even Henge had lost its magic with the passage of the years.

'Abury's so large,' she said, 'and it's been my world for so long, that any other will seem a dwarf beside it.'

Teina nodded. 'Aye, you'll not find a temple to match it anywhere in these lands. In Serapha's name the Tan once laboured with antler, flint and bone to dig ditches, raise banks, tombs and the Goddess Mound. And when it was done, their children's children dragged the stones from the hills and lifted them into place, more than half a thousand in number. And then the Dobuni came and were given Henge as a reward for aiding the Tan in their feud with us Cunei. But little has changed. Some of the tombs were filled with rubble to appease Bala, but every stone and tomb still plays its part in the Rites.' She paused, smiling. 'And now I'm chattering again.' She pointed to where the moon nudged the horizon. 'I must go. None of you'd forgive me if I let you go hungry on your last day as novices.'

For a while after Teina had left her, Morrigen stood alone in

* Silbury Hill, Wiltshire.

the night, content to savour its chill and her tiredness now that warmth and sleep lay ahead. Eventually she heard voices and turned to see the temple entrance suddenly brighten with colour. A moment later the other novices appeared, two carrying a shallow basin into which the remains of the fire had been ladled. She hurried to take her place in the circle as the basin was lowered to the ground and a slight, balding figure emerged from the darkness.

'It burns well.' Fram's first words never varied, nor did the response of those in his care.

'The Sun God Bala still sleeps. But these flames are proof of his glory and must be kindled at dusk and tended till dawn,' chanted the priestesses in unison.

'And soon he will wake.'

The seer turned and gazed out across the valley.

Knowing what would happen next, Morrigen watched and waited.

Fram's timing was uncanny. He never stirred from his pelts or left the temple until this precise moment. It was as if the words themselves, the act of turning toward the east, gave birth to the day. So she stood beside him, silent and expectant, as the wind tumbled her hair and the embers flared.

Suddenly it was morning. The stars shed their glitter. The sky lightened. In the distance, where the vale rose to meet the pleat of the downs, a pale orb of flame slowly lapped the skyline, dousing the last of the night.

The novices remained motionless, ears bent into the wind to catch the first sound of the day. Then it came, the rapid cry of a solitary jay.

Fram glanced at Morrigen.

She thought for a moment, remembering all he had taught her before interpreting the sound. 'It's an omen of fire,' she said finally. 'For the call of the jay can also be heard in the crackling of the forest as it burns.'

Fram nodded, hiding his sorrow at the passing of another night, that slow irreversible journey towards his own death, by smiling benignly at each of the novices. How many must have passed through his hands since he was first appointed their guardian by his brother seers? Their numbers blurred, leaving only memories – youth's optimism and folly. For three years they were his, raw clay to be shaped by his wisdom before being sent out from Abury as priestesses to serve the Sun God in the temples sacred to their tribes. The smile faded. Once they had kept him young, now they reminded him of his age.

Sensing his melancholy, Morrigen watched him as he stood framed between two of the stones. In the background she could hear Teina singing to herself as she bustled to and fro in the temple; preparing food, scouring cooking-pots, spreading fresh bracken over the clunch floor in the sleeping quarters. Teina and Fram, the servant and the seer, the two people no gratitude could repay. Loving Teina, she was sometimes confused by her inability to feel the same affection for Fram. He had sheltered her when weak with hunger, persuaded the High Priestess to let her be initiated as a novice after Aelina's death. He never angered or raised his voice, never begrudged the days spent instructing her in all she had missed when still a handmaid. But she could not love him. She was flawed, he was not, and in recent months she had come to think of his perfection as a knife that had laid bare both her conscience and her faults. And then there was Aelina, the accusation she had seen in his face . . .

Suddenly, as if waking from a trance, he turned towards the novices and said, 'That may be the last sunrise you will ever greet at Abury. By dusk you will have been replaced. This evening, as Bala sets, we will together walk along the Maiden Way and enter the temple to celebrate the advent of spring. Tomorrow you will leave here, not as maidens, but as women, priestesses skilled in the lore of the God whose name you bear. You have sacrificed much, the company of your families, marriage, the joy of having children. But the debt will be repaid. After divining the portents for three years those of you who wish to marry will be able to do so. In return for gifts to Bala, you will be given as wives to the sons of chieftains. Until then you must offer comfort to the people of your tribes and interpret the omens with truth.' He paused, glancing at each in turn. 'One Rite lies ahead of you. It will make you women. Don't be afraid of it. Without pain there would be no purpose to pleasure.'

Morrigen shuddered at the thought of what had to be done. Then the fear left her as once again she marvelled at Fram's timing. For the sun had cleared the horizon as he finished speaking, blinding her and forcing her to turn away from its light.

A distant drum began pounding. Others joined in as the villages scattered round Abury awoke to its noise. Soon both hills and valleys echoed to their music. Suddenly the runner serving the novices until the eve of the next full moon climbed the slope and took his place beside the fire. Shivering, naked save for the jet round his arms and throat, he stood waiting whilst Fram unrolled a lynx skin, revealing a burnished copper axe whose head he pushed deep into the fire, purifying it in the heat. The novices began the morning lament, linking arms and slowly circling in the same direction as the sun. Fram withdrew the axe from the flames and gave it to the runner, telling him to let it be known that a jay had been the first creature to welcome the new day.

The runner lifted the axe into the sunlight, then turned and began the descent towards the river. Morrigen watched him until he disappeared. In her mind she could see him dip the axe into each of the surrounding springs and streams to protect drinking livestock against disease, hear him tell those he met that the day boded well for the clearing of forest and undergrowth by fire.

The lament ended. One of the novices entered the temple, returning with a water-skin. Fram remained motionless until the first beam of sunlight struck the fire, then lifted his arms toward the sky. The water was poured into the basin. The embers spat steam; sodden ashes floated over its rim. Serapha had returned into the earth, Bala had risen. Morrigen's last day at Abury had begun.

*

'Morrigen.'

No answer.

'Morrigen.'

She said nothing. Breathing in, breathing out. In again, fiercely, stifling screams, the sharp pain in her belly. From beyond the low wattle walls of the temple came laughter, voices, the squeal of a pig. Then evening's hush. Dust drifting through the shaft of light in the courtyard. The distant chink of a carved length of chalk slipping from her own fingers. Still weak and in shock, she winced as another wave of pain flooded her body.

'The pain will pass.'

A tallow flared in the darkness. It was held low, lighting

Fram's face, the wisps of hair that clung to his skull like seaweed on rock.

Suddenly she heard her own voice boom with anger, filling the temple. 'You're a man. How can you know of such things?'

'But it is done?'

'Yes.'

He sat facing her. 'Now no one can take your maidenhood. Your own hand has made you a woman.'

'I feel no different.'

'That will come. One day you will take part in the Rites and the seasonal congress of the Gods.'

Morrigen lifted the phallus into the light. It was still warm, wet with her blood. She glanced at Fram, resenting his presence and the torment he had made her endure. 'Apart from the pain, what else should I feel?'

'No woman can feel what isn't in her heart. Some scream and cry out. Others cannot do it and call on Teina to help them. But you said nothing as you entered the temple. I saw no fear, you made no sound.'

'Perhaps I have no heart?'

'Or would like to think so?' The seer paused and clapped his hands together. The noise returned to them as an echo, dull and hollow. 'That is how you should feel.'

'For that is what I am?'

'Yes.'

He was right. She felt empty, detached from her own body. Even the pain seemed distant and remote, making her a spectator to her own suffering. His voice bridged the void.

'There is nothing you would like to tell me before we part?'

Morrigen shook her head, flustered by the suddenness of the question.

'Are you sure?'

Then she knew what he was going to say. She paled, hurriedly turning away.

'Two years have passed since Aelina was offered to the Gods,' said Fram softly. 'But both of us know what happened that day.' He paused, giving her the chance to confess. Her hands were trembling, her eyes evasive. 'When I woke and told you to rekindle the fire, you showed no surprise. You knew it was out. How?'

Morrigen held her silence, clinging to her guilt. Then release came, pouring out in quick sentences that hid nothing. 'I slept badly that night. Once I woke and saw no light from the fire. I went into the court. The fire was low. Aelina was sleeping. I wanted to wake her. But something seemed to lead me back to my bed. I couldn't stop it. It was as if Bala himself had taken my hand.' Her voice rose as she saw the accusation on Fram's face. 'So it was I who let the fire go out! How was I to know what would happen? When you ordered Aelina to be slain I felt that I was to blame. And yet, inside me, I knew that the fates had decreed both the Darkness and her death. Afterwards, when you made me a novice in her place, I was afraid to speak of it lest I be driven from the temple.'

Fram tipped her face toward his. 'A maiden dies that you may take her place. You show no joy in your womanhood. After three years you are still a stranger to me. Is it because there is evil in you? Or have the Gods chosen you for a task that none of us know about?'

'I'm no different from the others. Don't say such things. They frighten me, make me doubt what I am.'

'You are different. You say little, but think much. The others gossip about the warriors they mean to take as lovers. Some, like Ralla, had already lost their maidenhood when they entered this temple tonight. Many have forgotten what I taught them. But you have done neither.'

'Perhaps that's because they were sent here and I arrived like a dog with no home? You took me in. I want to thank you by serving the Gods.'

Fram smiled at her seriousness. 'I'm an old man whose bones have grown brittle and empty of marrow. No, Morrigen, you must do what is in your heart.'

She trembled, whispered, 'So much is still hidden from me. Sometimes I feel like a sheep lost in fog that can't find its way home to the pen.'

'The mist may be of your own making.'

'But if it lifts, what will I find?'

Fram frowned at her urgency. Gradually he became aware that she was staring at him and that the humility had left her face, leaving it as hard as stone. He felt that he was seeing it for the first time; its cruelty, guile, acceptance of evil. It was as if, he thought, she had answered her own question and in doing so prompted the birth of the woman she really was.

Suddenly he realized that her confession had been false. 'You lied!' he cried. 'You knew I would make you a novice if I had the chance. That's why you let Aelina sleep. It was cunning that led you back to your bed, not Bala.' Too feeble to control his rage, he began choking and gasping for breath.

Morrigen smiled as she watched him. 'And did I cause the Darkness?'

'Go!'

She did not move. Her stare seemed to make motion impossible, still even his tongue.

'It was you who made me what I am,' she said softly. 'But you can't destroy me; not now. I still bear the scars of my childhood, its poverty, the years as an outcast. Such wounds never heal. I'm glad, for without them I might never have understood that though many people yearn for power, few gain it. I intend doing so. I've learnt a lot whilst in your care. I know now that you Dobuni use the seers to cheat the tribesfolk of what's theirs, that even the seers are guilty of using magic and sorcery to gain power for themselves.'

'We're not all like that. Must you be as they?'

'The deer that doesn't run with the herd is the first to hear the wolves at its heels.'

'We're not beasts! Listen to me, Morrigen. You think sinners go unpunished for their wrongs and that the Gods forgive all evil. You believe evil will win you power over the tribes. You're wrong. The moth is drawn to the flame, but the flame destroys it.'

Suddenly her smile widened and the coldness left it, leaving behind it the full mouth, lean gawkish face, long-limbed body, the mane of hair that fell sheer to her waist – the imperfections three years had turned into beauty. Fram trembled, glad he was old and beyond the reach of love, the death of the moth.

Noting his tremble, Morrigen knew that victory was nearly hers. To seal it, she became a child again, all innocence and vivacity as she reached forward and kissed his brow. 'I'm pleased we spoke as we did, aren't you?' she said happily. 'It drove out the demons, made me realize my foolishness.'

It was as if they had never quarrelled, as if the cruelty he had seen in her had belonged to a dream. 'Yes, I'm glad.' Fram sighed as he let himself be disarmed. 'I'm sending you to Henge,' he added.

Morrigen grinned and threw her arms round his neck. 'Henge!' she cried. 'So you do still care for me? I was certain I'd be sent to a temple where both the seers and High Priestess would soon forget I existed.'

Fram freed himself from her embrace. To allow it at all seemed proof of his surrender. Despising himself, he said, briskly, 'You leave at dawn with a merchant. But you've the right to go home before taking part in the Rites.'

Morrigen frowned. 'No. I've had no news of my mother for nearly three years. What came between us can't be mended. Anyway, Teina is more of a mother to me now.'

'I thought that's what you'd say. And it's partly because of it that I'm sending you to Henge. You've no kin, no one of influence who can help you. Henge is the home of the High Priestess and the seers of the Sacred Rites. To the Dobuni it is more sacred than Abury. Your presence in the temple of your own tribe will be a mark of my favour. The rest is up to you.' Fram paused. 'Ralla will be joining you there.'

'No!'

'Yes,' said the seer sternly. 'You must resolve your quarrel. Enmity between priestesses is a threat to peace – more so when one is a Cunei and the other a Dobuni. You're both strong women. I have seen how the others obey you. Ralla is a warrior's daughter. Indulge your conflict when you've both become well-known and you risk provoking a war between the tribes.'

Morrigen begged Fram to reconsider, but he refused to listen. 'We've spoken long enough,' he said, lifting a small cup from the pelts beside him. 'It'll soon be dark and we must begin the serpent dance.'

Morrigen grimaced as she took the cup and swallowed the bitter infusion of wormwood and bull's blood prepared by Teina for the loss of maidenhood. But the drink revived her, and when the other priestesses entered the temple she stood and took her place in the circle as it formed in the central court.

'So, waif, we are yet to be parted.' She turned to see Ralla standing behind her.

'The day will come.'

'And this blade may help it dawn.' Ralla touched the knife at her waist, then gave a mocking smile as she spun on her toes and began the dance that imitated the slow uncoiling of a waking snake. In one hand she held its shape, the phallus with which each priestess had taken her virginity. In the other, the sloughed skin that proved it capable of renewal and rebirth.

Morrigen watched her for a moment, then joined her companions as each became part of a serpent waking from winter's hibernation. Dust rose, thickening the air, as they threaded their way past the stones and posts inside the temple and Fram walked amongst them, scattering bones to enrich the soil. The pace quickened as they neared the entrance, bare feet drumming ground worn smooth by centuries of ritual.

Outside, night had not yet fallen. Mist hung layered in the valley. Nearby, the bones given in offering to the temple lay piled in a long row that suggested the rotted, ivory carcass of a single monster. In the far distance, where down met forest, Morrigen glimpsed a pall of smoke rising from the fires lit that morning to clear land for cultivation. Groups of Tan, their voices muffled in the mist, loomed out of it to take their places in the procession. Some had brought ashes from their hearths. Others carried seed, flint and sprigs of hazel whose catkins fell as they walked.

Led by Fram, the journey to Abury began. The priestesses and villagers moved slowly between the two lines of stones that bordered the Maiden Way on its mile-long march to the temple. Alternately wedge-shaped or pillared to symbolize the sexes, each facing its partner, the stones merged with the twilight, leaving only their bulk to mark the route. The first torches were lit. The avenue bent, dipping through scrub and coppice before beginning the long uphill climb that led to the temple.

Ahead of her, raised on lengths of bark supported by stakes, Morrigen glimpsed the skeletons of those who had died during the winter. Many began wailing as the procession approached the mortuary racks. The corpses had been left exposed to permit the physical proof of the spirit's release from the body – the dropping of the lower jaw from the skull – and they faced to where Bala would rise on midsummer morn. As the journey continued, some of the skulls were hoisted on to poles by their kinsmen and carried aloft like misshapen banners.

The next halt was an ancient shrine where spring offerings were traditionally placed in a series of natural shafts that funnelled deep into the ground. A timber totem carved into the shape of the Moon Goddess rose above the villagers as they scattered flint flakes and shards of pottery, or tipped their gifts into the shafts. Having sacrificed the souls of what they most hoped summer's warmth would bring them – rich soil, food and tools – they moved aside and waited for the priestesses to breathe life into their gifts by trampling them with their feet.

A strange sensuality filled Morrigen as she danced. Her movements held a hint of abandonment, a recklessness that had no connection with her steps. It was as if the loss of her virginity had tapped a need she had not known she possessed. She sensed this herself, and for a moment saw it as a clue to the future, a warning that one day she might defy her vows in order to satisfy the need.

These thoughts faded when the procession moved on and she first glimpsed the temple. As always, its immensity took the breath from her lungs. The vast circular bank bestrode the scrub, its crest towering above the stones that ringed the inner ditch. The stones seemed gargantuan in the twilight, even human; a host of limbless giants that had quit the forest to welcome her arrival. The bank rose round her. Below her she saw a family of Tan placing a corpse in the grave they had scraped in the chalk and earth that time had tumbled into the ditch since its completion. Torches flickered against the darkening sky. The shamans chanted. The stones soared upward towards the God they had been raised to praise. She halted. Something seemed to hold her back, make her a Cunei again after the years spent surrounded by strangers. Tan villagers crowded round her, ahead a group of Dobuni were preparing for the mating of a bull and heifer as an offering to Bala. Nearby stood the Sun Stone their forefathers had brought to Abury as evidence of conquest, the hole near its summit describing the rounded shape of their God. She looked up at the moon, at Serapha, the Goddess she had abandoned by becoming a priestess. Shame made her turn away.

A Dobuni warrior stood behind her, idly slapping the flat of his blade against an open hand. Her shame became anger as she met his gaze. Gradually it came to her that one day the Cunei would be free again and that the dagger held by the warrior would be turned against him.

She entered the temple, hurrying on towards the shamans and seers gathered amongst the stones in its two inner shrines. The Spring Rites had begun. But whose birth had she come to celebrate? Those of the seasons, or her own? And if her own, what unplumbed future stretched darkly ahead of her?

# CHAPTER II

'Come, priestess. It's a three day journey to Henge. I gave offerings of an axe and some copper to your temple in return for the pleasure of your company. I'd hoped for more than silence. Or is your head so empty you can find no words to fill it?'

'It was you who set the pace.'

'But only to be rid of you sooner.'

For Morrigen such flippancy made the silence even harder to end. She glanced at her companion as she struggled to keep up with him. The years of travel had broadened his calves and lengthened his stride, making the rest of his body seem almost an afterthought. There was, perhaps, a hint of the dog fox in his face: a quickness, a shrewdness, an instinct for survival that spoke of storms weathered and chances taken. But the analogy suggested a slyness he lacked, and in the end his strength was the only constant: the dark windburned skin, the line of muscle squaring his jaw, the black beard deftly trimmed to match the crescent of beaten gold that hung round his neck. The gold was ubiquitous. It ringed the lobe of one ear, held his cape in place, glinted dully against the haft of his knife.

'Well?' he grunted, still waiting for her to speak.

'I'm honoured you considered me worth so valuable a gift.'

He growled his annoyance. 'If that's the best you can manage I'd rather listen to the wind, at least it doesn't flatter. You priestesses and seers are all the same. When you speak you sound as if you've a fish bone lodged permanently in the throat. What comes out is either pious nonsense or dislike masquerading as courtesy. You spend your lives worshipping the Gods, yet you can't tell the truth without first wrapping it in fine words.'

'I meant well.'

'You meant nothing.' Atius turned and began bellowing at his men.

Stung into silence, Morrigen splashed onward through the swamp. Sweat drenched her robes, mud covered her legs.

Insects the size of a thumb swarmed round her face. Apparently indifferent to the ochre she had rubbed on to it as protection against their bite, their buzz merged with the curses of the merchant's men as they beat a path through the reeds behind her.

She glanced over her shoulder at the long caravan of oxen plodding unhappily in her wake. Each carried a pair of basketwork panniers brimming with raw tin or unsmelted copper. The weight was so great that every now and then one of them would stumble and sink up to its belly in the marsh and have to be dragged to safety with ropes. Those spared the ores bore wooden chests laden with finished wares or the tools that had made Atius wealthy; bellows and casting moulds, crucibles and hammers.

Even after a day spent trudging at its head, the caravan still seemed to her like a village in motion. Hunters fed it, herdsmen drove the livestock that brought up the rear, women and children mingled with the smiths and miners whose skills replenished the chests.

'They've an appetite for mead and women no surfeit can glut,' said Atius suddenly, noticing her glance. 'Occasionally a knife ends what words won't settle. But none of them are afraid of me. I feed them well, pay for their wives and let them worship who they please. That's the difference between you and me. You trade on the fear of death. I peddle goods that make living easier.' He paused, grinning. 'Some of the men are still chattering about last night.'

'We were the guests of a Tan chieftain and his elders. It was my duty to light the first of the cooking fires and lead the villagers in their dance.'

'Duty be damned. You're a woman as well as a priestess. There wasn't a man there who'd have taken gold to stop watching you.'

'That's their concern.'

'One day it may be yours.'

'Do you always insult your fellow travellers?' retorted Morrigen sharply.

'Ah, that's better. Beauty without a bite soon loses its savour.' Atius laughed. 'I'm a merchant, a sorcerer who can turn two metals into a third. You're a priestess trained in magic and ritual. We both know what it means to play a part. And that's what you did last night. When you shed your robes and danced, it wasn't for any God, but yourself and those watching.'

Morrigen raised her sickle and slashed at the surrounding reeds. 'How well you appear to know me,' she said coldly.

'That's because we were cast in the same mould,' said Atius, amused by her display of temper. 'You're only half what you seem to be, and I was born a half-breed, the blood of two tribes. My father was a Dobuni, my mother a Cunei. My enemies accuse me of combining the arrogance of one with the fecklessness of the other. In truth I belong to neither.'

'Then I must pity you as being a man with no homeland.'

'Nonsense. I've no need of your pity. I've lands of my own. But home is where I lay my head – be it here in this bog or on an isle across the seas. I serve all masters, but am the servant of none. No tribal borders are closed to my men. Why? Because we're smiths whose hammers shape the bronze that no chieftain or warrior can be without.'

And when he tossed his head and began laughing Morrigen found it impossible not to be carried along by the freedom it seemed to evoke. He owed allegiance to no one, had breathed of a thousand winds, known pale women and dark, the heat of distant suns, shipwreck and mountains, rivers pebbled with gold. He had touched on a larger world and part of it had stuck to him like a burr, giving him a richness and resonance that made her own world seem drab by comparison.

Feeling curiously dissatisfied with herself, she began scrambling over the rotting bog-oak that lay waterlogged in the swamp as he dropped back to talk to his men. In places withy and sedge rose high overhead into a canopy of green. In others they vanished to reveal the river's flood-plain, or a heron, its wings brushing the surface, flapping lazily to where the river itself ran silt-stained and swollen. When it widened she saw wildfowlers in dug-out canoes drifting amongst the reeds in search of geese and mallard. Once, where a stream fed it, she passed some tooth-marked willow stumps and glimpsed a pair of beavers strengthening their dam, the buck in his moulting winter coat fastidious and fussy as he added another branch to its walls.

But no distraction allowed her to forget Atius.

Since joining his caravan on the previous morning, his ability to cut through the silence that masked so much of what she thought had forced her to endure the most unfamiliar of emotions. Ranging from resentment to a sense of liberation, the most pervasive was a gradual awareness of her womanhood that continued to nag even when he left her side. Fearful of betraying herself, she had taken refuge in a mixture of sarcasm and civility. They made poor allies, first failing her when celebrating the evening Rites as the guest of the Tan. By trying too hard to prove her loyalty to Bala, she had ended up dancing solely for the merchant's benefit. And now he had mocked her for it. She was young and inexperienced. The years at Abury had not equipped her to tame men like Atius.

And when he returned to the head of the caravan his presence seemed to menace her innocence, be a threat she could not indefinately resist. 'There's a small village ahead,' he said. 'We'll make camp there for the night. One of the oxen is lame and I must sell its load before slaughtering it.'

Morrigen grinned at the prospect of rest. 'Good. My feet are swollen. From toe to temple there's no part of me that doesn't reek of swamp.'

'I'm surprised you priestesses can still remember how to put one foot in front of the next. An excess of worship and those endless Rites have fattened you all up like calves for the pot.'

'Don't say such things!' protested Morrigen, as much dismayed by his honesty as she was by his blasphemy. 'Those who doubt the power of the Gods risk being destroyed.'

'Do they? I wonder . . .' Atius smiled, seeming both to mock her indignation and invite its denial. 'You make power sound like something only the Gods can possess. Yet even the sickle in your hand has the power to cut.'

'Now you're trying to provoke me again.'

'Only into saying what you mean, not what you think you should say. I've spent my life in travel, seen many faces. But I've met few who know where they are bound and won't be hindered from their course. You're one of them.'

'You presume too much. Yesterday we were strangers. Return to your men and leave me in peace.'

'And let you fall in the mire?'

A fallen tree blocked their path. Atius climbed on to its trunk and held out his hand toward Morrigen. She had to take it. And when she jumped and swung up beside him their two bodies touched, skin meeting skin where their robes hung open.

Atius smiled and pointed through the reeds towards the

river. 'Look,' he said softly. 'It runs to the sea and no man can stop it. Be as you are.' He released her hand.

Both remained silent as the trek continued. The merchant's words lingered in Morrigen's thoughts. Fram had taught her that the shards of a broken pot have an existence as real as the one they had just left. You can change the form of something, alter its structure, but you cannot deny its existence. As with the river, she began to perceive that she too was moving towards a destiny against which all struggle would be in vain. But what was that destiny? For an instant she gave full rein to her vision of the future, accepting the cunning that would have to be employed if her hopes were to be realized. And then Atius returned to her thoughts, leaving her confused and troubled as she remembered the press of his flesh against hers.

They reached the village in mid-afternoon. On its outskirts some women were cutting thatching reed and cropping nettles for net-making. Like their wives, the men were naked. They worked in a line, using antlers to break up the sod whilst their children gathered the stones into piles and separated the flints in readiness for knapping. The children were gaunt with hunger. Scanning their faces, a sudden sadness stirred in Morrigen's thoughts as she recalled her own childhood and that permanent emptiness in the pit of the belly no meal could ever fill.

As the caravan approached, the villagers dropped their tools and ran towards the stack of bows on the edge of the marsh. Atius ordered his men to halt. He clawed his way through the reeds, then raised the bronze axe-head that was the symbol of his trade as he told them who he was and where he was bound. 'I've an ox in need of slaughter,' he added. 'The ground is hard, the day long. By nightfall you'll be hungry.'

The villagers eyed him suspiciously. But the offer of fresh meat was irresistible. They lowered their bows, the children hopping from one foot to the next in their excitement as the long caravan slowly emerged from the swamp.

A thorn palisade surrounded the village. They entered it through a gap and Morrigen scanned the stilt-raised huts that rose from the mud. Pigs rooted through the filth. A line of smoked eels hung sallow and distended over a fire; beside it squatted two old women busy plucking and drawing the wild duck taken from the nets that morning. It was a task she knew well: the feathers and blood and glazed stare in their eyes, the dogs squabbling over offal already black with flies. Quickly turning away, she glanced at the canoes pulled up on the river-bank. Another was being built out of a length of oak; brushwood was being heaped over it to help burn it hollow and she could hear the rasp of the flints being used to shape its hull.

An old man with a bony face and dry papery skin hobbled forward on his stick as the villagers gathered round the caravan. 'I am Uba, and I sit on the council of elders,' he said, searching out Atius. 'We're a poor people. But we're Cunei, and would turn no one away who is in need of rest.'

Atius thanked him and indicated Morrigen, telling him who she was.

Morrigen smiled. Uba had a patience and a dignity that made her eager to help him. 'Please tell me if there is any way in which I can serve you.'

Uba welcomed her and placed his brow to hers as a sign of greeting. 'We must thank the Gods for having brought you here. Now that spring has come we're about to start sowing our corn. For years the harvest has been small. Perhaps you would bless the seed and ask the Gods to nourish the soil?'

'Of course.'

The courtesies over, Uba showed her to the hut kept empty for guests whilst Atius ordered his men to unload and water the oxen. The villagers crowded round as panniers were lowered and chests thrown open. From their eagerness to handle the contents, Morrigen guessed that most had never seen bronze before. Axes, arrow-heads and knives were gingerly touched and fondled as if too precious to function; a notion Atius hastily disproved by lifting an axe and quartering a log with two blows.

'Uba tells me,' he bellowed, as the crowd fell silent, 'that reavers have robbed your ewes of their lambs, that the Tan enter your lands when they wish, taking what they want and departing when they please. But how can you fight them with weapons that break or grow blunt? Your harvests have been poor. Why? Because the land is sour from use and to till more you must first spend your days bent double in the forest with only stone and bone to help you.' Like all skilled merchants, Atius knew exactly when to stop. The villagers were listening, excessive criticism could only alienate them and defeat its purpose. He raised his axe. 'With this you could defy the Tan, build your boats and clear land for corn. If it blunts, it can soon be sharpened.'

'What'll it cost us?' cried one of the villagers.

The question was always asked. Atius did not flinch from answering it. 'Nothing you can't spare,' he replied. 'For without it it may cost you your lives. How many lambs have been taken? How many babes did you bury when the harvest last failed?' He paused, allowing time for reflection, then added, 'Now listen to me, my friends, for like the oaf I am I now offer a bargain only an oaf would refuse. For each family here I've a bundle of arrow-heads, a dagger, an axe and a spear-head. In return I ask for the same number of pelts as have been lost this year because your arrows failed to kill, all the ewes that have been parted from their lambs, as much seed as was wasted last spring by being sown where the soil is weak. If you're ashamed of your losses, you won't heed what I say. But those who listen need never fear the Tan again. The axe will make fields out of forests. Those who hunt or fish will bear weapons worthy of their skills.'

The villagers withdrew and began debating amongst themselves. Apparently unconcerned at the outcome, Atius leant against his axe whilst they examined his wares and compared them to their own. Some shrugged and walked away, but most remained beside the chests and began shouting instructions to their wives and sons. Pelts were soon being unfolded and placed at the merchant's feet. Seed pits were opened, fish cut down from the smoking racks, sheep driven homeward from the spring pastures.

'You don't approve, do you?' said Atius, noticing Morrigen's dismay as she watched the villagers disperse to put their new weapons to the test, joking and laughing amongst themselves.

'No. These are my people. Last night you made the same promises to the Tan, only then you swore that your arrow-heads would add to their flocks and make it easier to pillage.'

The merchant grinned at her anger. 'So you think I'm an unscrupulous rogue who'd stop at nothing to add to his wealth? And so I am. But look at them, they're content. Why? Because they think they've outwitted me, that by giving me less than they lost they've proved me a fool. It's easier to forge an axe than to be sure of a good harvest. Human nature is a fickle creature. It begrudges parting with a handful of corn, but if you can make people believe they're cheating you they'd gladly sell their own daughters to prove themselves right.'

'But you're deceiving them, abusing their trust.'

'Am I?' said Atius, smiling wryly. 'And what will you be doing when at dusk you walk fields that have been ploughed until they're a wilderness and beg the Gods to make them fruitful? You might as well scatter salt as seed. It's dung, not prayers, these people need most.'

*

Frogs croaked in the swamp. The river ran black and as smooth as glass between its banks. There was no wind. The sun had nearly set, but colour still gilded the few places where its light still ventured: the ragged crown of the forest, the thatched dome of a hut, the angled corner of the field where Morrigen was standing, framed in a crimson shaft.

Listening to her ask Bala to grant the villagers their wishes, Atius smiled at the vanity that had made her select so theatrical a vantage for so pointless a task. But he knew he was alone in his doubts. The villagers stood round him, rapt and in awe. When she had finished speaking they started wailing and throwing themselves to the ground. The noise was hideous, and he was grateful when she silenced it by raising her arms and beginning the evening chant. Her voice deepened as she found and held the low sepulchral note with which those who served Bala greeted the night, the death of another day.

As the village maidens joined in and began moving in procession across the field, each beating the soil with the bone of an ancestor, Morrigen skimmed the faces of those watching the Rites. The men stood dour and solemn: she sensed that many were already imagining the harvest they would reap because a priestess from Henge had sanctified the soil before planting. The women stood apart, eyes covered so that none could profane or wish evil on one whose powers were so much greater than their own. Her gaze found Atius, the cause of her quest. That same cynicism remained, but it now shared his face with a question only she and the night could answer. She shivered, then lowered her arms and tightened her cloak, hiding her nakedness from his glance.

'Are you ready?'

She turned. A scrawny, pinch-faced man reeking of fish-guts stood behind her. Seeing the water-skin and bucket of seeds he was holding, she suddenly realized that he was the village shaman and that the two of them were now supposed to scatter and fertilize the first seeds to be sown. She took the bucket and backed away in disgust: had she arrived on the eve of the Spring Rites she would have been expected to mimic the sexual act in front of those watching.

The ground now warmed by the spirits of the dead, priestess and shaman began walking the first furrow; Morrigen scattering seed, her companion sprinkling it with water. Reaching the tail of the furrow, Uba approached with a torch so that she could light the field fire, the fire lit purposely to keep at bay both the demons of evil and any beast likely to trample the growing corn. The chanting ceased as she took it from him. She turned towards the villagers, plunged the torch into the fire, then stepped aside from its heat as the villagers broke ranks and began running towards her.

The men reached her first. Crowding round, they held out the tools Atius had sold them and asked her to bless them. She complied, then attended to the pregnant women whose bellies she must rub with ochre and the unmarried girls whose loins had to be smeared with fish roe. As on the previous evening, she felt the gentle almost imperceptible touch of power seem to settle inside her as she did these things and saw the fear and reverence on their faces.

She raised her arms in a demand for silence.

'I am Morrigen, whom some call the waif,' she whispered, forcing them to draw closer. 'When you are old you will remember this day and tell your children's children that I once stood amongst you.'

The whisper became a shout as someone repeated her name. Others took up the chant, and, as the crowd parted before her and she stepped into the dusk, she could hear its sound lapping round her like an echo that cannot be silenced.

*

It was dark inside the hut when he came to her. She had known he would come, known also that she would not turn him away. The beaver pelts given to her by the elders were soft against her skin. She rolled on to her back, adding to the distance that kept her from the shadow standing solitary in the entrance. She did not speak. Darkness enclosed her. From outside in the night she could smell the carcass of the roasted ox being charred by the flames, hear laughter, the songs of the villagers as they celebrated the portents that had brought them both bronze and a priestess. A pig shuffled beneath her, then rubbed its back against one of the stilts supporting the hut. A dog howled, drowning the soothing murmur of a mother trying to settle her children into sleep in the neighbouring hut.

Finally she was ready.

'Atius?'

'My face is hidden from you. I've yet to speak. Yet you knew it was me.'

He moved forward, bringing with him the river's tang and the drip of water.

'You've bathed?'

'A month's dust had made a midden of me.'

She closed her eyes as he knelt beside her. A hand brushed hers. She tried to find it, groping, uncertain, knowing that it was wrong but that she could not stop herself. Yet the words had to be said. 'I'm a priestess, no man can lie with me.'

There was movement. For a moment she thought he was leaving. She let her head sink deep into the pelts and opened her mouth as if to call him back. She lifted a hand to hush the thump of her heart. Then his fingers knitted with hers and she cried out and pulled him towards her.

'I'm frightened,' she whispered.

'Of the pain?'

'And the pleasure.' His body was damp and chill against hers and she whimpered slightly when his fingers pressed into her flesh and began tracing the long shape of her throat.

Atius's voice seemed to reach her as if through a mist. 'The river was cold, the current strong. I hoped it would bring me to my senses. Watching you at dusk I made up my mind to sleep elsewhere, with my men, anywhere but here. I've known many women. Learnt when to walk away. But tonight, even as I left the water, I felt myself turning towards this hut. Perhaps I'm asleep already? A man who walks when asleep can't be blamed for his blindness or the snares into which he stumbles.'

'Three days ago I was still a novice. We were strangers. Yet now you call me a snare?'

'Yes.'

'Then stumble . . .'

Morrigen's eyes flashed green and exultant as Atius shifted position, placing his weight above hers. She had triumphed and tamed him and could no longer be wounded. And now duty demanded that she please him and give herself to him in atonement for her victory.

So fierce was her joy it made her spread her limbs and pull him towards her, locking him in place. His fingers forked through her hair. She could feel his teeth at her neck and shoulder, his chest flatten her breasts, his body rearrange itself to match and merge with hers.

Yet inside she felt nothing, only that same sense of being detached from all that was happening to her as she had felt when taking her virginity. She pressed his lips to hers, hoping the rasp of his stubble would awaken her, give life to the pleasure now coursing her body. But the feeling of remoteness refused to vanish. He was a stranger, invisible, no part of her history. All that made him real would soon cease, his spent breath in her hair, his quickening rhythm within her. And in that rhythm she began to hear the echo of the villagers chant. So that when she finally cried out and rose to meet him and he fell exhausted beside her, her mind was empty of everything but the sound of her own name being endlessly repeated.

*

The shame came with morning. He had left her bed, but his seed still glazed her thighs and she could feel the marks of his teeth on her throat. The rhythms returned to her through sleep's haze, gradually becoming the sound of flints being knapped by a hammer. She began weeping, pulling the bedding over her head so that her world became dark and she need not search for him or show her guilt and the shame on her face. And then there was the fear. 'What if I'm with child?' she whispered, finally surrendering to it . . .

'Priestess . . .' It was a man's voice, muffled but close.

'Please go.'

But the voice persisted. 'You've brought us a miracle. Even as you slept, you healed. A village woman who yesterday was blind has woken to find her sight restored.'

And when Morrigen's head finally emerged from its hiding-place, Uba mistook her tears for joy at the woman's deliverance.

Her face was white. 'I have done this?' she murmured.

'Yes. Look.' The elder turned.

A young woman had entered the hut. She walked slowly, as

if familiar with no other pace. Her eyes were hollow and heavily lidded, but they were open, she walked unaided and her tears and bewilderment were proof of Uba's claim. She knelt beside Morrigen, kissing both her brow and eyes.

Still haunted by her sin and its consequences, Morrigen laid her cheek to the woman's and let their tears mingle as she struggled to overcome her shock and gain control of her thoughts. She knew she hadn't caused this miracle. Until now the woman had been a stranger to her. She had made no offering on her behalf, nor begged Bala to restore her sight. She had done nothing, nothing but defy the Gods and allow her womanhood to be despoiled.

Between sobs, the woman began speaking of her blindness.

'For five years I've seen nothing. The magic of many shamans has failed. My own husband, who today will return from the hunt to find me healed, once journeyed far to bring me the eyes of the eagle and the sharpness of their vision. They were placed over mine. But it made no difference. It's because of you that I'm cured.'

'I . . .' Morrigen's voice faltered. What could she say? Horror-struck, she pushed the woman aside and hurriedly pulled on her robes. What had Fram once taught her? As the sun rises, so the moon must set.

Suddenly certain what had happened and visibly stunned by the swiftness of Serapha's retribution, she began questioning the woman, making sure that nothing she said gave a hint of her thoughts. Yes, her husband was away hunting. For three days he had been stalking a wolf that had savaged their sheep . . .

Suddenly Morrigen could listen no longer. Ignoring the woman's cries, she fled the hut and her praises, running past the startled villagers without once looking back until the palisade was behind her and she was stumbling knee-deep through swamp and could collapse unseen in the reeds.

It was there that Atius found her.

Seeing her mud-splashed body, he knelt and began wiping the filth from her face. 'Are you so modest that you must flee from someone who tries to thank you for mending their sight? Uba is distressed. He thinks you've been angered in some way, that you want payment as well as praise.' Atius paused and lifted her hair from the water. 'Is there nothing you want to say to me after what we did last night?'

'Only that it was wrong.' Morrigen straightened and turned her face towards his.

'What is done cannot be undone,' said Atius softly. 'The same is true of this woman. Did you really heal her?'

'No!' cried Morrigen. 'You did! I have slain her husband! Don't you understand? Serapha has judged what we did. Now she's punished us. We sinned, but it's the woman and her husband who've been chosen to bear our burden. For as she has had her eyes opened, so have mine been opened to my shame. There's no pleasure without pain, no darkness without light. The husband has been killed by a wolf and when his corpse is brought home they'll know what I've done and curse not praise me. That's my punishment for lying with you. I meant well. It was done to please you and make you mine. But the man is dead, Atius, dead.'

The merchant gripped her arms and began shaking her as he hauled her to her feet. 'You're mad! You think you've done wrong and must justify your shame. A blind woman can see again. Nothing else has happened. Nor will it.'

Morrigen broke free and began splashing deeper into the swamp. Suddenly she turned. 'I may bear your child, Atius; but I'll still be a stranger to you. For you're right about only one thing. There is madness in me. And it's the kind of madness that cannot be cured and will always make me sin, even when I try to do good.'

# CHAPTER III

The two men lowered their fishing spears and stood to one side as the long caravan of oxen forded the stream. Both felt their seclusion had been violated; partly by the effect of the disturbance on their occupation, but also by the young woman, dressed in the pale hides of a priestess, who walked silent and wretched beside a black-bearded merchant at the head of the procession.

The emotions she aroused in them were very different. To the younger it seemed unnatural for anyone of such beauty to be sad on so perfect a day. But the old man, the rainmaker, saw more than her sorrow as she waded the shallows. Their eyes met, and for a moment he sensed a plea for pity so strong that he instinctively opened his arms as if to offer her shelter. She halted. He had a worn open face no blemish could age. But it was the simplicity of his gesture that held her, for it evoked someone who placed instinct before knowledge, intuition before reasoning. She stared at him, still undecided, then hurried on, her expression giving way to an embittered glower that seemed to reproach him for his peace of mind when her own was in such turmoil.

The rainmaker did not speak until the forest was quiet again.

'You're still thinking of her, aren't you, Hyra?'

'It's hard not to.' A pause, and a puzzled frown to accompany it. 'We must have met when both novices at Abury, but I'm sure I've seen her somewhere else. But where and when I don't know.' Irritated by his lapse of memory, Hyra sighed and lifted his spear. 'Something was troubling her, Tuah. That's all.'

The wrinkles on the old man's face deepened as he stared into the stream. 'That's twice in a day that others have spoiled our pleasure,' he said, remembering the wolf-mauled corpse that had been carried past them for burial earlier in the day. 'I sometimes think I spend too much time questing for portents in the sky and not examining my fellow men. I may make rain for the villages in the forest, but what's the point of my work if it doesn't answer to the needs of those I serve?'

Hyra smiled. 'I suspect you of rebuking me, not yourself.'

'Because you're a seer and I'm only a shaman? No, such tricks are beyond me. That woman needed help. That's common enough, we all cut sticks to lean on. But she knew it, and that's much rarer.'

Hyra laughed. 'Come, the water has cleared. No fish worth the name will wait all day to be caught.'

'An old man's ramblings, is that what you're saying? Yes, you're probably right.' But though Tuah tried to dismiss the woman, he again glanced in the direction taken by the caravan as the two of them waded into the current and took up position, one at the head of the pool, the other further upstream where fish in flight would first pause and take cover.

The water glittered, eddying slightly as it splashed round the lichen covered boulders in its course. Standing motionless, spear raised, eyes narrowed against the dazzle, Hyra soon forgot the woman. A lifetime of the moods and capriciousness of priestesses awaited him when he finally reached Henge. And that would be soon enough. His years as a novice had ended when he left Abury after celebrating the Spring Rites, and only the chance meeting with Tuah had delayed completion of the journey . . .

A sudden swirl beneath the water returned him to the present. He scanned its surface in search of the undulating motion of a tail that meant a trout was feeding within range. Then he saw it, lying long and sleek with its jaw to the current. He took aim, balancing his spear in the fold of one hand before finally releasing it. It cut the water. The fish vanished. His spear bobbed to the surface, weed impaling its head. A moment later he heard a second splash and turned to see Tuah sloshing towards him, his fifth trout of the day pinned to his spear-head.

The rainmaker grinned. 'You've spent so long being waited on at Abury that you've even forgotten how to fill your own belly.'

'Let's try again,' said Hyra eagerly.

'You'd stand here till dusk if I let you. But you're young and I'm old. Anyway, I've the weather to read.' Tuah climbed the bank and threaded the day's catch on to a length of hazel.

Hyra relented and took the fish as the two of them plunged through the forest towards the rainmaker's dwelling. Tuah's right, he thought: the years spent cloistered at Abury had blunted his instincts, made him forget even the simplest of skills. He smiled, too happy to let self-criticism long mar his pleasure. Sunlight filtered between the budding leaves of the oaks overhead. The air was pungent with sap and the blossoming limes. Once he glimpsed a herd of deer move silently through the shadows. He could hear the call of a cuckoo, see bees drift amongst the flowers that patched the glades. 'The forest makes me feel like a child again,' he said. 'Like someone reborn.'

'That's because, like a child, you're seeing it as if for the first time. Abury has dulled your senses. Even a pot of water becomes rancid if left too long. To be filled, it must first be emptied. By travelling alone and hunting your own food you've been forced to live by instinct, just as a child does.'

'But I'm a grown man: A seer of the Sacred Rites.'

'And I make rain. Others give us our titles, but the words mean nothing.' Tuah glanced at his companion. 'Do you really believe that you can best serve the Cunei by growing old in the Sacred Dwellings?'

'Of course,' answered Hyra: but his reply lacked conviction. Since becoming a novice he had lived in a world in which the power of the seers was taken for granted. It was hard to admit that the last few days had been amongst the happiest he could recall. Tuah's company, the appetite and aching muscles that marked days spent stalking fish or deer, the frugal simplicity of woodland life; all these things were like a cleansing wind after the formality and ritual of Abury.

The contrast became even more pronounced when he caught sight of the rainmaker's home. A hollow lightning-scarred oak, it sat alone, a mutilated finger pointing upwards to the sky, in a small clearing in the heart of the forest. The trees surrounding it had been festooned with branches that hung like deformed leaves from its still bare branches.

Tuah indicated the skull on its summit, empty eyes facing to where the next full moon would rise. 'My father's father. When I was a child I used to sit at his feet and listen to him gossip with the other elders in our village. They were old men. Some of them remembered being told stories of the building of Henge. Only one stone had been raised in those days, and that stood outside the temple.'

'Where it still remains.'

'To be treated like an old man who must be honoured because of his age,' said Tuah angrily. 'Once, when only Serapha was divine, the seers used that stone to plot the Goddess's movements as she travelled the heavens. They could even give warning of the nights of the Darkness. They shared their knowledge, telling the shamans so that they could calm and prepare the people before the moon dimmed. Sacrifices were prepared. The women who then ruled the Cunei gathered inside Henge, each squeezing her breasts until milk came and it could be poured into the pits that used to circle the temple. In this way Serapha was suckled and her light grew brighter again. Now what happens? The Dobuni are masters of Henge and the sun is worshipped as a God. Who was consulted when the temple was rebuilt so that the Serapha Stone aligns with the midsummer sunrise instead of the rising of the moon? Neither the Council nor the shamans. Yet it is we who serve the people. If I say it will rain, it does so. If I warn of a tempest, it comes.' He paused, smiling in apology for his outburst. 'And perhaps you can summon up sufficient wind to blow life into the fire?'

Hyra did so, then wrapped mud round two of the trout and placed them in the ashes.

But his thoughts remained muddled as he watched them bake. He had left Abury convinced that only the seers could placate the Gods. And here was an old man who could forecast rain from the motion of a fish or the slot of a deer, a man who lived alone in a forest but whose words rang truer than any he had been taught as a novice, and who, in a few days, had made him question Henge's purpose, ask himself if it was merely a statement of power sustained by fear and superstition.

Unable to resolve these doubts, he turned towards Tuah. The rainmaker was squatting on his haunches with his face tilted to the breeze. He was motionless, every muscle was at rest. Occasionally he sniffed the wind or glanced at the sky. Once or twice he placed his hands to the ground and snapped a blade of grass, rubbing it between his fingers. Hyra watched spellbound as the silence lengthened. Tuah had told him that every sense had to be employed when trying to predict any change in the weather, and for a moment it seemed to him that the rainmaker had withdrawn into a state of limbo in which he was neither man nor nature but a combination of both. Finally he spoke.

'The rains have ended. I must go round the villages and tell the elders to sow their corn before the night of the full moon.'

'Can't they come to you?'

'I'm their servant, not their master.'

How unlike any seer, thought a chastened Hyra. 'And how do you know that the weather has changed?' he asked.

The rainmaker's smile showed how accustomed he was to the question. 'Now you would like to outwit me, prove me a sham who picks clouds from the sky as a herd picks fleas from his swine. If I say something is about to happen, it does so. A rainmaker exposed as a fraud would soon pay for it with his life.' He paused, lifting an arm. 'Look at the trout, the sheen on their scales. Look at the shape of the clouds and the colour of the sun as it sets. Remember the tracks and calls of the creatures we saw during the day. Feel the dryness of the wind on your cheek, breathe its scents. Listen to the thrush, the bark of the stag. Watch the worm, study its cast. Alone, each of these means little, but together they're the voice of the earth and sky, of which wind and rain are just a part. From them, and many other things, I now know that the sun will remain with us until the moon is new again.'

'And after that?'

'We must wait. The corn will have started to sprout and the villagers will need rain to make it grow. I'll help them, putting away the limes that disperse damp clouds, burning no fires lest they dry up the moisture in the air. Even the bones of my forefathers must be taken down from the trees. Rain discomforts them. They grow angry, turning back the clouds.'

Tuah's words kept Hyra awake that night. Tossing restlessly beneath his bedding, he thought of his father and mother, his sisters and Lyla, the woman all hoped he would wed; finally, for no logical reason, the face of the priestess he had seen earlier in the day passed fleetingly before his eyes.

The night was warm, the stars in the constellation of the Herdsman stretched its limbs overhead. Once he heard the scrape of a wild-cat sharpening its claws on a nearby tree; once the snuffle of boar foraging for roots made him reach for his bow. But though the unfamiliar nocturnal sounds of the forest added to his unease, it was not they but Tuah who kept him from his sleep.

Until now he had never questioned the way of life that awaited him at Henge. Until now he had thought the seer's dedication to prophecy and the completion of the temple to be the noblest of destinies. In his years at Abury he had learnt how to use a tally stick to subtract and multiply numbers. He had been taught how to measure ground, how to understand the relationship between lines, surfaces and solids. He could speak fluently on the motions of the stars, the phases of the moon, the sun's annual cycle. Without faltering he could recite each of the rituals that governed the performance of the seasonal Rites. He could do all these things – but he couldn't spear a trout without the help of an old man or make the rain fall when it was needed.

'Very well,' he decided, before sleep finally claimed him. 'I'll renounce my vows and remain in the forest, becoming rain-maker in Tuah's place when he grows too old to make it himself.'

*

Tuah laughed when the seer announced his decision.

'You'll do nothing of the kind. It's to Henge you're bound and it's to Henge you must go.'

'But yesterday you told me I'd be wasting my time!' protested a crestfallen Hyra.

'And so you might be. You're young and eager to please, a reed to be shaken by each wind as it blows. Be patient. One day you may become Lord of the Rites. Perhaps then you'll remember our friendship and find a way to bridge the abyss that divides the seers from the people. You've a task now, a track to travel. You've the strength for it, and the will. You can remain here until the moon is full, then you must go.'

Hyra accepted this judgement. Kindness had lessened the sting, and for the next few days he was content to explore the forest with the rainmaker and go with him to the villages he served. During that time his affection for Tuah increased. There was something of his own father about him, that same mix of commonsense and straightforwardness, a complexity made simple because it dealt only with truth. Together they set snares and tracked a bear in hope of slaying it and being able to extract from its liver the oil used by the rainmaker when attempting to end a drought.

On the fifth day they rose early, intending to cross the forest and spend the night in a village on its far border. Tuah had yet to visit it that spring, for its inhabitants grew no corn, depending for their livelihood on cattle and leather.

They had nearly completed the journey when he suddenly halted in mid-stride and began sniffing the breeze.

'Can you smell smoke, hear women screaming?' he asked anxiously.

Hyra looked at him in amazement. The forest was silent but for the shuffle of leaves. Its only scent was of arrested decay. 'No.'

'I can. We must hurry.'

Tuah began running, barely slowing pace as he swerved between the trees and forced his way through the undergrowth.

Still mystified, Hyra hurried in his wake. Suddenly he heard someone cry out and glimpsed smoke in the distance. A few more strides and the forest parted to reveal a cluster of huts, one of them on fire, and a group of wailing women gathered round a man lying sprawled in the middle of the clearing. Some of the villagers were using branches to try and beat out the flames. Others appeared wounded and two lay prostrate near the blazing hut.

Seeing Tuah, one of the women ran towards him, arms outstretched and eyes wide with terror. He began comforting her, but her sobs made nonsense of her explanation. Finally she blurted, 'They came at dawn . . . as Bala rose. They gave no warning. They might have been demons. Most of us were still asleep. The first we knew of it was when they fired Caedor's hut . . .'

'Who came?' demanded Tuah.

'The Dobuni. They've slain Caedor and taken his daughters. They said they'd return, and would keep coming back until all the elders are dead or we obey the will of the seers . . .'

Tuah turned and stared searchingly at Hyra as the woman continued.

'. . . The Spring Lottery has been drawn. We were drawn first. Caedor refused to let anyone begin the Toil until after the herds had been driven onto the Plain to graze. He had no choice. We've no corn. Without the cattle we'd starve . . .'

A small but angry crowd had gathered round the rainmaker. Still troubled by Tuah's glance, Hyra stood quietly on its rim. Finally someone indicated the amber armlet that marked him as a seer. He backed away as a spear stabbed close to his chest. The mood worsened. The villagers began threatening him, shaking fists and sticks. An old woman hobbled forward. Her once grey eyes had paled with age, but in them he read the stunned and horror-struck look that signalled her loss. Suddenly she reached forward and spat in his face before Tuah could intervene.

'Be grateful that Tuah has befriended you!' she cried. 'If you had come here alone you would not leave. I would kill you myself.' She paused, pointing to the corpse at her feet. 'Look carefully at the work you seers have done this day. My husband lies dead in his blood. My daughters are to be sold as slaves.'

'Hyra knows nothing of this!' shouted Tuah sternly.

The villagers refused to listen. Some spoke of revenge, of holding him hostage for the daughters. Tuah tried to calm them, but their shouts drowned his words. He turned grim-faced towards Hyra. 'You'd better leave at once. I can't save you. Enough blood has been shed, but yours will spill if you stay here much longer. But do as the widow says. Look well. Tomorrow it may be your turn to draw the tallies that spare some and make others toil. Stones aren't people. They cannot starve or watch their husbands die. You may be a seer, but you were born a Cunei. Serve the Dobuni too long and you'll become as ruthless as they. Now go.'

Hyra started to speak . . .

'Go!' Tuah's arm rose sharply towards the forest.

But still Hyra hesitated. A stone struck his forehead. He turned and began running, lowering his head in shame when he reached the edge of the clearing and looked back to where Tuah stood staring at him. He hurried on through the forest. Suddenly he glimpsed the Plain through a break in the trees. Until meeting Tuah he had been longing for this moment. But today, wind-swept and desolate beneath clouds banked slate overhead, it seemed grey and forbidding, almost sinister: a landscape to match what he had fled from and the temple that lay hidden in its folds.

# CHAPTER IV

'You owe a lot to Atius. He brought you here safely, even delaying his journey until the fever had left you. Wouldn't it be courteous to show your gratitude before he goes?

'Must I?'

'Yes, Morrigen. You must.'

Ishtar was High Priestess, but she was also a Dobuni who boasted all the imperiousness of her tribe. It was not in her nature to humour the whims of those in her charge, least of all when they questioned her authority so soon after arrival.

Morrigen forced herself to appear calm as she walked through the small crowd that had gathered to watch the caravan as it left the Sacred Dwellings. The oxen were already in motion, their half-empty panniers slapping against their flanks as they crossed the causeway, skirted the servants' tents and began the descent to where the river looped back on itself as it flowed past far below.

Atius was standing near the livestock pens supervising the herding of the cattle he had acquired in exchange for his wares. Behind him rose the high chalk bank that enclosed the encampment. He smiled as he saw Morrigen approach. 'Worry can only make it worse,' he said gently, determined to end the hostility that had grown up between them since reaching the Dwellings on the previous day.

'I can't stop myself.' Morrigen's fever had drained the colour from her face, leaving it pale and drawn. Her eyes were swollen, but they glittered angrily as Atius wrapped her hands in his.

'It'll be a month before you can be certain,' he said.

'How convenient,' retorted Morrigen. 'Just enough time to forget that it was you who made love to me.'

'You could have ordered me to leave. You can't rearrange the past to suit the needs of the present. If you're with child, so be it.'

'Is that all you can say?'

'You've no proof yet. I'd save your anger till you have.'

'It won't be you who has to bear it, who has to serve as a priestess and act as if nothing has happened.'

'But it was you who demanded punishment.' Atius paused. 'I sometimes wonder if you enjoy your suffering, indulge it to gain sympathy or excuse your guilt. Did seeing the hunter's corpse really cause your fever, or was it a purge, an attempt at salving your conscience? Cry wolf too often and you'll make foes out of friends.'

'I have no friends.' Morrigen's eyes lifted to his, as if beseeching him to deny what she had said.

But Atius refused to be tempted. 'No, Morrigen. I've been snared once by you. It won't happen again.'

'Then leave me and go.'

Atius did not move as he surveyed the encampment. The ground sloped uphill to where the ramparts formed a high irregular circle round the thatched huts and log-framed storehouses that sprawled within its circumference. The huts were circular, with pitched conical roofs and wattle and daub walls incised with patterns. Their shapes, he recalled, indicated their function: the Council Dwelling, the Dwelling of Mysteries where the Rites of puberty and initiation were celebrated, the dwellings that housed the priestesses, seers and their acolytes. Some were entered between short avenues of posts shaped like serpents and horns. Other posts, intricately carved and also painted, reared up against the blue of the sky. Pedlars and visiting elders bustled to and fro through the quag. Two seers, both old and oblivious to the noise, were plotting the sun's motions from inside the circle of sculpted timber posts that constituted the Temple of Bala.

'I'll be glad to be gone,' he said finally, glancing through the entrance to the wilderness beyond. 'It may be sacred, but this place smacks of sanctimony. It always has and it always will. One night here and I feel like a finch in its cage.'

'You care for no one but yourself,' said Morrigen quietly.

'Whilst you believe that by serving the Gods you've renounced the devil. You're wrong, there's a devil in all of us. Without it we'd have no need of a God.' The merchant laughed. He stared at Morrigen for a moment, placing her image amongst those of the other women he had known. Suddenly he released her hands and joined his men. Dust rose, hiding him from view as his cattle were driven over the causeway. When it had settled, he was gone.

Morrigen remained where she was. Handmaids pushed past her, a dog licked the hand hanging limp at her side. She was aware of neither. The reality of Atius's departure had yet to root, but she could feel the beginnings of reaction, the need to sever him from her thoughts. Soon she would be calm again, as impassive and empty of feeling as the mud at their feet. Aware that she was being observed, she scanned her new world.

'Atius is a wealthy and successful merchant, but he's also without shame. I hope he hasn't persuaded you to disregard your vows.'

Morrigen turned to see Ishtar standing silently behind her. 'No, of course not,' she said quickly, lowering her gaze as the High Priestess's eyes bore deep into hers.

'Good. But you wouldn't have been the first. Since I took office at least two of the priestesses have had cause to regret meeting him.'

'What do you mean?'

Ishtar gave a clipped smile. 'He seduced them. They had to be banished to their villages to bear his bastards. Now come, it's time you were taken to Henge to give thanks for your safe arrival.'

*

Morrigen never forgot that first visit to the temple, nor those that succeeded it. For almost a month she daily walked the two miles from the Sacred Dwellings, sometimes standing alone lit only by the dawn, head bowed towards the stones in the entrance, hair lifting in the wind, as she waited for her body to disprove her worst fears.

The fear was obsessive. She was friendless, there was no one in whom she could confide. Ralla arrived, bringing with her a truculence and petty vindictiveness that deepened the divide between Morrigen and her fellow priestesses. The traders and shamans and tribesfolk who thronged the Dwellings only added to her loneliness. Even when she woke to discover that she wasn't pregnant and the panic left her, the fear remained – inspired now by the conviction that she must be barren. There seemed no escape. She ate little, slept less. Her skin lost its lustre and her cheeks grew wasted as if with disease. Caged by her misery, she began to think of herself as the most accursed of women. Gradually, like a stunted child conceived solely by the mind, this belief took on a life of its own. She grew used to it, accepting it as her true nature and drawing a measure of comfort from the peace it seemed to bring.

Only when at Henge did her fears return, and today, as was now her custom, she paused for a moment before following the other priestesses into the temple.

Two months had elapsed since her arrival. Spring had given way to early summer. Hawthorn blossom drifted snow-white in the breeze and a green haze marked the edge of the forest. Sheep grazed the scrub. The tents in the Village of Shamans were again occupied after being left empty throughout the winter. More tents rimmed the water-holes in the valley and round the nearest villages the thin tilted fields shaped the rise and fall of the downs, the Plain weathered to its curves by wind and rain.

'Hurry up, Morrigen!'

Ishtar was standing beside the trench dug to hold the next pair of stones to be raised in the still unfinished circle. She was aquiline and intolerant, with a sharp sallow face and even sharper temper, and her scowl was sufficient to end the banter that welcomed Morrigen's entry into the temple.

Morrigen joined her companions, only to be deliberately jostled by Ralla in the hope that she might trip and fall into the trench.

'Stop it! Step forward, both of you.'

They did so, Ralla shuffling uncomfortably as Ishtar rebuked them for bickering and threatened asking the seers to prepare the embers. But even the threat of having to undergo the Mastery of Fire by walking on heated coals to purify the mind made no impact on Morrigen. Ishtar watched her for a moment, finally sensing in her some inner strength that had known too much pain to still be panicked by it. She continued speaking.

'Until the eve of the new moon you two are responsible for dousing the fire every morning and coming here to offer guidance to the tribesfolk. The first hay has already been cut. Soon the Cunei will leave their villages and bring their herds to their summer grazing grounds on the Plain. It's the season of the hunt, of felling timber and raising tombs for those who died in the winter. But it's also the time of the Toil, and I won't allow your dispute to mar its success. Is that understood?'

Both nodded contritely.

'Good. Yesterday the first of the stones passed the Dwellings on its journey downriver from Abury. As priestesses of the fifth month it's up to you to watch over it as it's dragged to the temple. Do you remember your duties? Morrigen?'

'We must obey the seers, help prepare the food for the toilers and gather blossom to sprinkle on their cooking fires.'

'And wash the stone and take part in the Rite of Propitiation,' added Ralla, permitting a self-satisfied smile as she poured the ashes from the preceding night's fire into the trench. Since her arrival two of the priestesses had died of contagion. As a chieftain's daughter it was she who had benefited. Morrigen was now her inferior, and therefore expected to mix the remaining ashes with chalk and daub it in her hair, leaving it matted and unwashed until the stone stood upright in its socket.

But her triumph was brief. Once Morrigen had puddled the mixture and combed it into place, the streaks of black and white that now fell to her waist framed her entire body, giving it a grave but dazzling beauty.

Later that day the two of them left Henge and began walking along the Sacred Way towards the river. Once out of sight of Ishtar, Ralla resumed their quarrel. 'You reek of filth and look ridiculous. That merchant of yours would mock if he met you now.'

Morrigen tried to ignore the mention of Atius. Since hearing others gossip about his reputation her infatuation for him had turned to contempt. Hating him for all she had suffered, she had tried to banish his memory; but even hate needs something to sustain it and he still troubled her thoughts. He was a liar, a libertine who had taken advantage of her innocence; but she would admit it to no one, least of all Ralla. 'My duty is to Bala, not Atius,' she retorted.

Ralla sneered unpleasantly. 'Has he made love to you yet? No, of course not. I forget, the waif's much too prim to take a lover.'

'It's not your concern.'

'It may be one day. I've a mind to make him my own. He's wealthy, there's Dobuni blood in him. I'd show him such pleasure he wouldn't stray from my bed until I grew weary of him and pushed him from beneath the pelts.'

'You flatter yourself.'

'I speak the truth.'

Morrigen checked her reply. Ralla's affairs were an ill-kept secret. Ridicule, perhaps even disgrace, might follow if Atius seduced her when he next visited the Dwellings. 'Take him then,' she said finally.

Ralla frowned suspiciously. Morrigen's humiliation was the main motive for her plan. Like many women who boast of their promiscuity much of it was fictional. 'Are you trying to trick me, or do you mean what you say?'

'Find out whilst you've still the time. For the day'll come, Ralla, when no man will look at you again, be he young or toothless. I swear it.'

'So now you threaten?'

'Or prophesy. You must decide which.'

Ralla's retort died on her lips as she met Morrigen's gaze. She was smiling. But it was a hard, cruel smile that lacked any hint of emotion. Not for the first time she questioned her wisdom in choosing Morrigen for an enemy. There was a ruthlessness to her eyes that promised ill for the future. She fell silent, a temporary truce patching their feud as they recalled Ishtar's instructions and hurried on towards the river.

Entering a wood, Morrigen glimpsed the flash of sunlight on water at the far end of a broad track. The track was furrowed, flakes of stone lay in the ruts and the ground had been cleared of all trees and their stumps. 'There's the river!' She broke into a run, only slowing pace when she reached the tents on its bank.

The Cunei chosen for the Toil ignored her. Squatting disgruntled and morose in a circle, the women were plaiting nettles and cutting hide into strips, the men binding the finished ropes round the timber baulks that were to act as sledge. A group of seers, silent witnesses to the labour they had ordered, lined the river-bank, but she paid them scant attention as she peered excitedly up-stream.

Floating towards her were three dug-out canoes lashed one to the next. Their hulls were low in the water from the spread weight of the great stone they were carrying. Those on board were singing, and their paddles dipped and rose in time to their voices as they let the current carry them slowly round the long meander made by the river. Its course straightened. Half the oarsmen back-paddled, carefully turning their craft broadside to the stream before piloting them to where the bank shelved and their cargo was to be landed.

Morrigen watched as Ralla left her side and went down to

the water's edge. Behind her she heard some ewes stamp their hooves in complaint as they were robbed of the warm milk she was supposed to offer the toilers when they first stepped ashore. The paddles flashed, throwing up beads of water that glittered in the sunlight. Suddenly one of the canoes caught the full force of the current. A green wash sluiced over its sides. Morrigen's fist rose in alarm to her teeth . . .

'I am called Hyra. I'm the seer of the fifth month and will be staying with the stone until it reaches Henge.'

. . . the stone shifted slightly, pulling against its ropes . . .

'Are you listening . . . ?'

Morrigen nodded. Two men switched canoes, hurriedly correcting the balance as lines were tossed ashore and willing hands dragged them into shallow water . . .

'Priestess, please . . .'

This time she relented. The fist fell.

She did not recognize him for a moment; the contrast between the two places, the years in between, her own excitement, all conspiring to dull her memory. And then pine torches lit the night and she was in the Maiden Lines again, standing naked before a young bearded stranger whose appearance had fed her hopes and whose abrupt departure had changed her life.

'I've seen you before,' he said.

She turned away, now certain of betrayal, of having to relive her shame.

'I was fishing. You were walking beside a merchant.'

'I don't remember,' she stammered.

'Nor should you.' Hyra smiled and asked her name.

She shivered but said nothing.

'Is it a secret?'

She paled, closing her eyes. 'Morrigen.'

Hyra nodded. 'I already know Ralla. We met when still novices.' Disapproval sharpened his voice as he watched her dance amongst the toilers as they waded ashore. 'Time hasn't changed her.'

So her name hadn't reminded him of their first encounter in the Maiden Lines! Morrigen felt her numbness begin to ebb. By rights she should despise him for his behaviour in the Lines, but she found it impossible. Today, as then, there was a quiet and gentle dignity to his manner that made her feel instantly at ease. She indicated Ralla. 'Must I do that?'

'Are you as vain?'
'I hope not.'
'Then no. Such a dance has no place in the Rites.' Drenched in water, Ralla was swirling amongst the toilers. Her robes clung to her body, contouring its shape, rounded breasts, the wedge of shadow linking her thighs.
Morrigen turned towards the seer. Atius had made her wary of men. Those who had humoured her since his departure she suspected of regarding her as someone to be challenged or subdued. Yet Hyra's friendliness seemed too open to be critical. He had not flattered or questioned her, he shared her dislike for Ralla. But how long would pass before he heard rumours of her past and connected them to the girl he had met in the Lines?
'What happens next?' she asked him.
'I'm not sure.'
'There's so much we have to remember.'
'Too much, I fear.'
As if conspirators, they grinned as a pole-ramp was placed against the canoes and ropes were slung round the stone. The ramp was greased with pig fat. The toilers picked up the ropes and began to heave. The stone moved, the sudden shift of weight forcing the bows of the canoes deep into the river-bed. Fresh orders were shouted. A group of men swam across the river, ropes round their waists. After clambering through the reeds, they turned and held the stone in place whilst the ramp was forced beneath it. They began slackening their ropes, teasing them out through their fingers as the stone slowly slid down the poles to where the sledge stood waiting in the shallows. As the sledge took its weight, the canoes jerked upwards, spilling men and mud into the river.
Morrigen clapped her hands in her excitement, then began laughing as the toilers rose dripping from the water.
Hyra frowned at her enjoyment. 'I last saw these men on the day the Dobuni slaughtered one of their elders and took his daughters for slaves. You laugh, they mourn. They'd refused to take part in the Toil. All but one of their elders was killed before they finally gave in.'
Morrigen's laugh faded as she heard the anger in his voice. 'We serve the Gods, why shouldn't they? Henge is theirs. It's up to them to help build it.'
'Is it? I'm not so sure.'
Hyra remained silent whilst the Rites were celebrated. But

watching Morrigen ladle milk into bowls for each of the toilers, he tried to recall where he had first seen her. One image stuck in his mind, that of a copper-haired girl suddenly shedding her robes and standing brazen in front of him. But he could not place it, and so discarded it as being a role he must have invented for her, a fantasy worthy of only the most prurient of his dreams.

Disgusted at his own weakness, he purposely walked beside her when both seers and priestesses finally began the homeward journey along the river-bank towards the Sacred Dwellings. Since leaving Tuah, he had kept his thoughts to himself. Yet he felt that Morrigen had some connection with the days he had spent in the forest. Like the toilers, she linked past with present, gave perspective to the doubts that had turned slowly to discontent since arriving at Henge. So her presence loosened his tongue. He spoke openly, first trying to persuade her that his brother seers regarded their occupation as a kind of game, a means of outwitting one-another by predicting the motions of sun, moon and stars.

'They've been pampered too long,' he said angrily. 'The fate of the toilers means nothing. They're lazy, self-seeking and arrogant. No one questions their power. Why? Because they've surrounded themselves with an air of sanctity that none dare criticize lest they incur the wrath of the Gods.'

'You preach sedition.'

'I'm telling the truth.'

'And what do you intend doing about it?'

'I don't know.'

'You could fight.'

Hyra shook his head. 'No, my neck is too precious to risk it on a call to arms against the Dobuni.'

'So the brave words mask a man who'd play the craven?'

The question was important to Morrigen. Hyra's anger had shifted from the seers to the Dobuni themselves. It was dangerous ground. Dissent was forbidden. The last Cunei uprising had been brutally quashed by the nomadic and well-armed Dobuni.

'You were born a Cunei, but you serve Bala. We're both guilty of renouncing our people,' he said.

'To be a priestess there is no other choice.'

'So we're trapped.'

'Power can lead to carelessness.'

'In which case we must wait until the chieftains unite and Serapha's will is made known. No tyranny can last for ever.'

Morrigen smiled to herself. She had found her first ally, the first rung on the ladder by which she intended to climb. Pity and exultation crowded her thoughts. Already she knew that it would not be difficult to woo and win him: his eagerness to befriend her was proof of that. But she would have to be careful, and cunning. Otherwise he might suspect her motives, realize the extent of her ambition. Patience, she thought. Do nothing to encourage, nothing to hinder. Let love blind him to her faults, then manipulate and taint it, make use of it in any way that would best serve her interests.

She took his arm. 'You're the first friend I've made.'

Hyra reddened, then turned away to where the Plain sloped upward towards Henge. 'Something is going to happen. I can feel it. Not just to the tribes but to the temple itself.'

Morrigen remained silent.

Hyra looked at her. 'Why don't you answer?'

Morrigen pantomimed apprehension. 'I'm afraid for you, for both of us.'

'Why?'

'You might act on what I say. I don't want to cause you to suffer.'

Morrigen smiled as the seer squeezed her hand. It was all so easy. He was doomed and did not know it.

*

When the next two years were finally over Morrigen saw that they had been no more than a marking time, the stillness that precedes the storm. That first encounter with Hyra had been followed by many. Their friendship flowered, withered, commenced a second birth. Indeed, their relationship began to imitate the seasons, and there were moments when she thought that the process of growth and decay had absorbed them into its cycle.

Even her moods became changeable. Her lowly place amongst the priestesses, the tediousness of her duties, Ralla's scorn, her inability to exploit her status, all affected her, yet they never combined to become the sum of what shaped her. Laughter would turn to tears for no reason, her beauty become blemished by a sudden shift of expression. It was as if, noted Hyra, she was a tree whose branches put out leaves but whose roots remained invisible. For gradually it dawned on him that her exterior was a mask, that beneath it was something vulnerable and confused, the genesis of tragedy, a lack of peace that left her restless and mercurial.

After the evening Rites they would often walk along the banks of the river and watch the local tribesmen haul in their nets.

'Atius has returned again,' she said once.

Hyra detected the anger in her voice. For some reason Atius's presence made her curt and short-tempered. She would hear his laughter and scowl, catch his eye and stalk back to her dwelling. 'You make him sound worse than he is. The banter hides shrewdness and an understanding of the tribes.'

'He's Ralla's lover.'

'Forget them.'

'She's broken her vows. Ishtar should punish her.'

'She can't harm you.'

'She hates me. I don't trust her.'

'Atius must discover her faults for himself. She's a powerful woman. The warriors respect her, two more sources of copper were found after she last led the Bull Dance. The Council see her as a future High Priestess.'

Morrigen stared along the river. Down-stream, goats were being unloaded from a raft. Beyond it a group of boys were swinging from the Bridge of Peril, the cat's-cradle of ropes over which the seers walked blindfold on the eve of the Winter Rites.

She deliberated confessing. Until now she had remained silent about her one night with Atius, telling Hyra that they had quarrelled on the journey to Henge. But although time had dulled her hate, the merchant's brashness continued to attract her, and whenever he was resident in the Dwellings she felt as if she was being pulled towards him by emotions she could not muzzle.

In the end she said, 'But why does Atius spend so much time with her? To her he's a conquest, a trophy to be flaunted when we meet.'

'Does it matter? Try and destroy her and you risk destroying yourself.'

'But you'd make me whole again, wouldn't you?' said Morrigen softly, reaching for Hyra's arm.

He smiled, not certain what she meant but content in her

company. At such moments he knew he was in love with her, the broken creature only he could mend. But he never spoke of it. He had yet to tell her about Lyla, the childhood friend and sister to Ceruduc it was assumed he would finally marry. And then there were the occasions her melancholy spilled over into rage, exposing a second more sinister Morrigen. He would draw back from her then. Yet even as he did so he sensed the closeness between fear and desire; that same inexplicable attraction that made her stand close to the river when its waters were in flood, laughing like a mad-woman. He would call her back and hold out his hand, only to be ignored as she screamed her delight and the river's mudded roar tossed trees and bloated cattle high into the air.

*

Whilst Morrigen's ambitions remained thwarted, Hyra climbed swiftly through the ranks of the seers. Theirs was an insular world, sustained by tradition and the power of the Dobuni. In order to allay their suspicions and add to his knowledge, he befriended one of the oldest and most respected of the seers.

Leoid was wizened, myopic and lame; his infirmities and shrunken body suggesting someone who had purposely conserved his strength by preserving only its most essential features. Despite his age, his reputation was assured. It was he who had redesigned Henge for the Dobuni so as to align its axis with the Serapha Stone and the rising of Bala in midsummer, he who had positioned four stones in a rectangle outside the circle, the Element Stones, to mark both sunrise and sunset on each of the quarter-days. The two men became a familiar sight. Hyra carrying his measuring lines and sighting wands, Leoïd hobbling in his wake propping up the staff in which he cut his tallies.

North of the temple two parallel banks ran for a mile across the Plain. Now abandoned, they enclosed a funeral way where the Cunei had once carried their dead in procession before burial. Other funeral ways, survivors of a ritual that had died with the coming of the Dobuni, still scattered the countryside. One of them lay a three day journey from Henge, and, two years after first meeting Morrigen, Hyra and Leoid left the Dwellings to visit it.

They went alone, Leoid evading all discussion about the

reason for the journey until late on the third day. By then the high downs lay behind them, and only scrub and a wedge of forest separated them from their destination when he finally spoke.

'We worship two Gods, the sun and moon. We've learnt a lot about their motions, but most of it dies with us and is soon forgotten.'

'But what of the chants and Rites I was taught as a novice?'

'Can you still recite all you were taught? No, until we invent a means of recording knowledge there is much that will always be lost.'

Hyra smiled to himself. Leoid's belief that if words could be spoken they could also be transformed into shapes written on slate was one of the reasons why many thought age had dulled his wits.

'For instance,' continued the seer. 'I had the entrance to Henge altered to align with the Serapha Stone. But the results are inaccurate. You and I will have died and been reborn time and again before the sun rises over its summit. No, there are many riddles that need to be solved before we can claim that Henge will predict all the actions of our Gods.'

'How can a Cunei funeral way be of help?'

Leoid frowned, wagging a chiding finger. 'You doubt what you've yet to see. It's six miles long. It was built when Henge was first new, young men labouring into old age with only ox bones and antlers to raise its banks. For what? Why is it so long? We may never know, but I believe that those who ordered it dug once used it to plot the precise motions of the sun and moon . . .' Leoid had warmed to his theme and could not be stopped. If Hyra interrupted, he huffed cantankerously in retaliation. Left undisturbed he spoke of lunar cycles and the cycles that govern the nights when the moon's face grows dark. He explained its link with the tides and the movements of the sun. But so abstruse was much of what he said that Hyra sighed gratefully when he suddenly broke off in mid-sentence. 'We're there,' he said. 'Now you can see it for yourself.'

Hyra followed the sweep of his hand. Ahead of them, a pair of high banks a stone's throw apart ran eastward across the countryside. Only one section was visible. Dipping into a valley, it then rose towards a grass-covered long tomb straddling the crest of a hill. Turf had yet to hide it, and in places, white and gleaming with chalk, the banks modelled the roll of surf as it breaks. Smoke drifted from the villages in the valley. Sheep cropped the pasture. In the far distance he noticed tents and a group of recently dug round tombs still strewn with the garlands left behind by the mourners.

Leoid broke the silence. 'The locals still think it sacred and bury their dead within sight of it. Once a year the village girls gather inside it and strike out with whips at the unwed men from their villages as they race from one end to the other. Those who draw blood will never be barren.'

For the next few days the two seers walked back and forth along the way in search of the alignments Leoid believed it incorporated. During those days its sheer enormity made Hyra marvel at his ancestors' achievement. Here, on flint-scarred scrub thick with gorse and thorn, men had once endured a lifetime of toil to offer their dead a safe passage into the Underworld and learn what they could about the nature of their God. To walk its length took most of a morning. Gradually its secrets began to unfold. Leoid found a line that tracked the setting of the midwinter sun, then a second line that marked the moon's rising midway through its cycle, an alignment he himself had built into Henge.

One afternoon he asked Hyra to light a beacon on a nearby tomb in hope of confirming his findings. As Hyra set off to gather brushwood from the forest he noticed a procession of mourners begin climbing the valley in readiness for a burial at sunset. The corpse lay on a litter. Behind it walked shamans, seers and a solitary priestess.

Reaching the edge of the forest, he passed a swineherd driving his pigs in search of mast. A squat, surly looking man with blackened teeth, his swine snuffled with hunger as he cursed and drove them on with his whip in the direction of the procession. By the time Hyra had collected sufficient fuel for the fire the mourners had drawn closer. A shock of copper hair hung stray and wind-blown beneath the priestess's hood.

Hyra dropped his load and tried to attract her attention. She waved, spoke to one of the seers and started running towards him. The swineherd shouted at her as she passed him. Morrigen quickened pace. The swineherd raised his whip and gave chase. Hyra ran to meet her, bewildered and slightly alarmed. Her legs were shaking, and in her face he saw the haunted hunted look of someone who has stepped back into a past they had hoped to forget.

'What is it?' he demanded.

'Let go of me!'

She tried to side-step. He tightened his grip on her wrist. 'You're frightened of the herdsman. Why? I need to know if I'm to help you.'

As if in answer, the swineherd lashed out with his whip at Morrigen as he approached. 'Come here!' he bellowed. 'You're mine, woman. You may have fled from me once but you won't do so again. Don't pretend you don't know me. You've changed though. You're not the wretch I met in the Maiden Lines any more.'

Morrigen went limp as she tilted her face to Hyra's. Her eyes held his, slipped away, then returned. For an instant she thought he had forgotten. His brow folded in on itself with confusion, then, as memory returned and he slowly released his hold on her, she realized that the swineherd's words had finally betrayed her . . .

'I would have told you,' she whispered.

Hyra turned away, momentarily too stunned to know what to say.

'I didn't want you to think of me like that,' said Morrigen. 'The swineherd's right. I'm not the same person any more.'

'It was night.' Hyra closed his eyes as he spoke. 'You seemed so unhappy. I couldn't understand that. I felt sorry for you and wanted to calm you whilst Ceruduc chose a wife.'

'It wasn't your pity I wanted.'

The whip cracked overhead, its tip curling and forcing them apart. 'Leave her alone,' shouted the swineherd. 'She's mine. There's a husband's pleasure I've yet to enjoy with her. I won't be cheated of my rights.'

Morrigen turned to Hyra. 'Now do you understand why I couldn't tell you? After you left my mother sold me to this. Look at him, Hyra! Is this what your pity intended for me? Smell him! He'd have treated me no better than a whore. I fled to Abury. Fram made me a novice.

The swineherd stepped forward to claim her, whip stock slapping idly against his calves.

Morrigen backed away. Hyra seemed frozen, unable to intervene. She turned, searching for escape. The swineherd lifted his whip, then stretched out a hand.

'Come quietly and I'll spare you the thrashing you deserve.'

Morrigen stared at him, caught between flight and confrontation. The absence of teeth made his face seem unfinished, his manner less threatening than his pose suggested. The scar she had noted in the Lines cut a deep uneven seam through stubble and little tufts of bristles. It was a face of surfaces, even his eyes were set shallow and close to the brow. Watching them, she suddenly sensed a weakness that prompted the answer she was searching for.

'Give me your dagger, Hyra,' she said softly. The uncertainty ebbed from her face, leaving it calm and impassive. She repeated herself.

'What do you want it for?'

'To open the scar on his cheek.' The words were deliberately brutal, but Hyra did not realize that they were a means of concealing her fear.

'No, Morrigen. You can't,' he whispered.

'So you'd rather I went with him into the forest and was raped until I fainted? I'm a priestess, not an object who can now be sold to right the wrongs done a swineherd.' Morrigen started walking towards Hyra. 'Or are you ashamed of me?'

'No!'

'Prove it.'

As Morrigen spoke, the swineherd bellowed with rage and swept the back of his hand across her cheek. She fell back, straightened, touched her face, then snatched Hyra's dagger from his belt and turned to confront her attacker.

'You're an old man who's grown slow on his feet,' she said evenly. 'Do that again and you die.'

She dropped to a crouch, wrapped both hands round the hilt of the dagger and raised its blade in readiness to strike. Her red hair hung dishevelled over her face, veiling one eye. So wild did she seem, so similar to an animal stalking its prey, that the swineherd glanced anxiously at Hyra before reversing and lifting his whip. He had left it too late. She leapt forward. He screamed, reeling backwards. Hyra jumped between them and tried to block Morrigen's path.

'Leave me alone,' she whispered, turning the dagger on its owner. 'Try and stop me and I'll do the same to you.'

Hyra looked at her in dismay. She was smiling at him, but her eyes had slewed, pushing the pupils up under the lids, and her lips had curled open to show the white of her teeth. Suddenly he sensed that some form of illness had temporarily affected her mind, that she was not responsible for what she was saying. 'I'm trying to help you.'

'Then stand aside and let me finish what I've started.' She side-stepped and continued her advance on the swineherd. He had fallen to his knees, discarding his whip, and a crimson line marked the long wound in his cheek. As she approached, he began scuttling backwards through the grass. The dagger slipped from her fingers. She started laughing. Still moving crab-like in retreat, the swineherd hurried away to his pigs and the safety of the forest.

*

The laughter ceased. But its echo lingered, making Morrigen shiver and press her hands to her ears as if unable to accept her behaviour. One cheek was very pale, the other livid and already beginning to swell from the blow. 'I had to do it,' she murmured.

'Why?'

'You think I'm cruel and without pity. Perhaps I am. The Gods made us. It's they who must take the blame.'

'And is it the Gods who made you laugh at him?'

'I couldn't stop myself. For years I've lived with the memory of that night I spent in the Lines. But you're a chieftain's son. You wouldn't understand what it meant to be sold for two piglets by a mother who despises you.'

'Would you have killed him?'

'If I had to, yes.'

'And me?'

'I don't know. We do things we don't mean to do but cannot stop ourselves.' Morrigen had become abstracted and distant. It was as if she was musing, thinking out loud. 'Death means less to a woman, we draw so close to it when giving birth. But I'm glad you've learnt the truth. It's strange, seeing him again has reminded me of what I hoped to become when I first fled from him. I feel cleaner, stronger, less uncertain of what lies ahead. It's two years since I reached Henge. I hoped for power, I have none. I wanted to lead my people, but still serve the Dobuni. The time has come to take what can still be mine. If blood must be spilled, so be it.'

Hyra gazed out over the scrub as she spoke. The sun was low and lit with flame. The forest's shadow lay long and perfect in the twilight. All was emptiness, desolation.

'You seem sad,' said Morrigen. Her eyes locked with his, seeming to draw him into her spell. 'Why?'

'Because I know that there is good in you as well as evil, but that the evil has conquered the good. Because I know that I should walk away from you now and never speak to you again, but can't.'

'Kiss me, Hyra.'

'What would that prove? That I'm willing to help rid you all of those who obstruct you?'

'It would be for both of us.'

'And a kiss would seal our complicity?'

'It would be proof of love, proof that what made you take pity on me that night in the Lines still lingers inside you.'

'It would prove my weakness, nothing else. If I truly loved you I'd force you to join the swineherd. At least you'd be spared your own destruction. To destroy others you must first destroy yourself.'

'The choice is mine.'

'But I needn't witness it.'

Hyra turned and began walking away. Morrigen watched him, but did not follow.

# CHAPTER V

Morrigen shaded her eyes and watched the kite as it soared over the Dwellings in the still spring air. With tail forked and head arched, it swept effortlessly on, scanning the grass below for any sign of movement. It circled again, then steadied. Suddenly it collapsed its wings and began falling, sheering earthwards in a plummet of rust and yellow. She lost sight of it. Finally it rose from a patch of briar and flapped ponderously southwards towards the refuge of the forest, the dun shape of a leveret clenched in its outstretched talons.

She smiled as it grew smaller. A bird of prey seen with its kill was an omen of change, proof that the Gods favour self-help. But how? Scrambling down the ramparts, she made her way towards the hut that housed the priestesses. How could an unknown and powerless priestess gain the influence she sought? She sighed wearily. A month had passed since her encounter with the swineherd, but the question still lacked an answer.

She glanced at the post in the centre of the encampment. Heaps of coloured sand marked the creep of its shadow. It would soon be noon, time to go to Henge and celebrate Bala's daily journey across the sky. She passed a serving-girl carrying a basket of oyster shells towards the midden, some women coiling cooking pots near the pit-kilns, deft fingers smoothing wet clay into the cracks before placing them in the sun to dry. Outside the Council Dwelling, a group of elders sipped tassine, a fermented drink made from berries and honey, as they awaited an audience with the Lord of the Rites. Nothing changed: new pots replaced old; worship and ritual and the daily bustle still punctuated her days – the beginnings of another summer.

Noticing Hyra and Leoid emerge from one of the huts, she slowed pace to avoid the reproaches and bitterness that now greeted her whenever she and Hyra were forced to speak; and met Ralla instead.

Her old rival appeared sullen and preoccupied. In the last

two years her cheeks had darkened, exposure to the sun giving her the gloss and sleekness that her features alone could never have provided.

So petty had the feud between the two women become that they both halted, each refusing to budge and make way for the other. Ralla sneered. 'No doubt it was you who persuaded Ishtar to have me sent from the Dwellings.'

'What do you mean?'

'The constellation of the Virgin has risen. The seers have asked that a priestess be sent on a tour of the villages. They've chosen me.'

'And you don't want to go?'

'Of course not!' Ralla stamped a foot in anger. 'Atius has been seen with his men. By the time he gets here I'll be scattering corn or listening to the complaints of the elders.' She paused, grinning slyly. 'But you could go in my place.'

'Whilst you lie in bed with Atius? I'm not that much of a fool.'

'You sound jealous.'

Morrigen scowled and pushed past the priestess. But what if the answer she was searching for lay outside the Dwellings? If her name was well known, the Cunei, her own tribe, might flock to her cause when she finally acted. She halted, turning towards Ralla. Her shoulders sagged. Defeat joined despair on her face, and when she spoke she sounded broken and cowed.

'Would you forget our quarrel if I went?'

Ralla's grin widened into conceit. 'You're afraid of me, aren't you?'

Morrigen bowed her head. She nodded. 'Please don't hate me. I don't mean to upset you.'

'So the waif has need of affection?' Ralla laughed and gave a braggart's smile, going on to promise her friendship if Morrigen toured the villages in her place.

Later that day the two of them went to see Ishtar. At first the High Priestess refused consent to their agreement, and only when Morrigen pointed out that her own low birth might make it easier for the Cunei to accept her, and prove Ishtar's respect for their beliefs, did she finally relent.

Morrigen left the Dwellings in late spring, taking only a guide and two servants to escort her and carry her baggage. She spent the first part of the summer moving from village to village; blessing crops, lighting fires, dancing in praise of the Gods.

Attentive, courteous, as willing to worship Serapha as the Sun God she served, her reputation grew as she continued her progress. An unlikely innocence surrounded her. Old men trembled as they watched the sway of her body. Only in the privacy of the sleeping-huts was she able to discard the mask. Eyes that smiled by day turned hard and cold and bereft of all kindness.

Her travels revealed much. Not all was as peaceful as it seemed in the villages. Beneath their apparent submission to the will of the Dobuni, many of the Cunei she met nursed a deep and enduring hatred for their masters. Time and again shamans came to her with their grumbles, their distaste for the Toil of the Stones. Gradually she realized that the tribesfolk were like tinder that needed only one puff of the bellows to burst into flames. The further she travelled from Henge the greater their hostility. In some places no Dobuni would willingly have ventured far from his tent without the benefit of a guard. Their merchants had been robbed, slaves set free, garrisons strengthened in the hill-forts by which the warriors kept watch on the trading routes and a subject tribe.

One night she heard two elders discuss their fears of a second uprising.

'Who'll lead us?' asked one. 'There's no one who can wage a war and unite the other chieftains.'

'What about Ceruduc?' suggested his companion.

'No. The man's too feckless. Anyway, the Dobuni are watching him. He shouldn't have refused to allow any of the seers to attend his father's burial. He may preach insurrection, but the moment he leaves those marshes of his he'll be slaughtered.'

Listening to them, Morrigen remembered the fierce hooded eyes of the warrior who had snatched Hyra away from her in the Maiden Lines, his arrogance and strength. A week later she heard his name being mentioned again. That night, as she tried to sleep and the drums pounded outside her hut, she began to perceive that Ceruduc might be the ally she needed; that one day fate would bring them together to drive the Dobuni from their lands.

As she journeyed, the beginnings of a plan evolved in her thoughts. For a while the fear of retribution made her hesitate. Finally she acted, consulting the soothsayers and rainmakers in an attempt to discover whether storms, disease, drought or a failed harvest were likely. The portents were all favourable. The corn began to ripen, the cattle grew fat as they grazed their pastures. Showers alternated with sunshine as midsummer drew closer.

Returning to Henge and convinced no disaster was imminent, she waited for a few days then went to Ishtar and offered her body for use in the celebrations that marked the coupling between Sun God and Moon Goddess during the Midsummer Rites.

The High Priestess scanned her face for some trace of her motive as they sat together in the quiet of her dwelling.

'Why are you doing this?' she said finally.

Morrigen smiled gravely. 'To thank Bala for all he has given me. Most of the other priestesses are the daughters of chieftains or warriors. Their fathers give thank-offerings to the temple. I'm poor and can only offer myself.'

'The risks are great. You know what happens to those who fail to bring pleasure to the Gods. It's you your people will blame if the harvest blackens or a murrain spreads amongst the sheep. I won't be able to save you.'

'I'm Bala's handmaid. He must do with me as he pleases.'

And so it was agreed that Morrigen, in place of the offerings she was unable to give, should be coupled with one of the shamans during the Rites.

Uncertain of Morrigen's intentions, but aware that she had somehow been tricked, Ralla tried to persuade Ishtar to change her mind.

The High Priestess laughed at her fears. 'You think I'd sit idly by and let Morrigen become our mistress?' she said. 'No, a beast is best hobbled by giving it too long a tether. Anything may happen. One tempest would destroy the harvest, and Morrigen with it.'

But the weather held, blue skies and a warm breeze accompanying the tribes as they converged on Henge to celebrate the solstice.

The night was cloudless. Torches lit the Plain and the lines of tents clustered round the temple. The moon rose, climbing the darkness like a mystical deity no man could confine. Mead was broached, oxen were spitted and the meat hacked hot from the bone. Towards dawn, the revels ceased as the drums called the crowds to attendance of the Rites.

Within the temple, another stone lay beside its socket. Hyra tapped it nervously with his knuckles, then peered to where Leoid stood amongst those gathered on the grass beyond the ditch. The alignment found at the funeral way was now to be permanently recorded by the raising of a large timber post that would act as a sighting line and mark the midsummer setting of the moon. He half turned . . . but again he could not look at her. He scanned the crowd. Their faces appeared grey and blurred and trenched with shadow. Their eyes glittered in the cones of light made by the torches. The night muffled all sound, turned all he saw into quick half-formed images, the fragments of a dream. He lowered his gaze to the notch on his sighting wand.

Morrigen glanced at him as he started tracking the descending moon. She had already guessed that his concentration was pretended, an excuse for not watching her couple with the shaman so that the sun would be reborn. Dressed in pale deerskin robes that fell vertical to the ground but had been cut to leave her thighs uncovered, she stood motionless in the centre of the temple whilst the shamans and other priestesses danced slowly round her. Chalk had been rubbed into her hair and face. She could feel its weight, feel it moist and cold where it whitened her cheeks; the symbol of her purity. She shivered slightly, closing her eyes as the first hint of dawn began to break in the north-eastern sky.

The Lord of the Rites began intoning the Chant to Bala. Hyra did not listen. The moon had started to wane, its body growing pale and almost translucent as the sun strengthened. Darkness had become light. One God sleeps, another wakes. The day of ritual coition between sun and moon had dawned again, repeating the circle duplicated in the shape of the temple, the cairns in the Place of the Dead, the still unfinished ring of stones.

A hand touched his shoulder. He turned to see Leoid snuffling anxiously into his beard. 'The wand, Hyra, the wand! Come, come, man! You're my eyes. We must hurry.' Leoid grinned. 'This is a triumph. I may be palsied, but none of the other seers would have known where to place the post . . .'

'Are you ready?' Ishtar joined Morrigen as the dancing ceased.

She nodded. 'Yes.'

One of the shamans stepped forward. A bull's mask covered

his face. Its four hooves trailed behind him in the dust. He held an axe in each hand, one of jet, the other of bronze.

'Step fretting, Hyra! Move the wand . . . more. There, that's perfect.' Leoid was hopping from foot to foot like a small boy.

Suddenly the sun's curve breasted the horizon, its light pouring upwards in tapered shafts that lit the belly of the sky. Hyra started trembling.

Morrigen commenced her dance, the watching crowd following the swirl of her robes as she wove between the stones.

'Take this.' Hyra struggled to forget her as Leoid handed him a coil of rope. 'Quickly now. There's no time to watch Morrigen.'

Hyra pushed his way through the crowd and hurriedly measured the distance between the stone hole and the spot where the post was to be raised.

Sunlight brushed the summit of the central stone.

The shaman joined Morrigen in her dance. They merged, parted, drew close again. She felt his heat, glimpsed dark eyes hidden beneath the slits in his mask. The phallus was of chalk, its whiteness softened by oils.

The moon nudged the horizon, growing paler as it sank. Leoid hobbled over to Hyra and began shouting at the toilers gathered round the post. They started digging, clawing at the turf with their picks and bare hands.

Hyra glanced over his shoulder.

Morrigen stood ready. She rose on to her heels, finding balance and poise as the shaman juddered into trance and the flight of his soul from his body.

'Lift!' The men hoisted the pole on to their shoulders.

She could hear nothing, see only a blur. Her mind emptied, leaving it free to be filled by the spirits of the dead.

The base of the pole was lowered into the hole.

Her thighs parted. The stench of animal and perfume caught in her throat.

'Heave!' The men ducked beneath the post, their arms jerking upwards as they forced it into the air. Hyra turned as it swung upright behind him.

Morrigen was screaming.

She began tugging her hair. It came free in her hands, sheaves of newly cut corn that floated to the dust when her fingers splayed.

Suddenly sunlight filled the temple. Her mouth opened,

becoming a perfect circle as Hyra lifted his head to where the sun was now mounting the sky, misshapen and blood-red with the proof of its birth.

*

'Sit down.' Ishtar smiled as Morrigen crossed her hut and squatted opposite her on a pile of pelts.

The hut was cool and spacious. Only the noon sun falling through the blackened smoke hole high overhead gave a hint of the heat outside. Both women were content to indulge its peace for a moment; to listen – but be no part of – the din and bustle that had pervaded the Dwellings since the first of the corn had been carried in from the fields to be threshed and winnowed.

Ishtar retrieved a sprig of beech from her lap and started fanning her face. 'I'm fortunate. Not all can be High Priestess and have an excuse to escape the heat.'

'It can't last.'

'Of course not.'

The fanning stopped, and with it the small talk.

'The harvest is nearly in,' said Ishtar. 'Most of the villages on the Plain have already filled their granary pits. More will have to be dug if nothing is to be wasted. The Gods seem to favour you Cunei. The leaves have begun to wither, but the sheep are still in milk. Cattle still graze. No beast has had to be slaughtered for lack of fodder.'

'We should give thanks to the Gods.'

'And so we will.' Ishtar paused, vainly searching Morrigen's face for some sign of pride or conceit. 'But the people believe that those who act for the Gods are themselves blessed. That means you.'

'I repeat what I said before,' said Morrigen warily. 'It's Bala who should be praised.'

'But it's your name not his that's now heard in the villages. Everywhere I go I hear tales of Morrigen, of what you've done for your tribe and may yet be able to do.'

'You can't blame me for that. I don't control their tongues.'

'But what of their minds? You're one of them. The pauper and handmaid, the waif who became a priestess. For years the people have despised us and envied us our wealth. But no one's jealous of you. They seem to think that you're their servant and will help and comfort them.'

'I've heard what they say. It means nothing.'

'You should be flattered, but seem indifferent.'

'My life belongs to the Gods.'

'The perfect answer. But is it what you mean? You're a mystery to me, Morrigen. And I'm not certain that I can risk being baffled by you or anyone else whilst I remain in this office.' Ishtar rose and began walking to and fro through the shadows. When she turned, her manner had changed and her voice sounded brisk, almost abrupt. 'Your years as a priestess are due to end after the Midwinter Rites. You can only stay here after that with my consent. Most are glad to leave. But there are always a few who choose to remain; the ambitious, those fitted for no other life, those willing to sacrifice a husband and children in order to serve the Gods. Which are you?'

Aware that Ishtar was trying to trick her, Morrigen remained silent.

Ishtar stared at her for a moment, then said, 'Very well, as you won't answer I'll do so for you. I've decided that you're to be wed on the day of the Rites, returning with your husband to his lands as soon as they're over.'

The blood drained from Morrigen's face as she slumped against the pelts. Tears shone in her eyes. She straightened, forcing herself to appear indifferent to Ishtar's decision.

'Very well,' she murmured.

'Is that all you can say?'

Morrigen shrugged. 'I have no choice.'

'None.'

'Then I must do as you say.'

But once outside the hut the indifference left her. Feeling weak and dizzy, as if struck by a blow, she stood for a moment as she emerged into the sunlight. Four months remained, four months to prevent Ishtar arranging her marriage and forcing her to leave Henge. But how was it to be done? Still dazed, blind to where she was going, she crossed the causeway and stumbled down the slope that led to the river.

'Morrigen!'

She glanced angrily across the slope. Hyra and Leoid were approaching. The old seer hobbled on, leaving his pupil and Morrigen to fumble for the words that might yet mend their friendship.

'Leave me alone!' snapped Morrigen, picking up speed.

Hyra followed her. 'Let's stop bickering. I've forgiven you for what you did. The swineherd should have left you in peace.'

'How noble of you to say so!'

'Stop it, Morrigen!'

'It doesn't matter what you think of me any more. I'm to be wed. Ishtar has ordered it.'

'She can't!'

'She can, and will. Banishment! So much for her reward for all I've done for her.'

'You could marry me . . .' Hyra was hardly aware of what he was saying. 'A seer's wife can't be banished.'

Morrigen halted, spinning to face him. She brushed a hand across his brow. 'No, Hyra,' she said gently. 'You once told me I was evil. To marry you now would be to kill our friendship and add to the evil. I couldn't do that.'

'Then you must love me.'

'Perhaps I am and am blind to it. Nothing makes sense to me. I couple with a stranger, a shaman who hides himself behind a mask. But you, you who are always beside me and hide nothing, with you I have never lain. For nearly three years I've turned to you when in need of comforting. Why do you never complain? Is it because you're weak, or are you stronger than you think? Sometimes I can see in your eyes the pain I've caused you. It wounds me, but I can do nothing to stop it. It's as if by hurting you I'm spared the need to hurt others. But for you I'd have long ago given in to what I am. You make me fight it. The fight wouldn't end if I married you. One day it would devour us both.'

Hyra smiled and took her hands in his. 'That's the longest speech you've ever made, and the prettiest.'

'Perhaps that's because I know it may be the last?'

'I'm going home tomorrow. Come with me.'

'I can't.'

'Why not?'

'We'd start arguing again.'

'It would do you good to leave the Dwellings for a while.'

'You won't try and persuade me to marry you?'

'I promise.'

'Very well, I'll come.'

Each lost in thought, they walked in silence along the river-bank. Every now and then Morrigen tightened her grip on Hyra's arm. Thinking she was trying to make amends for disappointing him, he smiled sadly and drew her closer.

Morrigen went where he led her. Blind to the river, unaware of his presence, Ishtar's decision looped endlessly through her thoughts. Marriage meant being sold to some chieftain prepared to pay well for the privilege of making a priestess his bride. And she had four months to stop it taking place. Seeing Leoid in the distance, she slowed pace, then lowered her eyes as the germ of a plan swept Ishtar from her mind.

'You must go home alone,' she said suddenly. 'I'm staying here.'

# CHAPTER VI

Green eyes tracked the old seer as he limped slowly across the Dwellings. He had spent the day at Henge. Fresh tallies notched his staff. His measuring lines trailed behind him in the mud, as if absent-mindedness had made him forget to make his customary neat ball of their length. It was nearly dusk. The women in the kitchen quarters were laughing amongst themselves. Dogs prowled near the middens. A servant appeared and began lighting the tallows outside the dwelling huts as Leoid hoisted himself up the ramparts. He stood preoccupied and alone on the summit, first placing some pegs in line with the setting sun, then turning to where a thin autumnal moon had begun its ascent.

It was the seventh day since Hyra's departure, the sixth Morrigen had spent observing every move made by the seer: his daily trek to the temple to adjust the fan-shaped ranks of posts he had set up in its entrance, the sense of urgency that betrayed both his excitement and nervousness. But she still lacked proof of the reason for his labours. Old men attempting celestial prediction were commonplace in the Dwellings. Without evidence, instinct had been her only guide. Throughout the week, as if a wolf stalking its prey, she had watched, followed and waited in the hope that carelessness might give a clue to his actions.

She stepped silently into the shadows as he left the ramparts. His unease was obvious. Worry rimmed his eyes. As he shuffled past he lifted his staff and peered short-sightedly at the tally marks he had cut in it with his knife during the day. She smiled to herself, again glad that she had silenced Hyra's confusion at her change of heart by walking away from him. The explanation could wait. It was Leoid who now concerned her.

That night, a bitter wind reminding her of the coming of winter and the need to outwit Ishtar before the Rites, she decided to act. She woke early, creeping through the deserted encampment and by-passing the guards before turning towards Henge. The sky was leaden, the wind cold. Mist lay pressed against the grass and the dew sloshed round her ankles. She halted only once, retrieving a staff and a coil of plaited ivy from their hiding-place in a copse.

A flock of starlings rose noisily from the mist as she approached the temple. It was forbidding and ghostly in the gloaming, and the wind blustered and pulled at her as if trapped by the encircling stones. Withered garlands tumbled round her, quickening her step as old fears found nourishment in her mood. Henge belonged to the Gods. Their presence gave it sanctity and forestalled their anger. If all went as she hoped, would they not judge her and punish her for her sins?

The mist slowly dispersed, revealing the thatched roofs of the villages that nestled near the temple. The clouds thickened overhead. Her heart drummed against her breast. Yet still she waited. Suddenly she saw the distant figure of Leoid coming towards her across the Plain. She hesitated, still uncertain of her ability to brave the consequences of all that now lay ahead, then unravelled the ivy, hurried over to the entrance, and pretended to be engrossed in the placing of the posts that blocked it.

'Leave them alone!'

She ignored Leoid's command, only turning to face him when he started waving his stick at her.

'I haven't moved them, I promise,' she called. 'Hyra asked me to come here.'

Hearing a woman's voice, Leoid lowered his stick and hastened blindly on, finally drawing close enough to identify the trespasser. His suspicions faded: no priestess would understand the purpose of the posts. She seemed flustered, was obviously harmless. But he spoke sharply.

'And how can Hyra give you orders when he's half-way home by now? And just when I most need him.'

Morrigen grinned foolishly. 'When he comes back I'm going to take this tally staff he gave me and break it over his head. I'm cold, muddled and wretched: and all because of him. I should never have listened to him. But we're friends. I wanted to help. Before he left he asked me to come here and watch the sun when it rose. And now look!' She pointed to the clouds. 'The sun might still be abed for all I can see of it.'

Leoid chuckled at her annoyance. 'Hyra's no fool,' he said. 'He's learnt a lot whilst helping me. It was he who cut these posts. He knew I needed them for my work. He must have thought that by observing the sun you would be able to tell him their purpose.'

'So we both were to be his victims!' cried an outraged Morrigen. 'I was to stare at the sun whilst he feasts, you were to be deceived, and he was to take the glory! Well I won't do it!' She tossed down the rope and marched indignantly from the temple.

'Wait!'

'And prolong my misery by helping Hyra cheat the man who taught him all he knows? No, I'm going back to the Dwellings.' Morrigen walked on. Suddenly she halted and lifted her hands to her face. She turned, blushing and visibly ashamed. 'How thoughtless of me,' she said. 'You need Hyra's help. The least I can do is offer to replace him until he returns.' She shrugged. 'But no. I'd be no use. My ignorance would be more hindrance than help.' She hurried on.

Leoid reflected for a moment: ignorance was a virtue he needed. He called out to her.

She halted again and glanced back over her shoulder; bright-eyed and innocent, with the long mane of her hair gusting like a pennant in the wind.

Leoid hobbled towards her. 'I'm an old man. The posts are heavy. But only they can provide the answer I'm looking for. I'd like to finish what I've started. Time is short. I need hands to help move the posts, legs still able to run. Without them the riddle may remain unsolved.'

Morrigen gave a diffident grin, hiding any hint of her triumph by the choice of her reply. 'I'll do what I can. But don't be angry if I make a mistake. I'm a woman not a seer. The heavens mean nothing to me.'

And so Morrigen replaced the absent Hyra as Leoid's assistant. Day after day she accompanied him to Henge. When the weather changed and the sun reappeared, the sighting-posts had to be shifted, pegs and ropes employed to modify the pattern they made in the entrance to the temple. Leoid fussed busily round her. For hours on end he peered myopically at the sky, taking sightings, aligning the posts so that they recorded the height of the sun and its rate of climb. At night, wrapped warmly in cloaks, they stood together in the darkness and plotted the moon's motions as it rose over the downs.

Soon Leoid's staff was scarred by the lines of notches that

were intended as the permanent chronicle of his labours. Never once did he speak of its purpose. Nor did Morrigen risk questioning him. The foundations for her belief that he alone could save her from banishment remained as frail as ever. But gradually she sensed that patience might bring its reward. His apprehension increased. Occasionally, always when studying the tallies on his staff, a look of bewilderment and horror would pass fleetingly across his face.

The kindness she displayed during these days would have disarmed most men. The old seer was no exception. Always wary of women, he began to indulge her company; her youth and charm and eagerness to please. At night, he would smile sadly when they parted. In the mornings, he sometimes hobbled into the priestesses' dwelling and watched her whilst she slept, as if unable to wake her.

Two weeks passed. Morrigen became impatient. The story she had told Leoid was an invention, a means of gaining his trust. If Hyra returned, betrayal would follow. Fearful of being confronted by her lies when on the brink of success, she grew sullen and short-tempered. She began questioning Leoid. He told her that he soon hoped to predict an event that would cause widespread panic if no one was warned about it. She tried to prompt him still further. He refused to answer. One evening she noticed him staring at her. He was frowning, seemed thoughtful and troubled. Detecting suspicion, she grew cautious again, once more adopting the role of foolish priestess indifferent to all he had said to her.

On the following day they returned to the temple. Leoid appeared agitated and more uneasy than normal. Measurements had to be checked, pegs placed at intervals round the perimeter of the bank. For a while he sat examining his staff. He began pacing, sat, rose again. There was no sign of his lameness. Morrigen ignored him. Her hands were trembling and wet with sweat. She longed to shake the truth from him, force him to speak. Finally he did so.

'How many days are there to the eve of the Solstice and Winter Rites?'

'Ninety.'

He nodded. 'That's when it'll happen.'

Morrigen rose to her feet. 'What will?' she whispered.

He turned away, silently shaking his head.

'Don't you trust me?'

'I trust no one. Knowledge can heal, but it can also cause conflict and bloodshed.'

'And with you it's safe?'

'For the moment, yes.'

Morrigen slid a hand beneath her cloak, resting it on the only memento of her affair with Atius. She walked slowly towards him, unable to stop herself. He was an old man, defenceless, weak on his feet. It could be done and done quickly. She looked round. The Plain was deserted and the stones hid them from the nearest village. Dead leaves trawled the sky, smothering the dying grass and the humped tombs of the dead. Death surrounded her, cheapening and robbing it of meaning. She glanced at Leoid. His hands were gnarled. His body was stooped and his ancient cadaverous face and peering eyes made him seem like someone who was already dead. But if it was done, the secret would die with him – remain his alone. Suddenly she hated him; for his age and obstinacy, all she had endured, her continued dependence on him. She released her grip on her dagger . . .

'You're right. It's best if I don't know.' But even as she spoke she was already plotting, searching for a weapon that would persuade him to end his silence.

That evening Ishtar requested her presence in her dwelling. The High Priestess wasted few words. 'I've found a husband for you,' she said. 'His name is Zarxus.'

Morrigen remained speechless for a moment, then dropped slowly to her knees. 'Did no Cunei ask if he could marry me?' she whispered finally.

'It makes no difference. Zarxus saw you when you toured the villages during the summer. He's offered half his cattle to make you his wife. Dobuni chieftains as powerful as Zarxus usually get what they want. He wants you. You should be honoured.'

'When will I meet him?'

'On the eve of the Rites.'

'But that's when we're to be married!'

'Exactly.'

'Can I refuse him?'

'No.' Ishtar paused. 'Leoid has spoken to me of the help you've given him. But from the moment Hyra returns you're to remain here and prepare for the ceremony.'

'Does that mean I'll be confined to the Dwellings?'

'Yes.'

'But why?'

'Because I say so,' said Ishtar sharply. 'You may go.'

Morrigen turned and walked in silence from the hut. A raw wind blew across the encampment, flattening the smoke from the fires. Oblivious to the cold, she circled the ramparts, then stood and stared out over the Plain. Leoid, Ishtar and Ralla – now Zarxus: the numbers of those to be outwitted seemed only to multiply. And time was short: Hyra was already overdue. Away in the distance she could hear a wolf welcoming the night. Its howl sounded plaintive and almost despairing; the echo of her own predicament. Only Leoid could reprieve her. But where was he weakest, most fallible? She pressed her hands to her breasts as a sudden shiver greeted the answer.

The next morning he decided to record the position of the sighting-posts before they were removed from the entrance. The work was straightforward, but it left him weary and complaining of his age. Morrigen admonished him for exhausting himself. 'You've done enough for today,' she said. 'You need a rest. I've brought us some food. Let's leave the temple for a while and eat it where no one can trouble or question you.'

The suggestion appealed to the seer. The two of them walked slowly across the Plain. Morrigen took his weight, deliberately steering him towards a small dip hidden amongst the gorse. She lowered him gently to the ground, then opened her basket and spread out its contents: bread, mutton, two beakers and a goatskin.

She lifted the goatskin. 'Mead?'

'No more than a sip. I'm an old man. It goes quickly to the head.'

Sensing his mood, Morrigen said little as they ate. He needed to relax, lower his guard. Afterwards, her cloak his pillow, he lay back in the grass and stared vacantly at the clouds banked grey overhead.

Occasionally he lifted his beaker, unaware that though he had twice drained it mead still slopped from its brim. Unnoticed, Morrigen filled it again, then sat beside him, knees pulled up against her chest, her chin wedged between them.

'What are you thinking?'

Leoid shrugged. 'I should be at peace. But what I've learnt

grieves and frightens me. Such things are ordained by the Gods. But why? It would take a sibyl not a seer to answer that.'

Morrigen said nothing. She was wary of interrupting and breaking his train of thought.

'We know so little about the sun, even less about the moon. They're mysteries, but they're Gods as well, and if in conflict those who worship them risk destruction.' Leoid sighed. 'Sometimes I fear that what lies ahead may end in every stone in the temple being smashed and torn from the ground. Perhaps I should be grateful for my age? It's you not I who'll be forced to witness it.'

The mead was making him maudlin. Morrigen smiled to herself and said, 'Don't speak about it any more. It only upsets you. Tell me about your childhood.'

'It was a long time ago. It wouldn't interest you.'

'Oh but it would. I promise.' Morrigen placed a hand to his brow, lulling and soothing him by tracing its lines with her fingers. 'Your beaker,' she added, raising it to his lips.

Leoid emptied it, then glanced at her. As if through a haze he was aware of her beauty and the concern on her face, the first tremulous stirrings of feelings long dormant. He began speaking, telling her about his boyhood in his father's tents and the world he had renounced in order to become a seer. He grew sleepy, his memories blurred. When Morrigen finally interrupted him the softness in her voice only added to his drowsiness.

'Sleep will do you good, help rest your eyes. You deserve it. None of the other seers could have done what you have done.'

Leoid smiled. 'You flatter me.'

'It's true.'

'Perhaps Hyra will continue my work?'

'Could Hyra have found out the truth about this calamity you think is going to happen?'

'No one could. It was chance that led me to it. Such things are few and their pattern is still unknown to us. But woe to those who live to see them.'

'Sssh.' He was growing excited again. Morrigen rebuked him, pressing him back to the grass when he tried to rise. 'No more talking. I forbid it.'

Becalmed by the grin that had accompanied the order, Leoid nodded, then reached up and touched her: rough worn-out hands on soft downy skin that drew closer as she edged towards him.

For a moment she permitted his touch, following the route of his fingers before lifting them aside. 'You shouldn't have done that,' she said gently.

'I didn't mean to. But you're to blame. You made me speak of my youth. The older you grow, the more you long to relive it.' Suddenly Leoid began weeping as the mead and her warmth mingled with the fear still locked inside him.

She stroked his face. 'I want to help you. Share your burden. If touching me would ease it I will let you do so.'

'Can I trust you?'

'You must tell someone. Why not the woman beside you?'

'You'll tell no one?'

'I'd do nothing to hurt you. That's why I'm here. But surely you know that now?' Morrigen shifted slightly, her hair spilling out in an arc round her legs when she shook it loose.

Leoid stared at her. He felt bewildered and confused. There was something unnatural about their intimacy, her closeness, the dizziness that filled him whenever he closed his eyes. Yet for nearly a month she had taken care of him and helped him in his work. She wanted to comfort him. Someone had to be told. Soon everyone would know. Without her, success might have eluded him. She was tender and gentle and her eyes held the innocence of a child's as they peered over the tops of her knees. There would be no need for any more questions if he spoke. She might even let him hold her until his dizziness had faded. He began speaking.

'I was younger,' he said. 'The tribes had gathered here at Henge to celebrate the Spring Rites. That night, without warning, the moon's light dimmed and went out. It was as if a shadow had passed across it. Many panicked. Some were slaughtered to appease the Gods. Times have changed since then. The Cunei are restless, the Toil has angered them. If the same thing took place tonight they might rise against us. I fear that their shamans would see it as an omen, a sign from the Goddess Serapha bidding them to unite and drive us Dobuni from their lands.' The seer turned towards Morrigen. 'It's going to happen again.'

Morrigen's heart was pounding so loudly against her chest she felt certain that Leoid would hear it. She gazed up at the sky, searching for the invisible moon. 'When?'

'On the eve of the Winter Rites.'

There was silence. Her whole body was shaking. 'Have you told any one else?'

'Not yet. I had to be certain. But the seers and chieftains must be warned.'

'Of course.'

Morrigen's voice had changed. The gentleness had left it. She tried to think and plan what next had to be done. Leoid began pleading with her. Sensing his alarm, she suddenly smiled and collapsed beside him, offering no resistance as his hands fumbled for hers. But she knew nothing of his touch, heard only the wind as it swept through the grass.

*

The hovel stood deep in the forest. Turves roofed it, branches supported its walls. Its owner was a healer; a thin unpleasant looking man with a sloven's hair and a sallow face grown pale after a life spent hidden from the sun. A hog sprawled in the entrance. A litter of piglets scampered round it, then fled grunting into the shadows as the woman stepped over their mother and lowered the hood of her cloak.

The shaman watched her as she surveyed his hut. She said nothing. For some reason the look in her eyes made him feel threatened and uneasy. A strange shine flecked their irises, making them cold and expressionless. He spat into the mud at his feet, then slowly approached her.

'I've seen you before,' he growled.

'Who I am doesn't matter.'

'Maybe. But I'll place you.' He circled her; noting auburn hair, the slight shake of her hands, the embroidered cloak patterned in black and red stripes. 'I never forget a face.'

'I didn't come here to be stared at.'

'For what then?'

'A potion.'

'You seem well enough.'

'It isn't for me.'

'Who then?'

'Need that concern you?'

'No.' The healer grinned, then spat a flake of bark from the corner of his mouth before indicating the herbs hanging to dry from the roof and the assortment of small pots that lined one side of his hovel. 'There. Ask and it's yours. I've cuckoo-pint for the lungs. Henbane, bryony and wart-weed. Or is it hare's sweat and pike's gall for the barren that brings you here? Or boiled crow's feet to take the swelling from the bruises and the demons from oxen?'

'None of those.'

'What then?' He began lifting the pots in succession. 'Ravens' tongues for the bite of a mad cur . . . toads' legs . . . a drench of ivy-root for the fevered . . . dried dung to ease the palsy . . .'

'I need a venom.' The woman's voice cut sharply into his.

Still grinning, he slowly straightened and walked towards her, cunning narrowing his eyes.

'Those who sent me will make certain you're rewarded,' added the woman.

'I don't doubt it.' The healer drew closer. Suddenly he wrenched the cloak from her throat, revealing an amber necklace. 'So, you're a priestess from the Dwellings. I knew I'd seen you.'

'My name is Morrigen.'

The healer's smile broadened. 'Ah, the waif herself. And what does the waif want with a venom?'

'Others sent me. They didn't tell me.'

'You sent yourself, woman!' snapped the healer. 'That's why you're trembling. Why you came to me instead of one of the shamans who hawks his wares round the Dwellings.'

'I need poison. If you can give it to me, say so. Or are we to waste the day discussing the reasons for my coming here?' Morrigen turned, as if to leave the hut.

'Aye, I can give it to you.'

She halted. Outside the hut the trees tapered into shadow. Leaves side-slipped as they fell. 'The person who takes it mustn't know what it is,' she said, her back still facing the healer.

'Look at me!'

Morrigen turned.

'That's better. You and I need to understand each other if we're to part as friends. I may deal in words, but you trade in death. And death has its price. A healer's task is to lengthen life, not shorten it.' The shaman laughed. Morrigen's trembling had grown worse. She cringed and backed away from him as he spoke.

'Show me your venoms,' she whispered.

'Who's the wretch you want to get rid of?'

'It's not like that.'

'Tell me!' barked the healer. 'A surfeit can be as harmless as mead. I need to know his age, if it's a man or a woman. The amount must match the victim.'

Morrigen lowered her head. 'It's a man. He's old. That's all you need know.'

The healer stared at her for a moment, then crossed his hovel, returning with a lidded pot and a clump of glossy leaves. He lifted them into the light.

'Hemlock. The poisons are destroyed when the plant is dried. It only kills when still fresh. The breathing slows, the pulse quickens, the mind grows confused. Death takes less than a day.' He paused, exchanging the leaves for the pot. 'The Death Cap toadstool. The pain begins in the belly. Vomiting follows, the pulse weakens. The pain vanishes, perhaps for two days. When it returns a coma begins. Nothing can be done to stem it. Death takes place on the fifth day.'

'That's too long.'

'These are venoms, woman; not healing purges that can be given again if first they fail.'

'I'll take the hemlock.'

The healer held up the leaves. He grinned, then opened his hands and let them float to the floor. 'We've yet to discuss what they're worth.'

'I'll meet your price.'

'You're impatient. It's never wise to be rushed.' The healer smiled again. 'You shouldn't have told me your name. It'll add to the price.'

Morrigen did not answer for a moment. She opened her cloak, drawing a small bronze dagger from the belt round her waist. She laid it flat in her palm, blade towards the healer. 'Will this suffice?'

The healer's eyes widened with greed. He hurried towards her, intending to take it from her and inspect it. The blade moved, halting him in mid-stride as Morrigen's fingers snaked round its hilt and it lifted and slammed into his stomach.

A cry broke from his throat. His body sagged against Morrigen's. She closed her eyes, placed both hands on the dagger and pushed it as hard as she could. He began to fall. She could feel his breath, sense flailing arms gradually go limp. She pulled the blade from his jerkin, then stood with it in her hands as he slowly slid to the mud.

The sow lying in the entrance to the hut shuffled to its feet, sniffed the warm stain beginning to spread over its master's belly, then turned and ambled contentedly into the forest, only quickening pace when a sudden scream ended the silence.

# CHAPTER VII

'Let's hope that Hyra can bludgeon some sense into our masters when we finally reach that temple of his.'

'Don't be silly, Cronus. I haven't come all this way to let Hyra do the talking for me. I'll speak to the Council myself.' Lyla grinned at Hyra, then reached out and straightened his tunic: that hint of possessiveness that had once so irritated.

Cronus grunted. 'I've a seer for a son. After three wasted years he should have at least learnt how to placate the Lord of the Rites.' He paused and glanced at his son. 'Or is it only those damned chants and rituals that matter to you now?'

'It was you who sent me to Abury,' replied Hyra evenly, hoping to avoid an argument in front of Lyla.

'But it was your mother who made me do it.' Cronus was always like this when annoyed: 'A mastiff worrying a bone' was how his wife had once described him. 'It's the hills. They're a prison to her. She'd be happier in a bog as long as it was flat.' He paused, inspecting the empty Plain, the humped tombs breaking surface on the horizon. 'She's a fool. This place is worse than a graveyard. But even when you were a babe she swore that one day you'd leave us and become a seer.'

Hyra said nothing. In listening to his father he had again felt that familiar sense of having been rebuked by proxy, of having in some way failed him or been a disappointment.

Cronus was oblivious to the effects of his bluntness. Gruff and plain-spoken, quick to anger and slow to forgive, his temper was part of him, a characteristic that complemented his squat ox-like body, the contrast between the windburned skin stretched tight over his skull and his square bewhiskered face. And now he was mumbling to himself as he strode through the grass. Occasionally he glowered and glanced over his shoulder to bellow at the men looking after his baggage oxen.

Sensing Hyra's mood, Lyla drew alongside him. 'He's always like this when he has to leave his hills. I sometimes think they mean more to him than your mother.'

'It's not just that. I'm his heir. If I wasn't a seer they'd be mine one day.'

Lyla took his arm and tried to shake him from his thoughts. She laughed. 'Do you remember how we used to play in them as children when Ceruduc and I came to stay? There was nowhere to run in the marshes.'

Hyra smiled as an image of Lyla racing breathless and shrieking back to the village passed through his mind. 'You were the fastest.'

'I still am.'

Hyra glanced at her. Womanhood hadn't changed her. Her legs were as long beneath the boyish agile body. Russet hair fell neatly across her shoulders. Grey sensible eyes still humoured his gaze.

'You needn't have come,' he said finally. 'Father and I could have pleaded Ceruduc's case before the Council.'

'I wanted to. I haven't seen Henge since before father's death.'

Hyra scanned the familiar sweep of the Plain. Tombs surrounded them. Smoke spilled westward on the wind as it rose from the villages near the temple. 'We'll be there soon.'

'And gone as swiftly I hope,' growled his father.

'You should have stayed at home,' said Lyla.

'Someone's got to try and prevent that fool of a brother of yours having his lands taken away from him.' Cronus's eyes twinkled slightly. 'Anyway, there's no telling what might have happened if I'd left you alone with Hyra.'

Lyla glanced at Hyra. Their eyes met. She blushed, quickly turning away. Hyra frowned. The weeks at home and the journey to Henge had seen a renewal of their friendship, but the nearer he drew to Morrigen the greater his unease. Wary of being misunderstood, he had said nothing to Lyla about her yet, and though a meeting was inevitable he was beginning to suspect that his affection for both would be no guarantee of its success. He sighed, his stride instinctively lengthening as his thoughts switched to concern for Morrigen and anxiety as to how she had fared in his absence.

'Look! There's Henge!' shouted Lyla suddenly.

The temple was deserted, its only occupant an old widow burying her husband's bones in the Place of the Dead before winter set in. Mist wrapped the stones. High overhead some ravens were mobbing a buzzard, black shapes croaking and cawing as they wheeled against the slate of the sky.

'It looks different,' said Lyla, disappointed.

Hyra was not listening. The raven was an omen of threat, of the demons that lie in wait in hope of carrying off the souls of the dead.

'I've brought a gift from Ceruduc. Shall I leave it there now?'

Hyra forced himself to answer. 'No, we'll come here tomorrow. I promised mother I'd make an offering for Rhionan.'

Passing the temple, they began the long uphill climb that led to the Sacred Dwellings. Children from the villages ran out to watch them go by. Hearing the bells on the baggage oxen announce the arrival of a chieftain, a group of elders left their huts to welcome Cronus and offer him a site for his tents.

'You're thinking about Rhionan,' said Lyla, noticing Hyra's frown.

'It's hard not to. Do you realize she's never been here yet?'

'The journey would have exhausted her. Kirsten may be old enough to travel, but you've got to accept that one of your sisters is a cripple and always will be.'

'She once hoped to be a priestess,' said Hyra. He smiled sadly as he thought of her as he had last seen her, propped against the entrance of the hut and waving at him as he left the village: the drawn wasted face that never showed the pain, the body buckled out of shape by the softening of the bones is the legacy of rickets.

'When will I go before the Council?' asked Lyla, determined to halt Hyra's brooding.

'Tomorrow, probably.'

'Do you think they'll hold it against Ceruduc for sending me in his place?'

'You're his sister, that should satisfy them. Ceruduc would have lost his temper. The case is simple enough. Just tell them exactly what happened. Ceruduc wanted to drain part of the marsh. The Dobuni demanded cattle in payment. He refused them entry into the village. But that's no reason to try and rob them of the only pastures that never flood.'

'He behaved like a hot-blooded fool,' growled Cronus. 'Take a whip to a Dobuni and there'll always be trouble.'

'What is it, Hyra? What's wrong?' said Lyla. Hyra had slowed pace and was staring at the sky-line.

'The beacon's been lit.' Hyra paused, remembering the

ravens. 'The Dwellings must be in mourning.' He lifted an arm towards the pall of red smoke rising from the ridge ahead.

'Is the smoke always that colour?'

'No, only when the dead man is a seer. I must hurry.'

Hyra started running, followed by Lyla. Reaching the entrance to the Dwellings, he pushed his way past the villagers and camp servants who thronged the encampment. High on the ramparts he glimpsed some shamans tossing raddle on to a bonfire, their faces rouged by the smoke. Then he saw the corpse. It was covered by a rough woven shroud and lay on a raised wooden bier surrounded by seers, all of them naked and daubed with ashes in imitation of death. Most were wailing. Every now and then one displayed his grief by dropping to his knees and beating his head against the ground.

Hyra stared at them for a moment, then turned to Lyla and told her to remain where she was. He hurried forward, joining one of the seers. 'Who is it?' he shouted.

The seer straightened and stopped his wailing. 'Leoid.'

Hyra's legs weakened beneath him. For an instant he feared he might faint. Tired after the journey, unable to speak, he lifted his head and gazed horror-struck at the bier as the first wave of shock took the colour from his face.

'It happened yesterday,' added his companion. 'The priestess Morrigen returned for help. But he was dead before we reached him.'

Hyra looked at him in amazement. 'What was Morrigen doing with him? She hardly knew him.'

'Maybe, but they've rarely been apart since you left. They were on their way to the temple. Apparently he complained of a sickness and collapsed. He was an old man, too weak to move. No healer was near. There was little she could do.'

Hyra hung his head. It was all so final, so straightforward. He glanced at the corpse again, then looked behind him as if expecting the familiar stooped figure of Leoid to come hobbling towards him, staff rapping the ground, the measuring lines tucked into his belt dangling forgotten in his wake.

'He's dead, Hyra.'

'We were friends. I come home, find only a corpse. It's hard to accept.' Hyra pressed his fists to his eyes, staunching tears. 'Where's Morrigen?' he whispered.

The seer pointed to the priestesses' dwelling. 'She blames herself. No one's been able to comfort her. She's like a mad beast. She swooned when she saw him being brought back. She came to during the night, woke us all with her howls.'

'I must go and see her.'

Lyla caught up with him as he began crossing the encampment. 'I've found out what's happened,' she said. 'I'm sorry . . .'

Hyra forced a smile. 'Thank you.'

'Where are you going now?'

'To talk to Morrigen.'

'I'm coming with you.' Lyla placed a hand on his arm. 'I've heard of her. She came to the villages on the edge of the marsh during the summer. Do you know her well?'

'Please, Lyla! Leave me alone!' snapped Hyra, suddenly tired of being pestered by her questions, that sense of somehow being owned by her that had always been the price of her company.

'You know her well,' retorted Lyla coldly. 'You don't have to tell me. But I'm still coming with you.'

'Do as you please.' Too dazed to argue, Hyra swept past the two hand maids standing outside the entrance to the priestesses dwelling. Inside, beyond the ring of carved timbers that circled its centre, a reed partition divided the sleeping quarters from the rest of the hut. Behind it lay Morrigen.

She lay stiffly, as if hewn from stone. For a moment he thought she was sleeping, but then he realized that she was staring blindly upwards through dark hollow eyes that were bloodshot from weeping and exhaustion. Her fists were clenched, the knuckles white as bone against the skin. As he knelt, she turned slowly towards him. A glimmer of recognition crossed her face, then she began crying again, sponging away the tears with her hair.

'There's no need to speak,' he said softly. 'Leoid may be dead but he'd lived well, longer than most men. The fault isn't yours. You must sleep, it'll help you forget.'

'I'm glad you're back. You'll help me get better, won't you?'

Footsteps crunched in the bracken. Hyra glanced over his shoulder to see Lyla walking quietly from his side. When she reached the partition, she turned and stared at him for a moment, then vanished, hiding her bitterness.

'Who's there?' whispered Morrigen.

'No one. Try and sleep.'

She took his arm and pressed it to her cheek. 'I can't sleep.

Not now.' Sleep would mean being haunted by the souls of those she had slain; the convulsion that shook the healer as she picked the hemlock from the mud, Leoid's struggle when he realized he had been poisoned, the eternity spent holding him down until his body went still beneath her.

'What happened?' asked Hyra.

For an instant Morrigen verged on confession. Hyra would understand that she needed pity not punishment, that the evil that possessed her was a form of sickness no medicine could cure. 'I . . .' She stopped. Then the madness gained control of her again and truth became lies. 'He asked me to help him until you came back. The work wasn't important, but he wanted to finish it. Yesterday we were marking new sites for tombs. He stumbled as he walked and began to grow feverish. He asked me to stay. It meant watching him die . . .' She broke off and began sobbing again.

Hyra tried to calm her. The attempt was wasted. She was still suffering from shock and when another of the priestesses entered the hut he suggested she be given a potion to help her sleep.

'We've tried. She refused to drink it.' said the priestess.

'Warm it again. She may take it from me.'

'No!' Morrigen started whimpering and tugging at the pelts, pulling them round her face.

'You need rest,' insisted Hyra. 'It would do you good.'

But Morrigen cowered away, refusing to listen to him. Her guilt had worsened when she heard the sympathy in Hyra's voice. She started shaking. Cold sweat stood out in pearls on her forehead. Suddenly she screamed and tossed aside her bedding, forcing Hyra and the priestess to hold her down to prevent her fleeing the hut.

There was no sign of Lyla when Hyra finally retraced his steps and joined those mourning the dead seer. The shroud had been lifted. Leoid lay robed in his head-dress and ceremonial robes, his staff and mace beside him.

Hyra mounted the bier and kissed his brow. In repose, he seemed almost a child again. Death had smoothed the age from his cheeks and removed all trace of his infirmities, leaving him cold and pale and exuding the sweetness that perfumes all corpses.

Hyra grew pensive when he noticed Leoid's staff. It was covered with freshly cut tallies that had not been there when he went home. Every cut had a purpose. In combination they became a language capable of being deciphered and understood. The more he examined them, the more certain he was that they concerned the behaviour of the moon. Yet Morrigen had said that the work they had been doing was unimportant. He sighed. He was in no mood for riddles. Leoid was dead. No mark on a tally staff could resurrect him.

*

'Will you speak to me now? Or are we to stand here like strangers until Cronus returns? You didn't say a word to me during the feast, not one.'

Hyra said nothing. He walked over to the entrance to his father's tent and stared out over the Plain as the last of the revellers vanished into the dusk, torches lighting their way. Their laughter faded, leaving only the noise in the kitchen tent and Lyla pouring more mead into her beaker.

'Do you hate me so much you can't even look at me?'

Hyra turned. Debris scattered the tent; broken beakers, mutton bones and scraps of bread, the basin of sweetmeats that had been trampled into the straw during the feast. Lyla stood in the shadows, the tallows on the wall behind her lighting one side of her face.

She giggled and lifted her beaker, slopping mead down her robes. 'They've all gone.' She waved a stray hand at the emptiness.

'You're drunk.'

'Are you surprised? Oh, don't stare at me like that. Self-righteousness doesn't suit you. For the last three days you've done nothing but ignore me. We haven't even been to Henge yet. There's always been something else: Morrigen, the mourning Rites, meetings that can't be postponed – anything but me. Yes, I'm drunk. But at least I'm not afraid of the truth.'

'Do we have to fight?'

'That's up to you,' said Lyla tersely, suddenly draining her beaker.

Both Ishtar and the Lord of the Rites had attended the feast given by Cronus to thank them for allowing Ceruduc to retain his lands. In their honour Lyla was wearing woollen robes that hung loose and full round her body. Ochre coloured her cheeks, a single fragment of lapis lazuli lay blue against the white of her throat.

Shaking the plaits from her hair, she moved slowly towards Hyra, a half-smile parting her lips. She spun, hitching her robes high round her thighs then lowering them over her shoulders, exposing the hard curve of a breast. She giggled again.

'Is this what you want? A whore who'll play the slut and lie with you in the straw?'

'It would make a change,' said Hyra, humouring her.

'Well it's a change you'll have to do without until that priestess of yours stops her whining!' cried Lyla angrily, dashing her beaker to the ground and covering her nakedness. 'She's not ill. It's a sham. She enjoys watching you dance attendance on her. Are you better today, Morrigen? Try to sleep, Morrigen. Pah! She's evil, Hyra. Only you're too besotted by her to see it.'

'Is it evil to feel guilt because she was with Leoid when he died? Is it wrong of me to want to make her understand that she's not to blame for his death? The mead's made you hate her for taking me away from you. She means well. I owe her much. Without her I'd have left the Dwellings within a year of first coming here.'

Lyla stared at him for a moment. Unused to mead, it had muddled what she wanted to say, the need not to sound spiteful lest he mistake advice for jealousy. The flirt, the friend – both had failed her. And now she felt confused and wretched, too fuddled to argue. 'Do you love her?' she said.

Hyra shrugged and began pacing the tent. 'I don't know. Love to her is a sickness, something that weakens instead of strengthens. There's a wildness in her, a fear of being tamed or caught. She has some hold over me. When we're apart the knots that bind me to her seem to tighten still further.'

'A rope can be cut.'

'It's not always so simple.'

'But I don't matter?'

'I didn't say that.'

'You've said nothing at all that hasn't had to be squeezed out of you like water from a stone. Look at me, Hyra! Or are you blind as well as besotted? Why do you think I'm crying? What made me get drunk tonight? Why have I stopped Ceruduc from finding me a husband?'

'Please; the men may hear us . . .'

'Let them! All my life I've been thought of as the gentle,

constant, long-suffering Lyla, the woman you can turn to when in need of consoling and ignore when content. But that's what others have made me. It's not what I am. I'm a woman, with a woman's needs and a woman's faults. Yet even now you still treat me like a sister.' Lyla paused to sweep the hair and tears from her face. 'Why do you refuse what could so easily be yours? I love you, Hyra. I'd marry you now, tonight. But what I want doesn't matter. You want Morrigen, a woman who may never love you and might one day destroy you.'

'Listen to me, Lyla . . .'

'No! I've listened and waited long enough. I'm not a dog who must lie in the cold until its master takes pity on it. I'm leaving tomorrow. If you and I meet again it'll be chance, nothing more.'

Hyra started to follow her as she ran past him and disappeared into the night. He halted. Explanation would turn to argument again, end in her tears or his surrender. He deliberated going to see Morrigen, then turned and walked back to the tent. A dog slunk away at his approach, a bone clenched in its jaws. In the distance he could hear a low and toneless singing, the seers round the bier chanting the Song of the Dead. He slumped in the straw and placed his head to the wall of the tent . . .

'Eat.'

He looked up. His father stood in the shadows holding a stick speared with venison.

'I've no appetite.'

'For food, or Lyla?'

'Both.'

Cronus perched beside his son. 'I've just met her. She was crying. Something you said?'

'Or didn't say.'

'She's a good woman.'

'Does she need you to praise her?'

'Come, Hyra. It's our last night together. Let's say what we mean. You're your own master. You can do as you wish and wed who you please.' Cronus paused and tossed the venison into the straw. 'I've been speaking to Ishtar. She mentioned Morrigen. She told me that she had arranged her marriage to Zarxus because she doesn't trust her. Is she right?'

'No. Morrigen's harmless. Ishtar dislikes her because the shamans listen to what she says.'

Cronus smiled. 'I was like you once. Fobidden fruit is always the sweetest.'
'I haven't lain with her.'
'Perhaps you should?'
'She'd refuse me.'
'Admit defeat then, forget her.'
'I can't.'
Cronus chuckled to himself. 'I should never have given in to your mother. There's only two things that can ruin a man, women and Gods. They both need worshipping, and there's no place for worship in the hills. Come home with me. There's much to be done; sheep to be herded, bark to be peeled for forage, a byre in need of thatching. Simple tasks, but they'd help you forget her.'
'I've got to stay, at least until after her marriage.'
'To serve the Gods, or her?'
'I'm my own master, remember.'
Cronus laughed, then rose and crossed the tent. 'Perhaps you're wise. At least here you don't have Ceruduc for a neighbour. We may have saved him today, but there'll be trouble again soon. One sign from Serapha or a word from the shamans and he'll be marching on Henge. He'll march without me if he does. I'm too old and set in my ways to wage war.' He turned and lifted two ewers into the light. 'When did you last get drunk?'
Hyra smiled. 'A panacea?'
'It can help, sometimes. I'll join you. Father and son unable to stand, that should give the men something to gossip about to your mother when we get home.'
Cronus held out one of the ewers.
Hyra took it, grinned, then tilted it to his lips.

# CHAPTER VIII

Morrigen's recovery was slow. Always taciturn, her silences lengthened, seeming to isolate her from her fellow priestesses and enclose her in a private world. Forbidden to leave the Dwellings, watched closely by both Ishtar and Ralla when finally well enough to return to her duties, she spent much of the weeks that followed standing gazing at Leoid's corpse as it lay rotting on the bier. His robes flapped against his rib-cage, now an exposed fleshless hollow, as round and empty as a gourd, that sang its own lament when a bitter wind swept across the Plain and brought the first taste of winter to the encampment. But Morrigen did not hear it. Head bowed, hands and face discoloured by the cold, she would stand motionless for hours, silently pleading for atonement and forgiveness from the Gods. The two murders became a yoke she seemed unable to lift. Bewildered by her cruelty, the fear of retribution was as real as any of the images that still troubled her sleep and made her wake moaning and wet with fever in the night.

Hyra would walk across to her and lead her slowly from the bier. She rarely resisted, might even smile: it was like returning a somnabulist to her bed.

'I don't deserve your kindness,' she said once.

'Nor I your company when so soon you'll be wed.'

'The wedding will not take place.' She spoke softly, but with a conviction that made an answer impossible.

Such statements only added to Hyra's confusion. Lyla's admission of love had temporarily shaken his composure and steered him away from any entanglement, with either woman. But Lyla's departure with his father had left an emptiness only Morrigen could fill and the reality of her marriage had again begun to occupy his thoughts. Its approach was fact. One day a herd of cattle was driven into the Dwellings, Zarxus's wedding-offering to the priestesses of Bala. On another he entered her hut to find some shamans letting blood from her brow in order to release any demons that might mar the success of her marriage. And yet neither incident totally reconciled him to the inevitable. She still sought his company, still insisted they circle the ramparts together before nightfall. He had told her little about Lyla's visit, but she seemed curious for details about their friendship; a curiosity Hyra put down to her wish to avoid all discussion of her future.

'Tell me about her brother?' she once asked him.

'Ceruduc?'

'Yes.'

'We were close friends as children, even when I first met you in the Maiden Lines. But we've grown apart. I'm a seer, he's a chieftain. The two worlds don't mix.'

'Would he rise against the Dobuni if given the chance?'

Hyra frowned at the eccentricity of the question. 'Yes, I think so. Prudence isn't one of Ceruduc's virtues. But who'll provide the chance? Even with winter coming the Dobuni are keeping the hill-forts garrisoned.'

Morrigen nodded absent-mindedly. She stared out into the twilight, searching for the moon, the Goddess she had defied but who was soon to bring the portent that Ceruduc and the shamans were waiting for.

'What are you thinking?' murmured Hyra.

'About Leoid,' said Morrigen, acting a remorse that was beginning to fade.

*

A few days later it snowed during the night. Morrigen woke to a landscape that at last had no link with the afternoon spent waiting for Leoid to die. Sounds were less strident, whiteness dusted the Plain and broke the line of the forest. By nightfall the change of perspective had affected her view of what had happened. The healer had threatened her, his greed had caused his death. Leoid's unwillingness to share his secret excused his murder. Ishtar had no right to banish her from the Dwellings.

Propped by such arguments, her thoughts turned increasingly to the future. The preparations for her wedding took little of her time. One afternoon, with less than a week to go, a richly dressed Dobuni with a warrior's swagger and cropped wiry hair appeared in the encampment. She took no notice of Zarxus. On any other occasion his wish to make her his wife might have flattered her or inspired her curiosity. But although she ignored him, Zarxus's arrival saw the final exorcism of the past. She began to plan. The lies were rehearsed and their details amended until perfect, Hyra avoided lest he question her change of mood. Only Ralla succeeded in flustering her.

'You went to all that trouble to befriend Leoid. Then he died,' she said once, staring suspiciously at Morrigen.

'It was a coincidence.'

'Coincidences can be made to happen.'

Morrigen kept silent. Ralla mirrored her own defects, her cunning and calculation. The years together had taught her that it was their similarities not their differences that had made them such enemies. She also knew that if anyone was to guess the truth it would be Ralla.

The night preceding the Rites marked her gravest moment of doubt. Watching the pale winter moon as it rose over the Plain it seemed to her impossible that its light could suddenly dim and fade without warning. What if Leoid had been wrong? No mercy would be shown. She would be accused of sorcery, then put to death. She deliberated remaining silent. But even silence had its price: her marriage and banishment, a chance squandered that might never be repeated. No, it had to be done; and done so convincingly that everything that took place afterwards had a logic and momentum that lacked any connection with her.

She slept fitfully that night. Once a taper flared in the darkness and she heard two of the priestesses leave the warmth of their beds to watch over the fire. Melting snow dripped steadily from the thatch overhead. A cold wind touched her cheek as she tossed from side to side, waiting for dawn. Yet when morning came all the restless energy of the waiting again made her hesitate before lifting her pelts and adopting the bewildered slightly panic-stricken expression on which so much now depended.

Her companions soon noticed it. One asked her what was wrong.

She shrugged. 'I'm not sure. But I'm frightened.' She paused, wide-eyed and knuckles pressed to her teeth, the perfect facsimile of someone tense and on edge. 'Have the Gods ever spoken to you or visited you in your dreams?' she said finally.

'What are you talking about?'

Morrigen turned away, burying her face in her hands as if too ashamed to meet the stares of the small crowd that had gathered round her. 'Serapha came to me in the night,' she whispered. 'She spoke to me as I slept.'

'You're lying!' Ralla had pushed her way through the crowd.

'I'm not. I promise.'

Ralla sneered. 'And what did she say to you, this Goddess of yours?'

'It concerns the Rites. That's all I can say.'

'Don't be silly, Morrigen. You can tell us,' chorused her companions.

Morrigen refused. And though she remained pale and visibly agitated she couldn't resist a slight smile as she saw Ralla slip unnoticed from the crowd and leave the hut in the direction of Ishtar's dwelling.

The summons came shortly before noon. The High Priestess stood alone in the shadows. Her fire had been heaped with peat and smoke hung thickly round her. It eddied, lapping at her robes as she stepped forward. 'I want the truth, Morrigen; and I want it now. Don't look so surprised. You're not a fool. You knew that Ralla would betray you.'

Morrigen hung her head. 'You'll laugh at me.'

'Am I laughing now?'

'We're not the masters of what we dream. It probably means nothing. It was just a dream. I could easily be wrong.'

'Perhaps I should be the judge of that?'

Morrigen nodded, nerves arching her feet as they scratched through the rushes.

'Well?' demanded Ishtar.

There was silence for a moment, the hiss of peat, then Morrigen lifted her face and said, 'There's to be another Darkness. The moon's light will dim as we celebrate the Rites.'

Ishtar frowned. She trembled, tightening her cloak. She scanned Morrigen's face. 'And what will happen then?'

'It will brighten, be slowly reborn.'

'And what you've told me is what you dreamt, what Serapha revealed to you as you slept?'

'Yes.'

Ishtar began pacing. Each time she emerged from the smoke her face appeared paler, more strained. Finally she said, 'If you're proved wrong, you'll die. But you already know that, don't you?'

'I'm not afraid. The Gods gave me life, it's theirs to take.'

'And you'd risk losing it on the day of your marriage?'

'If that is their will.'

Morrigen's composure returned as she watched an anxious looking Ishtar spin into the smoke. Ishtar's imperiousness had deserted her. She was cornered, and knew it, and her voice showed the strain when she spoke. 'If what you've told me takes place and I've said nothing, the seers will accuse me of doubting your word and failing to give them warning.'

'Then tell them.'

'I intend to. But it's a pity your Goddess waited until now before troubling your dreams. You know as well as I that it's too late to send couriers to the villages.'

'Am I to blame for that?'

'No. But it's the seers who interpret the omens. None has predicted a Darkness. Why should Serapha speak only to you?'

'I don't know.'

'Nor do I. The Cunei are fickle, they bend with the wind. Thanks to your travels you're well known to them now. If the Darkness happens the shamans may exhort them to rise against us. Some will think that you're a Goddess yourself and demand that you be dressed in these robes and appointed High Priestess in my place.'

'That's not my intention.'

'What is?' Ishtar crossed her hut and stood in its entrance. The silence lengthened, to be ended when she retraced her steps and again joined Morrigen. She smiled thinly. 'Go outside and tell me what you see.'

Morrigen did so. Two men were cracking the ice on a water-trough. A group of shamans squatted disconsolately round a fire. Smoke seeped through the thatched roofs of the dwellings. Watching it rise, she suddenly realized the reason for Ishtar's request. She gazed up at the sky, frightened and unnerved.

'I'm not surprised you're trembling. So would I be,' murmured Ishtar. 'It's the one thing you'd forgotten. What was it you said? The Gods gave me life, it's theirs to take away. And take it they will if the weather holds.'

Morrigen turned away, unable to look. Beyond the ramparts thick grey-bellied clouds rolled remorselessly towards her, obscuring any hint of the sun.

'If they don't lift before dawn tomorrow the Goddess Serapha can do as she pleases,' said Ishtar. 'But you, Morrigen, you will be dead when next she rises. You may go. I fear that your marriage may be brief and it would be wrong to keep Zarxus waiting.'

As Morrigen left the hut, it began snowing.

*

Torches lit the night and glistened against the snow that had covered the Plain during the blizzard. It was still falling; muffling sound, buckling the tops of the tents in the Village of the Shamans, licking at the faces of those in the procession. But the wind had died, and, as Henge drew nearer, the drifts it had left in its wake could be seen rising smooth and sheer as buttresses where they met the stones, as if shoring them up. But the stones had also broken the force of the wind, and the shamans started wailing when the central stone loomed out of the darkness, capped with snow and as white and slender as an alabaster column.

The shamans wore furs. Grey-bearded like old men as their breath turned to hoar on their whiskers, each carried a basket filled with corn that had been soaked in tassine. Winter had begun, and the ghosts of the dead had to be feasted and placated as they rose from their slumbers to roam the land. Behind them walked the seers and priestesses carrying offerings for the Gods lest their light fail and be extinguished by the cold.

Amongst them walked Morrigen. The snow melted as it fell against her cheek and dripped into her furs. The wetness did not matter. She moved mechanically. Her hood had fallen, the weight of snow in her hair setting it into a lop-sided parting that was already beginning to freeze. She was aware of neither. The suddenness of the blizzard had robbed her of all belief in Leoid's prophecy. She was convinced that her death was imminent, so much so that she had already set in motion its processes.

'It was a threat,' whispered Hyra, drawing alongside her as she entered the temple. 'Try and concentrate. Withdrawal into trance won't help you. She won't do it. She daren't risk offending Zarxus.'

Morrigen shuddered and gripped Hyra's hand. 'She wants me dead.'

'You could flee. They'd never find you tonight. Most of the

warriors have been sent to the nearest villages to quell any rising.'

'It's too late.' Morrigen glanced at Ishtar. Torch-light lit the half-smile that had remained on her face since the blizzard first broke. Men with spears surrounded her. On the far side of the temple, where the snow had been trampled, she could see Zarxus waiting impatiently for the Rites to commence. She peered upwards, blinking against the snow.

'It won't stop now,' said Hyra, guessing her thoughts.

'I know.'

'Run. It's your only chance.'

'I can't. I've no food or bedding, not even my dagger. Look at her guards, they're waiting for me to make a mistake.' Morrigen hesitated for a moment, then stepped forward, taking her place beside the central stone.

The shamans started dancing, first turning to the four quarters of the firmament, then circling the stone and sprinkling corn as they asked the spirits of the dead to watch over them until spring. The seers began chanting, the priestesses placed their offerings at the foot of the stone.

Suddenly Morrigen realized that the steady trickle of snow down her cheeks had ended. She lifted a hand and held it into the light: the snow had stopped.

'It won't save you.' Ishtar appeared beside her.

'When will it happen?'

'At dawn. It'll be quick. Zarxus insists on being allowed to enjoy your company until morning. I've agreed. It's the least we can do for him.'

'And if I refuse?'

'You won't have much choice. Look at him. The delays have tested his patience. He's like a stag before the rut.' Ishtar smiled and melted into the shadows. The seers began intoning the Chant to Bala. The Lord of the Rites started beating the stones with a sprig of holly, warming them and filling them with life.

Morrigen scanned the sky. A light flashed, vanished. The flash was repeated. The seers' voices wavered, then faltered completely as high overhead the clouds slowly parted to reveal a backcloth of stars twinkling palely against the night. There was silence, a distant shout from one of the villages on the Plain.

'It must be done!' cried Ishtar.

The Lord of the Rites nodded anxiously, glanced at both Morrigen and the sky, then trudged through the snow towards Zarxus. The chieftain laughed at the sudden change of mood, unfastened the clip to his cloak and tossed it aside. Oblivious to the cold, he stood naked to the waist as the Lord of the Rites smeared his body with ochre and civet as a sign of his strength. Morrigen was crying. In a few moments her blood would be mixed with Zarxus's, she would kiss him in homage and be given the holly – the ceremony would be over. He would escort her to his tents. His handmaidens would wash and robe her and prepare her for his bed . . .

'Look . . . !'

Morrigen jerked round as one of the shamans began pointing at the sky. The clouds stood out in silhouette against the darkness. Light lit their ragged edges, the faint curve now visible behind them. The curve thickened, becoming a full and perfect moon that bathed the Plain in its glow.

For a moment no one moved.

Ishtar began whimpering, striking out with an erratic arm when Ralla ran forward to comfort her. Morrigen was still crying. The seers were silent. Only Zarxus seemed unaware of what was happening, for he suddenly turned and snatched the knife from the Lord of the Rites, drawing blood as he nicked his hand with its blade. Raising it again, he pulled Morrigen towards him . . .

'Wait!'

A thin sliver of shadow had started sliding across the rim of the moon. There were screams. The baggage oxen outside Zarxus's tents began bellowing. One broke free from its tether and ran trumpeting into the night, only falling silent when it sunk up to its belly in the drifts. As the noise faded, a wolf could be heard howling. Its cry was answered by another. Soon the Plain seemed to echo to their din and the terrified wailing of the tribesfolk in the nearest villages. An owl, a nocturnal phantom in its winter plumage, flitted through the moonlight, hooted, circled the temple, then settled on the stone standing alone in the Sacred Way. So ominous a portent caused instant panic. The owl was a hunter, a symbol of darkness, the stone was the Serapha Stone and had been raised by the Cunei in praise of their Moon Goddess.

Seeing it staring at them through its vast circular eyes, head slightly tilted, the priestesses cried out and began running.

Some tripped and fell to the snow; others, unaware of where they were going, floundered blindly through the drifts in search of escape from Serapha's judgement. The shamans wailed, the seers prostrated themselves before the stones, clutching at them with torn finger-nails as they begged the Goddess to take pity on them. As if to drown their pleas, a sudden wind swept the temple, lifting the snow into a fine cutting spray that doused the torches and left only the stars and the moon to compete with the Darkness.

But though the stars still glittered the moon had narrowed to an arc and its light was failing fast. Morrigen freed herself from Zarxus's grip and turned to watch it as its face was eclipsed by shadow. One of the seers threw himself round her legs. Screams pierced the night. She had expected to share their terror or feel some sense of her triumph, but instead felt empty and at peace, aloof from the surrounding confusion. The seer was babbling incoherently. Thrusting him aside, she began striding across the temple, cloak open, her hair streaming behind her in the wind. Hyra was terrified but still on his feet, and his last glimpse of her, before the moon vanished, was of someone who seemed almost a ghost, a creation of the dream that had heralded the Darkness.

The darkness was absolute. Nothing was visible but the continued shine of the stars. To those who experienced it its length was eternal. Even the stones merged with the blackness and those clinging to them did not move until a thin crescent of colour finally returned to the sky.

The moon began to swell again, its light brightened. The screams faded and gave way to tears. Ishtar was still whimpering, half-buried by the snow. Ralla knelt sobbing beside her, Zarxus had vanished. So had Morrigen, and Hyra only finally caught sight of her when he stumbled across to the entrance and peered into the shadows. She was standing motionless on the bank staring back at the temple. She smiled at him, then turned and began walking towards the Dwellings, her first steps matching the ascent of the owl as it rose from its perch and flapped silently into the night.

# CHAPTER IX

Despite his power, Ortus was a benevolent well-meaning man who had risen to be Lord of the Rites by his knowledge of the constellations and his willingness to compromise. But the diffidence concealed shrewdness, and one glance at the courier as he crossed the Council Dwelling gave warning of what he most feared. The Darkness had taken its toll: no sudden aberration of the stars or attempt at compromise could now juggle its effects. Smoke blackened the courier's face and in his haste he had forgotten to unbuckle his snow shoes. Small clues, but sufficient for Ortus to decide Ishtar's fate and for Ishtar to know that she was doomed.

Ishtar had broken-off in mid-sentence when the courier entered the hut. Now trembling slightly, she watched him for a moment, then scanned the half-circle of seers and priestesses squatting opposite her on the pelts. The Council had been in conclave since dawn; lined faces betrayed their fatigue, the memory of what had taken place during the night. Grateful for any distraction that lessened the tension, most were watching Ortus or whispering amongst themselves. The remainder turned away, evading her gaze.

Her eyes found Morrigen. The noon sunshine slanting low through the entrance lit one cheek but left the other in shadow. She seemed relaxed and at ease, as if indifferent to the outcome of the conclave. But Ishtar knew instantly that the constant fingering of the beads round her neck revealed nervousness not habit. The two women stared at each other until the courier finished speaking. Attention shifted again, all eyes fixing on Ortus as he gave his instructions to the courier, who then rose and withdrew. He turned towards Ishtar.

'You may continue.'

The High Priestess forced a smile as silence returned to the dwelling. Further argument was pointless, the decision had been taken. 'I've nothing to add,' she said. 'The Gods have heard me. Now they must judge me.'

'And what if they've already done so?'

'Then you must share the blame? You've spent your life studying the heavens, yet now you confess to being unable to predict its motions. How can you expect me to succeed where you have failed?'

Ortus spread his hands as if to accept her criticism. It would soon be over; he could afford to indulge her. But indulgence did not require him to allow her room for manoeuvre. 'So you admit your guilt?'

'I admit nothing!' Ishtar turned angrily towards the solemn faces of the seers. 'Last night you were pleading for your lives, all of you. Now it's I who plead and you who judge me. Of what am I guilty? You say that my powers have begun to decay and must be transferred to my successor before they weaken any further. You accuse me of doubting Morrigen's word, of being envious of her gifts. But I wonder what you would have done if you'd been told that the Goddess Serapha had spoken to her as she slept? During the Darkness it was perdition that frightened you. Now you're afraid of angering the Cunei and need someone to blame for your faults, someone whose death will salve your consciences.'

An embittered despairing speech, and truthful enough. But Ishtar knew that it was too late for rhetoric. Nothing she said could save her.

The seers shuffled uncomfortably as they saw the accusation in her stare. 'The Goddess must be appeased,' volunteered one. 'A pyre has been lit at Henge. It'll be kept burning until the eve of the Spring Rites. But it isn't enough.'

Ishtar sneered at him. 'So you've chosen to play the craven and pretend that my death will make you virtuous?'

'Silence, woman!' Ortus rose heavily to his feet. 'The will of the Gods may still be unknown, but the people's will has already been heard. The courier brought me news from the villages. What I most feared has happened. Two have risen in revolt. Dobuni tents have been burnt, a warrior murdered, some herdsmen slaughtered in their beds. Old grudges are being settled and the blood-letting may soon stop. But the shamans won't be silenced so easily. The Darkness has brought many portents: lambs born out of season, babes come early from the womb that refused their mother's milk and will now be honoured as martyrs for choosing to die rather than serve the Dobuni. Oxen, the very symbol of Bala's power, have been seen deliberately plunging themselves into the swamps and rivers. Even the clouds that hide the sun will be construed as evidence of our weakness. We have no choice. To please the shamans we must make an offering to Serapha. The alternative is insurrection and the risk of defeat.'

'And I am to be that offering?'

Ortus met Ishtar's gaze. There was no need for words. The loneliness of high office had brought them together as friends, their age and sense of duty fostering a closeness that both of them treasured. His head slumped, then straightened. He nodded.

There was silence. A few of the priestesses started sobbing. Ishtar buried her face in her hands. A moment later a group of shamans entered the dwelling. She glanced at them, then paled and backed away as if searching for escape as a line of warriors took up position in the entrance. Each had smeared his brow in imitation of death and wore a dagger at his waist. She screamed, then crossed the hut and threw herself at them, windmilling her arms and kicking out with her feet in an attempt to flee the dwelling. One knocked her to the ground. She lay still for a moment, then rose to her haunches and turned towards Morrigen.

'Are you content now?' Her voice was a whisper. Her cloak was torn, one lip was cut, dishevelled hair hung down over her face.

As prior to Leoid's death, Morrigen felt as if she was a stranger to her own emotions. She wanted to show sympathy, but instead saw only an old and frightened woman, without dignity or beauty, who knew that her death was close. She looked round. Everyone was watching her, awaiting her reply. First measuring her words, she said gently, 'What I said to you yesterday is still true. We serve the Gods. They gave us life, it's theirs to take away.'

Ishtar started cackling. Gradually her laugh turned into a prolonged and hideous shriek that filled the entire dwelling with its despair. At a sign from Ortus two of the warriors hoisted her to her feet. Her screams faded to a moan, allowing Ortus to speak.

'All of us know how well you have served us as High Priestess. Because of that it is only right that you be given the chance to end your own life. No demons will carry away your soul. One day you will be reborn and will be able to make amends for your errors.' He paused and indicated one of the shamans. 'A venom has been prepared for you. I hope that you'll find the courage to take it.'

Ishtar gazed at him. 'Do I have a choice?'

Ortus glanced at the warriors, who quietly drew their daggers.

'I see.' Ishtar trembled and momentarily closed her eyes before walking over to the carved post that rose from the centre of the dwelling. She pressed her brow to it and started weeping. The shamans began intoning the Song of the Dead. She straightened, then beckoned to one of them, taking a small rounded beaker from his outstretched hand. She lifted it to her lips. Her fingers began shaking and the venom spilled down her chin.

'The end will be swift,' murmured Ortus.

'But not swift enough. Death never is.'

Spellbound eyes followed the rise of the beaker as again Ishtar placed it to her lips. The colour left her face, leaving it ashen and drawn and creased with age. Her lips parted into a smile. The beaker slid from her fingers. 'I can't do it,' she whispered.

She did not move as the warriors closed in on her. She screamed. Ortus raised an arm. As it fell, her screams gave way to a hoarse muffled whimper. The warriors stepped back as she slowly collapsed to the pelts, the hilts of their daggers still protruding from her robes.

Almost in unison, and as if released from a coma by the presence of death, those watching drew breath, filling the gloom with a deep, feral moan that lingered on as an echo as Ishtar's body twitched slightly, and then was still.

Hyra turned away from the corpse. As he did so, he glimped Morrigen standing motionless in the shadows. Unable to conceal her elation, she smiled at him. Then the smile vanished and her heart quickened as she realized her error. Sensing her panic, still troubled by her smile, Hyra grew thoughtful. Much had happened since the autumn. The coincidences were many. Morrigen had been the only witness to Leoid's death, her prediction of the Darkness had led to Ishtar being sacrificed. Aware that the tallies on Leoid's staff could prove a link between the two events, he watched carefully as she pushed past the warriors and knelt beside the High Priestess, showing her respect for the dead woman by folding her arms across her breasts and making certain that her eyes remained open to permit the escape of her spirit. As always her courtesy disarmed him, and his suspicions faded as he saw her stifle tears and heard the seers murmur their appreciation.

The gesture had been deliberate. Since waking on the previous morning Morrigen's every action had been structured and examined for flaws. And as tassine and spitted meats were brought in and passed round, she knew from the glances of the seers that success lay close. The lies, the deceits, even the three murders of which she was guilty, all would be justified if she left the Council Dwelling as High Priestess. In no mood for food, she sat demure and silent as the seers plunged their faces into a basin of perfumed water to prepare themselves for what lay ahead. Finally Ortus rose to formally address them.

'Ishtar is dead. We must now appoint her successor. The Gods will guide us, but the threat of unrest amongst the Cunei makes the burden a heavy one. It has to be done though, and done before dusk lest Serapha be offended and fail to rise. As is the custom, each of the priestesses will be masked and called to stand before us. Those who believe she has been chosen by Bala to serve in his temple will remain seated, those who do not must stand and turn away.'

One by one the priestesses were paraded in front of the seers. Despite their inexperience, it was obvious from the start that Morrigen and Ralla were the main contenders for the appointment. When Ralla stood, most seers stayed seated. Morrigen trembled as she was led forward and the blindfold was lowered over her eyes. Unable to see, her sole clues were the shuffle of feet and a sudden flurry of whispers.

A drum began beating. She heard the shamans cry out, beakers being smashed to the ground. For an instant the knowledge of victory made her weaken and begin to stumble. Then she tore the mask from her eyes, blinking against the light as one of the seers lifted Ishtar's cloak over her shoulders and another held out her necklaces and raven's feather head-dress. Her fellow priestesses had fallen to their knees and lowered their heads, so that all that could be seen of them was a curtain of hair; hair which it was her duty to cut and plait into a gown as a reminder of their subservience and the powers of her office. She stretched out a hand to take the head-dress.

'No!'

Ralla had jumped to her feet and was advancing on Ortus. 'The waif is a Cunei!' she cried. 'It's those who share her blood who have murdered our herdsmen and burnt their tents. How can you be sure of her loyalty? Make her High Priestess and you risk the destruction of both Henge and these Dwellings.'

An expectant silence greeted Ralla's outburst. Those who questioned the authority of the seers faced banishment or the Mastery of Fire. But Ralla's anger had echoed Ortus's misgivings. He turned to Morrigen. 'Is this true?'

Morrigen shrugged. 'You must believe what you wish.'

'That's all she ever says!' protested Ralla. 'She's worse than one of the popinjays peddled by the merchant from Karnos* when we gather for the Rites.'

For once Morrigen had no answer. Suddenly vulnerable and defenceless, she felt her self-control begin to ebb. The emotions she had harboured inside her since befriending Leoid could be caged no longer. Convinced that Ralla was trying to cheat her of victory, she leapt towards her, fingers spread and aimed at her eyes . . .

'No, Morrigen!'

Hyra's warning cut sharp as a knife through the din. And it saved her. Regaining her balance, she stepped back and let her arms collapse to her side.

'The popinjay repeats what others teach it,' she said softly, turning to Ortus. 'All I have learnt I owe to the seer who instructed me when I was a novice, to Ishtar, to Ralla, and to you.'

'She's lying!' shouted Ralla. 'If Hyra hadn't spoken she would have tried to kill me.'

Morrigen permitted a smile. 'Or embrace you. Only a fool would judge what has yet to happen.'

'And only a fool would wait to find out.'

'Silence! Both of you!' snapped Ortus. Never before had he so profoundly detested the arrogance of youth; and never before had he felt so apprehensive when having to surrender to it. 'These are fearful days,' he continued. 'One of you is a Cunei, the other a Dobuni. Today of all days you must live in peace and set an example to your people.' He paused and lifted his mace, then turned towards the seers. 'Despite your choice, I have decided that from this day forth both Morrigen and Ralla shall be honoured as equals, sharing the duties of the High Priestess, its powers, title and dwelling. As I command, so shall

* Carnac, Brittany.

it be.' Taking two daggers from the seer beside him, he gave one to each of the priestesses.

Ralla placed hers in the flat of her hand, blade towards Morrigen. She smiled, her fingers circled its hilt. The burnished copper blade parried the light from the tallows as she lifted it into the air and moved closer to Morrigen. Then she laughed and pirouetted and began hacking at the hair of the nearest priestess, covering the ground with a carpet of gold.

*

'They must come soon. It's so cold just standing here.'

'Zarxus would have warmed you.'

'Men don't matter to me.'

'That's not what Atius told me.'

'Atius is a liar.'

'And a braggart.' Ralla paused, stamping her boots in the snow. 'Would you have killed me tonight?'

'Yes.'

There was silence, both of them instinctively retreating from further conflict. The long wait and the tediousness of the ceremonies that had filled the day had finally united into a sense of anti-climax that left them drained, weary and beyond argument.

Ralla peered out over the trampled, dung encrusted snow that stretched frozen into the darkness. 'What really happened to Leoid?' she asked, trying to play down the significance of the question. 'I won't tell any one. We're equals now.'

Morrigen did not answer. The chances of their intimacy surviving the night were slight. Anything she said would soon be distorted and used to hasten her ruin. Yet Ralla's self-confidence left her slightly unnerved. It was as if she knew that as High Priestess she was already invulnerable.

'That merchant is yours if you want him back,' continued Ralla. 'There's no pleasure in being wooed by a man who begrudges every night he has to spend in the Dwellings. As soon as we've made love he's more concerned with the welfare of his oxen than his mistress. Men are much the same. One moment they flatter, but as soon as they've enjoyed what they wanted they rise, robe and are gone.' She spoke with the authority of experience, afterwards pausing to glance at the outline of the tents pitched near the causeway. 'Zarxus is still here.' She grinned. 'You may not need warming, but I do.'

'But you can't! Not now!'

'Why not? He needs company. He's been complaining all day about losing you.'

Morrigen was too tired to show concern for Zarxus. She rested her head against the post behind her. 'Oh how Ortus went on. I feared he might never stop. I fell asleep once and when I woke his voice sounded just as dreary.'

'There were lice in Kelda's hair,' said Ralla. 'They kept tickling me as I cut it.'

Gossip surrendered to silence. Finally the cortège loomed out of the night, forcing them to leave the shelter of the dwelling and stand solemnly in its entrance. Ishtar's corpse lay balanced on the heads of her pall-bearers. The priestesses followed, stubbled skulls now shorn of hair glinting palely in the light from the torches. All were wailing, very softly, and the wind drowned their lament as it gusted over the ramparts and licked at the snow.

Morrigen and Ralla moved aside as the procession entered the dwelling. Some of the priestesses held bones that had been taken from the Tomb of the Priestesses to guard Ishtar as she slept. Others carried offerings; bread and tassine, a small carved phallus to prove her devotion to Bala. The torches flared in the darkness, casting flickering shadows that made the ceiling come alive to their dance.

Morrigen shuddered as she knelt beside the corpse. The shadows made her feel like a trespasser in a dwelling peopled by spirits. And now she was to share it with Ralla, sleep where Ishtar had slept. But Ishtar was dead. Dressed in fresh robes, there was no sign of her wounds. But her hands were stiff and unyielding to Morrigen's touch and her fingers lay hooked like talons across the rise of her breasts.

Morrigen turned away and ordered the waiting priestesses to begin digging the grave.

Ortus had already sited it. The priestesses gathered round, each arming themselves with an antler and pieces of flint from a basket. The constant treading of feet had compressed the earth beneath the rushes, leaving it hard and cracked. The women knelt and began chipping at its surface, tools rising and falling in time to their chant.

Morrigen grew impatient as the shaft slowly deepened. The monotonous scrape of the flints jarred at her thoughts. Her head was aching, waves of pain moving to and fro across her temple. She was exhausted. Like a snake sloughing its skin, she wanted to begin again, untainted, guileless, empty of evil. Leoid's bones lay entombed near Henge, the healer's corpse would have rotted and been forgotten. Only Ishtar remained to continue haunting her and remind her of what she had done. Her burial would banish the past, bring a new beginning and the peace of mind she so longed for.

Ralla joined her. 'It'll be dawn before it's dug,' she said, glancing at the shaft before gazing out into the darkness. 'Zarxus is still awake. I can see a light in his tents.'

Morrigen frowned anxiously. 'Don't go to him. Not tonight.'

'You're not my mistress, Morrigen. A High Priestess can do as she pleases.'

'Please stay. Just this once.'

Ralla turned and stared at her, as if to read her thoughts. She laughed. 'So the waif is afraid of being alone with a corpse. You bury her. It's you who wanted her dead.' Still laughing, she swept up her cloak and vanished into the night.

Morrigen ran after her, then halted and looked back over her shoulder. Shadows swirled against the pitch of the roof. Ishtar's body lay lifeless and abandoned on the floor. She hurried towards the grave, ordering the priestesses to speed up their work.

She began pacing, but wherever she walked Ishtar's still open eyes seemed to track her movements, reproaching her with their gaze. The noise of the flints grew louder, less rhythmic. The shadows became monstrous and misshapen, like giants created by the Gods to punish and torment her.

Suddenly she could listen no longer. Pushing past her companions, she jumped into the grave, picked up a flint and began hacking at the earth beneath her. The flint blistered her skin and her nails were soon torn. Dust filled her throat and her eyes. But finally it was done.

Breathing shallowly, certain that the madness had left her, she stood to one side as Ishtar was lowered into the grave. Her knees were bent, their joints cracking slightly before giving way. Crouching as in sleep, she lay gazing upwards as the offerings were placed beside her. Then she vanished, the earth drumming against her ribs as it was shovelled on top of her. For an instant one eye remained visible, then it disappeared, smothered and blinded by the weight of earth. Once the grave had been filled, fresh rushes were strewn over it and a single stone was placed in its centre to mark the site. The priestesses knelt and pressed their cheeks to the stone, then rose and returned to their dwelling. Morrigen was alone.

*

For a while she did not move. The wind moaned in the thatch, the tallows dimmed. But even in the darkness the chinks in the walls let in enough light to give life to the shadows. She rose and hurried over to the chest, again tormented. She removed a bundle of tallows and lit them, placing them round the dwelling and filling it with a brilliant blaze of colour that killed the shadows and turned night into day. But her delirium remained. She walked over to the water-trough and began washing her hands; scrubbing the fingers that had held the knife, mixed the venom, dug the grave. But the more she scrubbed, the more vivid grew the memories she was trying to erase.

She started pacing again. Reaching the entrance, she stared out at the snow. A giggle, man's voice, then silence. Moonlight traced the curve of the ramparts. A few stars patterned the night. She decided to wake Hyra. He would calm her and watch over her as she slept. But the darkness intimidated her and she began floundering panic-stricken through the snow, finally turning back when only half-way across the encampment. Once inside the dwelling again, she lay down and draped herself in pelts. She was High Priestess. Victory was hers. Sleep would heal and leave her refreshed. But she could not sleep. The last of the tallows burned steadily shorter. She rose to light more. It guttered and went out. She walked onwards in the direction of the chest. Suddenly she stumbled over the stone above Ishtar's grave. She screamed, collapsed to her knees and wrapped her arms round its coldness, too frightened to move or attempt returning to her bed.

*

In the morning she was found fully dressed and still clinging to the stone.

Throughout that day the humility of both High Priestesses was remarked on whenever their names were mentioned. Had not one spent the night guarding the remains of her predecessor whilst the other gave her body to Zarxus in compensation for his loss? But soon their courtesy was forgotten.

Two days later a runner collapsed on the causeway. He was exhausted and suffering from the effects of the cold. His veins stood out like the warp of a net and the constant intake of frozen air had doubled the size of his tongue. He could not speak at first. But when he did those who understood him trembled and touched their daggers: Ceruduc and another of the chieftains had risen in revolt against the Dobuni, even now they were marching on Henge.

# CHAPTER X

Hyra ignored the stares of the warriors standing guard outside the High Priestess's dwelling as he stamped the snow from his boots and ducked through the entrance. Their suspicion would once have surprised him, but in the three weeks that had elapsed since its new incumbents took up residence he had grown used to the unease that now pervaded the Dwellings.

The handmaidens combing Morrigen's hair melted into the shadows as the seer approached. They too had grown accustomed to the change of mood; but for them it took shape in the daily bickering between their two mistresses, the contradictory orders that made all attempts to please one certain to enrage the other. Hyra waited until their steps had faded, then sat opposite Morrigen and peered quickly into the gloom.

She smiled at his nervousness. 'No one can hear us. Ralla's out. Try and keep calm.' The past weeks had taken their toll. The strain showed on his face and the lines on his brow had slowly deepened to ruts as the crisis worsened.

Hyra sighed and lifted his hands to the fire. 'For once I've reason to be worried. Another band of warriors has just reached the Dwellings. That makes nearly a thousand camped outside the ramparts. Ceruduc's doomed. His every move seems to end in disaster.'

'Is there still no more news?'

'None. But Zarxus's couriers have confirmed that the uprising has spread into the Northern Vales. Tharah has driven the Dobuni from the hill-forts and is trying to link up with Ceruduc. But two men can't win a war. Unless the chieftains unite and join the rising the Dobuni will be strong enough to defeat Tharah then swing south into the marshes and begin hunting for Ceruduc.'

'Zarxus can't move until the snow melts,' said Morrigen. 'There's no fodder for his baggage oxen. Every hunting party he sent out would risk being ambushed.'

A month ago Hyra would have smiled politely at Morrigen's knowledge of strategy. He now knew better. Her aptitude for it was instinctive. Just as she had mastered the innumerable duties of her new office, so also had she grasped the problems of tactics and supply that confronted Zarxus.

'And what will happen when the weather changes?' he said. 'The Dobuni are still nomadic. Their winter quarters are scattered across the Plain and he's told the chieftains to be wary. No Cunei village in the land would be safe from attack if it chose to join the revolt.' Hyra paused and tossed more logs on to the fire. He stared into the flames. If his assessment was right, defeat was inevitable. For an instant he thought of Lyla, now a fugitive in hiding with her brother. Too despondent to add to his diagnosis, he instead asked for news of Ralla.

'She's with Zarxus again. They've stopped caring who knows that they're lovers. According to Dobuni legend an alliance between a priestess and warrior is permitted during times of war. Even Ortus has sanctioned it. At least I'm left in peace.'

Hyra glanced at Morrigen. Her hair hung in folds over her shoulders, falling in a cascade of coloured leather ribbons to below her waist. A copper serpent torque entwined each of her arms. Her lynx-skin robes had been patterned in red and white stripes and a spider frozen lifeless in amber stared out from the curve of her breasts. Yet she wore her beauty like a mask, so that in its opulence it seemed as mysterious and inscrutable as her features.

'The peace won't last,' he said gently. 'One day you may have to put aside your trinkets and be ready to flee.'

It was the first time Hyra had broached the possibility of Morrigen being caught up and engulfed by the rising, and he was unprepared for the anger that swept her face.

'No!' she cried. 'For years I was scorned and treated as an outcast. I'm the waif no longer. I'm a High Priestess. This is my home.'

'That's what Ishtar thought. It's now her grave.' Hyra paused, letting reality take root. 'What will happen to you if Ralla persuades Ortus that you're to blame for the rising?'

'Ralla means nothing to me. She and Zarxus can plot as they please. No one will listen to them. I dreamt of the Darkness. Serapha has spoken to me.'

'And Serapha is a Cunei Goddess. Ortus is no fool. He made you High Priestess in the hope that it would silence the shamans and prevent a revolt. He failed. You've already outlived your usefulness. He needs Zarxus's support. Zarxus and Ralla are lovers. If Zarxus demands your death Ortus will have to obey lest Zarxus takes offence and leaves us to our fate.'

Morrigen rose and turned away from his gaze. As she reached the entrance to her dwelling, the warriors stepped aside to let her pass.

Hyra drew alongside her. 'Today they guard you,' he whispered. 'Tomorrow they may become your gaolers.'

She trembled and quickened pace, stumbling through the snow. The logic of Hyra's words needed no explanation, similar thoughts had nagged at her for nearly a week. But until now she had chosen to ignore their warning. The rising had lost its momentum. By spring Ceruduc would be dead. To join him meant embracing his cause and the pointlessness of all she had done. She would be accused of treachery, hunted, shown no mercy if caught. For three years she had employed cunning and patience to win the power she wanted. In its name she had murdered, known guilt, risked the retribution of the Gods. Suddenly frightened, she climbed the ramparts and gazed out at the emptiness.

Hyra followed her. 'We should flee and find Ceruduc.'

She shook her head. 'I'm staying. Go and you do so alone.'

'We're Cunei, Morrigen. He needs our help.'

'The rising will soon be over. Even you admit that he's doomed.'

'Better to die for a cause you believe in than one you don't. Stay or flee, the outcome may prove the same.'

Yet still she clung on to her delusions, the belief in her own immunity. 'If anyone tries to harm me,' she said, 'Serapha will stay their hand and make certain that they're punished.' But her reply sounded hollow and contrived. As if to escape from what she knew to be a lie, she turned – only to find herself facing the shamans. After four days there was little to see: just the line of heads staring down from the poles that the Dobuni had placed in the entrance as a warning of what happened to those who defied them. But one seemed to be grinning at her, mocking her arrogance. She shivered, then reached for Hyra and pulled him towards her.

*

Throughout the next week she rarely ventured from her dwelling. The snow returned, roofing the heads of the dead with neat white skull-caps and isolating the encampment from the rest of the Plain. There was no news of the uprising. The warriors huddled in their tents. Hunters trudged towards the kitchen quarters with winter's gleanings: small birds that had fallen from their perches, deer and boar, the occasional carcass of a horse that had been found frozen to death, only its legs protruding from the drifts. One night the wind rose to gale force, leaving in its wake a savage but haunting expanse of snow-sculpted statues and carvings.

Despite its beauty, the snow transformed the Dwellings into a beleaguered fortress, and there were moments when Morrigen felt certain that when it finally melted it would take Zarxus and Ralla with it, leaving her triumphant and invincible. Again and again Hyra tried to make her see sense. She refused to listen, calling him timid, irresolute, even a coward. He debated leaving without her. No knots bound them, she had abused his friendship, her behaviour before and after the Darkness continued to puzzle him: but he knew he couldn't do it. In the end it was Ralla who at last drummed home the precariousness of her position.

She had left Zarxus's tent to celebrate the evening Rites. Once over, she swept unannounced into the High Priestess's dwelling and surveyed it with a proprietary smile.

Morrigen watched her uneasily. The past few weeks had taught her that every move made by Ralla had its purpose, usually malicious, always self-serving. 'What do you want?'

'You'll see soon enough.' The smile broadened as Ralla turned and called to the guards. 'Assist the priestess Morrigen find lodgings in another dwelling.'

Morrigen rose to her feet. 'Return to your post!'

'Do as I say!' cried Ralla.

The guards shuffled unhappily, but remained where they were.

Ralla grinned at Morrigen. 'I've spoken to Ortus. You're to leave tonight. As High Priestess it is mine by right. Another blizzard and Zarxus's tents will collapse. As overlord of the Dobuni he's entitled to a dwelling that befits his rank.' Once again she ordered the guards to gather up Morrigen's possessions; this time they obeyed.

Morrigen tried to stop them. It was pointless. They merely

shrugged her aside and started packing her robes and bedding pelts into a basket. Ralla began chiding her for harassing them.

'We're at war. Even you must be willing to surrender your comforts if the revolt is to be crushed.' An eye lifted. 'But perhaps you wish it success?'

'So now you accuse?'

'You accuse yourself. You're a Cunei, so is Hyra. Ever since the runner brought news of the rising the two of you have skulked in this dwelling and plotted treason.'

'That's a lie!'

'Disprove it.'

'I don't need to.'

'Brave words, but the day may come when you do. A woman's head is as easily spitted as that of a shaman.'

Morrigen said nothing. Ralla would never have acted without the support of the seers. The few shamans still in residence had been forced to swear loyalty to Bala. She'd been trapped, left no room to move. Quelling her rage, she accompanied the guards when they finally crossed the encampment with her belongings. Her new home was a small thatched hut standing close to the midden. As she entered, some men hurried by with buckets yoked across their shoulders, adding the stench of ordure to that of the kitchen refuse.

Still stunned by the ease with which Ralla had undermined her authority, she left the hut at once and demanded an audience with Ortus. She was refused admission to his dwelling. She protested. His guards were polite but firm: their master was discussing the war with Ralla and Zarxus, perhaps she could return in the morning? Finally accepting defeat, she returned to her hut and sat alone in the gloom. Anger gave way to despair. She felt humiliated and already condemned, virtually a prisoner in a hovel fit only for her servants.

It was Hyra, joining her at dusk, who first noticed its advantages. 'It's closer to the ramparts,' he said, after listening to her account of what had happened. 'We're less likely to be seen if we have to flee.'

Morrigen began crying. But despite her tears she had yet to admit to the inevitable. 'Can't we wait another week? We've heard nothing for days. The revolt may be over.'

'We must go!' retorted Hyra urgently. 'Every day adds to the risk. Give Ralla the time and she'll invent a means of proving that you're in league with Ceruduc. I'm in danger as well.

Ceruduc and I were once friends. Ortus knows that. Only today he asked me to stop attending the Council. He spoke courteously, but his meaning was clear. Wait a week and we'll be dead, both of us.'

'How will we find Ceruduc?'

'I'm not sure. Someone will lead us to him.'

'They'll use hounds to track us.'

'The cold should deaden the scent. It's a chance we must take.'

'And if we get lost?'

'Better to be lost than mounted on top of a spike.'

Morrigen lowered her head. The fight had suddenly left her. No questions or attempts at delay could win back what she had lost. Gripping Hyra's hand, she pressed it to her tears as he spoke.

'We'll leave tomorrow night. The moon's on the wane. We'll meet here after the Rites and scale the ramparts as soon as it's dark. We'll need food, snow-shoes and cloaks. I've a bow, we've both got daggers.' He paused, tilting her chin. 'Promise me you'll come.'

She shivered, then nodded. 'I promise.'

That night she lay awake in the darkness and listened to the measured crunch of boots as the guards circled the Dwellings, the yap of the dogs scavenging through the midden. One sniffed at the entrance to her hut, then crept into the warmth and placed its muzzle against her breast, tail thumping. For some reason it reminded her of the child who had watched her weep on the night she had fled Henge to become a novice. And now the circle had completed itself: once again she stood on the brink of departure from the world of the Gods. Then it had been spring, the season of rebirth, now snow covered the Plain and to flee meant abandoning the hope that had been born inside her when seeing the temple for the first time. The dog began licking her face, washing it clean, just as her tears had washed away the marks of her maidenhood all those years ago.

Past and present had blurred in her thoughts. As if to find focus, she closed her eyes and tried to summon up an image of Serapha. Perhaps then the Goddess *would* speak to her, give some hint of the future? But the images she conjured were of blood and fire, of men falling like corn before the sickle and oxen with horns ablaze rampaging through the night. Certain she had fallen asleep and was being troubled by a nightmare, she buried her face in the dog's coat and began crying. When she woke in the morning, both the dog and all memory of her dream were gone.

It had been agreed that she and Hyra should avoid meeting until evening lest the guards had been ordered to watch them. Without anyone to comfort her, she felt apprehensive and ill-at-ease. When she joined Ortus, the Lord of the Rites made light of her change of dwelling, blaming the weather and Zarxus's importance. But his manner aroused her suspicions and from that moment on every word spoken to her acquired fresh nuance: she was being followed, the guards would be in wait on the ramparts to kill her as she fled; her arrest was imminent, her death a certainty.

Such were the fears that nagged at her confidence as the short winter day drew to a close. After celebrating the Rites and telling her handmaidens that she was to be left undisturbed, she returned to her hut and waited for Hyra. The wait was brief. But the encampment lay in shadow when he finally slipped through the entrance, dressed in furs and carrying his bow beneath his cloak.

His face was drawn, his anxiety obvious as he quickly asked her if she'd remembered the food and snow-shoes.

She blushed, angry at having failed him. 'No.'

'The bow should keep us fed, but speed's vital.' Hyra disappeared, soon returning with a second pair of snow-shoes.

'I'm frightened,' whispered Morrigen.

'So am I.' Hyra smiled nervously and stared out across the encampment.

Dusk fell, reducing their world to the flicker of eyes and the beat of their hearts. The surrounding dwellings rose in silhouette against the darkening sky. Eventually they left the hut and crossed the midden. Above them they glimpsed the guards on the ramparts. Reaching the shelter of a byre, they stood waiting in its shadow. The guards moved on, leaving their route deserted.

Hyra tapped Morrigen's shoulder. They started running, floundering upwards through the snow until they reached the top of the ramparts. Morrigen paused to look back at the wooden temple in which she had spent so much of her life. Certain she would never see it again, she lowered her head in homage to Serapha, silently begging her mercy for her crimes. Then Hyra was tugging at her arm and she was pushing her way through the thorn palisade that surrounded the encampment. No one cried out and no one followed them. A moment later they rose to their feet and vanished into the darkness.

*

Dawn found the two fugitives huddled beneath a pine tree on the edge of the forest. The nocturnal trek through powder snow and the miles that separated them from capture had left their legacy. They were hungry, exhausted and uncertain where they were. Weakened after spending much of the night hauling themselves out of drifts, morning only added to their misery. The cold persecuted with indifference, invisibly seeping through furs and cloaks and further draining their strength.

Waking from the brief sleep that had followed their collapse shortly before dawn, Morrigen at first feared that Hyra had frozen to death as he slept. He lay motionless; icicles hung from his beard and his face was livid with cold. His cloak cracked when she touched it and only after placing a hand to his lips and feeling the warmth of his breath was she certain he had survived the night. She called his name and began shaking him. 'Wake up, Hyra! You must stand!'

Bloodshot eyes finally opened. They stared up at her. 'I can't,' he murmured, not moving.

But Morrigen insisted, first dragging him to his feet and then supporting his weight as they shuffled back and forth through the snow. The exercise breathed life into her limbs, the colour returned to her cheeks. But Hyra's features remained unchanged and when she let go of him he slumped despairingly to his knees, complaining of tiredness and a fever. Yesterday so confident, he was now as helpless as a child, and when he looked up at her he seemed like a hunted animal that had relinquished the will to live. But Morrigen's fear of being alone and snow-bound in the forest added to her strength. Her head cleared.

'We must light a fire.'

Hyra fumbled for flints and tinder, finally pulling a clump of damp moss from his pouch. Tossing it aside, he said, 'It wouldn't have helped us. Most of our food fell from my bundle in one of the drifts.'

'What's left?'

'Only the flour.'

'We must eat.' Even flour would sustain them and blunt their hunger. Morrigen took it from his bundle and they both stuffed it into their mouths, forcing it down with snow. After they had eaten she asked him where they were most likely to find Ceruduc.

'He'll have taken refuge in the marshes. He's safe enough there. But even in summer it's a twelve day journey from Henge.'

'Time doesn't matter. The snow may hinder us, but it makes pursuit almost impossible.' Morrigen had already started thinking ahead, negotiating the obstacles she knew might delay their journey. 'We daren't seek shelter in the villages. Most have been occupied by the Dobuni and we don't yet know which are loyal to Ceruduc.' She reached for her snow-shoes.

Hyra placed a hand on them. 'Not yet, please. Can't we stay here for a bit?'

Morrigen stared at him. His eyes evaded hers. 'Remain here and this pine will mark your grave,' she said sharply, suddenly angered by his self-pity and change of mood. 'It was you who persuaded me to flee and spoke so boldly of the cause for which we both were to fight. Admit defeat now and you'll lie here like a craven until the carrion begin picking your bones.'

'I need sleep.'

'And so do I. Just as I need a roof and warmth and a full belly. But we won't find them here.' Morrigen swept the forest with her hand. Forbidding and silent, it stretched boundless on either side of them, leafless trees merging with the grey of the sky.

Hyra looked round, then hauled himself upright on to swollen feet. His toes felt numb, devoid of all feeling. He had seen frost-bite before and the memory made him tremble as he slowly strapped on his snow-shoes.

They headed deeper into the forest. The sun lay hidden behind cloud, and without it to guide them Hyra felt certain that each step they took was leading them further from the marshes. The trees seemed identical, every configuration of glade and thicket resembled the next. Occasionally they passed a shallow scrape in the snow where deer had foraged for grazing. Once a chain of tracks mapped the direction taken by a wolf. But they saw neither deer nor wolf, and heard nothing. The silence was oppressive, for it left only their thoughts for company. The swelling in Hyra's feet worsened and Morrigen kept having to halt to give him time to catch up.

At some point during the day the wind lifted and it started to snow again.

Morrigen pressed on. There was no point in stopping or retracing their steps. They had reached a break in the forest and an open ice-locked expanse of swamp now blocked their path. Dead rushes rimmed its banks, and their frozen razor-sharp edges tore at her hands as she plunged through them and stepped on to the ice. It cracked beneath her, leaving miniature crevasses in the snow. Hyra joined her, but the crack grew no worse. She took a second hesitant step, then began walking towards the distant safety of the trees. The marsh was bleak and windswept, and, as the wind strengthened, the snow came tumbling towards them, muffling sound and transforming the horizon into a confused, half-glimpsed blur that only turned into forest when they again began wading through the reeds that bounded the swamp. Hyra asked Morrigen to halt, but the wind whipped at his words and she heard nothing as she hurried on through the trees and began vainly searching for refuge from the blizzard. Suddenly the wind veered and his cries reached her. She turned to see him stagger and slowly collapse to his haunches. The snow started banking up round his waist. 'I can't go any further,' he shouted.

'You must!' screamed Morrigen.

There was no answer. Morrigen retraced her steps. His strength was ebbing fast, but she knew that if she gave way he would freeze to death by nightfall. Removing his snow-shoes, she began dragging him behind her as she turned and struggled onward through the snow.

After that both time and direction became irrelevant. She didn't know where she was going, nor did she care. The blizzard intensified. The snow lashed at her eyes, the wind shrilled in the branches overhead. Again and again she fell to her knees and had to force herself to rise. All that mattered was staying upright, the will to keep moving. To surrender meant death, for her as well as Hyra. Suddenly a shape too solid to be a tree loomed out of the snow. It vanished, reappeared, turned into a small hovel standing alone in a clearing. She cried out and quickened pace, finally letting go of Hyra when she had reached the shelter of its walls and was protected from the wind. She hurried towards the entrance, certain that welcoming hands would carry her inside, feed her broth, wrap her warmly in pelts. But the wattle door hurdle was missing and a carpet of leaves filled the darkened interior. The hut was empty.

For a moment she did not move. Her strength had failed. Better to lie down where she was, let oblivion numb her. But instead she returned to Hyra and pulled him inside. The cold had mottled his face and his lips were chapped and swollen. She rubbed his cheeks with her hands, then took the bedding from his bundle and covered him as best she could against the snow drifting in through the entrance. He smiled, gratefully, then closed his eyes.

She looked round. Snow and ice had patched the holes in the thatch. Withered plant stalks hung from the rafters. A snow-laden basket lay on its side in the corner. Up-ending it, a handful of nutshells fell to the leaves, the unwanted debris left behind by squirrels or mice. She held out the empty basket towards Hyra, but he was already asleep. She lay beside him and lifted the pelts round her shoulders. Memories of the day returned sharp and vivid to her thoughts as the blizzard raged outside and the wind buffeted the walls of the hovel, then came the sleep she craved.

She was the first to wake. It was dark inside the hut and until she heard the trees tossing to and fro overhead she could not remember where she was. She crawled across to the entrance. Snow had blocked it as she slept, and a bitter wind gusted into her face when she punched a hole in the snow and peered outside. But the darkness remained: night had fallen. Quickly scooping fresh snow into the hole to keep out the wind, she woke Hyra and asked him for his flints. She stood and fumbled in the thatch, fingers searching for the dry moss used to line it. Finding some, she took the flints from Hyra and began striking them, cupping them with her hands against the wind. A spark cut the darkness, the moss started smouldering. She began blowing it, only lifting her head when smoke turned to flame and the first flicker of light lit up their sanctuary. She asked Hyra to gather up some leaves. He did so, carefully placing them on the burning moss. The flames strengthened. A moment later Morrigen screamed.

Hyra turned towards her. Her mouth hung slack in the thin light and her scream had given way to quick jerky breathing that was almost a whimper. She began shaking. 'What is it?'

'We've got to leave,' she whispered.

Hyra frowned and knelt beside her, momentarily unaware of the pain in his feet. 'There's no one here. The place is empty.' He glanced round, noticing the clumps of herbs that had been hung up to dry and the broken purge pots lying forgotten amongst the leaves. 'It's a healer's hovel that's been abandoned and gone to ruin. We couldn't be safer. No one will find us here.'

Morrigen raised her head and slowly scanned the shadows. She started sobbing. Suddenly she heard the grunt of the sow that had sniffed his body as he lay dead in the entrance, her dagger in his ribs. Imagination. Both the pig and his corpse were gone.

She stifled her tears, forcing herself to smile and appear calm. 'How silly of me. The wind must have startled me.'

'We couldn't leave, even if we wanted to.'

Still trembling, her hunger and exhaustion forgotten as the past came back to haunt her, Morrigen began searching the hovel for any evidence of her visit. There was no trace of the hemlock, nor of the blood that had splashed the walls as he fell. Only his spirit remained, but that was sufficient, for it gave her surroundings an oppressive almost menacing aura that could not be assuaged. And now Hyra was talking to her.

'I've yet to thank you for what you did. I owe you my life. If you'd left me in the forest I'd be dead.'

. . . adding another death to those that burdened her conscience. 'You'd have done the same,' she said, indifferent to his gratitude. 'Anyway, we'd both be corpses by now if we hadn't found this hut.'

'The fates must have led us here.'

Morrigen closed her eyes. Fate or chance, her return to the scene of the healer's murder had left her prey to the knowledge of her evil, the past she had hoped to banish by fleeing the Dwellings. 'Hold me,' she murmured. Hyra did so, enclosing her still quivering body in the curve of his arms.

Her eyes sought his. 'Have you ever done something you can't justify or explain?' she said suddenly.

'Of course. We all have.' Hyra smiled, going on to misinterpret the question. 'Was saving me like that?'

'I suppose so,' she said vacantly.

'Does that mean that you love me?'

'Should it?'

'That's for you to say.'

But Morrigen could not answer. She was not thinking of Hyra, but of the inexplicable compulsion to kill that had made her rob the healer of his life.

That night they slept side by side near the fire, too weary to do more than heap it with the remainder of the leaves and bore a hole in the snow to let out the smoke. When they next woke it was morning. The wind had dropped and big snowflakes floated gently from a leaden sky.

Afraid of what might happen if left alone in the hovel, Morrigen insisted that Hyra nurse the fire whilst she gathered fuel for it. She squeezed through the entrance, then climbed to her feet and stood silent for a moment, stilled by the whiteness that encircled her. During the night the drifts had run together into ripples through the forest and the trees rose above them as if from the waves of a frozen sea. Icicles trailed from the limbs of the oaks. The weight of snow had stripped a pine of its branches, leaving only its torn trunk to mark the passage of the blizzard. Morrigen floundered across the clearing and began digging into the snow with her hands in search of brushwood and fallen branches. Returning to the hut, she disturbed Hyra attempting to remove his boots.

He reddened, then straightened his legs. 'I can't get them off.'

Morrigen stacked the firewood and began tugging at one of his boots.

Hyra winced at the pain. 'You'll have to use your knife.'

Morrigen frowned anxiously. The leather had swollen to the shape of his foot and though she had loosened the thongs the boot refused to budge. Using her dagger, she carefully cut the seams and peeled back the leather. She grimaced and turned away as the smell of decay reached her nostrils. The two of them stared at each other for a moment.

'It's frost-bite, isn't it?' said Hyra quietly. 'You needn't pretend. There was no pain, the whole foot was numb. I'd already guessed.'

'Why didn't you tell me?'

'What difference would it have made?'

Morrigen looked down at his foot. It was inflamed and discoloured and the toes had been absorbed by the swelling. The skin had ruptured near the heel and arch and a trickle of putrefied blood seeped from both wounds. She cut the boot from his other foot, slumping forward in relief when she saw no indication of any poison.

Hyra smiled at the irony of his predicament. 'We're in a healer's hut, but there's no healer to tend me.'

'Can frost-bite be cured?'

'I think so.'

'What with?'

'Bryony root.'

'Would I find it now?'

Hyra's smile faded. 'No. It's midwinter and snowing. You're weak with hunger. We've no digging tools but our daggers. Anyway, the plant would have died back in the autumn. You'd never find it.'

'But could it save your foot?'

'If it was steeped in boiling water and then used as a poultice to ease the swelling and soak up the poisons, yes.'

'Then I must search for it.' Morrigen rose and walked towards the entrance.

'Don't be a fool! You could dig for days and find nothing. You've no mittens and no spade.'

Morrigen ignored his protests. The alternative was confessing, explaining that if she had not murdered the healer he would have welcomed them to his hut and been able to treat Hyra himself. Wrapping strips of bedding round her hands, she stepped out into the snow.

Knowing that bryony grew amongst undergrowth, she began digging on the far side of the clearing, where the drifts were shallowest. The bedding gave scant protection, the feeling soon left her hands and both arms turned livid with cold as again and again she plunged them into the snow and fumbled for a fragment of stalk or a crimson berry preserved frozen beneath it. Occasionally she lost her balance and fell headlong into the drifts, to rise spluttering and a little weaker, snow clogging her eyes and weighed down by the ice-cold water that had gradually seeped through her clothes and filled her boots.

Her quest became obsessive: through it she could save Hyra and find atonement for her guilt. The snow stopped, but her search continued. She moved deeper into the forest, leaving mounds of leaf-flecked snow scattered behind her. Suddenly she saw a single hoof poking from the rim of a drift. She had eaten nothing but the flour since fleeing the Dwellings and the sight of the hoof reminded her of her hunger. She stumbled over to it and began clearing away the snow, finally uncovering the corpse of a young roebuck that must have strayed from the safety of its herd during the blizzard and fallen victim to the cold. The warmth of its body had melted the snow beneath it, which had then refrozen as ice as its body heat dropped. Embedded in the ice were some rotting leaves, a few twigs, and two scarlet berries.

Tears and laughter mingled on Morrigen's face as she pressed her cheek to the buck. The search was over: she had found both the bryony and food. Oblivious of her fatigue, she hacked one of the antlers from the deer, using it as a pick to break the ice and expose the remnants of the plant. She started digging, carefully loosening the frozen soil round the long tap-roots on which Hyra depended. Once they had been unearthed and placed in her pouch, she turned to the buck, first paunching it and then cutting a strip of flesh from its flank. Scattering snow over its carcass in the hope that wolves would not find it, she began the homeward journey to the hut.

It was nearly dark when she reached it. Hyra lay motionless beside the fire, too crippled to move. She glanced at his foot: the suppuration had grown worse and the swelling had spread to his ankle. 'I found it,' she said, swaying slightly as she banked up the fire and knelt beside it.

Hyra looked at her in disbelief. Her eyes were bloodshot, her robes sodden, and her hair had frozen solid where it tumbled from beneath her hood. 'Thank you,' he whispered. Their eyes met for a moment, then Morrigen turned away, the motives that had sustained her throughout the day leaving no room for his gratitude.

After finding an unbroken pot in one corner of the hut, she chopped up the bryony and boiled it until it had softened and could be bound as a poultice to his foot. He cried out at the pain as the hot roots touched the inflamed skin, then lay silent and pale whilst Morrigen spitted the meat and cooked it over the fire. In their hunger, they ate it when still nearly raw, afterwards paying for their greed by vomiting much of what they had swallowed. Their nausea drained them of all strength, and, after wrapping themselves in their bedding pelts, they both stretched out beside the fire and went to sleep.

*

That first day set the tone of those that followed. Morrigen succeeded in jointing the remains of the buck and hanging it outside the hut, where it was safe from marauding wolves. More bryony was found, and gradually the swelling in Hyra's feet began to subside and the wounds started to heal. Using needle and gut, she made both of them a pair of deerskin boots, as well as hats and leggings. One morning they woke to find sunlight glittering against the white of the snow, and though it remained bitterly cold the change of weather did much to restore their spirits. Hyra grew stronger, Morrigen impatient to leave. Finally she suggested that they move on as soon as he was well enough to travel.

'Why?' he retorted. 'Surely it would be better to wait until the snow starts to melt and we're able to hunt our own food? We're safe. No one will find us unless the healer returns.'

'He won't come back . . .' Morrigen broke-off as she suddenly realized what she had said.

Hyra appeared not to notice her error. 'Then we'll stay.'

Morrigen scanned the hut. It was only her guilt that had made her so eager to leave. Despite its associations, she had rarely been so happy, and it required little effort for Hyra to persuade her to accept his advice. During the past few days the constant presence of the snow-bound forest had worked a change in her mood, imparting something of its tranquillity and peace. It had isolated and harboured her, enabled her to forget Ralla and Zarxus and the world she had fled, even the uprising itself. The last year had seen the end of all simplicity in her life, the need for cunning and caution leaving her permanently on-edge. The forest made no such demands; and in nursing Hyra and gathering firewood at dawn when her breath froze in front of her in the chill winter air, she felt fulfilled and content, as if becalmed in a backwater.

'Sometimes I think we should stay here for ever,' she said once. 'We're free to do as we please. I don't have to serve a God I don't believe in. You don't have to study the heavens and remember the Rites.'

'And what about Ceruduc?'

Morrigen shrugged. 'I'm tired of always having to struggle for something, be it myself or a cause. The revolt means bloodshed and widows and having to goad the tribesfolk into taking up arms. The Cunei are strangers to war. Most would much rather stay in their villages and till the fields. Is power that important? Does the success of the rising really depend on you or me?'

'You'd soon tire of living in a hovel,' said Hyra. 'You're happy now. But it wouldn't last.'

Morrigen smiled and began arguing with him, but in her heart she knew he was right. Saddened, she closed her eyes and lay back on the pelts. The fire had dwindled to embers and it was warm inside the hut. She reached towards Hyra.

'No, Morrigen,' he whispered.

'Why not? There's no shame in love.'

He trembled but did not answer as she rolled onto her side and pressed softly against him. Her eyes opened, locking with his and making evasion impossible. Seeing his confusion, she smiled and kissed his eyes. Her robes hung loose round her shoulders and when she lowered them her breasts showed pale where the sun had not touched them.

'But you don't love me,' said Hyra.

'Must pleasure have a reason?'

Hyra looked at her, momentarily spellbound by her beauty; long sweep of her legs, the slight salt of her skin when he bent forward to kiss it. She lay silent, stretched beside him, one leg hooked over his. A tress of hair lapped one of her breasts, the other rose smooth and delicately traced with veins from where it merged with the pattern of her ribs. She trembled at his touch. Her breath quickened as she rose above him, fingers fumbling with the thongs on his robes before reaching down to lay her lips to his chest. He tried to halt her. A stillness and pause, ending when she said something he did not understand and gave a small cry. She grew fiercer, freeing herself from her remaining clothes before falling across him. She rose, fell, her body rocking above his when they met and became one. Then it was too late to turn back and pleasure became a harsh, urgent rhythm that left no choice but surrender.

Morrigen's sadness returned when they finally drew apart and lay in silence by the fire.

Hyra tidied the hair from her face. 'You're unhappy. It seems wrong.'

'I can't help it. I know that if we stayed here I'd become your wife and bear your children. Yet it was you who said we must go.'

'You'd love me for a year or two, no longer. In the end you'd flee. You can't disguise what you are by forsaking the world and hiding in a forest. We have to leave, and we both know it.'

A hesitant smile crossed Morrigen's face. 'So we're to be lovers until the snow melts?'

'Is that what you want?'

'Yes.'

'So be it.' Hyra turned away, concealing his sorrow at her acceptance of what lay ahead.

*

And if that acceptance of a fixed span to their affair shaped the theme of the month that followed, its variations were many. For once Morrigen had no need to act a part. She hid nothing, held nothing back. It was as if all the constraints on her had been temporarily lifted, leaving her free to be as complaisant and careless as she pleased. She was a child again, laughing and clinging to him for warmth as they tramped the forest. Then night would fall and the woman in her demanded tenderness and silence as they sat together by the fire, his lap her pillow.

One morning they decided to disguise themselves as a travelling pelt merchant and his wife when they finally left the hut. Armed with Hyra's bow, they tracked deer, boar and wild-cat through the forest. As the weather grew warmer and the snow started to thaw, they were able to set a line of traps along the edge of the marsh, adding beaver skins to the pile of pelts waiting to be cleaned, stretched and flayed. In the evenings they huddled round the fire and cut arrows and snares or prepared the skins for tanning.

Then came the morning when the last of the snow lay as slush in the clearing. There was now no reason for delaying their departure. Even prior to that moment both of them had sensed that their affair was drawing to a close. For as they drew closer, the season's wheel seemed to force them apart. Their relationship appeared linked to the vagaries of the weather. Sunshine left them pensive and withdrawn. Overnight frost or the threat of snow gave hope of postponing the inevitable. One evening, after two cloudless days, Morrigen separated her bedding from Hyra's and placed it in the corner of the hut.

Hyra watched her. 'Is it so easy?'

She shook her head and could not look at him when she spoke. 'No. What else could we do? We've spent a winter together. Winter's now over. Don't let's question what we've shared. I'll never forget this hut. But let's leave it as friends and begin the search for Ceruduc.'

Hyra smiled to himself. Her words explained her silence of the past two days. She had seemed distant and remote, but he now realized that she had been preparing herself for their departure.

'Couldn't we fight the Dobuni as lovers?' he said.

Morrigen hesitated, not wanting to wound him, then said, 'You're the only person I've ever trusted. You've never hindered me or demanded what I cannot grant. As your lover I'd have to give too much of myself. As your friend I need never be afraid of offending you or having to defy you. Do you understand what I'm trying to say?' She had tipped her head to one side; as a child does when sure of its own mind and puzzled by the indecision of others.

'I think so.'

'Today we saw a squirrel, the first of the year. It reminded me of myself. It takes refuge in the winter, just as we have done, and then comes out with the spring to continue its life, just as we will be doing when we leave the forest. What we've done belongs to this hut. There'll be no room for love once we find Ceruduc. It would become stunted, we'd quarrel. In the end I'd have to destroy you to save myself.'

*

They left at first light, Hyra dragging the pelts behind him on a sledge. On the edge of the clearing they paused to look back at the tumbledown hovel that had watched over the birth and death of their affair. A wedge of fresh reed marked a hole they had patched in its roof. The surrounding hazel was beginning to bud and spears of new grass coloured the floor of the forest. 'It'll be our secret,' said Morrigen. 'The one thing we need share with no one.' She smiled sadly, then turned and stepped into the forest.

That day they reached the moorland that bordered it. On the next, a small village where Hyra was able to exchange some of his pelts for a baggage ox. They asked for news of the uprising, but the village was too remote to attract pedlars or gossip and their questions remained unanswered. But four days later, still travelling westward, they finally encountered proof that the revolt had survived the winter.

They were crossing a ridge of downland when Morrigen

noticed smoke in the valley below. Hurrying downhill, they passed a cluster of slag heaps, then the first of some charred and still smouldering huts. Morrigen halted, suddenly frightened and apprehensive.

'It's a mining village,' she said. 'But there's no one here. Perhaps it's been abandoned?'

'Or deliberately destroyed.'

Hyra crossed over to the blackened remains of the nearest hut, then bent and began searching amongst the ruins.

'The Dobuni?' whispered Morrigen.

Hyra nodded, silently holding up a bronze-tipped arrow.

Morrigen shuddered, taking his arm as they walked slowly through the smoke and began the hunt for survivors. But the village was empty. In their haste to flee, some of its occupants had discarded their possessions as they ran: a quern and wickerwork cradle, a string of beads that wrote the direction of the exodus and now lay scattered amongst the rubble. Suddenly Hyra saw a kite flap clumsily from a dip in the ground, a scrap of flesh still clenched in its beak. Instinct held him back for a moment. He walked on, mounds of chalk slag rising round him when he stopped to stare down at the pile of bodies that had been thrown into a mine-shaft on the edge of the village.

Morrigen joined him.

'Don't look,' he said, holding her back.

She lowered her eyes. She could not stop herself. It was as if fate had brought her to this place and demanded that she bear witness to a crime in which she had played no part; her first taste of war. She cried out, turning away. 'Why?' she whispered.

'They must have been supplying Ceruduc with flints for his arrows and spears. This is their reward.'

'But where are the women, the children?'

'The Dobuni have taken them. They'll be sold as handmaids or whores.' Sickened by the jumble of limbs and faces that clogged the shaft, Hyra stared out over the burning village. In its centre he could see the circle of scorched stumps that had once been a shrine to Serapha.

'Would you have been happy in the forest after seeing this?' he asked.

Morrigen was still staring into the mine. In the death beneath her she had seen no trace of her own guilt. The arrangement of corpses was random and haphazard, a world away from the controlled cunning that had prompted her to murder. It was the Dobuni who were guilty, not she. Her crimes had purpose, theirs were casual and impartial in the choice of their victims. Hyra repeated his question.

Morrigen shook her head. 'No. And those who did it will die.'

'As old men in their beds, but not in battle. Unarmed villagers are no match for the Dobuni.' Hyra paused to look back at the smoke. 'This won't help Ceruduc. He's dependent on the mines staying open. He can't arm his men without them.'

'There are other mines. The Dobuni can't close them all.'

'They will if they need to. This is Zarxus's doing. It's more than a warning. He's trying to rob Ceruduc of any chance of being able to break out of the marshes and attack the Dwellings.'

'It's still not too late to return to the hut,' said Morrigen quietly.

In answer, Hyra entered the remains of the shrine and lifted his arms to the sky, first calling on Serapha to sustain the revolt, then offering into her keeping the souls of the men lying entombed in the mine.

A week later they took shelter in a copse on the edge of the Great Marsh.

*

Dim mist-ridden fingers of colour brushed the tops of the hills as the two figures dropped down through the scree. Darkness prowled in the foothills. A dog barked. A quick flicker of light crossed the valley below: a herdsman returning home after checking his sheep. The village was silent again, the thatched roofs and turf walls of the huts making it seem like part of the landscape: the wooded hills, contoured slopes, the world that Hyra knew best.

Loose stones rolled past him when he finally halted and waited for Morrigen to pick her way to his side.

'It looks safe enough,' she whispered.

'You can't tell. Father keeps two of the huts empty for guests. They could be full of Dobuni.'

They peered into the darkness; Morrigen uneasy, Hyra

expectant at the prospect of seeing his family – but both of them searching for any sign of the patrols that had forced them to turn back and seek shelter before entering the marshes.

'We've no other choice,' said Hyra, again reviewing the permutations that had made them retreat into the hills. 'Without father's help we'll never find Ceruduc. The marsh-folk were growing suspicious of us. Zarxus knows we're alive – how I don't know. But much more questioning and someone would have guessed who we were.'

They moved on, keeping low and silent as the hills gave way to the first of the fields that ringed the village. Its huts rose round them. Occasionally they saw a chink of light against the thatch or heard the murmur of voices. An ox lumbered out of the darkness, then lowed as its tether jerked it to a halt. Another dog began yapping, to be silenced by a curse and the sudden thwack of a stick. Hyra motioned to Morrigen as they reached the granary pits in the centre of the village. She knelt at his side as he again scanned the darkness for the glint of a spear, the careless gesture, a figure detaching itself from the mound of leaf fodder that blocked their route. 'How much further?' she whispered.

Hyra pointed towards the timber post that had been raised as an offering on the day he was initiated as a novice. Beyond it lay a large circular hut standing isolated from its neighbours. Its walls bulged outwards. Cowhide pennants trailed from the crown of the roof. 'I'll go first. One scream from Kirsten and the whole village will wake.'

Morrigen nodded as he started crawling towards the hut. A hurdle had been drawn across its entrance. Reaching it, he straightened, quickly counting voices before pushing it aside and diving through the entrance.

His mother's face was the first he saw. Her mouth had opened to cry out and one hand was already fumbling for a stick. He quickly threw back his hood and lifted his face into the fire-light. 'Ssh! It's me, mother!' he whispered hoarsely.

For a moment she could only stare at him, open-mouthed and unable to speak. Then her bewilderment turned to delight as someone called his name and a young raven-haired girl burst from the smoke and flung her arms round his waist. 'Kirsten!'

'Oh, Hyra! Where have you been? What are you doing here?' At six years old, Kirsten's voice was still that of a child's, almost a squeak when measured against the much gruffer voice that succeeded it.

'There's easier ways to enter your own home.'

Hyra turned to see his father emerge from the smoke, an arrow still in place against his bow-string. 'I was afraid the Dobuni might have posted guards in the village.'

'They left four days ago. Even they had the sense to believe that you wouldn't be so foolish as to come here.' Cronus paused as he saw Morrigen enter the hut. His frown deepened. 'So you're still together?' he said tersely, briskly striding past her to replace the wattle in the entrance.

'There was nowhere else we could go.'

'You'd better think of one. And soon. The Dobuni have sworn to level every dwelling in the village if you're seen here.'

'Stop it, Cronus! Let him speak. This is his home. And as long as it's mine as well I'll not stand by and listen to you turn him away.'

Hyra smiled gratefully as his mother gave a final pat to the grey of her hair and stepped forward to greet him. Her thin arms locked him in her embrace. Her body seemed frailer than in the summer, but it still gave off the familiar musty smell of smoke and old age that he had always remembered her by. As they drew apart, he introduced her to Morrigen.

She bowed her head. 'Any woman who serves the Gods is always welcome in this house.'

Morrigen acknowledged her kindness. Stern melancholic eyes stared at her for a moment. Reading their question, Morrigen deflected it with a lie: a chaste and irreproachable smile. The old woman appeared satisfied, for she suddenly pivoted and clapped and said, 'Kirsten! Fetch some corn and prepare bread for your brother and the priestess.'

Hyra patted his sister's head. She grinned up at him, her callused skin and lank cheeks making her older than her years. 'Where's Rhionan?' he said.

'Waiting to be kissed.'

A moment later his elder sister hobbled from the smoke. She smiled, and her smile was so fresh and unexpected that for an instant it was possible to ignore her twisted legs and crumpled back and see only her beauty. For although her illness had distorted her limbs and nearly destroyed her body, her face had been spared. Her skin was pale, almost milk-white, but the gaiety in her eyes and her corn-coloured hair gave her features a delicate, porcelain beauty that the pain had yet to blemish.

She lurched forward, dragging one foot behind her and gripping his arm for support. 'There, now you're my captive. And despite what father said I'm not letting go of you until you've told everything you've done since leaving Henge.' She smiled again. 'But first I must meet Morrigen.'

Aware that Rhionan's crippled body rarely inspired sympathy, Hyra watched Morrigen's face, searching it for any hint of repugnance. She smiled instead. The two women kissed, Morrigen taking his sister's weight and then helping her sit. 'How wonderful,' she said happily. 'I've not had a woman to gossip with since we left the Dwellings. The men can do as they please, can't they? Come and join us, Kirsten. If we all take turns at the quern we'll have bread that much sooner.'

It was flawless, and Morrigen knew it. The old woman smiled at her thoughtfulness. The two sisters laughed and gathered round her.

Hyra grinned and turned to his father, then his grin faded as he saw the anger on Cronus's face. 'What's wrong, father?'

'Do you need me to tell you that?'

Hyra looked round before answering. His mother had joined her daughters and Morrigen. Their voices rose as all four began chattering at once.

'Is it Morrigen?'

'And where you're going and what the pair of you have been up to since you fled. We thought you were dead. Your mother even went into mourning.'

'We couldn't get word to you. We hid in the forest until the snow melted.'

'Where Morrigen's bed kept you warm,' retorted Cronus. 'No, you don't have to deny it – it's there on your face. You could have been here a month ago. Twice the Dobuni have searched the village. Last time they came they killed Latho. Why? Because he was a rainmaker and refused to pledge fealty to Bala. Next time it'll be I or your mother. But for the waif and her dreams we'd still be at peace.'

'Morrigen had nothing to do with the revolt.'

'That's because she's cunning enough to let others wage her wars.'

'You're wrong, father. We're here to join Ceruduc,' said Hyra, going on to detail their attempts to enter the marshes.

But Cronus continued to mock him. 'Join Ceruduc and you'll be dead before this summer's leaves,' he said harshly. 'The man's a fool. Most of the mines have been closed. He's short of men. Another month and he'll be out of grain. The last ambush he mounted ended in Cunei killing Cunei.'

'But he's still alive?'

'Some would call it that. I don't. A grown man playing at war and skulking in a swamp is better in the grave.'

'Do you know where he is?'

'No, but I can guess.'

'Can you help us find him?'

'So first you come home, now you intend leaving.'

'Isn't that what you wanted?'

'Yes . . . No . . . Oh, damn the lot of you!' Cronus cursed and began pacing to and fro through the smoke, eyebrows drawn down into arches over his weathered face. Watching him, Hyra suddenly realized that Morrigen was merely an excuse for much of his anger, that its true cause was his own helplessness – the needs of a wife and two daughters. His father must have sensed his thoughts.

'I can't leave them,' he said. 'I wanted to. But your mother made me promise to stay and I'll not go back on my word.'

'But I've promised nothing,' replied Hyra softly.

His father nodded, then reached his decision. 'I'll help you find Ceruduc. There are some men in the villagers who've been supplying him with arms. They think I don't know. It'll take time to arrange. Until then you must stay in the hut.'

Hyra scanned its single room. Bracken covered the floor. A slate slab and some storage vessels were its only furniture. Suddenly he knew that he might never see it again; and so saw all the things that familiarity had blinded him too: the wicker basket filled with his mother's salves and healing herbs, sewing gut and needles, a bronze awl for punching leather, the cooking pots in the hearth, his father's axe and shield.

'What about Tarxien and the villagers?' he said finally. 'Tarxien's your steward. He has the right to enter the hut.'

'Tarxien will have to be told. The others can he kept away. You must be ready to hide.'

'How long will it take?'

'Two or three days.'

Hyra glanced at the circle of women round the fire. 'And mother?'

'Say nothing. I'll speak to her when you've gone.' Cronus paused, indicating Morrigen. 'I'll be glad to get rid of her,' he grunted. 'She's already bewitched your sisters.'

'You dislike her, don't you?'

But for once his father evaded the challenge, choosing to be elliptical instead of direct. 'You'll be with Lyla soon.'

'Is that all you can say? I'm not afraid of the truth.'

The two men stared at each other: one seeing the heir he had hoped would farm his lands, the other the father whose rebuke had always meant more to him than praise.

'She's turned your head,' said Cronus finally. 'Continue to befriend her and you'll live to regret it.'

'She saved my life in the snow.'

'For now you're more use to her alive. That will change.'

'You judge her too harshly. You don't know her as I do. 'She's a stranger to you.'

'And so was your mother when I picked her from the Lines. The waif makes me uneasy. There's something wrong with the company a man keeps if he feels ill-at-ease in his own home.' Cronus was staring at Morrigen. He turned away, shaking his head as if to free himself from a spell.

*

'Goodbye, father.'

'Go. Your mother's guessed that you're leaving. I must comfort her.'

Only Cronus's eyes were visible against the dusk. Hyra met their gaze, then backed away to where Morrigen and the four villagers stood grouped in the darkness. There was a thin, despairing scream – quickly strangled; then sobbing.

Morrigen smiled to herself as she heard it. The village faced out towards flat sedge-covered marshes and the distant sea, now black and an extension of the night. A sickle moon lit the dim outline of the hills behind her. The three days in the hut had left her tense and irritable. A woman's world: Rhionan's misshapen body, Kirsten's chatter, the old woman's eyes watching and following her. She shivered slightly, glad to be gone.

They left hurriedly, creeping in single-file through the deserted village. The four villagers were secretive and taciturn – a perfect match for her mood – and even the shaman offered no explanation as they began the descent down a steep, rutted track that zig-zagged the slope towards the marshes below. The track ended. They skirted a wood, then trudged up a long gorse covered coombe that led away from the marshes.

Hyra grew apprehensive and asked the shaman where they were going.

'To safety.'

'But not Ceruduc?'

'It's a night's journey to his camp. If we're not back in our beds by dawn we risk being questioned. Others will take you to Ceruduc. You'll be safe enough soon.'

They walked on through the moonlight, occasionally pausing to rest or sip water from a stream. Eventually the shaman halted and began imitating the screech of an owl. Hyra scanned the night. The gorse stretched away into the darkness, but he could hear a faint, muffled tapping that seemed to emanate from the ground beneath him. A moment later a wedge of scrub shifted position, revealing a glimmer of light. The noise increased, adding voices to the tapping. The shaman said, 'We're leaving you here.'

Hyra started to protest.

The shaman silenced him, grinning roguishly. 'Zarxus has threatened his warriors with death if they don't close all the mines. It's a threat that may spare us a battle. First they must find them.' He vanished into the darkness.

Still baffled, Hyra crossed over to the square of light and looked down. Beneath his feet a vertical shaft ran deep into the earth, its entrance heavily grooved where ropes had worn furrows in the chalk. Morrigen joined him, her impatience giving way to a smile as a wave of hot, stale air washed upwards into her face. 'So this is how Ceruduc puts the flints on his arrows,' she whispered.

'But father said all the mines had been found!'

'He was wrong. Just as he was wrong about me.' Morrigen smiled. Gathering her robes round her waist, she started down the ladder pegged to one wall of the shaft, climbing past deserted galleries where the flint seam had proved too thin to mine and only some worn antler picks lay forgotten in the gloom. Hyra followed her. High above him the sky gradually receded into a small black circle cushioned with a sprinkling of stars. Two men, both naked and drenched in chalk dust, stood waiting at the base of the shaft. One shinned up the ladder, quickly killing the night as he replaced the turf-covered wattle that concealed the entrance to the mine. His companion prostrated himself in homage to Morrigen.

'Welcome,' he said. 'You'll have known better lodgings, but none so safe.'

'How long has it been open?'

'It was closed when the uprising started. The Dobuni think it abandoned. We've been storing the waste in some of the old galleries and only taking Ceruduc his flints after dusk.'

When can we join him?'

'His men are coming here tomorrow night. You'll leave with them.'

'And until then . . . ?'

'Come.' The miner grinned and led them across the chipping-floor to an empty gallery. 'You can sleep here.' He left them for a moment, returning with a strip of dried meat and a goatskin of water.

Morrigen slumped gratefully to the ground. Hyra placed his chin to his knees and rubbed the dust from his eyes. The three days in hiding at home had been forfeit from the start, no more than a reprieve. Morrigen's eagerness to find Ceruduc and his father's suspicion of her motives had led inevitably to argument. He too had been ready to leave, but only when descending into the mine had he realized that he was a fugitive again, dependent on others for survival. He lifted his head and peered unhappily into the shadows.

The oil-lamps perched in ledges in the network of galleries that ran outwards from the shaft cast a dim and yellow light. Near its base, a group of men sat knapping core flints into flakes with precise taps of their hammers. Others shaped the flakes into arrow-heads, daggers and axe-heads. Slag lay piled round them. Every now and then a naked grime-engrained miner would stumble out of the darkness and slap another basket of flint-bearing chalk at their feet. Hyra knew that he lacked their skill and would be more hindrance than help, so after watching them for a while he lay beside Morrigen and let the monotonous chip of the hammers lull him to sleep.

Throughout that day they dozed, rested and gossiped with the miners. Time passed slowly. The rank air was sour with sweat and the smoke from the lamps. The heat was intense and both abandoned their clothes before crawling along one of the galleries to watch the miners work the face. Once, where the chalk had turned to rock, Morrigen was asked to place rough chalk carvings of a phallus and childbearing woman in the hope that an offering to Serapha would help locate a fresh seam of flints. The baskets grew heavy with finished weapons. Shifts changed. The rubble on the chipping-floor was shovelled into creels and taken away to be dumped.

The waiting ended with the abruptness of its beginning. The miner who had welcomed them suddenly rose and disappeared up the ladder. The lamps flared as cold air gusted down the shaft and into the mine. Accompanied by an armed Cunei dressed in the feathered goose-skins worn by wildfowlers, he finally dropped out of the shaft and walked over to his guests. 'One of Ceruduc's men,' he explained. 'The others are waiting at the entrance. They'll guide you to his camp.'

Morrigen was the first to reach the surface. Still balanced on the ladder, she tilted her head to the night sky, breathing deeply of the cold clean air before pulling herself out of the shaft. A chill wind squalled across the moor. Hyra joined her, and they stood shivering in the darkness as ropes were tossed down the shaft and the flint-laden baskets were hauled to the surface and loaded on to the backs of the waiting men.

The nocturnal journey began. Leaving the mine, they tramped in silence through the gorse. Scrub gave way to withy and reed as they entered the marshes. A salt breeze swept the night, bringing with it the staccato boom of a bittern and the cry of geese rising honking into the darkness. Water lapped round them. It gradually deepened as they plunged further into the marshes. Once they scented smoke from a Dobuni fire and had to double back through the rushes. Eventually they halted. The men formed into gangs and dragged dug-out canoes from their hiding-place in a bed of osiers. They began to relax, joking amongst themselves as the baskets were packed on board. Fresh orders were given, some of the men perching on top of the baskets whilst the remainder picked up paddles and thrust them deep into the water, forcing the boats through the reeds that barred their route. Occasionally one would ground on the mud and everyone had to jump out and wade waist-deep through the water.

The channels that cut through the marsh gradually broadened, opening out into vast rush-locked lagoons that scattered the moonlight. The wash from the canoes shivered the reeds and sent geese rising up into the darkness ahead of them. It was the first time Morrigen had been in a boat since her childhood, and its unfamiliar motion left her becalmed and at peace. Paddles splashed. A salt breeze blew in off the sea. The men on the baskets squatted in silhouette, their faces lit from below by the water's reflection.

The water grew brackish, the tide marks on the stems of the surrounding reeds showing where the sea had breached the rim of the marshes. The leading dug-out veered into a narrow creek. Hyra peered ahead of him as a light stabbed the darkness and he glimpsed the outline of a wattle stockade rising sheer against the sky. He jumped overboard, helping the men as they dragged the boats through the reeds. The boats grounded. He heard voices, saw torches, then started sloshing his way through the mud as the familiar bearded figure of Ceruduc loomed towards him out of the darkness.

Morrigen remained seated whilst they embraced. She had waited seven years for this moment. She touched her hair, but it was beyond combing. Her robes were sodden where they traced her body. But in her unkemptness she appeared unshaken and unshakable; a woman to match the man. And the moonlight lit her smile when she finally stood and Ceruduc stepped forward to greet her.

# CHAPTER XI

Ceruduc's laugh was coarse and rumbustious, and it echoed back out of the night as he grinned at the grave face on the far side of the fire. 'So sober a face doesn't suit you, Hyra,' he said, tipping more mead into his beaker. 'Forget them, both of them. Ralla's no better than a whore and Zarxus is an oaf. All Dobuni are, it's bred into them like muscle or blood. Let them boast. They haven't won yet. They'll pay for their folly when we leave the marshes.'

'And so will you if you don't listen to what I say.'

'Nonsense! Wars aren't won by murdering shamans and posting warriors in the villages. I know we Cunei are sometimes too timid for our own good, but once cornered the tribesfolk will stop at nothing to drive out the Dobuni. We may be few, but we're not dead yet – nor will we be. One victory and every chieftain in the land will point his boots at the marshes. You wait, another two months and even Cronus will see sense.'

'The mead has dulled your wits. You talk of victory when you've yet to win a skirmish.'

'A dozen corpses don't make a war. The Dobuni will only be conquered when we meet them in battle.'

Hyra shook his head and switched his glance to Morrigen. After being welcomed by Ceruduc, she had grown pensive and distant, as if content to enjoy the fire's warmth whilst the two men discussed the course of the rising. But in the last few moments Ceruduc's self-confidence had begun to work a change in her mood. Her eyes had brightened, and the rapt smile that edged her lips suggested indifference to his own warning of the dangers that threatened. He turned to Ceruduc, determined to make both of them see sense.

'The revolt's on the brink of collapse,' he began. 'Your own words have condemned you. You've told us about ambushes failing for lack of planning, men deserting within days of joining you, hungry, disenchanted, armed only with cudgels and flints. Chieftains who had sworn to help going back on their word, others refusing to acknowledge your leadership and abandoning you to your fate.'

Ceruduc smiled, then drained his beaker. 'And will you do as they?'

'Of course not. But you must take the offensive whilst you've still the chance. Leave it too late and the Dobuni will buy off the shamans with gifts and offer a reward for your head.'

'They've done that already. I'm worth forty oxen, twice that dead.' Ceruduc laughed and waved an arm at the encircling stockade. 'They'll never find us here, not even if we're betrayed. No one could mount an attack through the marshes and live to tell the tale.'

'So you think you're safe. But you won't outwit Zarxus by hiding in a swamp. How many men have you? Seven score and a handful of women and babes. There were nearly two thousand Dobuni camped near the Dwellings when we fled, more in every village we passed.'

'We're well armed. If Tharah breaks through we'll have enough men to abandon the stockade and march on Henge.'

'Tharah's irrelevant. Another chieftain as feckless and hot-headed as you won't trouble Zarxus. He's as good as cut off, you told me so yourself. It's only a matter of time before Zarxus surrounds him and either starves him into submission or slaughters his men in battle. What'll you do then?'

Ceruduc growled angrily at Hyra's persistence. 'You've yet to fight!' he cried, stabbing a finger at him. 'But already you presume to judge what we've done. Men have died for this rising. Where were you when we laid them on the racks and made widows out of their wives?'

'Now you're provoking me. You know I couldn't leave the Dwellings until certain of not being caught.'

Ceruduc dismissed the excuse. 'You've changed, Hyra. Pampered seers who've grown idle serving the Dobuni don't wage wars, nor can they help win them.'

'And what of priestesses? Can they aid your cause?'

Both men had forgotten Morrigen. As she spoke, she tilted her head to one side so that her hair caught the glow from the fire. Its light mirrored her eyes and played on one cheek, giving her a soft lambent beauty that shamed them into silence and washed the scowls from their faces.

She smiled at Ceruduc, purposely drawing him into her

spell. The boar's tusk once pinned to his hair had vanished – the hair itself, like his beard, running to grey where it lapped his shoulders. But sinew still thickened his neck and his features still echoed the strength and arrogance that were her only memory of their first encounter. His eyes met hers, shifted away, then returned – his failure to outstare her making him toast her question by again emptying his beaker. Her smile broadened into a first measured hint at invitation. This time his gaze did not flinch, it was she who turned away. Where once his arrogance had mocked her, it now seemed a virtue, proof that he remained undaunted by the prospect of defeat. How different to Hyra, grim-faced and sullen in the darkness.

'The rising must go on,' she said finally. 'It's like a child that needs to be taught how to stand and fight back. To admit defeat now would be to disown the Goddess we serve. Men have died in her name. More will join them, but when the last is taken to the Place of the Dead the Cunei will have won Henge and sacked the Dwellings.'

'But how?' cried Hyra. 'Words aren't deeds. Flint is no match for bronze.'

'And is Serapha no match for Bala?' retorted Morrigen. 'You doubt what you've yet to discover. Ceruduc's the warrior. He launched the rising. Let him finish what he started before condemning it.'

'The ally I need!' applauded Ceruduc. 'If you and I had met earlier we'd now be at Henge giving offerings for our victory.'

Morrigen turned towards him, her eyes showing passing anger before fixing on his. 'We have met,' she said softly. 'In the Maiden Lines. "Lying with her would be like bedding the bones left untouched by the dogs." Your words. You don't remember. Hyra does, he was with you when you spoke.'

Ceruduc glanced at Hyra for confirmation, then frowned and lowered his head. She knew that he was sifting the past, searching for her face amongst those of the women he had known. But memory's sieve had not held it, so he grinned and said, 'You see how foolish I am? I confuse beauty with bones and now have to apologize for my error. But the youth is not the man. The man is not so blind.'

A pretty speech: Morrigen's first premonition of what lay ahead. She smiled, acknowledging his flattery. 'Nor is the woman.'

Ceruduc turned and looked up at the dim shapes of the sentries patrolling the stockade. He seemed uncomfortable, momentarily off-balance. He grew fidgety. The buckles on the two lines of throwing daggers that crossed his chest required tightening, his beard demanded a tug. Suddenly he rose and said, 'I must wake Lyla. She won't believe me when I tell her who's here.'

Morrigen watched him vanish into the darkness. She could hear water slapping on mud, the faint cry of a gull. Once, when the wind lifted, she thought she could pick out the distant boom of sea on shingle. She tried to empty her mind, be calmed by its melody. But it was no use. The calm was fraudulent, an imposter. All she could do was plot and plan and debate how best to profit from Ceruduc's recklessness. Or was his levity a fault, a sign that he lacked the stamina to outwit Zarxus and turn defeat into victory? Unable to yet answer the question, she began pondering her own position. She was an exiled High Priestess who owed her rank to predicting the Darkness. Only if the revolt succeeded could she hope to become mistress of Henge. The alternative was death. Alone she had no chance of reaping the harvest she had sown by claiming a link with Serapha through her dreams. But Ceruduc could help her, just as Hyra had done when fleeing the Dwellings. Now certain of what had to be done, she smiled to herself, then glanced at Hyra as he stared into the fire.

'You judge him too hastily.'

Hyra snapped a twig and tossed it to the flames. 'He's not what he seems.'

'Are any of us?'

'I used to think so. Meeting you changed that.' Hyra paused, hoping to goad her into tenderness or affection. She did not answer. 'You forget,' he said, 'I've known him since we were boys, had time to accept him for what he is. You hope for too much from him. The brave words are a mask. No one can hide in a swamp and not be scarred by it.'

'And do you carry the scars of the winter we spent in the forest, hiding in a hut?'

'You want me to say yes, admit that loving Morrigen must have its price.'

'You protest too much.'

Hyra sighed, too tired to fight her, then said, 'It's not Ceruduc's courage I doubt, but his wisdom.'

'Or are you merely envious of all that he's achieved?'

Hyra laughed. 'He's achieved nothing. Bickering has led to blunders, blunders to waste: of both men and supplies. The rising's no nearer success than on the day it was born.'

'You're wrong, Hyra. Henge will be ours again. It may take a year, even longer. But one day the stones will be torn from their holes and a new temple raised . . .'

Hyra straightened, silencing Morrigen's prophecy as a slight, cloaked figure hurried out of the darkness, rubbing her eyes and escorted by Ceruduc. One quarrel was over, another was about to begin.

'Hyra . . . !' Lyla ran towards him, her hood falling from shoulder length hair as she opened her arms to greet him. Then she remembered their last meeting and saw Morrigen and halted in mid-stride. Her arms dropped to her side; pleasure giving way to a bitter and reproachful smile, the muttered words of welcome that had to be said. Her glance shifted to Morrigen, then returned to Hyra in an attempt to define their relationship. Something in his face made her move on again and embrace him. Her body stiffened as he breathed her warmth. Sleep still touched her, her hair was rumpled and the impress of a pillow creased one cheek.

'So you've come?' she said finally.

'Yes.'

'Choice, or necessity?'

'Choice.' They stared at each other for a moment, then Hyra turned and steered her towards Morrigen.

'We've met before,' said Lyla quietly. 'You were unwell. I'm glad to see you mended.'

Morrigen said nothing as grey shrewd eyes slowly scrutinized her face. Meeting their gaze, she felt as if on trial for her sins, for they seemed both to recognize her cunning and denounce her as an imposter. Unable to deflect them, aware that she had encountered someone it would be hard to deceive, she reached forward, kissing Lyla's brow.

'You're a brave woman,' she said.

Lyla smiled at the compliment. 'You flatter me. A woman's place is beside those she loves, even when at war. Don't you agree?' She paused, gesturing towards the huts that lined one wall of the stockade. 'There's little I can offer that would prove our welcome. A swamp boasts few comforts.'

'I've grown used to their absence.'

'Of course. We'd heard rumours that you'd fled. The journey must have been arduous to take so long.'

'We . . .' Morrigen stopped herself just in time. 'It was. Our lives were in danger.'

'They still are.' Lyla smiled crisply, then sat beside the fire and began questioning her guest about her flight from the Dwellings.

Listening to their small-talk, Hyra realized that each was employing it as a means of probing the other's weaknesses. One would provoke, the other rebuff or turn her reply into an attempt at ridicule. But Lyla's eyes kept lifting, as if searching for his. He tried to evade them. He had been too preoccupied since reaching the stockade to have spared her much thought or prepared himself for their reunion. Both in the forest and during the journey west he had occasionally speculated on her fate, even sensed that each day brought them closer. But his concern had been slight: only Morrigen had mattered. And now Morrigen was no longer his and both women had to be humoured lest their antagonism add to the difficulties that already bedevilled the rising. He turned, suddenly aware that Ceruduc was talking to him.

'How much power does Morrigen still have?'

Hyra shrugged. 'I don't know. The people seem to remember her. I'm sure most of the shamans would do as she asked.'

Ceruduc nodded. He was watching her; smiling when she smiled, frowning when fatigue made her press her knuckles to her eyes or a sudden shift of expression spoilt her beauty. 'Did I really mock her in the Lines?'

'It was a long time ago. There's no reason why you should have recognized her. I wasn't even a novice. We'd gone to Henge to find you a wife.'

'Perhaps I found one and didn't know it?' Ceruduc smiled hesitantly. 'And you and her . . . ?' He paused, hoping to avoid precision.

The silence lengthened as that same hesitancy spread to Hyra. The question had been posed: and his answer? He glanced at her, remembering and simultaneously trying to forget, then said, attempting a carelessness he did not feel, 'We're friends. Nothing more. But it would make no difference. She does what she wants and takes what she wants.'

'A warning?'

'The truth.'

Morrigen had turned to watch them. She knew that they were discussing her, just as she also knew that Lyla's every gesture and word was a proclamation of her love for Hyra. The thought unsettled her, left her strangely dissatisfied. She gazed out into the night. Away to the east the sky was beginning to lighten, black meeting yellow and a slick of crimson. A new day. She should feel content, less as if some part of her had been torn out by meeting Ceruduc . . .

'You're shivering.'

'I'll be all right, Hyra. We're both tired. We need sleep.' Still thinking of Hyra and all she had lost, she looked up. She smiled at him, then trembled and closed her eyes as she realized her mistake and Ceruduc held out his cloak. She took it and wrapped it round her shoulders. But her shivering grew worse.

*

'Some's stale, the rest is beginning to sprout.'

'And the other pit?'

'Empty.'

Hyra dismissed Ceruduc's steward and frowned as he again bent and looked down at the rotting corn in the granary pit. It was too late to tell the man that it hadn't been properly covered against the rain; just as it was too late to curse him for only half-smoking the eels in the store-hut. Small wonder four more of the men had deserted during the night and the rest were complaining of hunger. He turned, angrily shaking his head as he carefully quartered the stockade to make certain the sentries were in place.

Three weeks had passed since his arrival. During that time high tides and a gale had smashed one of the walls, adding their flotsam to the black ankle-deep mud that had washed through the encampment and still hampered every step. Through the breach he could look out over the marshes. Reeds ran level to the horizon. Snipe swerved in mid-flight, drumming their alarm as an osprey swept low over the creeks, wings outstretched, talons splayed to snatch an unwary mullet from its lair. But he took no pleasure in watching it hunt, and scowled as he tightened his cloak against the threat of rain and sloshed on through the quag.

In Ceruduc's absence it was he who had to tour the encampment in the mornings and make sure that the men were occupied. It was a thankless task. Some had been wounded in a clash with the Dobuni on the edge of the swamp, and the remainder, now less than a hundred in all, were either with Ceruduc, setting snares for wild-fowl, or sitting disconsolate and sullen in small groups outside their huts.

'You look as wretched as they.'

He glanced round to see Morrigen emerge from the wattle and reed round-house that had been set aside for the women. 'I've good reason to be,' he said. 'And so have they. We've grain for a week and no chance of getting more. The fish are fit for the midden. We need fresh meat, fodder and healing swabs.' He paused, wary of provoking her, then added, 'Ceruduc's taken leave of his senses. No one else would go searching for Tharah when we lack the food to feed even ourselves.'

'You should have gone with him.'

'He insisted I stay. You know that.'

'You're his equal, not a chattel who must do as his master bids.'

Hyra growled at her petulance. 'Leave me in peace,' he snapped. 'Ever since we arrived you've done nothing but nag and pick a quarrel when we meet.'

'I don't mean to.'

Morrigen swung round, eyes narrowing in self-disgust as she saw one of the shamans duck from beneath the thatched awning that sheltered the wounded. In one hand he held a pestle filled with fish-scales ground to pulp for use as a linctus, in the other a blood-soaked length of fleece. She switched her gaze to the saltings. She was lying, just as the shaman was deceiving his patients by patching wounds no medicine could mend.

She tried to smile, mock her own predicament. Until a few days ago she had thought she was free of Hyra's shadow, the memory of what they had done. But even his presence seemed to trammel her freedom.

His silence accused, pre-empting her actions and the conviction that he had outlived his usefulness and that it was Ceruduc she must now woo and court and bend to her will. But it was hard to do. They had shared so much, known a happiness she could not easily forget. Yet the links had to be broken.

She turned towards him again, renewing the attack by accusing him of idling outside the round-house until she appeared.

Hyra laughed at her conceit. 'Are you mad? At dawn I was rousing the men and helping them mend their nets. Since then we've cut thatching reed, shaped axe-shafts and gathered driftwood for the fires.'

'And now your conscience is clear and you can spend the day trailing in my wake like a dog might its keeper. That's been your usual occupation since Ceruduc departed.'

'Don't be absurd, Morrigen.'

But she would not be halted. 'We made love,' she snapped, 'but that doesn't make me yours. If this rising succeeds there's one law I'll see quashed; that which binds a woman to a man as if she's a creature in bondage.'

Hyra shouted at her, then clambered through a hole in the stockade and pushed his way through the reeds.

She followed him. 'You want a woman who loves you, one that you can love in return. Admit it! Go to Lyla. She fusses you enough, that's proof of love, isn't it? Lie with her, forget me, even hate me if it makes you leave me to do as I please . . .' She paused, momentarily unable to say what she did not mean.

Hyra halted and stared at her as she breasted the reeds. 'You're crying,' he said softly.

'Am I?' She touched her cheeks, licking the tears from the tips of her fingers. 'Why don't you hit me or lose your temper? Just once. It would make it all so much easier.'

'I know you too well.' Hyra lifted his head and looked out over the marshes. The osprey had vanished, leaving its hunting grounds to the greylag and heron, the breeze on the water. 'Do you remember telling me that there would be no time for love once we found Ceruduc?'

'It may not happen. He may not come back.'

'But if he does . . . ?'

'Am I to blame?'

'Maybe not. But you could prevent it.'

'I'm not sure I want to. Anyway, does it matter to you? We're friends, no more. I heard you tell him so on the night we first came here.' Morrigen smiled and retraced her steps through the reeds. They swung upright behind her, leaving Hyra stranded and imprisoned by their curtain.

*

The next few days were spent waiting for Ceruduc's return. He was already overdue, and the uncertainty as to the cause of his absence added to Morrigen's own doubts as to what she should do next. After Leoid's murder the laws of cause and effect had carried her along like a leaf blown by wind. Her actions had selected themselves, leaving no room for self-doubt. But on this occasion she felt mistress of her fate, of a decision that might shape her future if it survived the rising.

Much depended on Ceruduc, and at night, lying awake in the hut that housed the widowed and unwed, she would pull the pelts over her head and gaze unnoticed at Lyla, seeking in the sister some echo of the brother. But it was as if they owed their conception to different mothers. One was massive and wayward and strode cluttered with weapons; the other slender, prudent, almost pernickety.

The days passed as tedious and dull as the encircling swamp. As High Priestess, she was asked by the shamans to intercede with Serapha on behalf of the Cunei and make offerings for victory. A timber Goddess post stood in the centre of the encampment. Round it she heaped gifts: of flints and arrows, a Dobuni corpse found bloated and belly-up in a nearby creek. But her sense of isolation made her worship seem meaningless. Apart from the wounded and the weapons stacked in the mud, there was little evidence of the revolt to add weight to her pleas. It felt distant and remote, an event that had by-passed its own birthplace and those who were fighting for it.

Tempers frayed; a blood-feud left two men dead and the rest disgruntled. The tension increased as the days slipped by. Morrigen avoided Hyra. Hyra paced the stockade to escape a confrontation with Lyla. Lyla's concern made her listless and tearful.

And then it was late afternoon again and the encampment echoed to the squeals of the last of the pigs as it was caught and butchered. The women sat weaving rushes into shields, the mothers suckling their babies as they worked. The men gossiped, mended nets, drew their bows at the butts lining one wall of the stockade as Lyla rose to fetch another bundle of reeds. She glanced casually across the marshes, shading her eyes against the sun as she glimpsed three canoes moving slowly towards her.

'Someone's coming!'

Hyra looked angrily at the sentries: one was whittling a handle for his dagger, the others had their backs to the swamp. He jumped to his feet, cursing their carelessness as he reached for a spear. The men scurried into position, snatching at stones and their bows as they went.

'Who is it?' demanded Hyra, joining Lyla.

'They're too far away. I can't be sure. It must be Ceruduc.'

'Or someone from the mines. Ceruduc took six of the canoes.'

Lyla clutched at his arm. 'Something's wrong,' she whispered.

'Wait. We'll know soon enough.'

They watched in silence as the dug-outs approached. They moved sluggishly through the water and the action of the paddles was ragged and feeble. No one waved or shouted a welcome. A man stood, tried to lift an arm, then slumped out of sight.

'It's Ceruduc!' Lyla started running, stumbling as she gathered speed and floundered blindly through the mud.

The dug-outs had vanished behind the reeds before Hyra gave chase. Hearing moans and a sudden yelp of pain when one of the canoes grounded on the mud, he halted, angrily shaking his head at Ceruduc's foolhardiness. It was all so pointless. More men had died, been butchered by axe and dagger as neatly as the hog intended for his supper. And for what? He walked on, anger giving way to dismay as Ceruduc hobbled through the reeds, supported by his sister.

The two men stared at each other for a moment. Ceruduc's tunic was torn, his eyes were hollow and bruised by exhaustion, blood smeared his face. But even in defeat a hint of his brashness remained.

'Tharah's dead,' he said suddenly. 'I've seen his head – what was left of it. It sat on a Dobuni spike. You can forget his men; most lie dead, the rest have fled to their homes. There's more . . .' He paused, giving a quick sharp laugh as he saw the amazement on Hyra's face. 'The mine's been taken. We went there yesterday to take refuge for the night. Many of the men were wounded and could go no further. We were wasting our time. Dobuni tents stood beside the entrance.'

'And the miners?'

'Food for carrion.' There was no more to be said. Ceruduc fell silent, once lowering his head when the wounded were carried past towards the stockade.

'What happened?' said Hyra quietly.

Ceruduc shrugged. 'We were seen and had to fight our way

back to the marshes. There were Dobuni everywhere. We couldn't have made it much easier for them. All they had to do to find us was follow the fallen.'

'Are we safe here?'

'Let them come! Better to die fighting than have to grovel before Zarxus.'

'The men may not agree.'

'They'll do as I say, and so will you.' Ceruduc shook his sister aside and splashed onward through the mud. Hyra watched him for a moment, then turned to Lyla.

'It's over. We should leave tonight, before it's too late.'

'He won't give up.'

'For fear of injuring his pride by having to admit defeat? Or has he some reason none must know for condemning us to the grave? The revolt's as good as crushed. We've won nothing, changed nothing.'

'He needs time,' insisted Lyla.

'And what about men and arms and provisions? He's had time enough to wage war on every tribe in the land. Look where it's led him!'

Hyra's anxiety increased as darkness fell. Entering Ceruduc's hut, he tried to persuade him to abandon the stockade during the night. But it was no use. Ceruduc pleaded exhaustion, a shortage of canoes, the condition of the wounded. Feeling helpless and apprehensive, Hyra stormed from his hut and stood alone in the dusk. A flock of mallard dipped low overhead. The injured screamed and cried out as the shamans rubbed salt into their wounds.

'Shall I speak to him?' Morrigen stepped silently from the shadows.

Hyra stared at her for a moment. 'What will you say?'

'That the revolt must go on.'

'You're mad!'

'Or you are. What other choice do we have? Where will you go to if you flee, what will you do? It's too late to lay down our arms. Zarxus won't spare us. It's either fight him or die.' Morrigen smiled, then pushed past and entered the hut.

*

A single tallow lit the discarded axe and bloody robes strewn over the rushes. Ceruduc lay stretched beside it, arms hanging loose at his side and face to the thatch. She halted in the entrance, body framed against the darkening sky. Shifting slightly, but showing no surprise at the intrusion, he lifted a beaker of mead, grinned and said, 'So now Hyra has sent the priestess Morrigen to try and persuade me to turn tail?' The beaker was drained and quickly filled.

'Could I convince you?'

'No.'

'Nor do I intend to.' Morrigen moved into the light as behind her the shamans abandoned the wounded and began lamenting the dead. 'You yourself said that a dozen corpses don't make a war.'

'You think I should continue the fight?'

'Yes.'

Ceruduc smiled, drawing strength from her presence. 'And so I shall.' He hoisted himself on to his elbows and invited her to sit. She did so, a sudden curiosity crossing her face as she noted the few comforts that filled his hut.

'A man's world,' she said.

'And what would a woman do to it?'

She smiled. 'Scatter it with robes, her amulets, the things that appease her vanity or she can't bear parting with. Women grow uneasy in an empty room.'

'Are you?'

'No.' Her smile faded. 'Zarxus will find us. Not tomorrow perhaps, but soon.'

'I know.'

'What will you do?'

'Fight back. Kill him if I can.'

'And if you lose?'

'Flee, then gather more men and harry him again.'

'I intend going with you.'

'Women aren't warriors. A spear is not a sewing needle.'

'Nor does freedom concern itself with the sex of those who defend it. I'm a woman, but do I have to dress as a man and carry a bow to prove my support for the rising?' Morrigen paused, hesitant to commit herself any further. His ill-fated return had reminded her of his faults: the hot-headedness that marred his judgement, the single-mindedness that as well as a weakness was her sole guarantee that the revolt still lived.

She looked at him. His breathing had stilled and the beaker lay forgotten at his side. There was silence, the distant wail of those mourning the dead. He reached forward, eyes fixed on hers, then lifted the corner of his bedding.

Morrigen had anticipated a request, even force, not a gesture. But the meaning was as clear, and so were its implications. She had won him, and in doing so had established an alliance that would make her spiritual leader of the Cunei if the revolt succeeded. She drew back, pretending shock at his indelicacy. 'We're at war. Such pleasures belong to peace.'

'They can be given as a reward.'

'Rewards must be earned. Anyway, I'm a priestess not a prize.'

Ceruduc fell back against the rushes. 'Now you're tempting me.'

'Provoking perhaps. Temptations are for those who don't know what they want.'

It was true. The softness in her voice invited provocation, and returned it as openly as it was given. The tallow's flame lit the copper in her hair, the pale robes that shaped her haunches. Ceruduc lifted a hand, momentarily deliberating using force.

'Do so and you risk losing what you yet might win,' she said. 'The wait may teach you patience.' She smiled, then disappeared into the night.

*

She stood alone in the darkness, still smiling. The promise remained unspoken, but even now she knew that it would be enough to prevent Ceruduc's defiance giving way to despair. She gave a sharp brittle laugh and began crossing the encampment. The body, her body – what was it but currency, to be given or sold as her needs dictated? Ahead of her she could see the shamans still circling the Goddess post and begging eternity for the dead. Serapha herself, now risen as a quarter moon low against the horizon, lay flat and hazy behind the cloud rack scudding in from the sea. The wind had lifted, the sound of waves breaking on mud timing her steps as she walked back to her hut.

She slept fitfully, kept awake by the gusting in the reeds and an old woman who spent the night trying to comfort the bereaved. One had a daughter, a thin pinch-faced child whose steely hand gripped her mother's as if terrified that she too might be inexplicably snatched from her. Watching her, when again woken by sobbing and the low hum of voices, Morrigen felt her resolve begin to weaken. Everything she touched or took part in seemed doomed to tragedy. Even the child's tears could be traced to her via Leoid's murder and the prediction of the Darkness. Now the child had been robbed of her father and would be sold into slavery if the revolt foundered. And she would be to blame, and would still be to blame when the slave became a whore or died nameless and unmourned in some slave-pit beyond the seas.

She turned away, unable to watch any longer. She closed her eyes, briefly dozing before opening them again – suddenly alert and wide-awake. The wind squalled overhead, water lapped at the reeds. Not wanting to panic those sleeping, she silently pulled on her cloak and stepped out into the night. The clouds had lifted, stars patched the sky. She crossed the encampment and hurriedly climbed one of the ladders that led on to the stockade. Her hair billowed and whipped into her eyes as she slowly quartered the darkness. There was nothing; just the dark sweep of the marsh merging with the black of the sky. But she had heard something. Now heard it again: the splash of paddles as they hit the short choppy waves in the creeks. She remained motionless for a moment, too stunned to cry out, listening to the paddles. Their noise seemed to mesmerize her, help maintain the distance between herself and her first experience of war. But the delay could not last, for suddenly an observant sentry bellowed the alarm and she half-slid, half-fell down the ladder. She began running through the mud, aimless and in panic, as all round her women started screaming and the men burst from their huts.

'Pull yourself together!' Ceruduc blocked her path.

'I'm frightened!'

'So am I. So are they. But it's those who show it who'll first feel a blade in their bellies.' Jet and greenstone looped Ceruduc's arms, a copper torque hung round his neck. From the waist up he was naked and his vast wind-burned body dwarfed the battle-axes that dangled from each of his wrists.

Morrigen pressed her face to his chest, stifling tears. She straightened. 'What can I do?'

But Ceruduc was no longer listening. 'Someone silence those women!' he shouted 'We're at war not a wake! Where's Hyra? Damn the man! He's always somewhere else when he's needed!'

A moment later Hyra came running out of the darkness.

'They're attacking from the south on rafts!' Like Morrigen, he knew nothing of the abruptness with which peace can become battle, and his ignorance showed itself in the marriage of horror and disbelief on his face.

'How many men?'

'Four, five hundred. It's too dark to be sure.'

'So they've come like wolves in a pack. It's too late to flee. We'll stand and fight. You guard the stockade. I'll try and stop them landing.' Ceruduc turned and began bellowing orders at his men. The men cheered, then fanned out into a line as he led them through the marshes towards the rafts now clustered against the darkness.

Morrigen began shaking as she watched them approach. Archers in close-fitting pigskin that had been hardened in brine stood grouped in the bows. Behind them stood the warriors. Bare-breasted, their bodies greased with bear fat as a charm against being slain, each held an axe whose bronze blade gleamed sharp and menacing in the moonlight. She could hear their war chant, see a seer hold aloft the already blood-stained spike that would carry her head to Zarxus if the battle brought victory.

Hyra handed her a spear as he drew alongside her. 'What will they do next?' she said.

'Try and smoke us out.'

'Will it work?'

'How can we stop them? A few buckets of water won't douse the fires.'

They stood silent and impotent as torches were passed amongst the archers. A moment later the first of the fire-arrows streamed crimson through the darkness and fell harmlessly into the reeds. But the next struck the stockade, and soon it was pin-pricked with sparks that spread and licked at the wattle as the wind caught them and turned them into a single sheet of flame. Black smoke billowed in the darkness. A hut began burning, its roof lighting the night like a beacon as molten wedges of thatch collapsed into its blazing shell.

'Join Lyla!' screamed Hyra.

Morrigen nodded, shielding her face against the heat as she plunged towards the women, now gathered with their babies and children in the mud. The fires lit their faces and burned blood-red in the puddles. Driven back by the flames, Morrigen halted as through a gap in the stockade she glimpsed the first of the Dobuni splashing through the shallows, the Cunei charging forward to repulse them. Ceruduc led the assault, arms outstretched and axes scything the air. A warrior lunged at him with a spear, then dropped screaming into the water as an axe severed his arm and sent it spinning into the night. Three more took his place. Ceruduc's laugh rose above the din as he waded into the attack, his battle-axes clearing his path until two of the Dobuni lay dead and the third chose retreat. He was like a beast out of myth: black-bearded, implacable, brutalized by the scent of blood and the harsh rhythms of the drums urging on the Dobuni as each of the rafts nosed in amongst the reeds.

Remembering her errand, Morrigen hurried on in search of Lyla. She found her amongst the women. Smoke blackened her face and her robes were torn. But in contrast to her brother an unlikely serenity seemed to surround her as she moved slowly amongst the children, distributing bread in an attempt to calm them. Seeing Morrigen, she said, 'Find a goatskin! We need water!'

Morrigen glanced at the huts. Most were burning or had already been reduced to rubble. The heat was intense. Flames soared upwards, their roar merging with the screams of the children and the din of battle. She pondered fleeing, taking refuge in the marshes, then saw Lyla staring at her and forced herself towards the water trough. Suddenly part of a wall buckled and began tilting, spilling burning wattle across the width of the encampment. She backed away, cautiously picking her way towards Lyla as yet more of the stockade toppled into the mud. 'Stay here much longer and we'll be cut off from Ceruduc!' she shouted.

'Have the dug-outs been found?'

'I don't think so.'

'They're our only hope.' Lyla turned and began giving instructions to the women. For a moment none of them moved. Their faces were apathetic and cowed, and when they finally rose, gathering up their babies and the small bundles that contained their only possessions, it was out of despair not panic that they did so. The older children clung together, bewildered eyes reflecting the flames as Lyla and Morrigen guided them through the charred rubble that was all that remained of the encampment. Leaving the stockade, they formed into line and began crawling through the reeds so as to avoid being spotted. The noise faded. Mud oozed round wrists and ankles as each of them followed the dark shape of the woman in front. Ahead of them the sky was beginning to lighten. Behind her Morrigen glimpsed Ceruduc and his men retreating slowly towards the stockade . . .

'Watch out!' cried Lyla.

Morrigen turned. A Dobuni archer had risen from the reeds in front of her. She twisted, diving sideways as his arrow slapped into the mud. She stood and lifted her spear. The archer cursed, fumbled for a second arrow. Suddenly a horde of screeching women rose as one from the reeds and started running towards him. He fired again, one fell, but the others quickened pace. He panicked, stumbled, then vanished from sight as the first of the women reached him. Then it was over and his body lay battered and forgotten as the now hysterical women splashed onward through the mud and began clambering aboard the canoes . . .

Morrigen and Lyla had not moved. From start to finish the entire incident had taken less than a minute. Its speed had stunned them, and neither spoke as they lowered their spears and stared down at the archer's corpse. Then the first low sob of reaction broke from Lyla's throat. She began weeping, standing pale and shaken as Morrigen tried to comfort her.

Behind them, in silhouette against the flames and in danger of being surrounded, Ceruduc and Hyra were trying to stem the Dobuni advance until the women were out of range. Only a few of the men remained standing, the rest had been killed in the attack or cut-down when attempting to flee. Morrigen led Lyla through the reeds. Only two of the dug-outs had yet to be launched and water lapped her waist as she helped Lyla to safety and pushed them both through the shallows. She felt empty, indifferent to her own fate. No murder she might yet commit could match the cruelties of war. Arrows splashed round her as she clung to the boats and waited for the men to join her. Only seven succeeded, one being struck by an arrow as he waded through the water. He fell, bobbing amongst the reeds as his companions climbed aboard and picked up the paddles. Moments later the two canoes had left the encampment behind them.

Morrigen buried her face in her hands as the full horror of all that had happened turned to shock in her thoughts. Lyla was still weeping. Blood and smoke smeared Hyra's face. Ceruduc sat grimly silent. Morrigen raised her head, reached out and grasped his arm. 'It isn't over yet.'

'Isn't it?' He slumped over his paddle and stared back at the flames as they welcomed the dawn. The stockade was still blazing, the wind scattering the sparks as they cleared the smoke. The triumphant Dobuni swarmed round the ruins; cheering, beating drums, waving the grisly trophies of victory.

'Will they follow us?' asked Morrigen.

'For six men and a score of women and babes? Would you?' Ceruduc gave a bitter despairing laugh, then freed his arm from her grip and thrust his paddle into the water.

*

Gulls lifted crying into the air as the procession trudged along the beach. After wheeling overhead, some slipped inland on the wind to where the canoes lay abandoned in a creek and a pall of black smoke hung low over the marshes.

The procession moved slowly and in silence, heads bowed against the swirl of the sand. That sudden mass frenzy that had engulfed the women had left them humbled by what they had done. They could not explain it to themselves, so felt meek, even ashamed.

Morrigen walked behind them. At some point during the morning she halted and stared out to sea. Water seeped between her toes. Waves crashed, curling green into white as they broke and tossed up their spume. The wind buffeted her face, cleansing it with a cold salt spray that revived and strengthened. Suddenly she sensed that something inexplicable had taken place, that by allowing her to escape unhindered the Dobuni had at last made their first mistake. She laughed happily, then spun on her toes. And when Hyra heard her and glanced back at her, she was a blur of limbs and hair still turning against a backcloth of sea.

# CHAPTER XII

Ivy and twisted pine roots hid the entrance to the cave. Beyond their curtain it funnelled back into the rock-face, ending where water dripped into a small pool just visible against the darkness. Bats splashed droppings on to the rocks below before going out into the dusk to feed. It was damp and cold inside the cave; so cold that the children, huddled together for warmth, could at last forget the heat, the lazy blood-red sun sinking slowly over the woods.

The shaman stood naked in the entrance. The skin was still peeling from his shoulders, but the rest of his body had been so scorched by the sun that the pain no longer troubled him. At the start of the drought the evening rainmaking ceremony had bred optimism. No other ceremony would dispel the sunshine and summon up clouds. But that was a month ago: a month of fleeing from one sanctuary to the next, the constant search for shelter from the heat and the bands of Dobuni roaming the countryside.

So no one watched him as he placed sticks towards the four firmaments of the heavens and began chanting. To those who still lived, the daily ritual had become a macabre joke; an empty pointless gesture that seemed to add to their misery instead of subtracting from it – the corpses they had left behind them. They were fugitives. Withered leaves and dried-up rivers could not harm them. The drought was Bala's punishment for attempting an insurrection. No Cunei could defy the Sun God. Better to snatch some sleep and try to forget that dawn meant moving on and being burnt by the sun again.

But the shaman had grown used to their taunts. His task was to make rain. Finishing the chant, he pricked his thumb with a thorn and walked back through the cave, intending to dip his thumb into the pool so that his blood would mingle with the water and be reborn as rain. Suddenly an axe-head fell across his path, blocking his route.

'Your blood's too precious to waste. We need arms and men to carry them, the rain can take care of itself.'

The shaman turned, stared at Ceruduc for a moment, then stepped over his axe. Silence again. The children watched him, glad of the distraction. Moths danced in the fire-light and threw their shadows against the rocks.

'Find the weapons and we'll find the men,' said Morrigen suddenly. Until she spoke, she had been leaning against Ceruduc, her head sprawled on his shoulder, watching the women as they paunched and jointed a boar. The words had been instinctive, for she was still too tired after the journey through the woods to try to plan or think logically. But now she straightened and pushed herself upright, clear-headed again, her exhaustion forgotten. 'Flint's no use to us. Until we have bronze, and enough of it to put an axe or spear in the hands of every Cunei alive, we'll go on being hunted and bedding in caves.'

Cerudic shrugged, idly kissing her cheek. 'It can't be done.'

'Why not? There's been no rain since the Midsummer Rites. The Dobuni insist that only the Cunei are being punished. That's a lie. Their cattle are dying. Most of the water-holes are empty. Another month without rain and their herds will have been destroyed.'

'Dead cattle won't win us the war.'

'But living ones might.'

'Nonsense!'

'Go on, Morrigen . . .' Hyra had risen from beside Lyla and was now walking across the cave. The kiss had hurt; partly because it reminded him that their affair was as old as the drought, but also because he had yet to recover from feeling slighted and somehow debased by the lack of emotion she had shown when finally renouncing him in favour of Ceruduc. He tried to banish it from his thoughts, note only her manner, the nervous excitement that had always gripped her when a plan first took shape. 'What are you trying to say?' he added.

She hesitated, still probing for faults, then said, 'It's nearly three months since we fled from the marshes. We've mounted no ambushes, attacked no one: done nothing but bury the dead and go from cave to cave. The rising is over. The Toil of the Stones has been started again and all mention of our names has been forbidden. It's as if Zarxus has chosen to pretend that we don't exist. But he's still hunting us. The tribesfolk haven't forgotten what we did. Most would risk a second rising if they were properly armed. The Dobuni depend on three things; fear, bronze and cattle. But their cattle are threatened. We've seen them driving their herds from the summer grazing grounds into the valleys, where's there's still water in the rivers. If we could steal them and exchange them for bronze we'd be closer to victory than at any time since the Darkness.'

Morrigen was standing with a peculiar stillness that seemed entirely disconnected from the noises round her. A child was crying. Water dripped monotonously in the gloom.

Ceruduc launched himself from the wall. 'And how can five men and a handful of women rob the Dobuni of cattle?' he demanded. 'Even if it succeeded, where would we drive them? No merchant on the Plain would risk supplying us with weapons in exchange for stolen cattle.'

Hyra was staring at Morrigen. Her face suggested distance, ignorance of the interruption. 'You're thinking of Atius?' he said quietly.

She nodded, then turned to Ceruduc and gave him a brief but distorted summary of her friendship with the merchant. 'If we can provide the cattle, he'll sell us what we need. He's afraid of no one. His mines are too far away for even Zarxus to close them.'

The silence returned as each of them pondered her words. Ceruduc watched her uneasily. Her eyes had been evasive when describing Atius and he sensed that some things had been left unsaid. Since the night she had first slipped naked into his bed, saying nothing as she made love to him whilst the others slept, she had evolved into an obsession that seemed incapable of exorcism. It was impossible not to love her. But for her vigilance they would all be dead, victims of carelessness or a Dobuni trap. Time and again during the past three months she had sensed danger before it struck, consoled the sick, forced them to continue the fight when defeat appeared certain. Yet despite her strength, or perhaps because of it, her company left him ill-at-ease and aware of his own emotions; the jealousy and possessiveness he had always despised in others. At times he felt that he was being used to satisfy some private vision, that her protestations of love would turn to scorn when he could serve her no longer. But she was right. Since fleeing the marshes all attempts to revive the rising had been thwarted by the lack of weapons. He went back through her words, patrolling them for flaws.

'We need more men. If the cattle stampede it'll take days to round them up and begin the drive.'

'That's a chance we must take. Even women can be taught how to fight and herd cattle.'

'No! The whole idea is ridiculous!' Lyla had risen and was glowering at Morrigen. 'What will happen to the children? Half have died since we left the marshes. The rest are sick and short of food. Ask their mothers to drive cattle and there won't be a baby alive by the time we get to Atius.'

Morrigen peered into the shadows. A boy born since leaving the stockade lay pressed against its mother's breast. The skin hung loose from its bones and heat-sores discoloured its skull. Every now and then its lips would fumble for a nipple and begin sucking, then it would start whimpering as instinct told it that the breast was empty of milk. The rest of the children lay crouched on the floor of the cave, the cold hard bed grown familiar with the months. Most were staring at the cooking pot balanced on the fire. A few met her glance, gazing at her through dark puzzled eyes made old by all they had suffered. She could offer them nothing, and so turned away and said, 'We remain together. How long would it take the Dobuni to find them if we left them here with the women? Someone would betray us. The guard on the cattle would be strengthened, the attack turn into an ambush.'

'You make it sound so simple,' said Lyla contemptuously. 'You're as good as condemning them. What gives you the right to decide who's to live and who's to die?'

Morrigen smiled. 'Death is not an end, only another beginning. You forget, the dead are seeds to be sown and brought back to life again.'

'And if one of those babies was yours?'

'It would make no difference.' Morrigen stared at Lyla. Her robes were ragged and one of her shoulders had been badly burnt by the sun. But any glance would have revealed a similar tale: the raw still festering sores on Ceruduc's cheeks, the ill-used women silently preparing the food, the scar above Hyra's eye that commemorated one of many encounters with the Dobuni. Yet still she felt the need to justify her lack of pity.

'Look at us,' she said. 'How much longer will we survive if we go being hounded and driven into caves? What'll happen when winter comes? Atius can help us. We either strike back as best we can, or admit defeat. Before leaving, the attack must be planned and rehearsed until every detail is perfect. We must all try and master the bow. We've made mistakes, but make another and it won't only be the children who'll suffer, but all of us. It's that simple.'

*

From high above it, the valley resembled the creation of a dream or the most surreal of hallucinations. The river meandered, flashed silver, appeared to be drowning in the waves of heat that rose from the surrounding scrub. Trees dissolved into scorched yellow grass or the lazy motion of the cattle, became mirage beneath the washed-out blue of the sky.

Dust hung thickly over the herd, but the sunlight was so bright it cut beams into the haze and picked out the glitter of water when another of the steers waded into the shallows to drink. The rest stood bunched in the shade that ringed the trees, or stayed motionless, too hot to graze, tails swishing against the flies. The herd was immense and sprawled unchecked between the slopes that trapped the heat in the valley. Through it, like a servant appointed to clear up the debris after a feast, walked a young naked herdsman who occasionally halted to pat the dung into bricks and then stack them to dry for fuel.

Morrigen tracked his progress for a little longer, then again switched her attention to the small black tent that stood beneath the trees. Seven men lolled idly outside it, just as two more sat with their dogs at the head of the valley.

'We ought to silence the dogs. They'll be turned loose at dusk. One bark and they'll give the alarm.'

'An arrow?' suggested Ceruduc.

'No. Silence the herdsmen and their dogs won't matter.' Morrigen paused to glance behind her at the rest of the band. The two oldest women, toothless and wizened, sat mothering the children in a thicket of gorse. The others, each armed with a bow and bundle of arrows, were binding their breasts against the whip of the bow-string. 'We'll attack at dusk. It'll be cooler. Wait till morning and the heat will slow us down.'

For an instant Ceruduc deliberated defying her; rebelling, however briefly, against her assumption of responsibility for the attack. But she was right, she always was. Common sense stayed his anger. 'And if we're separated?'

'Stay with the cattle.' Morrigen grinned. She had been waiting too long to feel nervous. Three weeks had passed since the birth of the plan: three weeks of daily archery practise and the slow tedious journey that had brought them westward in search of a herd that was close to Atius but large enough to merit the risk. 'Let's eat now. We won't have another chance before daybreak and it'll help take their minds off the ambush.'

Dried meat was shared out. The sun continued its descent. Shadows lengthened, slowly rippling the far slope of the valley and duplicating each of the cattle. No one spoke much. Thoughts became haphazard or surrendered to the sudden tightening in the throat that made them so quick to fidget whenever Morrigen crawled through the scrub to scan the valley. For the rest of the time she sat beside Ceruduc, a hand draped loosely over his knee. Hyra watched her. Once he turned away to see Lyla staring at him, the edges of her mouth drawn down into a sour smile.

'Do you still love her?' she said.

Hyra had been caught off-guard. 'I don't know. She saved my life in the snow. Just as she saved yours when the Dobuni nearly trapped us in the forest.'

'There's no need to defend her.'

'I'm not.'

'Then why not answer my question?'

Hyra shrugged. Lyla's smile turned winsome and hopeful. 'And what about us? You and I?'

'Please, Lyla. Can't this wait? We're at war: some, it seems, with each other as well as the Dobuni.'

When Lyla felt threatened her feet began twitching, suggesting a spoilt child forbidden its own way. They did so now. 'I can't help disliking her. Both you and Ceruduc have changed since you met her.'

'Is she to blame for that?'

'I want you to forget her, that's all.' Lyla paused, compelling him to react to the silence by meeting her gaze. 'I could help you.'

The offer was so blatant, and would have been crude but for the simplicity with which she spoke, that Hyra blushed. He lowered his head, suddenly too weary to continue fighting her. 'What if I'm killed tonight?'

'If we're doomed, does it matter what we do? You've lost

Morrigen. We all need someone to love, someone to patch and mend them when they're wounded.'

'And mourn them when they're dead?'

'Yes.' Lyla had heard the surrender in his voice. She moved closer, placing an arm through his: the act of possession.

Hyra looked down at her hand. Her fingers were worn and chapped, the nails torn to the quick. He gathered them into his fist, pressing them together as she smiled and said, 'I won't keep you for ever. I know that.'

'I won't leave you. Not now.'

'Ssh. Don't make promises you can't keep. I might believe you.'

Lyla glanced at Morrigen, scanning her face for anger or resentment. But Morrigen was busy with the women. Cheated of her triumph, she turned and lay against Hyra, finally content.

Hyra did his best to humour her. She was gentle and compassionate. Her love was so obvious he felt faintly embarrassed, as if he had been given something he did not deserve. But Morrigen still nagged at his thoughts as the sky changed colour overhead. Dusk fell. The heat gradually faded, giving form and shape to the cattle as they began to graze in the cool. A fire was lit near the tents and the herdsmen gathered round it to eat. The waiting was over. Bows were strung, children parted from their mothers as they prepared for the attack. Hyra called on Serapha to watch over them. Morrigen repeated the evening Rites as the last of the tassine was passed round in a length of horn and each of them sipped it to prove kinship with the cattle. Dusk gave way to darkness.

'Are you ready?' said Ceruduc.

Morrigen nodded, eyes shining in the moonlight. They began moving, voices falling to a whisper as they broke the sky-line and started crawling across the scrub. The fire flickered orange against the night. Reaching the perimeter of the herd, they fanned out, moving calmly and deliberately so as not to cause a stampede. Some of the cattle gathered to watch their advance, lowing softly; others lumbered aside and went on grazing. A dog barked and was silenced. Another pricked up its ears and sniffed the darkness. They halted, only moving on again when it dropped to its belly and turned its muzzle to the fire. Two of the herdsmen rose and started walking through the herd, a coarse parting jest causing a rumble of laughter. Another pause, then Ceruduc and one of the men drew their daggers, rubbed dirt on the blades, and began stalking the two herdsmen.

The waiting marked Morrigen's only moment of nervousness. Her heart beat painfully against her breast as she watched them flit silently through the shadows. Padding from cow to cow, they occasionally paused to avoid detection before hurrying on again, black shapes bent low in the moonlight. The distance shortened. One of the herdsmen began singing. His companion joined in. It was a lament, the tale of a young girl who had been snatched by an incubus. Suddenly two daggers jerked upwards behind, steadied, flashed, then fell – halting the incubus. There was a faint cry. The dull thump of a body hitting the ground . . .

Morrigen smiled and unshouldered her bow, waving forward the women on either side of her. Each of them placed an arrow to the string, slowly drawing it back as they walked on and the herdsmen came within range. She bent, picked up a stone and tossed it at the fire. A dog growled, then started yapping and dashing towards her as the herdsmen leapt to their feet.

'Now!'

The women fired, their flint-tipped arrows cutting the darkness. Some of the herdsmen staggered and cried out, then tumbled to the scrub. One dropped screaming across the fire, partially dousing its light. Still bewildered by the suddenness and direction of the attack, the survivors took refuge where they could. A moment later Hyra and the rest of the band opened fire on them from the rear of the tent. Trapped and defenceless, silhouetted against the fire, they rose and tried to scatter, only to be halted when the women loosed a second volley at near point-blank range. At any other moment the brutality of their actions might have made the women hesitate, revert to the instincts of their sex. But not tonight. They had suffered too much and known too much sorrow to show pity. Some even laughed as the men scurried forward, daggers lifted. A minute later it was all over. The last scream faded, leaving only the mooing of the cattle and the incessant yap of the dogs.

No time for delay. A whistle shrilled; the signal for two of the women to retrieve the children. Ceruduc appeared out of the darkness and began bellowing instructions. Hyra and his men started rounding up the cattle. Morrigen and the women dismantled the tent, transforming its posts and frame into a pair of pole-sledges. Two steers were roped and harnessed to the sledges. When the children arrived, they were lifted on to them and covered with bedding. The dead Dobuni were weighted with stones and tossed into the river. Torches were lit, staves cut from trees and distributed amongst the women. Speed was vital, but so often had they rehearsed the attack and its aftermath that a kind of heady exuberance gave precision to the most complex of tasks. And soon the cattle were moving, being driven forward by waving torches and the crack of whips. Unconcerned by the change of master, the dogs orbited the herd, rounding up strays, reducing the chance of stampede. Dust rose into the night. The sound of hooves and clashing horns mingled with the cries of the women. The men ran along the backs of the cattle, jumping from one to the next, using sticks to keep them moving. Ahead of them, the valley narrowed, then opened out into a vast desolate bog that had been cracked and baked by the sun.

'We must keep going till dawn!' cried Morrigen.

'What about the strays?' answered Ceruduc.

'Leave them be. We've enough cattle here to arm every Cunei alive. If we reach Atius.'

And if Morrigen's postscript spoke of doubts about the task that confronted them, she kept them to herself. The trek had begun. Even in embryo it had the quality of an epic, the sagas of past deeds recited by the shamans and elders whenever mead made them nostalgic. In the darkness it was impossible to guess how many cattle they had taken: Hyra was later to estimate it at two-thousand head, most of them steers. But for now they stretched away on either side of their drovers, splashing them with dung, clogging throats and nostrils and eyes with the dust-cloud stirred by their hooves. The dust pervaded everything. Nothing had existence outside the borders defined by the herd. Bushes loomed out of the murk, then vanished again, leaving only the stars to give direction to the journey.

That night the bog turned to woodland and the rim of a forest. When dawn finally broke, the sun rose flame and limpid over a landscape peopled with soaring pillars of ivy that reared upwards, then fell as canopies over the trees beneath them. No sapling had been spared. But the taller the tree the more savage was the ivy's grip. It strangled their branches, wrapped distended tendrils round their invisible trunks.

To Morrigen it was a landscape to match the trek, for the brightness of the foliage and the crimson sun leant an air of unreality to all she had initiated. But for the cattle it was an obstacle that both frightened and confused. Some halted, and soon the entire herd had come to a standstill: thirsty, exhausted, impervious to the whip or the teeth of the dogs.

'They won't budge!' shouted Hyra, returning from the front of the herd.

'We can't stay here,' said Morrigen. 'They need water. It'll soon be too hot to move.'

Hyra scanned the undergrowth. 'We could light fires and risk a stampede. The forest's too thick for them to pick up speed.'

A long arc of dead timber was heaped to the rear of the herd. The flames spread along it with an arid crackling. They licked at the ivy, causing a fervid wind that made the cattle start bellowing and thrusting forward in their panic, some even climbing on to the backs of those that blocked their escape. Their fear was like a contagion, for it quickly spread to the rest of the herd when the first tongues of flame swept high into the trees. Soon they were moving again, thirst and weariness forgotten as they careered through the forest.

The sun continued its climb. The heat grew more oppressive, the surrounding trees providing scant refuge from its attack. The forest became a furnace that sucked all the moisture from the air. Sweat dried to salt on the skin, the cattle grew sluggish. Clothes were discarded, only the children retaining the protection they offered against the insects that swarmed through the undergrowth.

Suddenly the cattle quickened pace, trampling the calves in their eagerness to gain on those round them. Morrigen peered anxiously ahead of her. The trumpeting of the cattle and the earth tossed up by their hooves made it difficult to detect a cause for their behaviour. The forest rolled endlessly ahead of her. It seemed boundless, an aberration of nature that denied even the laws of its own geography.

'They've scented water!' cried Ceruduc. Suddenly the trees thinned and gave way to a lake, stagnant and steaming in the sunlight. Yellow water-lilies made a carpet of its surface. Within minutes the entire herd had plunged into its waters, turning the lilies to mud. The band joined them, splashing and laughing as they sloshed through the shallows and the dogs barked at the din.

They remained there till dusk, dining on one of the steers and falling asleep in the shade. Though there was no evidence of pursuit, the heat made further movement impossible. 'We'll lose most of the cattle if we travel now,' said Hyra.

'In that case we'll travel by night,' said Morrigen. So at dusk the herd was goaded into motion, and as darkness fell it could be seen spreading out over a wilderness of scrub and open moorland that stretched away into the twilight.

That night's journey proved more arduous than the first. The jubilation that succeeded the attack turned into an unending struggle to keep the herd intact. Ceruduc and Morrigen trudged at the head of the procession, plotting the route and steering it away from the few villages that lay in the coombes. The women and dogs guarded the flanks, leaving the others to bring up the rear.

That night set the pattern for all that followed. Time and fatigue became meaningless. All that mattered was keeping limbs and cattle in motion. For two days and nights they found no water, only dry water-holes and boulder-strewn river-beds that loomed empty and serpentine out of the darkness. Calves lowed piteously. Bare-boned steers collapsed to their knees, too weak to stand, adding their corpses to the long line of offal and bones that trailed in the wake of the herd. No one was immune to thirst. One of the children was its first victim. Two more soon followed it to the grave. One of the women went mad, suddenly side-stepping and throwing herself beneath the interminable tramp of the hooves.

When dawn broke the herd would halt and the dust slowly settle. The survivors of the night would gather together, too weary to eat or mourn. None wore clothes, even their bows had been abandoned. Their feet were blistered, their groins swollen with sores. Bruised eyes stared out from dust-engrained faces and hair that was thick with lice. The days were spent listlessly beneath the sledges whilst an indifferent sun beat down on the cattle and the kites wheeled overhead. The heat cut conversation to a minimum. No gesture was squandered. It was as if the sun's fierceness had pared away any action not essential to survival. At dusk the trek continued. No one person inspired the others. Morrigen's tongue had turned black and bloated from thirst. Ceruduc and Hyra resembled carioatures of the two men who had started the journey. To Lyla it seemed that a collective will to live had possessed both man and beast, forcing them on towards a horizon that none could see.

And then came the night of the rains. The first clouds appeared in mid-afternoon. By evening the sky was sombre. Thunder rumbled in the distance and the air turned sultry. Suddenly lightning forked the darkness, lighting up the cattle and the panic-stricken faces of the children. The thunder grew louder, its drone giving way to sudden stentorian cracks that caused the ground to tremble. The rain fell softly at first, but soon it seemed as if every shower and cloud-burst that had failed to fall since the start of the drought had been fused into a single sheet of water. It splashed the scrub, sluiced dirt from faces, drowned the shouts of the men and the bellowing of the cattle. And then, as the thunder intensified, the cattle started stampeding. One of the women tried to halt them, only to be gored and tossed high into the air. Soon the moor was deserted and all that remained was the rain and the muddy tracks left behind by the herd.

The day was spent rounding up the cattle. Most were too weak to go far, and gradually they were herded together and left to graze the new grass thrust up by the rain. Watching them, Morrigen felt as if a great burden had been lifted from her shoulders. She sensed that the worst was over, that the deaths had not been in vain and that journey's end was approaching.

Her change of mood infected the others. That evening they supped on roasted beef washed down with as much water as they could swallow. From then on the trek proved uneventful. As their strength returned, so did their spirits. The scrub turned into a succession of valleys hemmed in by low undulating hills. Villages lay ahead, their stone huts and the bewildering speech of those who gathered to greet them marking them as strangers, neither Dobuni nor Cunei. They had reached safety. A sudden exhilaration swept the band as the vales were replaced by moor and a distant view of the sea. They began travelling by day, finally encountering a pedlar who was able to direct them to Atius's camp. Towards noon on the seventeenth day after the ambush they entered a small village. Granite boulders climbed the hillside beyond. Mounds of slag rose from the heather and in the distance they could see tents and timber-framed towers.

Morrigen stared at them, unable to believe, then turned to Ceruduc. 'Halt the cattle.'

Exhaustion made her stumble as she began walking towards the tents. The ground levelled, revealing shafts cut into the hillside, smelting pits, a line of furnaces. Gangs of men swopped jokes as they broke up rock with mauls and loaded ore into buckets. She halted, momentarily embarrassed by her appearance. One of them glanced up and asked her what she wanted. She told him. He looked at her, smiling broadly as he tried to reconcile her request with the dung in her hair and her mud-bespattered body. Finally he shrugged and led her towards the largest of the tents, ducking beneath its awning. A moment later Atius emerged into the sunlight. She called his name. He stared at her without recognizing her, as if she was an irritation come to trouble his day. She brushed the hair from her hair, attempting a timid smile. Suddenly he cried 'Morrigen!' and began running towards her. He reached her as her legs crumpled in complaint at having to bear her weight and she dropped slowly to the ground.

*

The tent was quiet and spacious and empty. But the sounds that filtered through its walls – hammering, mens' voices – tricked Morrigen into thinking that the journey was not yet over. She stiffened, then remembered where she was and fell back to the luxury of the furs that coddled her body. Water splashed cool and gentle as a lullaby. She listened to its music for a moment, then curled up on her side, too tired to search for its cause. The air was clean and untainted by cattle. The fresh-cut bracken on the floor still carried its scent. Beside her, on a granite slab, was a bowl filled with dark rounded fruits joined to a stem. She plucked one, curiously examining its bloom.

'Grapes,' explained a voice. 'Eat them. They're for you.' A hand passed in front of her face and dropped the entire bunch in her lap. She looked round. Atius smiled and sat beside her.

For a while she did not speak. Words would trespass on her peace, end the languor that had soothed her since she woke.

Finally she bit into the skin of the grape and said, 'I've never seen them before.'

Atius grinned. 'A merchant lives by trading. The work has its rewards.'

'How long have I slept?'

'Since yesterday noon.'

'I'm sorry. I didn't come here just to rob you of your tent.' Morrigen scanned her sanctuary as she spoke. The melody she had heard came from a spring that bubbled into a stone-lined pool, then flowed along a conduit and left the tent through a hole in the floor. The walls were of auroch skin that had been sewn into different coloured panels to mark the quarters of the moon. Bronze and copper axes hung from a carved kingpost. Urns lined the entrance and a wooden chest thrust its clawed legs into the bracken.

Atius laughed as he saw the astonishment on her face. 'Warriors die, those who provide them with the means to kill each other grow wealthy. Unjust perhaps, but true.'

'But not even the chieftains or the Lord of the Rites live as well as this!'

Atius shrugged as if indifferent to the trappings of his wealth.

Morrigen stared at him, remembering the worldly merchant who had taken her maidenhood and caused her such torment. The cynicism remained, but she had experienced too much and been the source of too much pain to be awed by his brashness any more.

She had lowered her eyes, as if drawing in on herself, allowing Atius to sense her thoughts. It was a long time ago. We've nothing to regret or be ashamed of.'

'And Ralla?'

'Ah, so that hurt. It was meant to. A way of teaching you something about the nature of men,' Atius smiled. 'I've had to ban Ceruduc from the tent. He's like a mad beast. I think he feared you were dying.'

'He's a brave man. There'd have been no rising without him.'

'And without you both he and it would be dead. I've spoken to Hyra. If all the seers were as wise there'd have been no need for your journey. I thought he was lying at first. To steal two thousand head of cattle in the middle of a drought and drive them through the Forest of Souls can't be done.'

'But we did it.' Morrigen grinned, then her pleasure faded as incidents from the journey invaded her thoughts. She shivered. 'The Forest of Souls, so that's what it was called.'

'According to legend, the trees are dead warriors who were slain in battle. The ivy is their shroud.'

'It was nearly ours.' Morrigen's shivering had worsened. She had suddenly realized that the trek was not yet over, that in the days ahead it would become a form of nightmare whose every detail would have to be relived. 'How's Hyra?' she asked.

'More bone than flesh, like all of you.' Atius hesitated, catching her glance. 'Ceruduc is your lover, but the seer's your first concern . . .'

She turned away. So the years had changed nothing? Atius's ability to sort masquerade from truth and plumb her thoughts remained as acute as ever. She took refuge by questioning him about the rest of the band.

'They've been scrubbed, robed and fed. Another night's sleep and they'd go anywhere: if you led them.' Atius laughed. 'I've tried to make them see sense, but they rose like dogs to their hackles. One of them even told me that the Goddess Serapha has chosen you to save her people. They seem to worship you.'

'And you don't?'

'What I believe doesn't matter. Are they right?'

Morrigen did not answer. She had long known of her talent for inspiring loyalty. But worship? That suggested sanctity, a link with the God-head. The notion flattered, made her feel virtuous and above reproach. Then she remembered the children who had died of thirst, the woman who took her own life.

'And the cattle?' she enquired, again switching the subject.

'A month on good pasture and they'll be fine.'

'Will you buy them from us, exchange them for weapons?'

Atius nodded. 'If that's what you want.'

'We need everything you can make,' said Morrigen eagerly. 'Axes, arrow-heads, daggers, spear-heads, oxen to carry them; as well as tools, spare ore and the loan of some smiths.'

Atius had started chuckling as the list lengthened. 'You take yourself too seriously. Be patient. The work's already begun. When you leave it'll be with enough bronze to fight every Dobuni who can lift a bow.'

'I intend winning this war,' said Morrigen solemnly. 'There'll be no more caves, no more days without food and nights spent fleeing from Zarxus's men.' She gripped Atius's arm. 'Join us. We need your help. Hyra is too cautious, Ceruduc too reckless to listen to reason. You may laugh at us, but one day Henge will be ours again. You bear Cunei blood.'

'And now you want me to risk shedding it?'

'Yes.'

'No, Morrigan. I live by selling my wares. I don't intend dying by them as well.'

She stared at him. 'You haven't changed.'

'Nor have you. I know you too well to be fooled. If you were honest you'd admit that you're fighting for yourself – not a tribe or a Goddess. Please, Morrigen, don't insult me by trying to deny it. You've tasted power. The taste lingers. It can't be drowned like wormwood by mead. It feeds on its own appetite. I wonder how long you'll be content as High Priestess if you do destroy the Dobuni? Victory can prove as hollow as defeat.'

'You're wrong. I've known defeat, you haven't.' Morrigen picked another of the grapes and said, 'Ralla will die if we win.'

'Killing Ralla won't bring you peace.'

And there the argument ended. Both had sensed that they were drawing close to a truth that might be better left muzzled, so they refrained from conflict, choosing instead to discuss the trek and the weapons Morrigen required. Finally Atius said, 'Come, Ceruduc's waiting. I promised to show him the camp.'

But the thought of Ceruduc fussing round her soured Morrigen's mood as she dressed and walked out into the sunlight. With Atius she could be herself. With Ceruduc the need for deception made it easier to submit to his embrace than invent emotions she did not feel: the sense of loss that marred her pleasure whenever they made love. Love was a compromise. Its rules had to be remembered.

She stayed close to Atius as he led her through the encampment. Even in the midday heat his men were hard at work; adding to the slag-heaps, preparing furnaces, shaping moulds for the weapons that would soon be hers. Seeing Ceruduc watching arrow-heads being cast, Atius waved, intending to attract his attention.

'Don't,' said Morrigen sharply.

'Why not?'

'I don't feel like talking to him.'

'He'll suspect me of being a rival.'

'He doesn't own me. It might do him some good.'

Atius looked at her for a moment. Her cheeks were thin, her lips blistered and ulcerated, but since their last meeting suffering had stamped her features with an authority he had not noticed before. He smiled, then steered her towards an open shaft that ran deep into the hillside. The shaft narrowed, opening out into a circular quarry where gangs of miners were hacking at the face with picks before loading the ore-bearing rock into baskets. 'Bronze is forged by adding tin to copper,' explained Atius. 'Look carefully and you'll see both metals in this one mine.' He pointed to a band of raw tin that gleamed dully in the sunlight. 'The tin's found in lodes in the granite. We have to break it up before using it. And here's some copper. Do you see?' He traced a line across the rock face, indicating a green seam that fell into uneven lumps when the miners prised it loose. Once the baskets were full, they were roped to a leather cable, hauled up towards the tower that stood astride the quarry, then swung away and upended, tipping ore and tin-bearing rock on to the mound of ore near the smelting pits.

Leaving the mine, they walked over to the pits and watched a group of men fill one of them with a mixture of copper and firewood in readiness for smelting. 'The ore has to be turned into metal,' said Atius. 'When the fire is raked out, the copper will have separated from the slag. It's the same with the tin. It's harder to work, but we use less. Bronze is nine parts copper.'

Listening to Atius explain the skills that had made him wealthy, Morrigen felt suddenly humbled. It was a world of which she knew nothing. Even his camp possessed an energy and sense of purpose that was all its own. It seemed almost magical, a place where alchemy transformed lumps of rock into the dagger she wore at her side. Until now she had been ignorant of the methods that shaped it. But she could still recall the arrival of the first piece of copper in her village; a simple pin so valuable and sacred its owner had buried it beneath the floor of his hut, allowing no one to touch it. And now copper had become bronze, a metal so hard no muscle could bend it. Looking round at the men mixing clay and dung for moulds, she realized that Atius and his smiths were perfecting a skill that would eventually change her world, win empires, make the flint mines and antler redundant, see forests become fields.

He led her next to a furnace heaped with earth. The two men

squatting beside it were working a set of bellow-bags to maintain the heat. He asked them what they were making.

'Axes,' said one.

Atius placed a hand to the earth. 'It's hot enough now. You can begin the casting.'

The men rose, gingerly removing the steaming earth from part of the clamp. The heat made Morrigen shield her face. Beneath the earth perched a line of crucibles waiting to be taken from the furnace. 'They're filled with both copper and tin,' explained Atius. 'The heat melts the ores. They fuse and become bronze. Watch.' One of the smiths drew a crucible from the flames, using a length of green withy as a handle, then stood with it whilst his companion skimmed the scum and ashes from the surface of the molten metal with a piece of bone. Holding it to one side, he walked over to a line of moulds that sat embedded in sand on the ground. He delicately tilted the lip of the crucible towards the funnelled entrance in one of the moulds and began pouring. There was a bubbling noise, a sudden hissing as a stream of molten liquid seeped through the vent in the mould. The action was repeated until all the crucibles were empty. The moulds were plunged into water and prised open.

Morrigen stared down in delight at the rough castings of the finished axe-heads as Atius listed what yet had to be done. 'They've been socketed. It'll make it easier to haft the shafts. Next they'll be heated again so as to soften the metal before shaping the blades. Once polished and sharpened they'll be yours.'

'How long will it take you to make what we need?'

'A month, maybe longer. If you're wise you'll make use of the time.'

*

The advice was heeded. For the next few weeks, whilst the smiths worked day and night to add to the finished weapons stacked in a store-hut, the small band of Cunei prepared for the return of their homeland. Chests were built to carry the weapons, baggage oxen were bought, handles added to the axes and spears. Birch was cut and bound to arrow-heads as fast as they were turned from the moulds, traps set for gulls and their wing feathers used as flights. New clothes were sown. Fish had to be netted and smoked.

But although the daily routine did much to restore the confidence of the band, it failed to ease the tension between Morrigen and Ceruduc. Its origins were simple, her refusal to marry him and her failure to become pregnant. Talk of marriage could be delayed, made dependent on the success of the rising, but the apparent permanence of their relationship made the issue of her fertility of more immediate significance. Afraid of admitting to her barrenness, she veiled it in mystery, baffling him with ambiguity, talk of divine will and the motions of the moon. But Ceruduc refused to be silenced. 'We've made love,' he said once, 'therefore you should be with child.'

'And if Serapha doesn't want me to bear you a son?'

'But I do. It's me you bed, not the Gods.'

Even so obvious a truth was open to doubt in Morrigen's mind, for the presence of the only three men she had slept with left her confused and troubled. Each gave her something that the others could not and there were times when the sum of all their virtues took on a life of its own, creating a fourth lover out of the three. Once, with Ceruduc, she imagined that it was Atius who was lying above her. She became fierce and uncharacteristically brutal, a mistress to match the man. Then the merchant dissolved into Hyra and she grew gentle, briefly finding pleasure in an act she had grown accustomed to regarding as an occasional necessity, to be endured but rarely enjoyed.

But for Hyra and Lyla the weeks spent with Atius brought an intimacy that flavoured their days. Hyra's surrender to Lyla's possessiveness, her understanding of its cause, both were forgotten as the links forged in childhood slowly drew them together again. The sea was a short walk from the camp. From the cliff-top they could look down at the black granite that tumbled to its bed. Gulls wheeled overhead. Shoals of fish drifted silver beneath the blue. White sand filled the coves. Together they searched for shell-fish and mussels, breaking them open and tipping them raw and still tasting of salt to their throats as the waves pounded the beach.

Atius would watch them as they left his camp after the day's work, grinning to himself as his men shouted quips that made both of them blush. Although self-contained, he knew that his cynicism had been born out of loneliness, and there were times when he envied their happiness, others when he would see

Ceruduc stalking sullenly across the encampment and feel grateful for his independence. But sadness tinged his gratitude. For Ceruduc's presence was a reminder that no one who loved Morrigen could ever truly be happy.

'She's miserable herself, it affects others,' said Hyra to him once. 'I doubt if she'll ever be content. She would see it as a weakness.'

'Yet no one else could have kept the rising alive.'

'That's the final irony. It's hard to live with her, but without her we'd be dead.'

'Have you considered what will happen to you all if you do defeat the Dobuni?'

Hyra shook his head. 'Not yet. It seemed foolish. Until now we've had to live each day as it came.'

'You should. The bronze has been given to you for the future, not the cattle. Drive out the Dobuni and the Cunei will be one of the richest tribes in the land. You've plenty of timber, a long coast, good pasture, the soil's easy to plough Abury may be more sacred than Henge at the moment, but it's obsolete and the Tan will do as they're told. In some ways Henge belongs to the future and Abury to the past. It has one thing that Abury lacks, a position on the trading routes. Act wisely and one day it could be the heart of an empire that embraces trade as well as the Gods.'

Hyra smiled: such sentiments were out of character. 'You make it sound as if it has a destiny.'

'It has. And Morrigen could shape it. Her vices are the virtues you need: cunning, ambition, a willingness to be ruthless.'

'She's not as strong as you think.'

'Maybe. But even if the attempt destroys her I think she'll turn Henge into something that men will wonder at when the Cunei are all dead and their Goddess has been forgotten.'

*

Atius's prophecy re-echoed through Hyra's thoughts during the days that followed, even doing so when the small band of Cunei finally left his encampment and began the journey home. Too practical to be a visionary, all that had seemed relevant until now was the success of the rising and the liberation of his tribe. And yet defeat of the Dobuni would not only free them, it would also provide the chance to build a new world on the foundations of the old. The notion was too large to be easily grasped. He tried to forget it, discard it as an extravagance or conceit; but again and again it returned to unsettle him as they retraced their steps over the desolate moor where the sun's heat had turned the cattle to carcasses during the westward trek.

Now only their bones remained. In his wake trudged a long cavalcade of oxen laden with the weapons for which they had been sacrificed. The children darted nimbly in front of the hooves, to be scolded by their mothers. Lyla and Morrigen walked on either side of him; one chattering, the other in silence. But Morrigen's excitement still betrayed itself in her mood: the fixed forward stare, the irrational laughter that underlined nervousness. Yet departure from the camp had ended the bickering with Ceruduc. Instead of being a fugitive, she was a High Priestess returning to claim what was hers. Ceruduc was a warrior and chieftain again, not merely her lover. Emotions could be set aside. Together with Hyra, they had started trying to plan the coming campaign, and in doing so had found a shared sense of purpose that left them buoyant and content.

The moor became forest, the forest turned to downland and the borders of their own lands. Scouts went ahead of the column, daily returning to report no sign of the Dobuni. Their luck held. Two weeks after leaving Atius they reached a small Cunei village set high on the downs. The villagers were at work in the fields; some weeding the corn, the others cutting flax and carrying it to a stream so as to rot it and separate the fibres from the straw. But all straightened and hurried towards their bows as the procession approached. A month earlier a Dobuni patrol searching for Morrigen and Ceruduc had camped overnight in the village, since then a pedlar's gossip had provided their only news. As they waited, the shamans chanted incantations as protection against any contagion the strangers might be carrying.

Morrigen led the procession. Her cream woven robes had been hemmed with jet. Quartz decorated her bodice. Copper bands twisted amongst her hair where it fell plaited to her waist. She had daubed one cheek the colour of her robes and painted a double spiral with red ochre on the other.

Seeing the amber round her throat and recognizing the spirals as the Helix of Serapha, one of the elders stepped forward to greet her. Her arrival bewildered the villagers. They began talking amongst themselves as she entered the village and placed a bronze axe at the base of the Goddess post. Then she turned and stood in silence as the chests were lowered from the oxen and thrown open, revealing arrows, spears, axes and daggers – all of them bronze and ready for use.

For a moment she was unable to speak. So much depended on what she said. The villagers gathered round, curious, staring at her. She glanced at the familiar weathered faces of those who had sustained her since the flight from the marshes: Ceruduc and Hyra, Ruah the rainmaker, the women whose courage was so much greater than her own, the urchin-faced children no tragedy could silence. And it was their grins that provided the cue she was waiting for.

'You know who I am. Some of you may think that I've returned from the dead, for since the night of the Darkness I've been an outcast, someone to be hounded and placed on a Dobuni spike. But I live. My head still rests on my neck. With me are those who first started the rising, the chieftain Ceruduc, Hyra – the seer of the Sacred Rites who helped me flee from the Dwellings. For a while we hid in the Great Marsh and tried to fight the Dobuni. Many died, mothers as well their children. Finally we were forced to flee and take shelter with friends. Now we've returned to finish what we started.'

As on all such occasions, the simplicity of Morrigen's words was matched by her manner. She spoke softly – conversationally, hands clasped neatly in front of her, a light wind pressing her robes to her legs.

'This time,' she continued, 'we bring weapons that won't snap or splinter. But arms mean nothing without men and women willing to use them. The Goddess has watched over us. But no Goddess can fight our battles. We need your help. Without you beside us, the Toil of the Stones will go on. Without you to halt them, the Dobuni will take what they want and be doing as they please when your children's children lie on the racks. But leave with us and I swear by Serapha herself that in a thousand dawns from now Henge will be ours and the lands of the Cunei will belong to the Cunei.'

There was silence, hesitation, a moment of uncertainty. Suddenly the villagers began shouting, waving their hoes and sickles. Hyra watched Morrigen as they crowded round her. She was smiling, tears streaked her face. Suddenly he understood that their response was a tribute to her, not their belief in the rising. By showing her frailty, her willingness to admit to defeat as she was to promise success, she had somehow strengthened them and given them back their confidence.

One of the elders tried to silence them. 'Follow the priestess and your homes will be burnt, your wives sold as slaves.'

'The women stay with their husbands,' retorted Morrigen. 'So will their children. A woman can draw a bow, a man nurse his babes. We're Cunei, not men and women who must act as others expect them to. Our sex does not matter. We fight as one or we don't fight at all.'

The villagers began chanting again. The shamans donned masks and circled the Goddess post, scattering ox-blood to summon up the spirits of war. But despite their eagerness to follow her, Morrigen felt guilty of deception. Disease would not cease if Henge changed hands; nor would hunger, hardship and poverty. Some of those applauding would soon be dead. She had a goal, they believed the lies that had foretold the Darkness and in promises she could not keep.

That afternoon they rounded up their livestock and packed their belongings into bundles. At daybreak, their huts blazing and fields abandoned to the weeds, they headed east to where the next village lay shrouded in mist. The rising had been reborn.

# CHAPTER XIII

Ragged clouds momentarily darkened the hillside, then the autumn sun returned to light their steps as the small group of Dobuni moved nimbly across the scrub. 'They're scouts,' said Ceruduc, carefully following their movements. 'Zarxus's eyes, chosen for their speed and trained to sleep as they run. Do we leave them alone or try and circle them before they flee?'

Morrigen smiled: a month ago any suggestion of an attempt to take prisoners would have verged on the ludicrous. 'They can't harm us. Hyra's instructed the sentries to make certain no one leaves the camp until they've gone. The livestock are safe. The women bringing in the harvest have been sent an escort.'

The scouts began climbing the slope, moving from boulder to boulder in an effort to gain height and a clear view of the encampment. Still dubious, Ceruduc frowned as he watched them. 'Leave them in peace and by this tomorrow Zarxus will know our numbers and the lay-out of the defences.'

'So much the better. We need time. We're not yet ready to withstand an attack. If Zarxus discovers that he's got more than a few fugitives to subdue he may think twice about leaving the Dwellings.'

Certain that the scouts posed no unforeseen threat, Morrigen turned and looked down at the bustling encampment that sprawled across the plateau. The site had been chosen within a week of their return from Atius. At the time it had seemed an unlikely and inhospitable home for the few tents that then shared it with the oxen and livestock given by the first villagers to join the rising. And now it was a fortress ringed by earth ramparts capped with thorn, the nursery of war: crammed with tents, cattle pens, grain-pits, field-kitchens and store-huts. Women hidden beneath bundles of birch arrow-shafts hurried past pigs and a flock of ewes that had been brought in to be milked. Children armed with sticks imitated their fathers as, under the watchful eye of their chieftains, they spent the afternoon perfecting the use of their new weapons. Spears clashed, axes gleamed bronze in the sunlight. A line of archers stepped forward and took aim at the rough wattle hurdles that served as butts.

Morrigen grinned as she heard their laughter. Morale was high. In the past ten days four more chieftains had left their villages and slipped past the Dobuni, bringing the total of Cunei in the camp to over two thousand. Initially the problems created by the numbers had seemed insurmountable. Old feuds had to be settled. All had to be fed, armed, divided into levies. Eventually Hyra had formed a council of elders to administer the camp, leaving Morrigen free to take part in the Rites and offer her advice where it was needed. But much of her time had been spent curbing Ceruduc's impatience. Suddenly she noticed another essential he had overlooked.

'Why haven't they been given shields?' she said, pointing to a group of spearsmen lining up to mount a charge across the stream that divided the camp. 'Lose them to Cronus's archers before they've had a chance to attack and we risk losing the battle.'

Ceruduc growled at her fussiness: the length of the arrows, the weight of the sling stones, the need for the shamans to be equipped with swabs and hartshorn for the wounded – no detail was too trivial to escape her attention. 'Wait here until we've provided everyone with a shield and we'll be here come midwinter. We can't stay here for ever. The men are as well armed as they'll ever be. We ought to strike now, whilst Zarxus is still at Henge.'

'No! Leave now and you'll march to defeat.'

'I'll do as I please,' retorted Ceruduc.

'Listen to me for a moment,' said Morrigen, turning angrily towards him. 'The rising foundered because of haste. You moved too quickly, attempted too much. The men lacked discipline, training, arms, even food. We're safe here. By the eve of the Harvest Rites we'll be a match for the Dobuni and have enough food to last us the winter. Hyra has sent out hunting parties, women to gather berries, nuts and bark fodder. The harvest isn't in. Most of the cattle need fattening before they can be slaughtered. We're short of timber, clay, hide for the shields. Hyra's right: nothing must be left to chance. He's ordered some of the men to travel by night across the Plain, digging food-pits as they go. Later we'll fill them with grain so that we're not totally dependent on the baggage oxen for supplies. He's thought before acting, just as you would act without thought.'

Morrigen's attempts to make Ceruduc see reason had become part of her day. But when she finished speaking he merely laughed and reminded her – as if to show up the contradiction in her criticism – of the act with which they had begun it. That silenced her, left her humbled by his arrogance and the vast carelessness that seemed to surround him. She also blushed. For in recent weeks, perhaps in response to the warlike mood that pervaded the camp, their few moments of physical love had acquired an almost military perfunctoriness, so that they might not have been lovers at all, but cattle who met, coupled and parted. And yet despite their arguments, the impersonality of the act had in some way drawn them closer. For Morrigen there was no need to feign a tenderness she did not feel, for Ceruduc the absence of emotion meant he could conceal the extent of his love.

Leaving the ramparts, they walked across the encampment as the drums boomed, calling home the working parties who had left at dawn to hunt, gather food or guard the livestock as they grazed. Reapers began returning from the nearest villages laden with sheaves of corn. Teams of oxen hauling timber emerged from the woods below the plateau. Their training over, some of those who had spent the day in camp sat binding wattle into frames for shields whilst their wives covered them with hide and dipped them in raw clay to help strengthen them. Others wove baskets, stacked dung, trimmed arrow flights, stretched sheep gut for bow-strings and fitted shafts to axes.

Outside the kitchen quarters, the task of butchering the forty sheep and steers that were needed to provide a daily meal for all those in the camp had already been started. Yet even as each carcass was jointed and distributed, the numbers to be fed were increasing. Beyond the ramparts, where the plateau dipped to open scrub and the edge of the Plain, small groups of Cunei could be seen hurrying towards safety. Most were exhausted and carried all they owned on their backs. Each family brought its hunger and anger; its children with the lost, bewildered eyes of the dispossessed; its tales of the brutal justice meted out by the Dobuni to those who had been caught on the journey from their villages.

Noticing another such group enter the camp, Morrigen and Ceruduc altered course, intending to welcome them. Amongst them was a tall grey-bearded man who had to be supported as he walked. He was whimpering softly to himself. His head hung low. Blood splashed a cloak that was torn and matted with mud. Morrigen halted. There was no purpose in greeting the wounded. By morning he would probably be dead, another nameless corpse to be mourned by the shamans and left to rot on the racks. She smiled inwardly at her own weakness. Since reaching the plateau, and as if in self-protection, she had chosen to deceive herself into thinking that war was best played as a game: let its realities impose and she feared she might prove unable to cope with them.

Ceruduc tightened his grip on her arm.

'It's Cronus!' he cried, already running.

Hearing the shout, Cronus looked up, to see Morrigen standing impassive and expressionless in front of him, the architect of all he had suffered. Still in shock, but needing someone to blame, he cried out, publicly cursing her as a sorceress. He shook aside those who were propping him and tried to walk towards her unaided. But he was too weak. He halted, then slowly collapsed to his knees.

'What's happened?' demanded Ceruduc, the first to reach him, cradling his head on his lap. 'Where are your men, your wife, Kirsten and Rhionan?'

Cronus did not speak. His eyes searched for Morrigen. To his dismay she met his gaze, even allowing him to try and stare her into admitting her guilt. And then he saw her sorrow and turned away. Sorrow could not comfort him. He had hoped to see proof of her cunning, anything that would nourish his hate and supply a reason to denounce her.

'My daughters are dead,' he said simply.

Morrigen shuddered, her mouth slackening and falling open as Ceruduc lowered his head to Cronus's. But Cronus knew nothing of their response, nor did he hear the whispers of those who had gathered round him. It was dawn again, three days ago, the village silent beneath the mist in the foothills. No detail had blurred; the warmth of his wife at his side, the sudden shout that had woken him. 'I was still asleep,' he said. 'There was no warning, nothing I could do. It was all so quick. They slaughtered Rhionan first, taunting her as they did so. Twenty Dobuni, under orders from the High Priestess Ralla. Then Kirsten.'

'But she was only a child!' cried Ceruduc.

'It made no difference. They bound me with ropes. I couldn't save her.'

'And your wife?'

Cronus straightened and stared blankly upwards, as if reminded of something that the shock had purposely excluded from his memory lest the grief become unbearable. And then his head sagged again. 'I don't remember,' he said emptily. 'I know she's dead. She was screaming. The village was burning. I pleaded with them, begged them to kill me as well. They refused.'

'Why did they come? Why kill Rhionan and Kirsten and spare you?'

'They came because of Hyra and the part he has played in the rising.' Cronus paused. The first flies had found the blood in his beard. Plump clouds floated against the sunset. Shafts of gold struck the craggs and bluffs on the surrounding hills, transforming them into half-formed faces that appeared to be staring down at him in silent mourning. He turned towards Morrigen. 'Another village has been sacked. Men have been killed, more women and children taken away to be sold. I've lost a wife and two daughters. You pretend to care, but I wonder if you really do?'

Morrigen smiled gently. 'My tears can't bring back what you've lost.'

'They'd prove you cared.'

Her robes rustled as she knelt beside him. 'You want to blame me for what's happened. I may not be able to weep, but I can understand your wanting to hate me. Do so, even despise me and call me a sorceress if it gives you strength, helps you forget.'

Cronus did not reply. For a moment he saw her as others might a chameleon, a set of paradoxes and borrowed personalities she could flesh out or discard at will. He stared at her in an attempt to force her into making an error. The silence lengthened. Eye to eye, they gazed at each other as those round them shuffled uneasily at so private a silence.

'You're fortunate,' she said finally. 'For years you lived in the hills with your family, a chieftain, free to hunt and go where you wish. I serve Serapha and must do her bidding, even when I don't understand it or know that the innocent are going to suffer. I'm a priestess, but that doesn't make me immune to pain. We've all lost something since the rising started, be it a child or the ability to weep. But compassion won't conquer the Dobuni. You once accused me of seeking power. So I do. But is it a sin to want the power to be able to give these people their freedom again?'

Cronus considered his reply. Her lies were so subtle it was difficult to fault them. He was about to speak when her façade appeared to peel away, revealing her as someone doomed to a torment that would not fade like his, but go on growing until it one day became madness. So in the end he remained silent, finally asking to be taken to Hyra.

'He went out with a hunting party at daybreak,' she said, lifting him to his feet. 'He'll be back soon. Come, let me take you to my tent to wait for him.' Expecting him to decline her offer, she stood to one side. But for some reason he held out an arm and let her lead him through the camp to where a circular tent sat ringed by Goddess posts.

News of Cronus's arrival had already reached his brother chieftains. They now stood grim-faced and solemn in line outside the tent. They were wearing the eagle feather headdresses that indicated their rank. As Cronus passed, each drew his dagger and tilted its blade to his chest, proof that they were willing to die in avenging his loss. Taking their daggers, Morrigen completed the ritual by placing them in a circle on the ground for the moonlight to hone.

Cronus lay down inside the tent. His presence seemed to assault its comforts, the hangings, ancestral skulls and thick bear-pelts that were an attempt at opulence. Handmaidens appeared, soft robed and respectful. Warm water was brought in and they knelt beside him and began bathing his face.

'I thought you were at war,' he growled, glancing round.

Morrigen shrugged. 'I'm not to blame. Others furnished it. A hovel would have served me as well.'

'And your servants? Some I recognize. They're all chieftains' daughters.'

'Their fathers insisted.' Morrigen smiled. 'I'd like to think that you might have done the same if Kirsten and Rhionan were with you.'

Cronus turned sharply away, hiding tears. He scanned his surroundings again, this time seeking some hint of his son.

Morrigen guessed his thoughts. 'He has his own tent. We're not lovers.'

'But he loves you, or did once.' Cronus had always mistrusted such apocalyptic words, *love*, *hate* – but there was no other vocabulary he could use. Not now, with his wife and daughters dead.

'And I loved him. Perhaps I still do and don't know it. But the past doesn't matter.'

Cronus had stopped listening. Her words had stirred his memory. No wonder he had hoped to forget. As if in slow-motion he relived it now. His wife, panic-stricken and too terrified to scream, staring up at him as they laughingly pulled off her robes and pegged her to the ground: war's most ancient outrage.

'Tell me about Ralla,' he said finally, trying to shut her image from his mind.

'Would that help?'

But he insisted, so Morrigen began pacing her tent and telling him all she knew about Ralla; her arrogance, her vanity. 'Even as a novice she used her beauty like a weapon. She needs praise, others to idolize her. I always thought that strange. Perhaps it goes with shallowness? For really she's heartless, almost without feeling. She decides what she wants then takes it.'

For a moment Cronus thought Morrigen was describing herself, employing Ralla to draw her own self-portrait. He said, 'Before leaving, one of the Dobuni told me that what had been done to my family was aimed at you. You were safe. The only way Ralla could strike at you was through Hyra, by murdering his mother and sisters.'

'I'm sorry.' And for once her regret was genuine. Rhionan, crippled and infirm. Kirsten, laughing and high-spirited; the child she might have been.

Cronus had started sobbing. Morrigen tried to comfort him, but could do nothing. The three day journey had delayed the effects of shock, but it now flooded through him, spilling out as a series of short moans punctuated by lapses into silence. Yet even in grief his dignity remained, so that Morrigen, though aware of his dislike for her, was unable to prevent herself admiring his courage. Men like Cronus were rare, she knew that. Somehow she had to win his friendship, persuade him to advise her and help plan the campaign. She smiled when next he spoke.

'Ralla's going to die for what she did,' he said suddenly. 'And I intend striking the blow that kills her.'

Morrigen was about to speak when a voice interrupted her.

'No, father. We strike it together, and will keep on doing so until every bone in her is broken.'

Morrigen turned to see Hyra standing in the entrance to the tent. The news had been given to him, but it had yet to lodge and showed only in the intense self-control that kept his face expressionless and his hands locked to his side. He stepped forward, kneeling beside his father. Cronus took a hand and placed it to his cheek. 'It was done quickly,' he murmured. 'They were very brave. Rhionan struggled. Kirsten tried to flee.'

'And mother?'

Cronus released Hyra's hand. 'I can't remember.'

Morrigen walked quietly from the tent, leaving them together. Archers stood in line in the butts. Even at sixty paces many of their arrows were falling short. She shook her head, emptying it of the scene she had left, then hurried towards them, already debating the need for longer shafts as a means of increasing their range.

*

Autumn was soon over. The arrival of winter was as savage and peremptory as any of the few skirmishes between the tribes. Gales stripped the woods. Rain flooded the parched uplands, turning every brook and stream into a mud-splashed torrent and the encampment into a quagmire. To Morrigen, now supported by Cronus in her insistence on patience, it seemed that even the elements had elected to play a part in the conflict. For the plateau offered scant refuge from wind and rain, and their constant presence appeared to foreshorten the days, making every dawn a drab facsimile of the next . . .

Scouts to be sent out. The shamans wanting her to take part in the Rites. Ceruduc's moods and affinity for mead, a lukewarm meal – the unvarying diet of chaff bread and boiled meats, the tour of the encampment with Hyra, the wounded to comfort, chieftains demanding firewood or more weapons for their men. Food shortages, arguments, worship, meetings that resolved nothing. The scouts returning to report. Then darkness again and Ceruduc's nocturnal visits to her tent: her arms swaying up to pull him down to her breasts, flesh to flesh and the warm curve of her thighs.

But despite the monotony, the encampment gradually acquired an atmosphere that was uniquely its own. Those who occupied it were no longer small groups of bewildered villagers, but a tribe, a nation bound together to wage war on a common foe. Like a stone dropped into water, its din and bustle had a purpose that sent ripples into every corner of the camp. Tents billowed in a wind scented by the smoke from the fires. Children dammed the stream or scrambled in the mud. Oxen trampled to and fro laden with provisions and arms. Women gossiped, bore babies, heckled the men as they trained.

By midwinter the stream of tribesfolk willing to abandon their homes and join the rising had dwindled to a trickle. Yet still they came. Each day brought its new arrivals. And for many their first sight of the priestess Morrigen was of a young cloaked figure eagerly scanning their faces. Only Hyra guessed the reason for her search.

'Your mother may be dead,' he said once, seeing her staring down from the ramparts at the fugitives in the entrance.

'She's alive. I know it,' retorted Morrigen sharply. 'Why doesn't she come?' There was an urgency in her voice that made Hyra refrain from challenging her. Her mother's absence had become obsessive. Eight years had elapsed since they last spoke, but the old woman's failure to join Morrigen had denied her much of her triumph. She felt cheated, as if even when apart her mother's contempt continued to mock all she had achieved. But one link with her past did reappear.

It was late afternoon, another short winter day slipping towards its close, when Morrigen heard feet shuffling through the bracken in her tent. She looked round to see a stooped rumpled old woman standing in the entrance. For an instant she was certain it was her mother – her stance seemed to suggest that she had the right to intrude – but the face was too full, the eyes too bright, her voice too friendly and rich with humour.

'Forgotten me, haven't you, lass?' she said. 'Fit for the racks, that's Teina. To each his span, eh? Then sleep. And long may it last. Eight days I've been tramping the ox-droves since leaving Abury. Thought I'd run out of fingers to count them before I found you.' She began cackling, enjoying watching the confusion on Morrigen's face switch slowly to delight. 'I'm not a ghost, lass. It's me, Teina. Flesh and blood and broth bones. Now stop gawping and welcome me like a friend.'

For a moment Morrigen did not move. Then she started laughing and ran forward into her embrace. Her skin was chapped, her fingers mittened with strips of hide against the cold. Most of her teeth were missing and the beginnings of a cataract hooded one eye. But despite the changes, her spark remained undimmed. Morrigen held her at arm's length, too overjoyed to speak. But Teina had words for both of them.

'Aye, you're as pretty as springtime,' she said. 'I knew you would be, always did, even when you were the waif following us homeward from Henge. I always promised myself I'd see you again. Now you're High Priestess and the cause of all that mud and caterwauling outside. You'll wake the Gods, that's if you don't deafen them first.'

Like a battered and slightly podgy insect emerging from its cocoon, Teina plumped herself down and began unravelling the endless lengths of assorted furs she had wrapped round her body before leaving Abury. Morrigen smiled as she huffed and snorted and spilled her wardrobe across the floor. 'You shouldn't have come,' she said. 'You're too old to travel.'

'But not to fight.'

'You can't!'

'I can, and will; and that's an end to it.' Teina grunted as she inspected the tent. 'I was right. I thought you'd be needing me. When was the bracken changed, the pelts last taken out for a thrashing? You should know better. I spent the best part of a year teaching you how to keep house. You're a priestess, not a beast who can bed down in a byre.'

'We're at war,' laughed Morrigen, in mock protest.

'Maybe, but wait much longer for the peace and you'll be dead of the pestilence. A night's sleep and a broom and we'll have it as clean as a new born babe.' Teina sighed as her exhaustion caught up with her. She swayed slightly.

'Let me help you.' Morrigen clapped, then knelt beside her as she battled with her clothes. A handmaiden appeared and was asked to return with fresh robes, food and tassine.

Teina smiled. 'You're making a fuss of me.'

'Of course.'

'I don't deserve it. Not from you. You've a war to win.'

Morrigen grinned. 'We'll win it, I can promise you that. Anyway, with you beside me the Dobuni will probably turn tail and flee.' She bent to kiss her, then closed her eyes as the old woman's fingers began combing her hair – just as they had done when she was still a novice and only Aelina's death troubled her conscience. The thought spoilt her pleasure. Suddenly she felt a temptation to confess. She trembled, testing the words as a bather might water. No, even Teina could not be trusted with the truth. She wouldn't understand, might forgive when she should condemn.

Teina began dozing, grunting to herself as she breathed. The tent was warm and she could feel the fire on her cheeks. The heat soothed her body, eased the stiffening in the joints. 'It was a long way,' she murmured. 'One night it snowed. I'm not the woman I was and winter's no time to be abroad. But I couldn't stay, not knowing where you were and what you're trying to do.'

'I'm glad you came,' answered Morrigen. 'I may be High Priestess, but I'm often lonely. I think I've forgotten how to laugh since we parted.' And in some way those few sentences were almost a confession in themselves. Loneliness and sorrow, even the foundations of her own self-destruction, all were hinted at.

Teina pulled her closer and they lay side by side as they had done when her sight was still sharp and both were servants. Morrigen snuggled against her shoulder: one mother might have failed her, but the other had returned. And when Cronus entered to speak to her and saw them lying together he felt as if he had stumbled on a different person, so tranquil and at peace was her face. He backed away, intending not to disturb her.

'Who is it?' she asked, hearing footsteps.

'We're back,' said Cronus. 'I thought you'd want to be told.'

For a moment she did not move. Mud spattered Cronus's cloak and there was blood on his face. Then she remembered and was instantly awake. Teina was led away to the sleeping quarters, grumbling and chomping on the last of her teeth. Cronus poured himself some tassine as Morrigen rose and began pacing, impatient for his news.

'It worked,' he finally announced, ending her suspense. 'We attacked at dawn. The Dobuni knew nothing. They hadn't even posted any sentries. We burnt the stockade and took a score of prisoners for the loss of two men.'

Morrigen clapped her hands together in her excitement. 'I don't believe it!' she cried.

'It's true.'

'And Ceruduc?'

'Safe, but now drunk.' Seeing Morrigen's frown, Cronus added, 'Can you blame him? That's the first ambush he's mounted since the rising began that's ended in success. Will you thank him? praise him for what he's done? No, so the mead must do it for him. You're at fault as well. Spend more time with him and he might not drink so much.'

Morrigen ignored the rebuke. She grinned happily. 'So now we've cut the trading routes between Henge and the west. That means that once it begins to snow the Dobuni will be isolated, unable to purchase arms.'

'Not completely. There are other routes they could use. With the Tan or Juba to the north, the Adana to the south and all the tribes east of the Plain.'

'But it's surely a victory? It must be!'

'But only because it'll make Zarxus realize that from now on no merchant can be certain of reaching Henge alive. It's a question of attitude. He'll feel uneasy, as if he's threatened and under siege. I've spoken to Hyra and most of the chieftains since I got back. They think we should plan a second ambush.'

'And you?'

'I agree. The men are growing stale. They need to fight. Not the battle itself perhaps, but skirmishes, ambushes that'll give them a taste of blood and a victory to boast of.'

*

And so, with the advent of winter and Ceruduc seeking refuge from Morrigen in mead, the Cunei went on to the offensive.

Though equipped by Hyra and led by Ceruduc, it was Cronus who had inspired the momentum for the change of tactics. The slaughter of his family had not been forgotten, and could never be forgiven. Yet one wound did heal. The ill-will he had borne Hyra for becoming a seer soon faded as their friendship flourished and ambush succeeded ambush. He also grew fonder of Morrigen. The mistrust remained constant, but there was a singlemindedness to her that seemed to shore up everyone in the camp.

The only victim of the closeness between father and son was Lyla. By instinct as possessive as her brother, she felt excluded from Hyra's life: by day too busy to keep her company, at night he was too tired to be sympathetic to her grievances. In desperation she turned to Morrigen, but was again rebuffed. Teina's arrival had worked a change in Morrigen's mood so subtle only Hyra noticed it. The old woman fussed round her, keeping visitors at bay and maintaining an unbroken monologue that she rarely silenced. Teina made her laugh, and if its currency was chatter the price was worth paying. So for a while she seemed to cloister herself in her tent, content to let others continue the rising she had fostered.

And the war went well. One night a small party of Cunei crossed the Plain, attacking the Sacred Dwellings and smashing one of the stones at Henge. The slave pits at the base of the ramparts were soon crowded with Dobuni. A thin seam of copper was found in the hills, providing much needed arrowheads for the men. A succession of attacks on the line of hill-forts that surrounded the Plain resulted in the liberation of its western edge. Other ambushes followed, to be answered by a sudden thrust at the encampment that verged on becoming a siege. For nearly a week the Cunei held out as fire arrows gutted their tents and the stench of putrefaction hung like a pall over the mortuary racks. And then, as if in response to the pleas of the shamans for deliverance, it began to snow and the Dobuni were forced to withdraw, trailing oxen and weapons in their wake as the Cunei severed their supply lines and harried their every step back to safety.

The coming of the snow changed the complexion of the campaign. For both tribes there was now a new enemy to be conquered. The snow was as ruthless as any weapon. It snatched the weak and the wounded, the young and the old; seeped into tents and through bedding; obliterated granary pits and fodder; buried sheep and cattle; made even the gathering of brushwood for cooking a debilitating and taxing labour. For some, like Morrigen and Hyra, it was a reminder of a past they had shared. For others, like Ceruduc and many of the men, it meant frustration, a battle against the cold, a quickening of temper. In the evening, ignoring Teina, he would storm into Morrigen's tent brandishing the goatskin of mead that was now his most enduring companion. There would be an argument, bitter and quick and ending in reconciliation, Teina being ordered to leave. Then they would make love, often standing and through vents in their clothing. Morrigen with her back to the wall, Ceruduc thrusting forward through the haze of his drunkenness. And when it was over there would be a tense cold silence that left both of them ashamed of what they had done.

'Now go,' said Morrigen once.

Ceruduc laughed harshly. 'Is that all I am? someone to serve you like a beast at stud.'

'What else can you be when sodden with mead?'

'You're not the only woman in the camp, not all would be so fussy.'

'Take them. You reek. You haven't changed your clothes in a month.' Yet even as she spoke Morrigen knew that part of her found pleasure in his debauchery. She was its cause. It made him her equal, each as shameless as the other. He treated her like a whore, but perhaps she was one? If nothing else it explained the eternal round of quarrel and contrition that kept them locked together.

But in reality it was the snow. For just as it had made her light-headed when trapped with Hyra in the forest, so now it affected her behaviour and invaded her thoughts. Like the howl of high winds or a full moon, it could madden, snap the links that moderated her wickedness. Frightened of what she might do if the snow continued, she would flounder through the drifts that lapped the ramparts and gaze out to where yet another blizzard squalled towards her across the Plain. Finally it would reach the plateau, sending everyone running for shelter as the wind flattened it and the oxen huddled together, their coats suddenly white.

Like the blizzards, the first signs of spring also appeared without warning. One night the wind veered to the west. The next morning the encampment woke to clear skies and a cool breeze. The drifts changed shape, finally exposing rock and bare patches of scrub as the thaw continued. The snow turned to slush. The women stopped having to crack the ice in the stream before filling their buckets. The remaining livestock were driven out to graze, the first scouts dispatched to gather news and gossip. By the day of their return, winter was over, its only legacies a cluster of burial tombs and the dabs of white beneath the tops of the hills.

*

Morrigen was celebrating the morning Rites with the shamans when the first of the scouts returned. He had run through the night, mentally withdrawing into a form of trance brought on by lack of sleep and the long lolloping stride that is the hallmark of the natural scout. The tribesmen crowded round him, eager for news. There was a sudden cheer that quickly grew louder as rumours spread through the camp. Deserting the shamans, Morrigen hurried towards him as Cronus and Hyra came running through the mud.

'Where's Ceruduc?' cried Cronus.

'I don't know. Why? What's happened?' said Morrigen.

'We must meet in Council, the chieftains as well.' Cronus grinned, shaking his head in bewilderment. 'The Dobuni have abandoned the Sacred Dwellings. Why, we don't know.'

'Are they advancing?'

'No, that's what's so strange. According to the scout they're falling back towards Abury and the forest.'

Despite the excitement that had swept the camp, Morrigen felt apprehensive and anxious as she joined Hyra and the chieftains in Cronus's tent. She sat cross-legged in the circle round the fire, the only woman amongst twenty men, listening attentively as the exhausted scout stammered through his report. Cronus broke the silence that followed.

'So what do we do?' he demanded. 'All hill-forts abandoned, the Dwellings deserted, the Village of the Shamans in flames. Zarxus is no fool, nor is he a coward. Yet there's no reason for what he's done. He has three thousand men, all well-armed and provisioned, and he chooses to retreat without a blow being struck. Is he trying to tempt us into battle? Has he used the winter to plot an alliance with the Tan?'

No one answered him. So much hinged on the correct interpretation of Zarxus's movements. The chieftains shuffled uneasily, wary of committing themselves. 'Are we ready to fight?' asked one.

Cronus nodded. 'Yes.'

'Then we should march.' The decision made for them, the other chieftains echoed their companion's militancy.

But still Cronus held back. He glanced at his son.

Hyra hesitated. An alliance with the Tan would mean the Cunei were outnumbered. Yet it seemed an unlikely marriage. The Tan had nothing to gain by the destruction of their southern neighbours. They worshipped the same Goddess, resented the changes the Dobuni had forced on them. Perhaps above all, they were peaceable and conciliatory, a nation of sheep-farmers and forest-dwellers who lacked the stomach for war. He looked round. Everyone was staring at him, awaiting his verdict. 'We should march,' he said.

Cronus turned gravely to Ceruduc. 'Do you agree?'

'Pah! We're wasting time. Always have been,' cried Ceruduc angrily. 'We could have been at their throats in the autumn. It's bronze that wins wars, not words, words, words!' He was drunk, his speech slurred.

Cronus swung to Morrigen; obeying Ceruduc, asking a question without words.

Morrigen closed her eyes, hoping for revelation, some portent from Serapha. Emptiness, her mind blank. She shivered, terror seizing her like a form of nausea. She nodded. 'When?'

'The sooner the better!' bellowed Ceruduc.

But she had been addressing Cronus. He tipped his head, nerves making him rub a sore at the base of his neck. His head straightened. 'At dawn tomorrow.'

The tension snapped, an audible sigh greeting its dismissal. Ceruduc laughed. Lifting his goatskin, he hurled it across the tent, splashing mead on the faces of those round him. 'And about time! A man needs company when surrounded by cowards. But it's only a sot who drinks when he fights.' Swaying slightly, he crossed the tent and dunked his head into the water bucket. He stood, water sloshing from his face. He grinned at Morrigen, suddenly sober and clear-headed again.

*

Abandoning the camp, the Cunei trudged eastward in the thin spring sunshine; men and women, children and livestock, a tribe at war that sprawled untidily across the empty Plain. By noon on the fourth day they were within sight of the first of the burial tombs that ringed their goal.

But, perversely, the nearer they drew to Henge, the greater Morrigen's fear. Thrown without warning into a battle, as when in the stockade, there had been no time for emotion. But the slow advance across the scrub had a premeditated, almost inexorable sense of purpose to it that left her permanently on edge. Beneath her, the white bull that was to carry her in triumph into the temple swayed from side to side as it climbed the downland. She gripped its neck, hoping for reassurance or release from her fear.

'What if it's a trick?' she shouted, as Ceruduc hurried by.

'There's no Dobuni within a day's journey of us. Stop fretting,' he replied, smiling at her. A stranger to fear, he found it endearing in others; proof of imperfection.

'Hold my hand,' she said.

It was wet and hot, too hot for so blustery a day.

For a while he stayed beside her, trying to comfort her, even forgiving her for the delay caused by her vanity at the start of the morning's march. Teina had plaited her hair into a single braid that had then been dipped in red ochre. It was almost scarlet, a florid blood-red contrast to the amber round her throat, bare legs, simple robes that had been soaked in brine to bleach out the colour. Raddle rimmed her eyes and her face had been streaked with thick black lines that switchbacked across her cheeks. Snake skins hung from her waist and the horns of the bull. In combination the effect of her appearance did not so much heighten her beauty as seem unnatural and disturbing, a notion that was echoed elsewhere in the procession.

For ahead of her, but to the rear of the scouts busily criss-crossing the scrub in case of ambush, were the shamans. The destruction of their village had prompted the appearance of a number of bobbing shrunken heads set high on spikes above their ranks: no quarter was to be given, no seer taken prisoner. They wore wolf masks, carried drums and whistles that offered a shrill and eerie counterpoint to the Song of the Dead. Behind her walked her handmaidens, armed and daubed; one of them the custodian of the greenstone axe she was to offer to Serapha on reaching the temple. Then followed Cronus and the other chieftains; Hyra, now robed as a Cunei warrior in ceremonial hunting cloak and with a bow slung over his shoulder. The levies succeeded their chieftains: the spearsmen and archers, the axe-men and slingers, their stone-pouches slapping against their thighs as they walked. Bringing up the rear were the women and children and livestock, and a long cavalcade of baggage-oxen laden with tentage and provisions.

Morrigen felt a shiver of nervousness as she turned from her inspection. Ahead of her, like sleeping giants blanketed in turf, a line of long tombs broke the skyline. Round tombs clustered alongside them, still chalk-white where the grass had yet to seed: the temple's approaches, the dead guarding the living and the necklace of stones that would be her share of the spoils if the Dobuni were beaten.

Hyra joined her. 'A year ago we were in flight from the marshes,' he shouted, smacking Ceruduc across the shoulder.

'Now look at us! If only Atius was here to see where his weapons have led us.'

But Atius would always be absent, thought Morrigen. Men like him had no need of a crutch, a God to prop their fears. She smiled at Hyra's excitement. Everyone appeared to have forgotten that the battle had yet to be won, that soon they might be dead.

'Look!' he cried.

The procession suddenly disintegrated as Henge loomed into view, its stones rising above the charred ruins of the Village of the Shamans. The shamans began chanting. Women fell and prostrated themselves to the earth, some tearing up the turf with their hands. Old men openly wept as they waved the bones they had brought as an offering for the Goddess. For an instant Morrigen was amazed at their fervour. And then, with the clarity that only tiredness and the knowledge of life's impermanence can supply, she knew that Atius was wrong; that men built temples not out of fear but because they believed that by creating something that outlived them they also survived, immortal, blessed with a divinity no scepticism could mute.

Kicking the bull, she goaded it forward as the villagers poured past her, axes lifted to smash the stones that symbolized their servitude.

'Stop!' she screamed.

They did so reluctantly, pausing on the summit of the bank as the white bull lumbered slowly into the temple.

Morrigen scanned their faces. Hysteria had sucked all reason from their eyes. She hesitated, then shouted, 'Offend Bala and we may lose the battle. We came here to destroy the Dobuni, not the stones our forefathers toiled to raise.' And then, as if the murders that lay on her conscience had taught her nothing else, she went on to remind them that all things are sacred and that those who harm them risk harm in return. One day, she told them, the stones will be removed and made into a tomb to honour those who died at the Toil. The Cunei listened in silence, their anger drained by her eloquence. And when she dismounted and placed the greenstone axe at the base of the Serapha Stone it was as if she was a Goddess herself, so composed and mystical was her appearance.

*

Evening. A half-moon lit the lines of tents that radiated outwards from the temple. Beyond them rose the palisade of thorn that had been hastily thrown round the camp during the afternoon. The Cunei had retaken Henge, but the celebrations had been brief. The soothsayers had driven themselves into trance in hope of gaining knowledge of the future. The healers had danced, a stag had been slaughtered and stripped of its antlers, offerings of flint and bone lay heaped round the stones; but a mood of quiet and uncertain expectancy had greeted the coming of the night.

'The men are in position,' said Ceruduc gravely, returning to the fire where the others were sitting.

'We've saved some broth for you,' said Morrigen, motioning Teina from the shadows.

Ceruduc took a bowl and cupped it in his hands as Teina filled it. Then he forgot about it, preferring to stand and peer anxiously into the darkness. 'I'm still uneasy,' he said. 'Perhaps I'd better check the sentries again?'

'Leave them in peace,' advised Cronus.

Morrigen agreed. 'They're as aware of the danger as you. There's nothing else we can do. Sit down and drink your soup before it gets cold.' Some trace of the aura that had surrounded her when alone in the temple still lingered. She was placid and unusually calm: too calm, Hyra had decided, watching her from across the fire.

Ceruduc shrugged and quickly emptied his bowl. 'I've waited too long for this moment to risk being caught napping now.' He sighed. 'I can't understand why none of the scouts have seen the glow of their fires. I've sent out more, but they won't be back before dawn. By then it may be too late. Zarxus *must* know we'd make camp when we reached Henge.'

Cronus glanced round: nothing but darkness and the Plain rolling emptily into the night. A child's cries, the low of the cattle, the murmur of voices in the nearest tents. 'I don't think any of us will sleep well tonight. Even those that aren't on watch are still awake, their hands on their weapons.'

'The silence makes it worse,' added Lyla. 'All the time I've the feeling I'm being watched.'

'You are.' Ceruduc rose and again scanned the darkness. 'Zarxus and his men are out there, somewhere. But where?'

And now everyone looked round; waiting for the glint of a

spear, voices, the one careless move that would betray the position of the Dobuni.

Lyla began trembling. In her mind she had evolved the idea that motion was the best technique for survival. Not this waiting, the purposeless fidgets that were energy demanding outlet. 'Do you think they'll attack tonight?' she said, voicing what all were thinking.

'No,' said Hyra.

'Why not?'

'They worship a Sun God. If they attack at all it'll be at dawn when he rises.'

There was complete silence, even their breathing seemed to slow. Hyra's reply had been almost casual, an answer at random.

And yet . . . ?

He frowned, his heart beat quickening. The others were staring at him as if stunned by his logic.

'They wouldn't!' he whispered. Yet even as he spoke he knew he was wrong.

'What would you do if you were Zarxus?' said Morrigen. 'It's brilliant, flawless. As Ceruduc said, the Dobuni must have realized what taking Henge would mean to us. To tempt us to leave the one place where we're safe, they withdraw from the Dwellings, leaving Henge unprotected. We cross the Plain. Camp here. Without water, ramparts, anything to help us withstand a siege. We've women and children within arm's length of the palisade. The livestock would stampede. There'd be chaos. How could we supply the archers with arrows and man the defences? At the end of the day the Cunei would have ceased to exist.'

Again the silence as Morrigen's summary took root. Lyla rose, shivering, a damp sweat on her face. 'We're trapped.' She turned to Hyra, hoping for contradiction.

Hyra reached out and gripped her hand, then looked round at the others. 'We can't attack them tonight because we've no clues as to where they are. Retreat across the Plain and we'd be as much at their mercy as here. Most of the women and children would never reach the plateau alive. So what do we do?'

Cronus sighed. 'I don't know.'

'We must leave the temple,' insisted Ceruduc. 'It'd be madness to stay.'

Another silence. Suddenly Morrigen lifted a finger. 'But if we were to seem to remain and yet not to remain . . . ?'

Ceruduc snorted, accusing her of riddles.

But Hyra was not so abrupt. Her eyes had begun to crimp, always a symptom of a plan's gestation. 'What are you trying to say?'

She leant into the fire-light. 'What would happen if we went now, under cover of darkness, but left the livestock and tents?'

'The Dobuni would spot us.'

'But if they didn't. If we went quietly, small groups at a time, through a gap on the southern side?'

'They'd attack at dawn as planned – and find no one. But we'd be without tents, oxen, most of the food.'

'And if we hid, out of sight in the woods in the valley, counter-attacking as soon as they had stormed the temple?'

'The . . .' Hyra ran dry as he suddenly understood what she was suggesting. He stared at her for a moment, shaking his head in silent admiration at the cunning that could invent so complex a plan.

'It's not perfect,' she said, at last smiling. 'But its faults may prove to be its strength. Would you suspect an attack having just overrun a deserted camp?'

'It'll work,' said Hyra, reassuring her. He looked round: Ceruduc was grinning, Lyla smiling, even his father had permitted himself a chuckle. He turned to Morrigen again. 'What do we do first?'

'Rouse the chieftains. So much depends on not being seen as we leave. Everything must seem normal. There must be no noise. The children and babies must be made to stay with their parents. The sentries must carry on patrolling, the fires kept burning. We'll take our weapons and enough food for one meal.'

The five of them divided, each walking a line of tents and whispering instructions. For a while the evacuation seemed doomed to disaster. Children had to be woken, babies fed and strapped on to their mothers' backs, the shamans convinced of the need to abandon the temple. But gradually order emerged out of chaos. Keeping low, as close to the shelter of the tents as possible, small groups of men and women started creeping through the darkness towards the southern arc of the encampment. A gap was cleared in the palisade. Finally, under orders from Ceruduc, a levy of archers broke from the shadows and began running across the scrub . . .

Ceruduc stared into the night. He waited for a shout, the cry of warning that meant failure. The silence stretched. He could hear a second levy forming up behind him. He turned, waving them forward as Morrigen appeared at his side.

'Send all the archers before the first of the women. Tell them to take up positions on the edge of the wood, but not to fire unless Cronus or Hyra give the order.'

'And if we're seen?'

'Then we fight.' Morrigen closed her eyes as the second levy began the dash to safety. It was her plan: she would be at fault if it went wrong. She forced a smile at her foolishness. There would be no point in apportioning blame. She would be dead, the Cunei scattered and broken.

She walked alone into Henge, silently begging Serapha's guidance in all that lay ahead. The stones rose round her, their shapes changing with the angle: now a coppice of bare elms, now bulk and girth, now bars on a slave-cage. Suddenly she sensed that even in victory they would continue to imprison her, make the temple the one place where she could never be absolved from her guilt. She was surrendering to self-pity, and knew it, so hurried through the deserted encampment to where the women and children stood gathered in the lee of the palisade.

The moon vanished behind cloud as they started to leave. The children clung to their mothers, enjoying the adventure. Once a baby screamed and those exposed to attack dropped in unison to the ground, nervously scanning the sky for the fire-arrow that would mean betrayal. A few of the older women stumbled in the darkness, twisting or snapping an ankle and having to be carried to the edge of the wood, a wedge of timber between their teeth lest the pain make them cry out. Finally it was Morrigen's turn to squeeze through the hole in the palisade. Lyla and Teina beside her, escorted by men with spears, she crept quickly through the night, pausing briefly to look back at the stone silhouette of the temple before dropping into the valley.

The wood was small, merely a chain of copses linked by pines. To Morrigen it made an inadequate sanctuary. Bodies packed it. Women and children were trying to find sufficient space to stretch out and sleep. Her unease increased. The noise was immense. Rotting timber snapped underfoot all round her, whispers multiplied as everyone relaxed after the journey. Accompanied by Cronus, she toured the temporary camp: posting sentries, pleading for silence, making certain that the chieftains were aware of their orders. Hyra emerged from the pines.

'We've done it,' he whispered. 'The last of the men have just reached the wood.'

His face was invisible, but the strain in his voice warned her that he was keeping something back. She frowned anxiously, searching for his eyes. 'Where's Ceruduc?'

Hyra shuffled uncomfortably.

'Where is he?' she repeated, her voice rising.

'He refused to leave,' admitted Hyra finally. 'He didn't want to tell you in case you insisted on staying with him.' He gripped Morrigen's wrist as she spun in the darkness. 'Leave him! Some of the men are with him. They had to stay. Someone's got to calm the livestock and stoke the fires. He'll flee as soon as they attack.'

Not waiting to argue, Morrigen turned and plunged through the wood, brambles plucking at her face. Her need for Ceruduc had bewildered her. Until now, though her lover, she had thought of him as a rung on a ladder, a stepping-stone to be used and then forgotten. Now it struck her – and no other word quite conveys the feeling she had of being reduced to dependance on him by a single blow – that the borders between her love for him and her hate were indistinguishable: she couldn't live with him, or without him.

But her longing to be with him – and her courage – left her when she reached open scrub. She retraced her steps and joined Teina. But the rest of that night passed as slow and agonizing as any she could remember. Ceruduc's absence made sleep impossible. She lay on her back, staring up through leafless branches as the moon wove between the clouds on its journey to morning. All round her she could hear the sentries pacing, mothers comforting their babies, Teina tossing in a short and troubled sleep. And then Cronus was tugging at her shoulder.

'It'll soon be dawn,' he whispered. 'The chieftains have started moving their men into position.' His face was wan, almost sickly; but there was a set look to it that she instinctively understood.

'You're thinking of Ralla,' she said, rising to her feet and tightening her cloak against the cold.

'Yes. I've waited a long time for this moment.'

'She may not come.'

'I'll find her.'

Morrigen glanced through the trees. 'Is there any sign of them yet?'

Cronus shook his head. 'None. We could be alone.'

We are alone, she thought. *We're born alone and die alone.* Tuah's words on the night she came to Henge to be sold. *But need others whilst we live.* Leoid, the healer, Ishtar: all dead that she might live.

Cronus sensed her mood. He smiled. 'Now it's you who are thinking of the past.'

She nodded. 'It's hard not to. By tonight we could be corpses.' She paused, again struggling with her fear. 'I must celebrate the Rites. The shamans will be waiting for me.'

Hoar silvered the trees and the leaves crackled beneath her as she walked through the wood. The women were dispensing food – bread and slabs of cold meat; the men smearing their faces with chalk. Some ran forward and touched their weapons to her robes. Away to the east, where the Plain met forest, a thin grey smear marked the horizon. In dawn's half-light the mens' faces seemed like images from a dream: white tousled hair, dark tired eyes. Envying them the masks that hid their fears, she hurried on in search of the shamans. She found them in a clearing, then stood with them in a circle as they turned to the dying moon and awaited the first sound of the day. The need for silence gave a dignity to their worship no chant could have improved; bare feet stirring the leaves, arms raised towards Serapha as if to imitate the encircling trees.

The sound came: the song of a thrush – a day for domestic routine and a gathering of friends. Morrigen frowned. Those who defied the portents risked accident and death. But it was too late now. The men had lined up along the edge of the wood, only the valley slope and an open expanse of scrub separating them from Henge. The women and children remained bunched in the gloom as axe and spear-heads were dipped in a basin of ox's blood being carried round by one of the shamans. Bow-strings, kept wrapped overnight as protection against the dew, were uncoiled and fitted to shafts.

Cronus and Hyra paced nervously. All they could do was wait. Occasionally they glanced eastward, silently urging on the sunrise. The men fidgeted, strapped on shields, touched talismans, calmed wives and children in hope of calming themselves. Hyra grew impatient, finally suggesting they advance.

'We'd be seen,' Cronus reminded him.

'And if Morrigen's wrong?'

'That's a chance we must take.' Nothing could fluster Cronus. Throughout the wait his thoughts had stayed fixed on the only act that concerned him, coming face to face with Ralla. The grey turned to gold above him. A glazed, rust-coloured sun canted the skyline. Morrigen and the shamans stopped dancing, lowering their arms. Sunlight spilled through the wood. No one moved. It was as if the sun's appearance had all but mesmerized them, locking limbs and making speech impossible. Bala had risen.

As if in response to a cue a drum boomed in the distance. Then came the deep, repetitive chant of the Dobuni war-cry. Cronus lifted his axe. The scouts posted at the crest of the valley began waving their spears, the signal that the attack on Henge had commenced. The chant grew louder, more strident. Apart from the din there was no hint as to what was happening. Eyes turned to Cronus, watching his axe, waiting for it to drop. Morrigen drew her dagger and stared down at the leaves in an attempt to conjure up the scene at the temple: the Dobuni breaking cover and charging across the Plain, only to find a handful of Cunei waiting to repulse them as they swarmed over the palisade.

There was a rushing sound, as of a blade cutting air. She looked up to see Cronus's axe plunge deep into the earth.

'Charge!'

An unrehearsed roar greeted his order. The wood emptied, spilling a ragged wave of cheering tribesmen who soon fanned out across the scrub as the pace quickened and they lifted their weapons. Morrigen started running, her escort and handmaidens in pursuit. Ahead of her the first of the levies began climbing the valley. Chieftains bellowed at their men, spears glinted in the sunlight. Suddenly a group of men burst over the top of the ridge. And then she was weeping and screaming his name as Ceruduc tumbled into a somersault and rose framed against the slope, his battle-axes hanging loose from his fists.

She ran towards him. He started laughing, pressing her to his chest when she reached him.

'They're all there!' he shouted. 'Like swine to the slaughter. Every Dobuni alive. Zarxus, Ortus, even Ralla.'

There was blood on his robes and she could feel its warmth on his cheek. 'I was frightened. I couldn't sleep,' she said, still clinging to him.

He grinned at her fears. 'It was simple. A fool could have done it. They came at sunrise, just as Hyra said. But there's some that won't see the dusk.' He turned, bellowing, 'Close up! We're at war, not hunting hind!' as the tribesmen poured past. He freed himself from her embrace. 'I must join them. Stay with your escort and keep well back.' She held out a hand, willing him to remain. The sight of him marked by the blood of those he had killed had stirred her desire, turned fear into exhilaration and awoken some unnatural libido only blood could arouse. And then he was gone and she was alone on the slope.

For a while she obeyed him. Then the noise lured her forward and she scrambled on up the valley until both Henge and the battle were visible above its crest. The Cunei archers were already within range and she glimpsed Ceruduc moving amongst them trying to discipline their fire. The Dobuni were divided; half were inside the encampment and the remainder spread out to the north of the palisade. They appeared confused and in disarray, as if still dismayed at finding Henge deserted. Scant thought had been given to the chance of a counter-attack, and, as she watched, those nearest the advancing Cunei reeled back as another volley of arrows cut its grim swathe through their ranks.

The palisade was soon breached. Smoke hung over it. Spear parried spear, stones drummed against the turf when the slingers opened fire. Arrows crossed in mid-flight as the struggle for control of the temple grew steadily fiercer. The dead sprawled forgotten on the thorn, limbs skewed, eyes without focus.

Morrigen moved closer. She could not stop herself. Reason rebelled, terror seized her, but the battle tugged at her the way a whirlpool tugs at the flotsam on its rim. As with her desire for Ceruduc, its sounds had disturbed some unfamiliar instinct it was impossible to evade. For the fighting was constant and the clash of the axes had set up their own rhythm, a harsh turbulent music that propelled her forward to the rim of the fighting. Her escort tried to turn her back. She refused. She was charmed, fate would protect her and still the vortex.

Gradually the battle splintered into images that her mind held for a moment, then released. A Dobuni archer toppling from the Serapha Stone, white gull's feathers garnishing his throat. The soft hum of the arrows as they curled lazily upwards to catch the sunlight as they fell. Ralla, her face painted to match the colour of her God, cowering in panic behind the stones. The dancing heads on the shamans' spikes; the wounded hauling themselves into shelter, often Cunei and Dobuni together; the blood splashing the thorn and making the ground slippery underfoot.

And it was the blood that turned the tide. For as the wind carried its scent to where the oxen and livestock stood penned, they started panicking, trampling the wattle and rampaging amongst the tents in an attempt to escape. Some entered the temple, flailing horns trailing torn strips of hide, to stampede between the stones and scatter the seers as they went. Now threatened by a second enemy and unable to reinforce the palisade, the Dobuni began falling back; only to find their retreat blocked by fallen tents, as well as sheep, pigs and the groups of oxen that roamed maddened and terrified through the encampment.

To Morrigen it seemed that the battle had been won. The retreat had dissolved into flight. Led by Ceruduc, the Cunei had ringed the palisade in order to cut them off. And then the Dobuni began rallying. For centuries they had known no home but the Plain, no temple but Henge. Faced with the loss of both and the certainty of death if they stayed, they formed into a column and suddenly swept through the palisade. The Cunei were too few to stop them, despair added to their courage, and soon they were hurrying north, seemingly impervious to the arrows and stones still falling amongst them.

Ceruduc cursed as he watched their departure. 'Let's give chase. Leave them to lick their wounds and we'll have a second battle to fight.'

'And what of our wounds? don't they need patching?' Cronus stood beside him, face ashen with pain, one leg bound with fleece where an axe had parted the flesh. 'We lost nearly a hundred men in that one charge.'

But his advice was wasted. Ceruduc and the other chieftains

refused to listen when he pleaded for caution. Scenting victory, they assembled their levies and gave chase, using slings and bows to check the retreat. Soon the encampment was deserted but for the dead and wounded and the few men who had remained behind to guard the temple.

Amongst them was Hyra. The fighting had terrified him; its noise, its waste, its almost casual butchery. But now it was over his fear had given way to an unlikely bravado. Grinning happily, he hurried over to where Morrigen was standing amidst a group of shamans on the Funeral Way watching the retreat of the Dobuni. 'We've beaten them!' he cried, too jubilant to note the concern on her brow.

'We've done nothing but take Henge, and that's ours anyway,' she answered crisply, pointing towards the battle. 'Look. Does Zarxus appear beaten? Ralla's still alive, so is Ortus. His men are sheltered by their shields.' The shields lifted as she spoke. There was a distant bark of command. A moment later the sky clouded with a volley of arrows that soared upwards, then dipped, straddling the Cunei as they gave chase.

'But if Ceruduc could get closer,' persisted Hyra.

'The bows would turn to spears and we'd lose men we can't spare. Zarxus knows what he's doing. By noon we'll be short of arrows and too weary to withstand an attack. It's the law of the hunter: first weaken, then turn for the kill.'

Hyra grew subdued as the logic of what Morrigen was saying finally soured his optimism. 'Shall I send a runner to tell Ceruduc to halt?' he asked.

'He'll ignore him.'

'I'll go myself.'

'Will he listen?'

Hyra shrugged, then shook his head.

'Forget Ceruduc. Halt the men and he'll be powerless. I'll try talking to them.'

The decision made, Morrigen removed her cloak and started running across the scrub. Crows rose from the corpses, black against blue, then settled again in her wake. The wounded begged for water or release from their pain as she vaulted their limbs. But despite their cries the battle seemed remote. The surrounding pasture rolled green and silent beneath a cloudless sky. Corn-buntings flitted overhead. The purple and gold flowers of the anemone sprinkled the turf. A hare loped parallel to her, ears folded back as if racing her, then veered sharply across her route to halt and rise up on its hind legs as the sound of the fighting grew louder. No more auspicious portent could have offered itself: to cross the path of a hare meant certain misfortune. Its moist timid eyes fixed on her for a moment, then it vanished. She snatched a shield from the ground and pushed past the men to where Ceruduc was trying to goad them into the attack.

'Let Zarxus go!' she pleaded, clutching his wrist. 'Can't you see what he's doing?'

'Leave me alone! We'll do as we please. We're men, not toothless old women who can't abide the sting of an arrow.'

'Listen to me for once! We'll attack later, when the men are rested and we know where Zarxus is going. It's madness to fight them now. You're squandering lives and risking defeat. A hare crossed my path.'

'Yours, not mine,' retorted Ceruduc, again shouting at the men.

Morrigen listened for a moment, then turned to the nearest shaman and cried, 'Sound the drums! Order the men to fall back!'

The shaman glanced anxiously at Ceruduc, then slipped into the crowd. A drum began beating. The men responded immediately. Exhausted after fighting continuously since daybreak and believing the order to have been given by Ceruduc, they turned and withdrew until out of range of the Dobuni. The distance between the two tribes increased. Ceruduc became hysterical, bellowing curses and shaking his axes. But his rage failed to persuade them. The reprieve was too welcome to be ended without reason. The men stood their ground, evading his anger by tending to the wounded. Suddenly he lowered his axes and spun round, striding grim-faced and alone towards Henge.

*

Later that morning, as the Cunei gathered on the Plain, Ceruduc commanded his tent to be raised and then sulked inside it. Morrigen entered it once, hoping for a reconciliation, only to find a goatskin empty on the grass and its owner as embittered as ever.

He ordered her to leave.

'Why?' she said, strangely hurt by his unwillingness to

forgive her. 'You've no reason to brood. We've proved that we can fight them. By tomorrow we'll have put them to flight.'

'But tomorrow you'll be their whore.'

She smiled. A light burnt in her eyes, a momentary flash of defiance. 'Not yours?'

Ceruduc's gaze lifted to hers. 'Mine now, theirs tomorrow.'

And so their quarrel was patched. But for once a sudden languor came over them as they lay together on the turf. The morning had drained them of the need to be turbulent. Ceruduc's arms felt leaden from wielding his axes, Morrigen was too tired for emotion. They made love slowly, finding in gentleness a pleasure so delicate that after it was over they did not move, but lay there, still welded, as if already aware that such moments were rare and worth treasuring.

Their own post-coital calm was echoed elsewhere. Outside the tent, the men idled in the warmth of the sun. Most went to sleep, content to let others decide their fate. Cooking fires were lit, cattle slaughtered to provide a hot meal when they woke. The livestock were rounded up, women and children reunited with their families. But despite the domesticity everyone knew that the dawn attack had proved indecisive. The Dobuni had been blooded but not beaten. Scouts had followed them, finally tracking them to an isolated hill-fort on the edge of the Plain. The rising had reached climax, and the knowledge that the final battle still lay ahead gave an edge to their mood. Spears were sharpened, stones gathered, fresh bundles of arrows distributed to the archers. In mid-afternoon the advance continued.

Once again the shamans led the procession as it moved northwards between windswept junipers and a stand of stunted oaks, oxen and livestock bringing up the rear. But unlike yesterday there was none of the celebration that had attended the return to Henge. Today they were leaving it again, and as the men glanced at their neighbours they were few who did not wonder which would return to it and which end the day on the racks. Yet Morrigen felt strangely dispassionate as she watched the temple recede. She had yet to sleep, and tiredness brings a lucidity and sparseness of emotion no fear can assuage. She knew that there could be no more retreats or failures made good. Her mind was alert and uncluttered, empty of anything not essential to outwitting the Dobuni.

Ceruduc did not share her singlemindedness. The renewal of

the advance had reminded him of her behaviour when pursuing Zarxus in the morning. He slouched sullen and disgruntled behind her.

Ceruduc's change of mood made Morrigen wary. Anger might make him impetuous or deaf to reason. She asked Cronus to try and mediate.

'Leave him be,' advised Cronus. 'It'll pass. He's like a hunting-dog, only content when snapping at heels.' He sighed, suddenly grey and older than his age. 'As for me, I've done enough fighting since the autumn to last me to the grave. I want peace, a day spent stalking a stag or sowing barley to the song of a lark.'

He was limping from his wound. Glancing at him, Morrigen noticed a great tiredness wash slowly across his face. She held out a hand. He took it, patted it, then lifted his head and smiled. And so boyish and eager was his smile that for a moment Morrigen thought he had come face to face with the vision he was searching for. Then his smile faded and she realized that it was not his hills he had seen, but the Dobuni encampment.

He released her hand. 'So much for the word of the scouts,' he whispered. 'They must have been blind to tell us it could be taken.'

Morrigen said nothing as she gazed up at it. She shivered, then turned to stare at Cronus as a sudden premonition passed through her thoughts, remembering him as he was now.

'Are you content?' sneered Ceruduc, drawing alongside her.

She looked up at it again. It lay ahead, massive and seemingly impregnable, a hill-fort crowning the summit of a long slope that fell away on three sides and was protected on the fourth by the forest. A high thorn palisade strengthened with daub-covered wattle surrounded its heart. Even from a distance she could see the warriors lined up behind it. All round her the men had fallen silent, awed by its size and the task that confronted them. She trembled again as Ceruduc invited her to speak.

'You brought us here. Now tell us how to take it.'

She lowered her head, unable to answer him.

He clapped in mock applause. 'Brilliant! We've a mute to lead us. I'll tell you what we do. You stand here at the bottom of the hill and we'll charge it. And by the time we've reached the palisade half of us will be dead. Those that survive . . .'

'Stop it!'

'Leave her in peace,' snapped Cronus, coming to her rescue. 'But for Morrigen you'd be dead already.'

'What's the difference? No one can enter that fort without an invitation from Zarxus. I'm telling you now, it can't be taken without a siege.'

'Then let's mount one,' said Cronus.

'And how long will it take for the men to lose patience? Who's going to sow the harvest and stop them sneaking home to their villages? How will we prevent Zarxus sending out hunting-parties into the forest, or even leaving if he chooses?'

'There'll be no siege,' said Morrigen quietly. 'We attack, and we do so tonight.'

*

'Do you think it'll work?'

'We've no other choice. Perhaps there never has been.'

'Fate then?'

'I suppose so. The Gods decide the omens for us on the day we're born. You can't defy them.' Hyra gazed out into the darkness as he answered Ceruduc. The moon had only just risen. Its light was pale, too faint to do more than sketch the shape of the fort. Then a torch flickered, giving it a human face: the hunched figures of the warriors moving quietly behind the palisade. 'Would it work if you were up there, expecting fire-arrows or a siege?'

'I don't know. I wish I did.'

'Would you be frightened?'

'Of course.'

'So would I.'

Ceruduc smiled. 'Only a woman could have thought of it. Men see obstacles as things they must confront. Women try and skirt them.' His voice changed tone. 'Are the shamans ready?'

'Yes.'

'And the cattle?'

'They're being herded now.'

'We'd better go.'

The two men rose and walked in silence through the darkness. Hyra sensed that even Ceruduc was apprehensive. His admission of fear, need for solitude, his absence from the line when all was ready: only nervousness explained them. Then he heard the drovers whipping the cattle into place and felt a sudden tightening in the belly.

Morrigen loomed out of the night. There was no decoration on her face, and though it was cold he noticed sweat standing out on her cheeks. Beneath her cloak she wore dark nettle-cloth robes and the boots and leggings she had made when alone with him in the hut. Memories stirred his affection. He smiled. She took his arm, threading the other through Ceruduc's. 'I'm coming with you,' she said. 'It was my idea. Let's at least die together if it fails.'

Hyra dropped back into the darkness, leaving them alone. Since pledging himself to Lyla he and Morrigen had purposely avoided any discussion of the past. But at moments such as this it was hard to remain silent, to pretend that he had exorcised her ghost. He began searching for Lyla, but as he did so he knew that even if he found her his thoughts would stay with Morrigen. Lyla had vanished, taking her place with the women. And then it was too late to continue his quest.

A torch flared, casting a dull yellowish light on the thick bundles of brushwood that had been tied round the horns of the cattle. More torches were lit, showing him the long line of men, six deep, stretched out in a half-circle round the base of the hill, weapons poised for the charge. He hurried to join them as the drovers moved quickly amongst the cattle, setting fire to the brushwood. The cattle bellowed their terror. Some dashed themselves against the wall of spears that held them in check. The spears were lowered, those holding them diving to one side when the drums began sounding. The cattle plunged forward, driven onward by fear and noise and the flaming fire-bands that brightened and licked at their faces as they gradually picked up speed.

They were a terrifying sight, even from the rear. Only the torches were visible, disembodied, tongued with flame, moving like fire-balls through the night. But Hyra knew that to the Dobuni, crouching bewildered and defenceless behind the palisade, they would seem like devils, cloven mythic monsters with flaming horns no weapon could halt.

He began running in their wake, stumbling over the turf tossed up by their hooves as on either side of him a wave of Cunei charged the slope, cheering and shouting to goad on the cattle. The distance shortened. The ramparts reared up above him. The first of the cattle crashed through the palisade, splintering the wattle and leaving flames to mark their passage where the tips of their horns had snagged on the thorn. Yet still they kept moving, trampling the sentries and the men spilling horror-struck from tents as they stampeded through the fort and vanished into the forest, singed heads flailing the trees in an attempt to douse the cause of their torment.

After such an event there should be a pause, thought Hyra, a slowing of time, a moment to assimilate what has taken place. But there could be no pause, for though the cattle had served their purpose the battle was not yet won. The Dobuni rallied, forming a ring in the centre of the fort as the Cunei stormed the palisade, shields lifted against the heat. Smoke confused, the blaze spreading quickly amongst the tents as the two tribes collided and the sound of combat rose above the crackle of the flames.

For Morrigen, standing surrounded by her escort in the smoke, the incidents that orchestrated the battle unfolded as they had done in the morning. But with the knowledge of all she had achieved to cushion her, the screams of the wounded and fallen gave a perspective to what she saw that sketched a more human canvas. The pained, almost quizzical expression that would cross the faces of the dying as they fell. The wounded clawing at the ground in their pain, then just turning and staring up at the sky, waiting for release, for peace, the will to live finally drained. The hesitation, and then the hardening into resolve, that made even the veterans hesitate before killing an opponent once he was disarmed and helpless. Suddenly Cronus appeared at her side, returning her to the smoke and the turmoil and the blood-loud present.

'We're gaining ground!' he bellowed, pointing to where Ralla stood behind Zarxus amongst the seers, her robes torn, wide-eyed with fear. 'I'm going after her before she escapes into the forest.'

'Forget her!'

'I'll do so when she's dead, but not until.' Cronus turned and began fighting his way towards the centre of the fort. Hyra tried to follow him. Ralla must have seen him and guessed his goal, for she knelt and tried to hide beneath her cloak. But the Dobuni were massed round her and Cronus had to pause and call for assistance before plunging forward again. In his mind he saw only his wife, Kirsten and Rhionan being tossed lifeless at his feet. No logic could have halted him. Suddenly he was outnumbered and alone. Lifting his axe overhead, he charged forward, his own momentum carrying him to within feet of Ralla when the first spear punctured his lungs. Hyra shouted a warning. But it was too late. A second spear followed the first and Hyra froze as his father toppled back to vanish beneath the feet of the Dobuni.

But Cronus's death marked the turning-point. Surrounded on all sides, the ring of Dobuni grew steadily thinner. Suddenly all but a few threw down their weapons and tried to flee through a hole in the palisade. Most were halted in mid-flight and the survivors were greeted by knives and clubs when they emerged. Even Ralla's reprieve proved brief. Smoke billowing through the fort, the battle lost and the dead heaped round her, she eventually surfaced from beneath her cloak to see Ceruduc standing above her.

'Look!' he ordered.

She did so, then fell whimpering to the mud as he held up Zarxus's head, hair clenched in his fist. No mercy was shown her. Her head joined Zarxus's on the shaman's spikes, to be borne aloft as the triumphant Cunei swarmed through the encampment, ruthlessly cutting down the few Dobuni still standing.

Hyra did not hear them. Too stunned to know shock or grief, he lay sprawled across his father, silently weeping into the black of his beard. It was there that Lyla found him when news of the victory reached the Cunei camp. Unable to comfort him, she helped him lift Cronus's corpse and the two of them carried it away with them – as those round them were carrying away the spoils they had found amongst the carnage.

*

At some point in the night Morrigen and Ceruduc walked alone down the hill and made their way towards Ceruduc's tent. The shamans were dancing in celebration. Moonlight shaped the smoke still rising from the fort. Many of its occupants had been women, and above the shamans chant they could hear the survivors' screams as the pleasures of rape replaced the search for spoils.

The memory of Cronus's death still lingered in Ceruduc's thoughts, marring his joy at the victory. 'We must bury him inside Henge,' he said.

Morrigen nodded absent-mindedly, too exhausted to plan

the future. In her thoughts she was still living the past: blood and fire, cattle with horns ablaze rampaging through the night . . . A dog, its muzzle pressed against her for warmth. She halted. Fatigue must have made her light-headed, prone to hallucination. She shook her head.

'What's wrong?'

'I don't know.' She walked on. One step, two . . . Snow on the ground and dogs scuffling through a midden. The past had distorted. Or was she dreaming as she walked? And then she remembered and her whole body felt seized as if by paralysis. On the night before fleeing Henge with Hyra in the snow, a dog had entered her tent, curling up beside her. As she slept she had dreamt of cattle whose horns were on fire, men falling like corn to the sickle . . .

She stumbled, a sudden incredulity making her stare up at the moon, the Goddess she served. She started laughing, delirious with joy. Serapha *had* spoken to her. Her dream had come true. The portents had been revealed to her and what had happened once would happen again and again until all revelation was hers and she was a Goddess herself . . .

Ceruduc asked her why she was laughing.

But she could not stop to tell him and so ran forward into the darkness, hair flowing behind her and the tears wet on her cheeks.

# CHAPTER XIV

'Who did this?' demanded Hyra angrily, an arm compassing all that was left of the Sacred Dwellings. 'You or Morrigen must order the looting to stop. We're meant to be grown men, not beasts or birds of prey.'

Ceruduc gave a resigned shrug as he surveyed the destruction and the abandoned corpses, the smouldering heaps of charred timber that were all that remained of the dwellings. 'Winning the battle won't end the hate. Let them do as they please for a while. Two days ago the Dobuni were still our masters. Revenge may be brutal, but it won't last for ever. A few days from now they'll be tired of pillaging. Even rape loses its lustre. The harvest has still to be planted. They'll go home soon enough.'

'Leaving us to rebuild what they've destroyed, what my father died for?' retorted Hyra, pointing to a line of blackened corpses hanging by their feet over the ashes of a fire. 'Is that what you fought for?' He turned, ordering one of the men sifting through the rubble for plunder to cut them down.

'We'd have had to raze the huts,' said Ceruduc. 'The shamans would have insisted. The Dwellings are theirs as well as yours.'

'Has Henge been harmed?'

'No.'

'The burial tombs?'

'A few, but only for trinkets.'

Hyra shook his head in despair, his anger at the burning of the Dwellings and the slaughter that had followed its occupation remaining visible on his face as he and Ceruduc walked on through the ruins. No building was standing. The timber temple to Bala had been set alight and only the stumps of the posts now protruded from the ground. Kites and ravens flapped through the smoke, too gorged to fly. The stench of decomposing flesh hung pungent and thick in the air. And once he had lived here and tracked the moon's cycle from the ramparts. Was he to stay and become Lord of the Rites as

Morrigen had asked him to do, fashion a new world from the rubble of the old, or go home to the hills?'

'What happens next?' he said, hoping for guidance.

'The Maiden Lines are to go, Morrigen insists. The priestesses are to be re-formed to worship Serapha, the same with the seers.'

Hyra smiled. 'I thought you wanted to sweep away anything that bore the taint of Dobuni?'

'Change too much and we risk angering the Gods.'

And suddenly it came to Hyra that despite Ceruduc's physical courage he was mentally timid, wary of doing anything that might offend Serapha. Even Morrigen, champion of change, had said nothing of amending the Rites. Everything was to go on as before, only the names and faces and God they praised would be different. 'It's always our beliefs that seem to hold us back,' he said.

'What do you mean?' said Ceruduc, uneasy in such shifting terrain.

Hyra snatched at an example. 'Look at our buildings, they're all circles; temples, tents, huts, even the sheep pens.'

'And so are our Gods, the moon and the sun. Any other shape might be mistaken for blasphemy.'

Hyra said nothing; the point had been proved. He remembered Atius once telling him that his dislike of all religions was based on their insistence on remaining stationary. 'They call it continuity,' he had argued. 'But it's really fear, the wish to cling to their powers. Only trade inspires change.'

Hyra smiled. Such scepticism was tempting, especially today. He glanced at Ceruduc. 'What about Atius?'

'The courier left yesterday.'

'He won't come. Bala, Serapha – all Gods are the same to Atius.'

'It's you that matters most. We need you here, both of us. We can't set up a Council and keep the peace between the shamans and chieftains by ourselves.'

Hyra sighed. 'I still haven't decided. It depends on Lyla,' he added, again trying to delay a decision.

'At least the Lord of the Rites can marry. Why shouldn't a High Priestess? It's all so stupid. There can't be a travelling pedlar who hasn't guessed that we share the same bed.'

'Laws can be changed. The shamans will do as she asks.'

'I'm not certain that she wants them changed.'

A bitterness had entered Ceruduc's voice that made Hyra study him for a moment. The gaunt, cadaverous face of the days leading up to the battle had gone, to be replaced by a pensive, slightly disillusioned expression that had rarely left him since the full extent of the adulation that now greeted Morrigen first became apparent.

Hearing further evidence of that adulation, he glanced to where the Cunei encampment sprawled untidily on the slope beyond the Dwellings. All day elders had been arriving from villages that had not joined the rising to offer her homage, each bringing with them a white milking-cow as a gift. One had broken loose and was now lowing piteously, its tether snarled round its hooves.

'She's never known such power,' said Ceruduc. 'Suddenly she's High Priestess, the most revered woman in the land. Three days ago she was still a fugitive. Now she's sitting in her tent giving an audience to the emissaries from the Juba and Tan. Marriage to me would mean turning her back on wealth, power, the worship of the people – everything she's always wanted.'

'Let the dust settle. She needs time. The two of you have been fighting the Dobuni since the day you met. The war's over. The peace will change her. Even praise sounds like flattery after a while.'

But Ceruduc was too troubled and in need of a confessor to heed Hyra's advice. 'Last night she made me leave her tent,' he said. 'Before going to sleep I swore I'd leave her, go back to the marshes and choose a wife. But this morning she embraced me as if we'd been together all night. I was angry. She started weeping, made me promise to stay.'

'Here she comes,' said Hyra.

Both men watched in silence as she left her tent and began walking towards the entrance to the Dwellings, flanked by the retinue of handmaidens that now ministered to her needs. The tribesfolk cheered as she passed their tents, some darting forward to scatter branches of hazel in front of her as she walked.

Hyra turned away, irritated and disapproving. There was something gaudy and unnecessary about the pomp that accompanied her whenever she emerged from her tent. It seemed contrived and actively encouraged, a denial of the motives that had inspired the rising. Suddenly he noticed a staff lying amidst the rubble. It had snapped, but the two halves lay side by side. Tally notches had been cut into it and the foot was worn, as if it had been used to support weight as well as record. Perhaps already aware in his subconscious of what it was so soon to reveal, he idly stared at it for a long time before picking it up: a distraction, two sticks to slap casually against his thigh.

By the time he had retrieved it Morrigen had abandoned her retinue and entered the Dwellings. She grinned happily, a quick skip bringing her closer to Hyra. 'I've promised the Tan that you'll take office as Lord of the Rites,' she said.

'But I haven't discussed it with Lyla yet!' he protested.

She pouted, sulking. 'She'll agree, you know it. I won't let you desert us. Anyway it's the first pronouncement I've made. The Tan will think that I can't be trusted if I go back on my word.'

'You should have waited.'

'I'm waiting now . . .'

Hyra stared round at the scorched ribs of the huts, as if answers were broken staffs and could be found amongst rubble. He had fought for peace and was being offered ceremony, a life of public worship and private doubts. Morrigen was smiling at him and her face wore a frailty and innocence that was hard to resist. His answer changed, then switched again. Finally he said, 'Yes, I'll stay.'

Morrigen clapped, kissing him. Ceruduc embraced him. But their gratitude did little to buoy his spirits. He looked down at the two halves of the staff, intending to drop them. Then he noticed that Morrigen's gaze had shifted to his hands. Her face paled, the grin fading. He lifted the staff, again glancing at the tally marks. Suddenly he recognized them and knew who had cut them.

'It's Leoid's!

Morrigen gave a brittle, nervous laugh. 'Is it?' she said carelessly. 'How strange to find it here.'

Even then he might never have discovered the truth if Ceruduc, feigning interest to ease the tension, hadn't asked him to explain the meaning of the marks.

'I don't know,' he replied. 'Last time I tried to read them they meant nothing at all.'

'Try.'

'Throw them away. They're worthless, fit only for kindling,' insisted Morrigen.

But instead of discarding them Hyra humoured Ceruduc and began examining the marks. For a moment they remained a mystery, as much a riddle as when he last had studied them. Suddenly they focussed into a single unity, cross-checking, documenting, each clue linking to the next. The blinkers fell from his eyes and he felt as if suddenly given sight, so clear and defined was their meaning. He turned to Morrigen, still refusing to believe. She backed away, arms outstretched as if torn between fleeing or wrenching the evidence from his grasp. For a moment he thought he might have made a mistake. Then he saw the sudden chill in her eyes: and knew the truth.

'Leoid had foreseen the Darkness,' he whispered. 'These marks predict it. Yet he died before telling anyone.'

'What are you talking about?' demanded Ceruduc.

But Morrigen knew, and so did Hyra. Their eyes locked, ignoring the interruption. There was silence, no one moved. Then Hyra swung his arm and struck Morrigen's cheek with the broken staff. She cried out, then turned away and hid her face in her hands.

'You murdered him, didn't you?' said Hyra. 'How I don't know. Everything you told me when he was lying on the racks and I came to comfort you was a lie, all lies.'

He raised the staff, intending to strike her again. But suddenly his rage turned to horror at what she had done and he let it slide from his fingers. Yet he went on talking, remorselessly piling fact on fact until no deception could save her. He reminded her of the dream she had invented, the night of the Darkness, Ishtar's death; all the lies and half-truths she had told in order to save herself from detection.

There was a second silence when he finished. Then Morrigen lifted her head.

'You've forgotten something,' she said quietly. 'Leoid was a Dobuni. Even if he had lived he'd now be dead. The shamans wouldn't have spared him.' She paused, nodding slightly. 'Yes, you're right. The dream was a lie. But does it matter? Without it there'd have been no rising, no battle or victory. I'd be married to Zarxus, you'd be a seer, Ceruduc a corpse. Is that what you wanted?'

Hyra stared at her in amazement. He had taken too long. In his eagerness to confront her with every detail of the truth he had supplied time to invent answers, justification, reasons for what she had done. Again he tried to provoke her into an admission of guilt. 'You deliberately murdered Leoid. You can't excuse yourself. We weren't at war. He was harmless, an old man, the one friend I had.'

'I couldn't stop myself. Ever since reaching Abury I had wanted power, to end being treated as an outcast. But because Ishtar was afraid of me, I was to be married and banished from Henge.'

'And does that justify murder?'

'Oh, to you it's all so simple, isn't it, Hyra? Lines which can't be stepped over. The Gods may have made us, all of us, but when they made me they cursed me as well. There are things inside me I'm unable to fight. Sometimes they cause good, at others they make me sin. If people are hurt or have to be killed, it does not matter to me. What I want I must have. At first I thought the Gods would punish me. But they've spared me and given me what I wanted. Are they also at fault?'

She spoke very slowly, often pausing to deliberate the choice of a word. Hyra backed away, appalled by her lack of emotion. He now realized that after four years of friendship and thinking he knew her she was as much a stranger to him as on the day they first met.

'So now I'm a disease you're frightened of catching?' continued Morrigen. 'Perhaps that's right? I am diseased, but sicknesses such as mine have their home in the mind. If I am evil, I cannot rid myself of it. If I do wrong, I'm unable to guard against it. You tell me I'm ruthless. But how can you judge what you don't understand? I need your help, Hyra, not your hate.'

Hyra refused to give way. 'After the first lie all others are simple.'

'It's the truth.' And then Morrigen did speak the truth, eyes bright and wide as a child's with the longing to be believed. 'I dreamt about the battle. I promise. I saw the cattle, the torches tied to their horns. Serapha revealed it to me as I slept. You must believe me!' The words were pitched higher and her fingers were plucking at Hyra's cloak.

He shook himself free. 'You're lying.'

She swung towards Ceruduc. 'I did. I promise you. Serapha spoke to me.' It was suddenly very important to her and she kept on repeating herself.

Ceruduc had so far said nothing, content to observe her. At first he had tried to pardon her. Love pulled one way, then the weight of evidence against her corrected the balance. As doubt faded he deliberated walking away, cutting her from his life as a healer might a sore. But he couldn't. He felt as if bound to her by knots no knife could part. His arms opened, offering her refuge.

'Leoid's dead,' he said. 'We can't resurrect him. What Morrigen did belongs to the past.'

'Listen to me, Ceruduc . . . !' Hyra stopped. The protectiveness on Ceruduc's face denied further argument. There was no point in warning him that what she had done once she might one day repeat. If nothing else he had salvaged one truth from the lies: he was finally absolved of her, and could return to his father's hills and leave others to rebuild the Dwellings.

*

Later that day, leading an ox, Hyra and Lyla left the encampment with Cronus's corpse strapped to a pole-sledge. Morrigen and Ceruduc stood side by side on the ramparts and watched them grow smaller.

'Have you forgiven me?' said Morrigen.

Ceruduc nodded, drawing her closer.

'It'll never happen again. There's no need for it now, not with you beside me.' Morrigen trembled: another lie told and Hyra gone, leaving no one to act as her conscience and curb the evil in her. Still trembling, she tilted her lips to Ceruduc's, sealing the past with a kiss.

# BOOK II

# HIGH PRIESTESS

# CHAPTER XV

The formalities were over. Gifts of a ewe and barley had been distributed to the head of each household. A set of antlers framed the summit of the Goddess post. Dogs snarled and showed their fangs as they were muzzled and roped. Nets were furled, the women hoisting them on to their shoulders and setting out in single file for the woods, thick scollops of mesh dangling between them. Children raced excitedly through the village and the men made ready to start. Only Hyra seemed unwilling to exchange the warmth of the Harvest Hunt fire for the crisp autumnal air sweeping down out of the hills. He appeared preoccupied and withdrawn, and merely nodded absent-mindedly when his steward reminded him that the herd had been sighted near the ridge above the village.

The men watched him impatiently, feet stamping against the cold. They began complaining, forcing his steward to jerk a callused hand at the cloaked stranger on the far side of the fire. 'Blame the courier,' Tarxien said. 'That's the fifth she's sent since the Midsummer Rites. You'd have thought that after four years apart she'd have learnt to fend for herself. Not a bit of it. Ceruduc may share her bed, but it's Hyra she turns to for advice.'

Tarxien was rarely so outspoken, or so coarse, but he was worried, and if he suffered from one fault as a steward it was an over-protectiveness towards his master that at times verged on still treating him like a boy. He was a burly man, with a shambling gait and rounded features that the cruel might have mocked as proving him a simpleton. But the face concealed common sense and a measure of shrewdness. Few of the villagers were aware of the rift between their master and mistress, even less had realized that Morrigen might be its cause.

'Look at him,' said one of them, pointing at Hyra. 'A tempest would budge him. Why did he have to choose today to start fretting about the waif? No stag'll wait for us. If I was he I'd send the courier packing.'

'It's Morrigen he's brooding on,' added another. Five couriers in half as many months. Present of oxen and bear-skins. They may not have met since the Dobuni were beaten, but she wants him back. No wonder Lyla had the skins thrown on the dung pile.'

His companion chuckled. 'Old Elmek the pedlar told me that that brother of hers has so taken to the mead you could put to sea in his belly.'

'It's Morrigen that's done it to him. No one can tame her. She's half Goddess, half she-devil. There's not a woman to match her. If I was Hyra I'd leave that shrew of a wife of his and do as she asks, return to Henge.'

'That's enough of this chatter!' growled Tarxien. 'You've a hunt to prepare for, not a day to waste gossiping.'

But if loyalty could silence the men, it could not disguise his concern when he saw Hyra rise from the fire and push his way through the crowd towards the large thatched hut in the centre of the village – and Lyla, standing scowling in its entrance. More trouble, he thought, before bellowing at the men.

'Well? Have you decided?' said Lyla, as her husband approached.

'Not yet.' Hyra shrugged, evading her gaze. In recent months he had come to dread confrontation, the sudden petulance that greeted any reference to Morrigen, however oblique.

'Is that all you can say?'

'Please, Lyla. Can't it wait until after the Hunt?'

A gesture can accuse as easily as words. So when Lyla ruffled the hair of the small boy at her side Hyra was in no doubt as to her meaning.

Cronus was only three years old, but in temperament as well as name he was already a miniature of his grandfather. Hyra smiled affectionately at him, then scooped him into his arms.

'You may hold him now,' said Lyla quietly. 'But I'm warning you, you'll never do so again if you leave us. He'll grow up a stranger to his own father. So will Kirsten and the babe I've yet to bear.' She paused and pressed a worn hand to the swollen hump of her belly.

Hyra turned away, to see Tarxien observing him. 'This is folly. The men are watching us. If we must fight, let's at least do so alone.'

'I don't care.'

Hyra sighed, thrown off balance by her bluntness. 'You can't use the children as a weapon to keep me here.'

'Stop me.'

'It won't work. They're mine as well as yours. It's they who'd suffer if we stayed together for their sake alone. Children can't patch up a marriage.'

'But Morrigen can break one.'

Lyla's stare was so stern and so direct Hyra could evade it no longer. They gazed at each other for a moment, the men and their son forgotten.

'Can't we begin again?' said Lyla. 'For three years we were happy. Why dismiss them and pretend they didn't happen?'

'And what of the fourth? Month after month we've done nothing but bicker.'

'Have you ever asked yourself why?'

Hyra did not reply as he tried to remember those years and see in her face some token of the youthful attractive woman who had accompanied him back to the hills with his father's corpse. But her attractions had vanished, blunted by the effects of child-bearing and the imprint of middle-age; the care-worn face and pendulous breasts still heavy with milk, the greying hair held primly in place by a bone. The ageing was inevitable, he accepted that, and his affection for her would not have dimmed if her light-heartedness had not deserted her as well. But time had soured her and traded humour for gravity. She had grown dour and critical. Her possessiveness had become obsessive. Perhaps he was being uncharitable? The death of their first child after a troublesome pregnancy, her concern for Ceruduc and resentment at Morrigen's sudden interference in their lives had all affected her. But somehow he felt that none of them justified her behaviour over the past year; her ability to find fault with everything he did, the constant nagging that could only be silenced by inventing excuses to keep them apart.

He lowered his son to the ground. 'I must go. The men are growing impatient.'

But Lyla refused to be dismissed. The courier's arrival had stirred up too much dust for it to be laid so easily. 'Let them wait for once. Morrigen wants you to return to the Dwellings. Are you going or not?'

'I don't know yet.'

Lyla gave a bleak smile. 'You'll go. What Morrigen wants,

she gets. You'd think she was a bitch on heat the way you and Ceruduc gather round her whenever she calls.'

'I haven't spoken to her for four years.'

'That hasn't stopped you thinking about her.'

'Don't let's argue,' said Hyra, struggling to stay calm. 'The Harvest Hunt is meant to be a day of feasting and celebration, not bickering.'

Lyla's smile became a shrill laugh. 'So what do you want me to do? Celebrate the death of our marriage? It's Morrigen who makes us argue. She's destroying us.'

'She means nothing to me any more.'

'You're lying, Hyra. Only you're too much a coward to admit it. You'd like to think you've forgotten her, but now that she's given you an excuse to leave us you can't fool even yourself.'

'And if I take it it'll be you who's to blame.'

Tears brimmed in Lyla's eyes. But they were the result of frustration rather than anger. It was all so obvious to her; and she was helpless. Her voice had risen as she spoke, attracting the attention of the men. Suddenly she gathered up Cronus and vanished into the hut, leaving Hyra alone in the entrance. He debated following her. But in his mind he could view what would follow too clearly to have faith in it. She would weep, he would apologize for wrongs he had not committed. Reconciliation would end in an act of love that would cause her pain and leave him ashamed. But their quarrel had ruined his pleasure at the prospect of the hunt. He angrily shook his head, then turned and barked instructions at Tarxien.

The hunt began, the villagers falling silent as they fanned out across the slope and began climbing the scree behind the village. The climb was steep, but Hyra welcomed the exertion. The chill air and a day spent stalking might clear his head, help him reach a decision. A brook tumbled amongst the stones. The deep blue of the bilberries punctuated the purple of heather. He reached the foot of the ridge and began crawling towards its crest, accompanied by one of his huntsmen. And gradually the chase succeeded in lending clarity to his thoughts. On any other day the need for stealth and concentration might have eluded him. But the Harvest Hunt was the most important of the year; an occasion when all those who owed him allegiance took part in a ritual that was part celebration and part thanksgiving.

He lifted his head above the skyline, carefully scanning the open moorland ahead. A herd of red deer stood browsing the heather. A grizzled matronal hind stood guard to windward. The stags were all with their hinds, long branched antlers brushing the turf as they grazed. He pointed to one of them.

The huntsman nodded. 'A good choice. Its coat's in poor colour. It'll be out of condition after the rut and should weaken quickly if the dogs keep close to it.'

Hyra smiled. His companion was taciturn and begrudging of praise. The choice of stag proved that the last four years had not been wasted. He too had mastered the blend of skill and instinct that can make the difference between success and returning home empty-handed. As a seer, the rutting of the deer, the partition of the herd into stags and pregnant hinds during the winter, the birth of the calves in early summer, had all been part of a seasonal ritual intended to influence the Gods and bring success to the hunter. It was an act of worship, not something that acknowledged the quarry's courage and the weight that stiffens muscles after a day spent running in its wake. Again he posed the question: was he to return to that world, as Morrigen had asked, or remain with Lyla and accept a failed marriage as the price of his liberty?

The advance continued, only the dogs and their handlers staying hidden below the ridge. Many of the villagers were naked. Some had marked their faces with chalk as proof that they would not rest from the chase until the stag lay dead. Hyra studied it for signs of weakness; a limp or old wound he could exploit. Its summer coat was beginning to thicken. Its antler points shone white after fighting off rivals for its hinds at the height of the rut. The herd grazed peacefully. Some lay on their haunches, replete, oblivious of danger. Once the old hind flicked her ears and began circling, the first sign of concern.

Her restlessness increased as the villagers drew closer. Suddenly she turned towards the ridge and gave a short nasal bark; the wind had eddied, carrying the taint of danger to her nostrils. Hyra rose and began running towards the stag. The herd remained frozen for a moment, then scattered as the villagers hurried forward across the heather, yelling and waving their spears. Panic turned to flight. The deer gathered speed, long bounding legs lifting them clear of the scrub.

Hyra halted and lifted his bow: another skill the years had

perfected. He drew back the string until it was level with his shoulder. The bow slowly bent, the yew heartwood on the inner face compressing as the elastic sapwood on the back stretched outward to take the strain in the curve. He took in air, holding it in his lungs until his body felt balanced against the spring in the bow. As the stag sped past him, he released the string. The arrow caught the wall of its neck and remained there, hanging slightly. Suddenly it swerved in mid-stride and hurried along the crest of the ridge. The dogs were unmuzzled and let slip. Yapping as they went, noses low to pick up scent, they ran as a pack before spreading out and following the stag when it vaulted the ridge. Hyra shouldered his bow and began sprinting in pursuit.

'Slow the pace!' cried the huntsman.

Hyra obeyed, then watched enviously as his companion swept downhill, agile and graceful, sturdy legs barely touching the ground between strides. The task was simple. The stag had been blooded and separated from the herd. It was now a matter of keeping it in sight until it started to tire and could be driven towards the woods. But success might still elude them. Two years earlier the chase had continued without pause for nearly three days. The deer might outrun them or take refuge in the bed of another and set a fresh stag in its place. Once cornered it could maim or cripple with one blow of its antlers.

The stag had heard its pursuers and veered. It was now running parallel to the slope, head raised, hooves pounding the turf. Dust rose round it when it suddenly turned and began climbing the scree, dislodging stones and slowing the pace of the dogs. But Hyra had anticipated the change of direction, positioning men to turn it back. The dogs drew closer. The fastest snapped at its heels, then it lengthened stride, quickly shaking them off as it careered downhill, scattering sheep as it went.

Hyra followed with the men. The running became easier. The thump of heart against chest gradually lessened as his legs found their rhythm. Only once did Morrigen and Lyla distract him, and that was when he glimpsed the scarlet wind-torn pennons on the summit of his father's tomb. It sat overlooking the village, the hills he had loved; and seeing it, and remembering the intimacy shared by his parents during the long years of their marriage, Hyra felt a sudden disappointment at the deceptions Lyla had forced on him. Their own marriage was a fraud, nonsense he should never have permitted. As chieftain he could annul it or take other wives, but both choices seemed a compromise, an evasion not a solution.

Noon came. The sun vanished. The first shadows flexed in the foothills. The stag took sanctuary in a copse and only when its tracks had been traced could the chase continue. By late-afternoon it had led the villagers to the far end of the valley. It now stood motionless, head lowered as it gathered breath.

Hyra approached it. Its bewildered eyes and almost human expression awoke his sympathy, some vague echo of his own predicament. 'I misjudged it,' he said. 'It's as fleet now as it was on the moor.'

The huntsman disagreed. 'We've winded it. It'll be ours by dusk.'

'Why doesn't it move?'

'It will.' The stag broke into a trot. 'It'll make for the stream,' added the huntsman as it doubled back and turned towards the base of the valley. 'It's beginning to weaken. Water's the one place where it can stand and fight.'

But the stream was too narrow. The stag hurried on, dragging a foreleg. Blood and mud splashed its coat. Occasionally it shook its antlers and bellowed as it ran. The villagers closed the gap, driving it nearer to the woods. Believing itself finally safe, it gathered the last of its strength into a gallop, then gave a defiant bark before crashing into the undergrowth: where the women stood waiting in the gloom, armed with rocks and cudgels.

The end was swift.

One moment it stood at bay, antlers rising from bramble, legs entangled in the nets that had been slung between the trees to impede its escape. When Hyra next looked it had been brought to its knees by the stones. He turned away. The women engulfed it, their cudgels lifting and falling.

And as the stag died, Hyra made his decision. Morrigen's image inexplicably rose up to haunt him as it fell. He shuddered, appalled that his thoughts could still conjure her portrait after the years apart and all she had done when they were together. But the past now lingered inside him like the fading memories of an oppressive dream. The present was Lyla; always pregnant, her voice shrill and querulous as she heaved herself around the hut on veined, thickening legs.

Hyra knew that he might never attend the Harvest Hunt

again. Regret became a sense of loss as he joined the women. Again he blamed Lyla. He grew angry, for once slitting the stag's throat without feeling pity or passing squeamishness. He ordered its antlers to be cut out and given to the village shaman, then thanked it for the food, tools and clothing its carcass would provide. The villagers skinned and butchered it. Its heart was buried, returned to Serapha as a spirit-offering to be resurrected if famine culled the herds; its entrails were thrown to the dogs.

Hyra's mood remained unchanged as they began the return journey to the village. The hunt had become a symbol of the pleasures he was forsaking: the camaraderie of the men, the rewards of being their chieftain, the love of farming and the hills he had inherited from his father. He looked round, determined to remember them as they were now, their tops washed by cloud. He was being sentimental, and knew it. Tarxien would have to be told. The confrontation with Lyla would at best be unpleasant, the parting from the children even worse.

The men began singing a hunting song as he entered the village at their head. The old and infirm stood propped in doorways and nodded their approval as the stag's carcass was carried past towards the cooking fire. Its flames lit faces he would soon forget; the children clinging to their mothers, Kosta the old wet-nurse whose breasts had nourished nearly half the village. But even Kosta's welcome could not sway him. He walked towards his hut, mentally preparing himself for the conflict ahead before ducking beneath its entrance.

It was hot and airless inside. Smoke masked the light from the tallows. Kirsten was crying in her cradle. Lyla sat sewing by the fire. Hyra removed his cloak and stepped on to the bracken, unwilling to end the silence. Lyla tilted her face and he could see that she had been crying. For a moment both tried to behave as if nothing had happened.

'Where's Cronus?'

'Playing outside.' Lyla paused. 'Did the hunt go well?'

'Yes. You should have watched. It would have done you good. You could have seen us from behind the hut.'

'I wasn't in the mood. Perhaps next year.'

'Of course.'

'I only enjoy it when I can run with the men. Yes . . . next year I'll join you.'

Hyra hesitated. Then, 'There won't be a next year, not for me. I've decided to go back to Henge with the courier.'

Silence. Lyla's sewing needle fell from her fingers and swung unchecked from the thread.

'Nothing need change. You can hold the land until Cronus is old enough to be sworn in as chieftain. The livestock are yours, so are the oxen and the rights of pasture on the summer grazing grounds.' In listing practicalities, Hyra discovered that emotions could be repressed. They also suggested that even in his absence life would continue as before. 'The thatching straw has been cut but needs pegging. Most of the forage has been gathered. We've ring-barked the trees in the middle wood. The granary pits are full and you should have ample food for the winter. Tarxien will know what to do.'

Lyla retrieved her needle and placed it neatly beside her. A fragment of wool was plucked from a sleeve, the smoke fended from her face. Then such mannerisms could no longer assist her. Her head slumped. 'Tarxien will know what to do.' She was barely whispering.

'Yes.'

'And if I choose to go with you? You forget, I'm your wife. You can't discard me at will or just walk out and abandon me because it suits you.' Lyla paused. 'Have you spoken to Artus?'

'No. He'd gossip.'

'He's the village shaman. You can't leave without examining the portents.'

'They don't matter. Nothing you can say or Artus can foresee will make me go back on my word.'

'Don't touch me!' Hyra had brushed Lyla's shoulder.

'Please, there's no need to fight.'

Lyla's voice lifted. 'Of course! That's what you'd like! The complaisant wife who does as her master bids. Oh, you can go. But before you do let's at least speak the truth and not hide it behind meaningless chatter about the forage and corn. You're going because of Morrigen. Admit it.'

'I'm going because you and I are unhappy together, because we'd be best apart.'

'That's a lie. You're trying to justify yourself by blaming me. I don't matter, nor does Ceruduc. It's only Morrigen, Morrigen, Morrigen. Go back to her. One day you'll find a way to excuse her for murdering Leoid. After that it'll be easy. You'll wait until Ceruduc is too drunk to know what he's doing, then try and make love to her again. I hope she laughs at you. I'd laugh myself if it wasn't so pathetic . . .'

'Stop it!'

'No! I haven't finished yet. You're a weak man, Hyra. The first courier that came should have had his tongue cut out and been sent back to her a mute. She'd have understood that. It would have proved that you meant what you'd said; that you'd forgotten her, despised her, didn't care whether she lived or died. But instead you welcomed him in and did as she asked. From that moment on you were hers, not mine; someone she could pick up and put down whenever she chose to. But you didn't notice, or didn't want to. Morrigen still relied on you for advice, that was all that mattered. And vanity made you believe that you could have us both, share us. You can't and you never could. You've lost me, Hyra. But I've your son and your daughter and you've only Morrigen, and one day you'll realize that by going back to her you lost her as well . . .'

There was no more to be said. Lyla had grown too distraught to add to it – and was too sure of herself to contemplate subtraction.

But her outburst had left Hyra increasingly uncertain of his motives for leaving her. For a moment he even wished that the years could be turned back and their quarrels forgotten. But it was impossible. Lyla began weeping. Kirsten had climbed from her cradle and was crawling towards him through the bracken, inspecting it as she went. He bent to meet her. Her plump pink fingers reached up and tugged at his beard. She giggled. Then the reality caught up with him. He wouldn't applaud her first steps or again tuck in her bedding as she slept. He rose, gently returning her to her cradle before hurrying blindly from the hut.

For a while he stood in the entrance, numb with grief. Night had fallen and the dancing had begun, but above its din and the beat of the drums he could hear Lyla crying as she tried to calm Kirsten. Cronus joined him. Normally he would have been asleep by now; the thumb wedged firmly in the corner of his mouth was an attempt to prevent himself yawning. He grinned happily at his father, his young face sparkling in the fire-light. Hyra stared at him for a moment, then turned away, tainted by self-hate. He tried to follow the dancing. The men were stamping as they circled the fire. The women swirled. Artus had donned the dead stag's antlers and its charred carcass had blistered and split open in the heat. A curved moon lay over one of the hills, reminding him of a jewel on a woman's breast; pale skin, a snow bound hut . . . He trembled, shaking his head as Tarxien approached out of the smoke.

'We've kept a place for Lyla by the fire.'

'She's not well.'

'Perhaps Artus . . . ?'

'No, it'll pass.' Hyra's gaze shifted as he read the question on his steward's face. 'I'm needed at Henge. I'll be leaving in the morning.'

Tarxien digested this with ox-like slowness. 'How long will you be gone?'

'I don't know.'

It was much less than the truth, but Tarxien seemed to grasp what he was trying to say. He nodded wisely, scrutinizing his master, then vanished, returning with a goatskin of tassine which he thrust into his hands. Its sweetness cloyed. But it burnt his throat and dulled his grief, so Hyra sipped it until it was empty and the motions of the dancers appeared sinuous and fluid. The fire glowed on their bodies. Some of the women had abandoned their robes and were swaying from side to side, carelessly, languidly, fingers clicking the rhythm. Amongst the unmarried was a young woman with raven-black hair and a pert open face. She returned his smile, then held out a hand and plucked him from the crowd. The villagers laughed at her audacity and closed the circle, urging them on. The drumming quickened. There was sweat on her body and when he touched it it felt warm and moist. Again they touched. Again he sensed a sudden intoxication in himself, an agreeable and unlikely recklessness. He glanced round. His hut lay in shadow and there was no sign of Lyla. He stood in silence with her after they had danced and tried to remember her name and whose daughter she was.

She grinned, gripping his wrist. 'Come.'

The noise receded as they walked. Hyra tried to halt. It was thought an honour amongst the unwed to lose one's maidenhood to their chieftain, something to be boasted about and likely to raise their value when they finally took a husband. It was a prerogative he had never enjoyed. But the tassine and his bitterness towards Lyla combined to make refusal impossible. He went where she led him. Then the wall of a byre hid them from the fire and she was smiling at him, her small breasts flattening as they pressed against him. His hands found her waist. It was firm but supple, not swollen in pregnancy or made flaccid by child-birth. She was no more than fifteen and youth's freshness gave its bloom to her skin. She giggled coyly, concealing her nervousness. But tonight he was drunk and wanted to forget, seek solace where he found it. So he grasped her haunches and thrust brutishly against her. She whimpered, shifting position. One last propriety to be observed . . .

'What's your name?'

She giggled again. 'Morrigen.'

He stumbled, falling forward. Then the vomit was splashing back into his face from the small of her back and her body had screwed round to avoid him as he fell.

*

They left at first light, Hyra leading, the courier goading on his baggage-ox as they began the descent into the valley. There was no wind, the air was cold. Mist climbed the hills the way a flock of close-packed sheep push on up a slope in search of grazing. There was frost in the valley and rooks clattered from the pines as they passed.

Hyra did not speak as the village receded. His memories of the night had blurred, but his nausea remained and he could still recall the girl's scream and the unbroken silence that had been Lyla's response to his behaviour. Her refusal to speak had been more damning than scorn, and he had finally fallen into a drunkard's sleep, unwashed and still reeking of his own sickness. He had woken at dawn, rising and staring down at his children for a moment before creeping from the hut and rousing the courier.

But departure did little to dispel the shame and self-disgust Hyra felt that morning. Throughout it, as the track twisted along the bank of a stream towards the woodland below, the events of the night looped endlessly through his thoughts, distorting and humiliating him. He now perceived that the girl's name had not been coincidence, but the portent he had refrained from seeking; a means of punishing him for abandoning Lyla. Yet an instinct he could not place seemed to steer him away from the four years of his marriage. At times he felt that a stranger was forcing him on, insisting that he keep moving and not weaken or return. His self-pity started to moderate, a warped logic helping to raise his spirits: Lyla's possessiveness had caged him, she resented his friendship with Morrigen, separation would supply time in which to begin rebuilding his life.

The courier soon soured his mood. By nightfall it had become apparent that despite having nothing to say he intended saying it. Silence left him uncomfortable, he explained – at length; and for the next eight days Hyra travelled accompanied by the sound of the courier's voice detailing an autobiography that lacked either incident or purpose. Aided by repetition it carried them to the edge of the Plain, at which point Hyra dismissed him and continued his journey alone. Two days later he reached Henge.

At first he could not enter. The walk across the downs in the crisp autumn air had purged the last of his guilt, leaving him expectant, even excited. But as he drew closer to the temple the intervening turf became a bridge between past and future: Lyla, Morrigen.

He hesitated, then crossed the entrance and added his offering to the bones that lay heaped round the stones. And suddenly the years contracted and he knew he had come home. He stood and surveyed the familiar landscape he had last seen when leaving for the hills. Goats grazed the stubble in the fields. The Village of Shamans was crowded with rainmakers and soothsayers who had assembled for the Harvest Rites. Corn was being winnowed in the nearest village and the chaff blew like smoke in the wind. A party of tribesfolk bearing branches of rowan was approaching along the Sacred Way, their children laughing as they switchbacked to and fro between its banks. Nothing had changed. The scars left by the rising had healed over without trace. Then he saw Morrigen and came face to face with changes no rumours had prepared him for.

She was sitting on a litter slung between two white oxen. Their hooves were crimson, lynx skins decked their bodies and coloured cloth hung from their horns. Shamans blowing long curved whistles walked ahead of her. A pair of roped lynxes padded in her wake, snarling at those who darted forward and tried to touch her as she passed. Seers attended her, followed by a line of white-robed priestesses tossing sweetmeats to the crowd.

Hyra followed her progress with mixed delight and apprehension. The villagers began chanting to the music of the whistles. The years in the High Vales had starved him of the atmosphere of carnival that accompanied her, and for one heady moment he believed that he had returned to help fashion a world that would do justice to all that had been achieved since defeating the Dobuni. Contentment showed in every face, no one was armed and no one oppressed. He smiled, waiting for her to acknowledge their cries before going forward to meet her.

The wait grew longer, then longer still. At first he could not bring himself to admit his error. But the more he watched her, the harder it became. Her beauty had not dimmed, but the realities of power had added an austere grandeur that seemed chill and forbidding. Her smile was fixed, her expression impassive. Her cheeks were pale and the amber necklace of her office had been augmented by a silver torque describing a serpent at the moment of striking. One breast was bared, the other covered by a bead-inlaid bodice and a single scarabaeid beetle. Weld streaked her hair and its length had been extended by the addition of feathers. Only once did her expression change, and that was when a young woman in the crowd held out her own new born baby as a gift. The gift was refused, but the flattery served to force an empty, measured smile to pass fleetingly across her lips.

Hyra turned away. His journey had been pointless. He knew Morrigen too well to be fooled by the adulation of the crowd. The changes he had seen in her were no more than externals, the Morrigen they concealed remained as self-seeking as ever. Lyla was right. Stay and Morrigen would destroy him. He looked round. In the Village of Shamans, an oasis of calm amongst the pomp, a group of rainmakers were preparing to purge themselves with ashes before attempting to still the wind. Their clothes were plain, their manner dignified. Hyra smiled, then left the temple and turned north towards the forest.

*

'I want advice, not criticism,' retorted Hyra angrily. 'Tell me what to do. Go back to her and I'm doomed. Return to Lyla and we'll argue more than ever.'

Tuah chuckled as he heard the irritation in Hyra's voice. 'Don't take yourself so seriously. The fault's yours. The unhappy have a way of inflicting their misery on themselves and blaming it on others. It makes it easier to bear.'

'So now I'm in the wrong!'

'Partly.'

Hyra snorted and kicked at the leaves. Since his arrival he had been pacing between the blackened fist of the oak and the edge of the clearing. He retraced his steps, then noticed Tuah's amusement and halted, hands on hips. 'You're laughing at me.'

'I'm laughing with you.'

'That's meaningless.'

Tuah's chuckle grew louder. 'It's ten years since we spoke. You can't appear out of nowhere and expect me to put your life in order as if it was a pile of logs that needs stacking. It can't be done. Sit down. Stop worrying. Let tomorrow wait on today.'

Hyra started pacing again, then realized his folly and relented. He sat beside the fire and glanced at the rainmaker. Although the bones still dressed the surrounding trees and the oak remained Tuah's home, he had aged considerably. His hair had fallen, exposing a rounded scalp that was as smooth as the skull overhead. His eyes had retreated deeper into their sockets, time and the vagaries of the weather engraving long fluted furrows into the line of his cheeks. 'I meant to visit you,' said Hyra finally. 'I'm sorry. The rising made it impossible.'

Tuah nodded but didn't reply, and when he finally spoke there was a concision to his words that suggested a demand on his strength, a wish to savour them and choose them with care. 'Morrigen came here once. It was before the Darkness.'

'She never told me.'

'I'd seen her before, when you and I were fishing.'

Hyra smiled. 'So you remembered?'

'Oh, yes. She had a strange face, sad but somehow proud of it. I sent her away. I didn't trust her. She tried to question me about the rain. I refused to answer. It wasn't for the good of the people that she asked, but herself.'

'She murdered a man that autumn, the seer Leoid.'

Leoid gave a slow nod of his head, as if to emphasize the pause. Then said, 'And you left your wife to go back to her . . . ?'

Hyra blushed. 'It was a long time ago.'

'And you've forgiven her?'

'I don't know.'

Silence. A squirrel scampered across the edge of the clearing, cheeks bulging with pouched nuts.

Tuah poked at the fire. 'So she killed? I should have guessed. She wouldn't look at me. Those who are about to die or take someone's life are like snakes, they never look you in the eye.'

Suddenly Hyra realized that this was something that Tuah had discovered in himself, not merely Morrigen. For since his arrival the rainmaker's gaze had always avoided him, shifted, failed to meet his.

Tuah smiled, sensing his thoughts. 'Only the Gods are immortal.'

Hyra turned away, searching in vain for words of sympathy or consolation. 'Is there nothing that can be done?' he blurted, embarrassed.

'No. Nor would I permit it if it could.' Tuah paused. 'But let's live again while we can. Tell me what's happened to you since we parted.'

And so, with dusk descending and the forest silent, Hyra repeated the story of his years with Morrigen and his marriage to Lyla. But this time, with Tuah to act as inquisitor, he found that the blame seemed to shift from Lyla to himself, that the reasons for their quarrels were as much his as hers. He tried to resist it by involving Morrigen.

Tuah was quick to stop him. 'Morrigen, Morrigen! How tired I've become of her name. A cow only has to drop its calf in midwinter and it's her the herdsmen praise. She's a strong woman, but she's not the cause of your misery: you are. Leave her be. Get away, from both her and Lyla.'

'But where to?'

'It's not important. Let the wind blow you where it will. Cross the seas, travel to other lands and live amongst other tribes. Learn of the Gods they worship. Enter their temples and tents. See how they build. Hold their tools and dress in their clothes. You must make your own way in the world. Don't turn for home until the name Morrigen means nothing to you.'

*

Later that autumn, on a cold blustery day when the last of the leaves had finally fallen, the old rainmaker took down his grandfather's skull and lay down beside the fire, holding it to his chest. He closed his eyes, smiling as the wind sang to him from the empty branches. By nightfall the leaves had banked up round his body, smothering it and hiding it from the moon. In the morning he was still there. Some days later a party of huntsmen found his corpse. Silver snail tracks criss-crossed his face. Rain-water had filled the skull.

That same autumn Hyra took his place amongst the oarsmen on a boat bound for the far side of the Dark Seas. The boat was frail, of planking sewn together with withy and caulked with fat. He peered longingly towards the shore. There was a sea mist, but black cliffs rode out over the water and the scent of thyme came out from the headlands. He raised his oar. The cliffs vanished, leaving the splash of oars and a long undulating swell that lifted the boat then dropped it in the troughs between waves.

# CHAPTER XVI

The seer remained silent as his High Priestess approached. She was hysterical. Anything he said would be ridiculed and perverted until truth became distortion and the distortion unrecognizable.

'Answer me!' she demanded. 'You promised to bring me his head before noon. Yet now I learn that he's still alive. Why? Why does no one do as I say?' She spun, encompassing the line of priestesses and seers in a single glance.

Still no one spoke. Morrigen's temper had grown increasingly unpredictable. The off-handedness with which she had spoken of Naxos's head made the timid finger their throats. Anger might yet turn to laughter, even remorse. But there was no certainty of that. The last priestess to contradict her had left the Dwellings a slave.

But the question had to be answered. The seer hesitated, shuffled, prevaricated for as long as he dared. Then said, 'I was told you'd ordered Naxos to be freed.'

'Freed! Never! There are to be no burials at Henge. None! Naxos knew that. He defied me on purpose. The temple is sacred. I won't allow it to be desecrated by a shaman's bones.'

'There is a precedent,' ventured the seer. 'The shamans will be offended.'

'Let them! They're fools, all of them. I'm surrounded by fools.' Morrigen paused to lift a knuckle and pinch it between her teeth. 'Who speaks to the Goddess? Who can predict the portents and foresaw the Year of the Comet?'

'Not all can be so fortunate.'

'Not all can be so stupid. You do nothing. You're useless. Imbeciles. Your last attempt to align the Serapha Stone with a post and the quarter-day made fools of us all. Now get out and fetch Naxos.'

The seer hurried from the hut. There was silence. His companions waited to be dismissed. The priestesses fidgeted and tried to evade their mistress's scrutiny. She began pacing, again nibbling her knuckle as she moved to and fro through the shaft of sunlight coming down through the smoke-hole overhead. It was stuffy inside the hut, an unseasonal fire burnt in the hearth and the sweet-smelling herbs she insisted be sprinkled on it gave a pungent scent to the air. The hut owed its construction to a wattle frame and sheepskin walls that had been stitched into panels and then painted with images of Serapha; spirals, eyes, the moon in its various phases. A caged hawk stared down from the angle of the roof.

'Bread!'

The bread was produced, then tossed into a small stone-lined pool in one corner of the hut. The carp rose to the surface, open mouths sucking it down.

'My cloak.'

A handmaiden hurried forward, wrapping it round her shoulders.

The silence returned as she resumed her pacing. Sunlight . . . shadow . . . the way the lynx skins brushed the soles of her feet as she walked. No use. The bid to regain control of herself had failed. The torment was always worse when in public. They were watching her, hating her, waiting for her to show signs of a flaw that could be used to hasten her ruin. She closed her eyes: opened them. A recurring nightmare had recently been troubling her sleep and even by day she was not immune to its prophecy. In it she was deranged and old, obsessed by the twin fears of insomnia and being poisoned. She shivered. Stared up at her hawk. Pointed to its cage.

'Why is Caedor without food?'

'He has eaten what we gave him.'

'Fetch more.'

Food was brought. Morrigen sampled it, then stood beneath the cage and tossed up pieces of meat, clapping and giggling when the hawk caught them in his beak. As he ate, she spoke to him continuously, maintaining the one-sided tittle-tattle of a mother talking nonsense to a baby until finally the chatter gave way to snatches from lullabies which she sang softly.

She could not stop herself. Her 'lost days' she called them, for after they were over she could not remember how she had behaved or what she had done. They had become frequent since the spring, and when incidents from the past entered her thoughts she was so appalled by the contrast they offered with the present that she sometimes wondered if they had ever taken place. Her months a fugitive, the cattle-drive and rebirth of the rising, such achievements seemed remote and implausible. She was approaching middle-age and still childless. Fear propped her power. At times she felt that she was being slowly suffocated by her own defects.

There was a shout. She turned towards the entrance as a young seer was brought into her dwelling by two members of her bodyguard. Rope linked his wrists and his cheeks were bruised, but beneath the bruises lay the defiant stubborn face of a man with nothing to lose. He sneered, then lifted his wrists. 'By what right am I charged?'

. . . and in the end there was only the power to fall back on.

Morrigen smiled at him, calmly, then tossed the last of the meat to her hawk. 'You have no rights.'

'By whose command?'

'Mine.'

'The seers are answerable to the Lord of the Rites and the Council, no one else. That is the law.'

'And who made the law?'

Naxos did not answer. During the last two years he had grown practised at skirting the traps she laid for the unwary.

'The Dobuni. And now I revoke it.'

'You can't do that.'

'I've done it. The Council will accept my advice. They're meeting now. And until I've spoken to them my decision remains final. By then you will be dead.

Naxos's existence might already have terminated, such was the abruptness with which Morrigen spoke.

She turned to the priestesses and remaining seers. 'For seven years, ever since the defeat of the Dobuni, I have done my best to serve the Cunei. The Dwellings have been rebuilt. The Toil is over. No woman is sold in the Maiden Lines. The poorest herdsman has the right to grazing and lands. I attend the Rites, meet envoys, travel to the villages, encourage trade. I'm your slave not your mistress . . .'

Naxos interrupted, laughing contemptuously. 'Some slave! One day the villagers will realize that by defeating the Dobuni they lost one tyrant and gained another, you. The Juba are given corn to leave us in peace. The Tan raid the northern villages when they please. The shamans can no longer be buried in the temple built by their ancestors. All study of the heavens has been halted, all prophecy forbidden.'

'Who led the rising?' cried Morrigen.

'And what of Cronus and Hyra and Ceruduc?'

'Where are they now? Cronus is dead. There's been no word of Hyra for nearly three years. Ceruduc lies in his tent too drunk to stand. The choice is yours. I either remain your High Priestess, or leave the Dwellings and abandon you to the Juba.'

As always, even the threat of such a move was sufficient to dismay those listening. If some felt sympathy for Naxos, they did not show it. Morrigen spoke for the Gods. Again and again during the past seven years she had proved her ability to communicate with Serapha and forestall the Goddess's anger. In their world there was no distinction between the real and the supernatural, the secular and the divine. If corn had to be given to the Juba, it was because the Gods saw it as a means of balancing the rhythms of the world. So too with Naxos's death and Morrigen's moods. Both were necessary, a means to an end.

The priestesses had grown agitated and started talking amongst themselves. Morrigen listened for a moment, then silenced them. She pointed at Naxos. 'Take him to the wolf pit.'

'No!' Naxos tried to protest, but the warriors propelled him through the entrance, still cursing and shouting at Morrigen. The hut emptied. Outside, all was bustle and routine; some women grinding corn in their querns, thatchers tossing bundles of reed on to the roof of a new dwelling, hay-laden oxen lumbering homeward from the fields.

A small crowd gathered to watch as the procession crossed the causeway and turned towards the river below. Morrigen went with it. A life was to be taken and tradition insisted that she be present lest the victim's soul return to torment her after his death.

The wolves barely stirred when the procession first reached them. Their pit was shallow and the posts that ringed it offered scant refuge from the sun. The months of captivity had robbed their coats of their sheen. Flies hooded their eyes and swarmed thickly round their droppings and the hunks of meat that lay untasted in the dust. One stretched lazily, snarled, then rose and stood staring upwards, panting in the heat, as the entrance hurdle was removed and Naxos was thrust into the entrance.

The condemned seer began struggling. Until now his self-control had not failed him. But the sight of the wolves and the warm foetid stench rising from the sun-baked bowl beneath him drained him of his courage. Despite the heat, a cold sweat stood out on his face. He began shaking. A few more of the wolves started circling. It was an unlikely scene, made unreal by its setting. Fishermen were shooting their nets in the river. Children splashed naked in the shallows. Sunlight laced the branches of the willows along the bank . . . and all the time the wolves were prowling their prison, mouths drawing back round yellowed fangs when they gathered in a pack beneath the entrance. One leapt, snapping idly at Naxos's feet. The guards watched Morrigen, awaiting her nod. To Morrigen, as to those round her, death was never conclusive. Evil spirits had possession of Naxos. The manner of his dying might be brutal, but the wolves would free the spirits and allow him to be reborn, cleansed of all sin. A second wolf snapped at his feet . . .

Hyra detached himself from the crowd.

His movements were precise, almost fussy. But at least his composure had returned and he knew what had to be done. It had been a long day; arrival at dawn, the need to question all those he met before reaching a decision, his sudden entry into the Council Dwelling. And now this. He lifted his bow, carefully taking aim at the guard nearest Naxos.

'Release him.'

The two words were spoken with a calmness and authority that made the bow an irrelevancy. The crowd fell silent. The guard glanced anxiously at Morrigen for instructions. Naxos remained poised over the pit. The bow shifted, the flint-tipped arrow sweeping the crowd until it was pointing at Morrigen.

'Do as I say. Order Naxos's release.'

'Who are you?' demanded Morrigen. Even the voice was no longer familiar. Sun had darkened the skin and bleached the colour from the hair. His legs were grey with dust. A water-skin and bedding pelt hung from the belt round his waist.

Hyra smiled, prolonging the mystery by purposely being elliptical. 'I'm the Lord of the Rites. No seer can be punished without my consent. That consent is not given.'

But the smile had betrayed him. For a moment Morrigen's bewilderment made her deny the evidence, then she called his name and ran towards him, undeterred by the bow.

The bow lifted, tracking her approach. 'First free Naxos.'

Morrigen halted. 'You wouldn't dare.'
'If Naxos dies, so will you. That's a promise not a threat.'
In any confrontation there is always a moment when hesitation can determine the outcome. And Morrigen had hesitated. Her gaze slipped away, then returned. The crowd was watching her. The silence lengthened, but the bow did not waver. She turned. 'Let him go.'
Hyra lowered his bow. Would he have fired it? He could not be sure. Surrender had left her vulnerable, and the anger he had felt when first hearing reports of her ruthlessness had dissipated as soon as he saw her. But its residue remained. He met her gaze.
'A short while ago I went before the Council and offered to become Lord of the Rites. They accepted. As from today both the seers and shamans are to continue their work without hindrance. You're High Priestess, nothing more, nothing less. I want the wolves slain, their pit used as a midden. Is that understood?'
Those watching began whispering. Naxos had backed away from the pit, too overwhelmed by his reprieve to yet speak. But Morrigen and Hyra were staring at each other, barely a pace apart. Morrigen was trying to coerce him into submission, re-establish the hold she had once had over him. But his gaze defied the attempt, and she suddenly realized that during their years apart he had finally stepped free of her shadow. He appeared stronger, more resolute, matured by experiences of which she knew nothing and could never share. The thought startled her. It was as if time had reversed their roles, made her the weaker.
She reddened, nodding obediently. 'Of course.'
Hyra took her hand, frowning as he noticed the imprint of teeth on the knuckles.
'I can't help it,' she whispered.
Hyra smiled. How defenceless she was when she blushed.

*

'Ceruduc.'
Another snore.
Hyra left the tent, walked over to the nearest water trough and filled the bucket beside it. Much of the water slopped from its rim as he picked his way round the filth that littered the tent;

the remainder he tipped over the figure lying sprawled amidst bracken. The snores subsided into a series of grunts. Ceruduc cursed, opened his eyes, hauled himself upright – water spilling from his beard.

'What the devil d'you think you're doing!'

Hyra clapped. A servant appeared. 'Take out the bracken and burn it. Add the clothes to the flames. I want your master scrubbed and dressed in fresh robes by dusk.'

The servant's eyes widened in horror. All previous attempts to tidy the tent and wash its occupant had resulted in his being kicked unceremoniously through the entrance.

'If he threatens you, tell me,' said Hyra, sensing his nervousness. 'If he asks for mead, refuse to get it.' He removed a goatskin from its hook on the wall, then tossed it to the ground.

Ceruduc lurched towards it, bellowing and demanding to be told what was happening.'

'We're turning you back into the chieftain who began the rising,' retorted Hyra. 'You may not like it, the role of hog may suit you, but it's going to be done and that's all there is to it.'

'Take this idiot away and have him thrown in the river!' shouted Ceruduc.

The hapless servant glanced at his master, then at Hyra, then chose compromise and vanished.

Ceruduc's bellows grew louder. His face was blotched and his eyes were bloodshot. A pair of lice ventured from his hair, then scuttled to safety. Fat clung in gobbets to his beard. Filth caked his robes and the reek of decay hung on his breath. He advanced towards Hyra, fists clenched.

Hyra smiled. 'I wouldn't risk it. You've been drunk so long that you'd probably damage yourself.'

'Who are you? What are you doing in my tent?'

'Have you so poisoned yourself with mead that you can't even recognize a friend?'

'What friend of mine would wake a man as he slept?' Ceruduc paused, eyes narrowing as he shuffled closer to Hyra and began scrutinizing him with the solemn, exaggerated fastidiousness of a drunkard trying to concentrate. A hint of recognition lit his eyes . . .

Hyra grinned. 'At last! I was beginning to fear you'd forgotten me.' He lifted his arms.

To have them felled by Ceruduc's fists. 'Pah! So the prodigal returns! Come to mend me or gloat?'

Hyra stood his ground, determined to weather the storm. 'Mend you. If I can.'

'Well it can't be done. You're wasting your time. And you can tell that to Morrigen. It's she who made me what I am. I've served her long enough, now I'm serving myself. I might have been a bull at stud for all I meant to her. What use is a woman who can't breed and can't marry?'

A long moment of silence. Then Ceruduc's bluster drained from his face and he became what he was, a self-pitying sot whose world had reduced to the dark comfortless haze that was his only defence against Morrigen.

'Isn't it worth a try?' said Hyra quietly.

Ceruduc slumped to the bracken as the haze lifted for a moment, recalling the derision and daily fights that had been the sum of their relationship before abuse drove him to take shelter in his tent. 'It won't work,' he said finally.

'So you've admitted defeat?'

'I've accepted the inevitable. No one can avoid his fate.'

'And this is yours?' Hyra indicated the filth on the floor.

'You should never have come back. You and Morrigen are much the same. She's abandoned me, you left Lyla.'

'So that's why you're angry?'

'Because of Lyla?' Ceruduc laughed. 'No, even my own sister has deserted me.'

Guilt made Hyra remember her as he had last seen her, pregnant with their fourth child. Despite his inquiries, one question still remained unanswered. 'And the baby . . . ?'

Another silence. 'It was a girl.' Ceruduc averted his head, suddenly ill-at-ease. 'She was born dead.'

Hyra swung away, Lyla's face encroaching on his thoughts as he mourned the dead daughter he had never seen.

'Does Lyla know where you are?'

'No.' Hyra glanced at Ceruduc, expecting to see either anger or accusation. Their absence made his shame seem harder to endure. 'I had to leave her,' he blurted.

Ceruduc shrugged. 'I had to leave Morrigen, there was no other way. You chose travel, I chose mead. It comes to the same thing in the end.' He paused. 'After the burial Lyla came here to look for you.'

'She would never have found me. I was in Karnos by then.'

'Karnos! That means you crossed the Dark Seas.'

'And many other seas.' Hyra closed his eyes as the memories of his three years in motion drove Lyla from his thoughts. He smiled. 'I've travelled so far and seen so much that I don't yet know where to begin.'

Ceruduc shook his head in mock amazement. 'You haven't changed. You left an imbecile, and only an imbecile would return.'

'I had to. And I'll tell you why when we see Morrigen.'

Ceruduc gave a scornful laugh. 'You forget, she won't allow me in her hut.'

'That's where you're wrong. And by the time you've scrubbed the lice from your hair she'll be waiting for us.'

*

'They'll be here soon. Is everything ready?'

Teina slapped her hands to her hips, releasing a flurry of dust which then lifted in the draught and took up residence on her bosom. 'That's the fifth time you've asked me. I've never known such a fuss. Move this, tidy that. It's not natural.'

'I can't help it.' Morrigen rose to her heels and spun through the soft light cast by the tallows. 'I'm so happy it almost hurts.'

'And hurt you it will if you don't stop chattering.'

'Now you're being cross.' Morrigen smiled as she saw the stern look on Teina's plump face. 'I told you he'd come back.'

'And not too late.'

'Stop it. Have they started the cooking?'

Teina grumbled suspiciously. 'Not thinking of changing your mind again, are you? It's me who has to keep the peace in the kitchen quarters.'

'Of course not.' Morrigen inspected her reflection in the carp pool. 'Are these robes all right?'

'They should be. It's taken half the day to choose them.'

'Why aren't they here yet?'

'One more question and I'll forget my own name,' said Teina, snorting impatiently. 'Hyra's one thing, but Ceruduc's another. Don't expect me to carry him back to his bed. Last time he came he took half the hut with him when he left.'

'Oh, stop fussing and comb my hair again.' Morrigen laughed. But in her excitement she could not remain still and so began circling whilst Teina scurried after her, rearranging her bodice, patting a loose hair into place, tightening the cross-gartered lines of blue beads that climbed her legs.

Teina was as baffled as anyone by the transformation in her mistress. For nearly a year she had been morose and short-tempered, prone to sudden tantrums and a casual ruthlessness that had shocked even the most hard-hearted observers. Only Teina – whose vantage was unique – had had the perception to realize that at the root of her behaviour lay her failure to become pregnant during her five years with Ceruduc. 'A woman without children is only half a woman,' Morrigen had once said to her, in a rare need to confide. But all that had changed since seeing Hyra in the morning. Teina was reminded of the freshness and clarity left by a summer storm, for in a similar way the abruptness of the change in Morrigen provided a contrast by which the past could be measured. Teina had not heard her laugh since the spring. The inclusion of Ceruduc in her invitation to Hyra would yesterday have been unthinkable. But when the two men finally entered her dwelling she greeted Ceruduc first. Then she turned to Hyra, clapping excitedly. 'I want to hear everything, every detail.'

Hyra laughed at her enthusiasm. 'We'd be awake at dawn.'

'Then let's! Do you remember how the three of us used to stay up all night when trying to plan the rising?'

The awkwardness had been dispelled, and though the need to find common ground confined their table-talk to reminiscence, no hint of it returned. They ate well. Roasted pig and a haunch of venison surrendered to strawberries and sweetmeats washed down with tassine. Afterwards, still nursing their beakers, they squatted round a charcoal fire that cut the smoke to a minimum. Morrigen smiled fondly at Hyra. 'I've fed you, now you must keep your promise.'

'But where to begin?'

'The day you left Lyla,' suggested Ceruduc.

That posed certain problems. Hyra reflected for a moment, finally deciding to refrain from all mention of his visit to Tuah and the deserted overgrown clearing he had returned to. 'First I went west and stayed with Atius. Through him I met a silver merchant bound for Karnos. I crossed the Dark Seas working an oar on one of his boats and stayed in Karnos for the winter.

'And is it as magnificent as they say?' asked Morrigen.

'More so. Their houses are built of stone and they bury their dead in chambers concealed beneath a cap-stone. The people worship both sun and moon, as well as the whale and the sea itself. Near the coast they've built two temples quite different from any others I've seen. Each consists of parallel lines of stones, more than a thousand altogether, that would stretch from here to Henge. Nearby they've raised a single standing stone that's taller than any tree.'

'That's impossible!' cried Ceruduc.

'That's what I said, until I saw it. It's visible from the sea and they use it as a sighting post to plot the motions of the moon. Their wise men are taken from their mothers at birth and trained from childhood in the use of numbers and the study of the heavens.

'The temple stones have been placed so as to record what they've learnt. They can even foresee the nights of the Darkness. An old rainmaker once told me that we Cunei used to do the same at Henge, using the burial pits round the outside and placing posts in the entrance, just as Leoid was doing when . . .'

Hyra halted, unable to say it.

But the sentence did not need completing. Its meaning was clear, and it evoked a past they had carefully skirted. Morrigen blushed, lowering her head. Ceruduc sensed the tension and hurriedly switched subjects, unaware that he was again acting as Morrigen's protector as he coaxed Hyra forward to the day of his departure from Karnos.

'I travelled south, first through forest, then scrub. The weather grew warmer. I fell in with a party of merchants carrying skins to the Two Lands*. We reached another sea, known to the tribes as the Sea of Jade.'

'I've heard its name,' said Morrigen.

'It's the biggest sea known, and thought to be shaped like a cradle. To the west the world ends in the Seven Fires of the Underworld. On its southern shore are the Two Lands and a land so hot only sand will grow there. To the east lies a great river and an island called Kerete.** I tried to reach it. Some traders had told me that the men there leap over cattle on the feast days and that the wealthiest of them live in painted houses that have one room raised above another.'

* XIth Dynasty Egypt ** Middle Minoan Crete

'Oh, Hyra! Tell us about it!' cried Morrigen.

'I can't. The Gods made a storm and our boat was driven on to a rock in the night. Many died. On the eighth day we were rescued and taken to a small island called Epius.* Fate had sent me there for a reason, and it's for that same reason that I've returned. I stayed there for a year, living as the guest of a merchant and learning all I could.'

Hyra paused as memory bore him back to its thin sun-scorched soil and the scent of vines and olive groves. Once again he had left a gap in his tale. For it wasn't a merchant he had stayed with, but his widow; the gentle Sallerno in whose company he had found safe anchorage after the years of travel, whose kindness and simplicity had made it so hard to leave.

Ceruduc was speaking.

'And what did you learn on Epius that you couldn't have learnt amongst Cunei?'

Hyra smiled at the irony in the question. 'How arrogant you've become. One example. Their temples are shaped like a clover-leaf. The outer walls are of stone, each dressed to lock with its neighbour. They're entered through an arch flanked by two stones with a third laid over the top. The insides are roofed and consist of a series of chambers linked by courtyards. The walls are carved or painted.'

'What Gods do they worship?' asked Morrigen.

'That was the strangest thing of all. They have no seers or shamans, only priestesses who are fed entirely on goat's milk so that they grow fat with fertility and are unable to walk. At dusk they're carried into underground catacombs filled with the bones of the dead. The dead send them dreams as they sleep. In the mornings, what they have dreamt is turned into a prophecy and the islanders act accordingly . . .'

The fire had dwindled to embers but no one stoked it.

Their beakers forgotten, Ceruduc and Morrigen sat spell-bound as Hyra guided them through the final years of his travels. It was as if a door had been opened in front of them, beckoning them into a new and exotic world of which they knew nothing. He spoke of ships with sails that were blown by the wind. He described a mountain that smoked as if a furnace had been lit in its heart; a sea strewn with amber so charged with life that the flotsam that clung to it gave off sparks as he

* Malta.

voyaged through it. He spoke of waterspouts and whirlpools and suns that had burnt him, of forests and mountains and a land deep in snow.

And when he had finished Morrigen felt that she was still in motion, still at sea or exploring the world he had shown her. He had reminded her of her ignorance, made Henge seem commonplace and her power appear petty. Once, whilst he was still speaking, she had reached out and gripped Ceruduc's hand as if in need of a rock to hold on to. He was still sober, and when he smiled the hair hanging and lopsided round his face made him younger than his years: the man she once had loved.

Suddenly Ceruduc became aware of the press of her hand. 'So now you're back,' he said, flustered and glancing at Hyra. 'To do what?'

'Build a world as fine as any I've seen.'

Ceruduc laughed at Hyra's earnestness. 'You're not a milk-fed oracle who can turn dreams into prophecy.'

'It needs to be done, and it ought to be done soon if the Cunei are to stay free. Before I came here I travelled through the villages and spoke with the elders. They agreed. Since the defeat of the Dobuni we've become like children grown drunk on liberty. There's chaos. The chieftains quarrel. The Juba are paid to leave us in peace. Morrigen punishes without realizing that if you become a tyrant it's your own freedom you destroy. You, Ceruduc. Did you lie a sot in your tent when there was a war to fight? Was Morrigen content being flattered during the months we spent hidden in caves?' Hyra paused, turning towards her. 'I haven't forgiven you for murdering Leoid. I never will. But I now know that no one person should be permitted or expected to rule an entire tribe. You need help. When I left with Lyla for the hills I was too angry to give it. Now I can.'

'How very generous of you!' snapped Morrigen, irritated by Hyra's criticism. 'You abandon us, travel, reappear without warning, have yourself made Lord of the Rites, and now you assume that we'll fall in behind you like dogs at heel. I've served the Cunei for seven years. Yet now you accuse me of oppression and cruelty. A nation is not built out of kindness, nor can it be made in a day.'

'Whip an ox and it dies. Feed it well and it'll pull a sledge and answer to its drover.'

'You're as guilty as me, Hyra. The villagers aren't oxen to be used like beasts of burden until they're fit for the racks.'

Ceruduc rose, shaking his head in dismay. 'And you wonder why I stay drunk. You're meant to be friends, not at war with each other.' He turned toward the entrance.

Morrigen held out a hand. 'Stay.'

Hyra watched her, alerted by the sudden softening in her voice. So much had happened since his return that there had been no time to observe her. Outwardly she appeared unchanged, and the years might have passed unnoticed if the tallows hadn't disclosed some inner stress that age had helped launch on its plunderings. Her cheeks had drawn tighter over the bone, pinching the skin round her eyes. The eyes themselves were more restless than he remembered. Scant evidence. But forced to diagnose the cause he would probably have said that only intense self-control now held her in check.

Ceruduc had stared at her for a moment, then returned to the fire. He glanced sideways at Hyra. 'So you think you can succeed where we have failed?'

An odd question, uncharacteristic of Ceruduc and proof that he was ill-at-ease, but to Hyra, now alert for nuance, the choice of words suggested complicity with Morrigen and the birth of a new alliance.

'Yes. We'll begin on the high ground above the Dwellings, on the site of the cattle pen used by the Dobuni for the mating of the heifers.'

'Why there, not inside the ramparts?'

'The ground is already sacred.' Hyra leant into the fire-light, eager to convince them. 'We were wrong to stop worshipping Bala. At Karnos the sun is regarded as Serapha's equal. We ought to do the same. Both Gods must be appeased. I walked round the pen this afternoon. To the west it aligns with the Funeral Way; chance I know, but surely propitious. Tomorrow I intend laying out the planning-pegs for a new roofed temple that will serve the Dwellings and prove what the Cunei can do.'

Morrigen was no longer listening. Despite Hyra's account of his travels his company had fallen short of its promise. Since finishing speaking he had gradually shed his attractions, becoming typical of all seers. Ground plans, alignments, the relationship between lines and numbers; all were so complex they both baffled and bored her. She glanced at Ceruduc, remembering the warrior who had once waded into battle with axes raised: 'the bull of combat in the field of slaughter' was how one lay had described him. Building temples suggested pedants with their tally staffs and tedious pernickety minds, not warriors. Everything Ceruduc did or failed to do courted the risk of death. Even as a drunkard some animal energy had still possessed him. Like her, he was blemished and imperfect. She tightened the pressure on his arm.

Dawn had broken when Hyra finally left the hut. Mist hung over the river and he could hear fishermen calling to one another as they beat the shallows with sticks and drove the salmon up-stream into their nets. The air had the warmth of a summer morning and the first birds had begun singing. He walked on towards his dwelling, thinking that Ceruduc would soon follow him.

But Ceruduc had halted in the entrance in obedience to a whisper from Morrigen.

He stared out over the mist. 'Why now?'

'Does that matter?' She was standing behind him, her head propped on his shoulder.

'Are you sure it's not Hyra you want?'

'Yes. He's good for us, both of us, and I'm glad he's come back. But I don't love him.'

'You make him sound like a potion.'

'Look at me.'

Ceruduc sighed. For a moment the memory of all the fights and arguments they had had circled through his thoughts. The cycle would repeat itself. They'd be happy for a few days, then the recriminations would begin and he'd take shelter in mead. He turned, to see her staring at him.

'The pleasure's gone,' he said finally. 'What I want when I'm drunk is not the same as when I'm sober.'

'And you're sober now?'

'Yes.'

'So what do you want?'

'A son. But you can't give me one.'

'Please . . .'

Ceruduc had broken free, but there was a plea in Morrigen's voice, almost an intuition, that made him halt and turn to her again.

'Once more. Just once.' She held out a hand, willing him to stay.

Ceruduc did not move. His face was grey and uncertain in the dawn. She brushed the hair from it, not daring to speak or do anything that might send him away. She touched his tunic, slowly releasing the toggles. Her fingers climbed his chest, searching for a scar, the memento of a quarrel. She kissed it, raising her eyes to his but keeping her mouth to his chest so that her words were almost inaudible when she finally risked speaking. 'Sons aren't created by the Gods. If you want one, you must make him.'

Ceruduc had yet to move. Nor did he now. Her eyes were holding him in place. There was no invitation in them, only an appeal and desperation that made them flinch when he broke the silence. 'How can you be so sure . . . ?'

'I can't explain . . . Another woman might understand. But not you.'

Morrigen hesitated . . . then turned and took a greenstone axe from its hook on the wall. The sun had now risen and she lifted the axe into its light as a symbol of the fertility she lacked. Gradually Ceruduc realized that what they were about to do had become ritual instead of pleasure, acquired a solemnity and importance to Morrigen that verged on the sacred.

She lowered her robes from her shoulders. She was naked beneath them and her hair rearranged itself so as to follow the flow of her body. She pressed the axe to her breasts, the dark fold of her thighs. The axe clattered loudly to the floor. She padded towards her bed, towing Ceruduc in her wake. She lay down and stared up at the thatch overhead. Ceruduc dropped to her side, passionless and bewildered, even slightly afraid. Her heart was lifting against the line of her ribs but her eyes were expressionless and barely blinked when he passed a hand in front of them. And when she finally shifted and pulled him across her he felt as if he was in the presence of death, so cold was her skin and impassive her face. Morrigen felt nothing; neither his entry nor his rhythm. But only when it was over did Ceruduc understand that by withdrawing into trance she had detached herself from her body, separating soul from flesh and leaving it empty to receive his seed.

*

'It can't be done!' cried Ceruduc. 'The posts'll work loose, they won't take the strain. Build too high and you expose the roof to the wind.'

'I've seen it done,' retorted Hyra. 'If the holes are deep enough and well packed with chalk the length of the posts doesn't matter.'

He paused and again checked the open skeleton of the temple. The din made concentration difficult. In the last month a temporary village had sprung up round the site of the cattle pen where it sat overlooking the Dwellings. Women plaited ropes. A group of miners were flaking cutting flints. Goats and sheep wandered untended amongst stacks of thatching reed. The two inner circles of posts were already upright and carpenters swarmed through the lattice of hazel scaffolding that enclosed them; some carving motifs of the Goddess, others chipping away at the tops of the posts to correct the height and shape the projecting stumps so vital to his design. He pointed to one of them. 'The tenons will slot into mortises on the underside of the joists. The joists'll help spread the weight.'

Ceruduc was unconvinced. 'I'd agree if the temple was circular, but it's not. It's the shape of an egg. The stress will vary from place to place. You're making it worse by using such tall posts for the third ring. They're the length of a fully grown tree. I'm using a hundred men to fell and haul them.'

'The third ring is the most important. The roof will slope down on either side of the posts, on one side to the outer wall, on the other to the central courtyard. Once up they'll reduce the load and absorb most of the stress.'

'Why eighteen of them?'

'Look at the pegs marking the ground plan. There has to be harmony between the spirits and the things we build, hence the six rings of posts; two for the Gods, four for the Elements. Each ring grows in equal proportion to its predecessor. In combination they're like a nest of eggs each larger than the next. Once finished, the gaps between some of the posts will create sighting lines, with Midsummer sunrise, the setting of the Midwinter moon. The break in the west points to the Funeral Way. Look along it and you'll be able to see fixed seasonal motions of both the sun and the moon. Not only will we have built a temple, but a form of calendar.'

Ceruduc knew nothing of calendars and felt at sea in such complex terrain. He scratched the wall of his nose, staring round at the pegs and ropes that littered the site and plotted Hyra's design. 'I still say it can't be done.'

Hyra grinned. 'You build. I'll tell you what to do and how to do it.'

Ceruduc was content. The hard work and demands on his concentration made by the last month had left neither time nor inclination for mead. The reflection that greeted him when washing in the mornings no longer returned to him as a befuddled and slovenly blur. Mead had never been an addiction, merely a refuge. His eyes had cleared, his wind and strength had returned. The nocturnal visits to Morrigen's hut had grown in frequency, the arguments rarer. At first he had felt that none of it could last, that it was tenuous and somehow suspect. But time had lowered his guard and made Morrigen an obsession only her company could absolve. Still chuckling, he turned and gave instructions to the men dragging the first of the main posts on to the site.

By mid-afternoon they were ready to raise it. It was a single oak whose bark had been peeled and whose branches had been cut back to the spurs. A sloped ramp had been dug down to the base of the post hole and the foot of the oak now rested above it. Hyra and Ceruduc paced uneasily, surrounded by the work force and the crowds who had gathered to watch.

'You'll never lift it,' growled Ceruduc.

'I'll wager a dozen cattle that we do.'

'They're as good as mine.'

Hyra smiled, concealing his concern by ordering the crowd to move back. He walked over to the men lined either side of the oak. 'Are you ready?'

They nodded, grins and coarse jokes belying their nervousness as they wiped the sweat from their hands and bent to the ranks of poles that straddled the underneath of the timber. There was a sudden disturbance in the crowd and a woman hurried forward carrying a large pottery urn. She quickly upended it, tipping the cremated remains of a human body into the post hole. The skull was still intact and she held it loosely in her hands as she stared down into the hole.

It was a strange incident, both public and private, an offering to the temple and a farewell to a husband or kinsman. But the atmosphere changed as she retreated into the crowd, celebration surrendering to tension and expectancy.

Hyra lifted his arms, asking for silence. 'The soil has been enriched, the Gods placated. Now it's up to us to honour that woman's gift and finish what she has begun.'

A drum began beating. The men knelt. Hyra waited, allowing them time to gather breath and correct their grips on the poles. Then cried, 'Lift!'

The end of the post furthest from the hole rose sharply upwards as in one fluid, practised movement the men straightened, snatching their poles from the ground. A baulk was jammed beneath it. Again the men took the strain, lifting the post still further. A second baulk was wedged on top of the first. One end of the post was now knee-high from the ground, dispersing the dead-weight towards the foot and reducing the demand on the men. Soon it had risen still higher and they could rest the poles on their shoulders. The post suddenly shifted, the angle making it slide down the ramp until it rested on the base of the hole. It steadied, then hung suspended, only the men beneath it preventing it from falling.

Hyra turned away, momentarily unwilling to watch – to see Morrigen moving through the crowd, her eyes shining above an exultant smile that all but spanned her face. She began running, stopped herself, then approached Ceruduc and tried to attract his attention. Thinking the temple's progress to be the cause of her elation, Hyra quickly forgot her as another group of men lashed ropes round the summit of the post.

But Morrigen ignored them. She too was constructing something, but its own alchemy would shape it and it lay in the dark cradle of her womb, invisible and unformed, still only an embryo. The Gods had heard her, and at times her joy was so great that she felt uncertain of her ability to endure it. The pain it provoked did not matter. Over the last few days her body's chemistry had undergone a change so subtle and profound that even the nausea that swept her when she woke was a welcome pleasure, the proof she had been waiting for.

Again she tugged impatiently at Ceruduc. Again he silenced her.

'Listen to me for a moment!'

'I've work to do.'

'Can't it wait?'

'Of course not.'

'Please . . .!'

Ceruduc had walked away. He lowered his arm. The post inched upward as the ropes stretched and tightened and the men kicked their heels into the ground. 'Heave!' he bellowed.

Hyra stood alone on the far side of the site. The crowd was

close and he could hear snatches of conversation in the pauses between Ceruduc's cries.

'They're wasting their time. Timber rots . . .'

'It'll finish its days as firewood . . .'

'I'll only put my hands to the ropes when it's stone we're hauling and it's at Henge that we're doing it . . .'

The post swung into the vertical. Even its critics began chanting and stamping their feet to attract the attention of the Gods. The ramp was filled in, chalk rammed round the post, the ropes pegged to hold it in place . . .

Casual eavesdropping. Chance. The notion was so vast that Hyra's first instinct was to ignore it. Would he live to see it finished? Would the Cunei accept the sacrifices and hardship it would entail? In his mind he could already see it: stone vaulting space. Disown it now and it would never be done. Then grow old regretting his weakness and being haunted by its unbuilt ghost.

Some ideas come in stages, each suggesting the next; others arrive perfect in the mind of their creator. With Hyra it was the latter. If eventually he was to realize that some fading memory of the lintelled arches leading into the temples on Epius had prompted at least part of it, he had no clue as to where the rest of it had come from. But its image was clear in every detail: the pillars flanking the entrance, the outer circle capped by lintels so that it formed a continuous circle, the inner arches each divided from its neighbour and shaped into a set of horns.

He stared up at the unfinished temple. But its symmetry had palled. In his thoughts it was already a matrix, a means of rehearsing and perfecting what now lay ahead.

'You were right. You've a dozen new cattle to add to your herd . . .'

Hyra turned, still dazed, to see Ceruduc striding towards him, Morrigen in his wake. He started to reply, then stopped as he realized that Morrigen was trying to speak. Yet he had to say it –

'We're going to build a new temple at Henge.'

It came out in a rush. Ceruduc snorted, unimpressed. 'You've taken leave of your senses. Let's finish this one first.'

'Two circles. Both of stone – the largest we can find. We'll cap them with lintels and . . .'

'Both of you listen to me for a moment!'

Morrigen's voice had cut into Hyra's, halting him in mid-sentence.

They turned towards her, silenced by her urgency. She could not say it. The words were all muddled inside her and when she rehearsed them they sounded awkward and inadequate. She walked towards Ceruduc, hands reaching for his. She smiled. She blushed. Then she said it. 'I'm going to bear you a child.'

# CHAPTER XVII

Summer became autumn and a winter so mild that many Cunei saw Morrigen's pregnancy as an omen of fruitfulness, proof that the Gods favoured them and that all their days thereafter would remain halcyon and fair. The new building acquired a name, the Temple of the Heavens. Once the posts were in position the joists and rafters were swayed into place and pegged with dowels. Thatchers replaced the carpenters. Symbols depicting the sun and moon were painted on the walls. The central courtyard was paved with white pebbles dredged from the river. The inside of the roof was hung with skulls, the outer thatching daubed with an immense elliptical eye that had the pebbles for a pupil and a single quartz-stone for its iris.

To the Cunei, the new temple was a living creature, in possession of both flesh and a soul. On their behalf its eye saw shooting stars and moons in wax and wane, the Comet of the Eighth Year and the Constellations of Winter. Spared the need to observe such phenomena themselves, Hyra and the seers spent the winter in a labyrinth of mathematics and astronomy. Lyla had yet to contact her husband. If he missed her or knew loneliness he did not show it as gradually the lessons he had learnt when constructing the temple were distilled into his plans for Henge. Night after night, in the hut he had inherited as Lord of the Rites, he squatted by the fire and plotted its shape on pieces of slate. By day he returned to Henge; measuring, recording, searching for the alignments he intended it to commemorate.

For Morrigen and Ceruduc there was no need for distraction.

'I've sinned. I don't deserve such happiness,' she said to him once.

'Give way to it,' he advised.

For a while she did so. Like a flower preparing to bloom, her beauty softened and colour warmed her cheeks, lending her features the delicacy they lacked. Even in repose she emanated the mystery taking place inside her. Serenity shaped her moods as her belly grew larger. She felt whole again, cleansed of guilt. The Gods had forgiven her and imbued her with their fertility. The prospect of motherhood became proof of atonement and even when it was unnecessary she paraded her acquittal by wearing the loose-fitting robes of the expectant mother.

One night she felt her child move inside her. She made Ceruduc placed an ear to her stomach. 'Can you feel him?'

Ceruduc's breath stayed locked inside him as a slight tremor disturbed the hump beneath his ear. He smiled in amazement. He had been brought up in a stern and disciplined world that thought all displays of emotion to be a weakness. A man of war at his best in the company of warriors, the past months had disclosed a tenderness in his character that had surprised all who knew him. It was he who prevented Morrigen taxing her strength, he who rationed her duties.

A second tremor, almost a thump. He straightened, carefully. 'Are you sure it's a son?'

'Of course. I'm a woman. To serve both Gods I must make what I'm not.'

Ceruduc smiled at her heresy. 'The healers say that children are created by the Gods breathing life into a man's seed as it enters the woman. Daughters are made at night by Serapha, sons by day when Bala is in the ascent.'

'It's a boy – I know it. You forget, we made love at dawn, in the half-light, the one moment when neither God is master of the spirits.'

Ceruduc indulged her, such confidence was hard to question.

But from the evening of that first movement inside her Morrigen's joy was marred by self-doubt. Since reaching Abury she had employed cunning to obtain and maintain her power. She had murdered twice. Until Hyra's return her years as High Priestess had meant calling the roll on priestesses banished, criticism silenced, men become slaves or victims of the wolf pit. *There can be no pleasure without pain*: Fram's words. Reminded of them now, she began to believe that retribution was approaching, tragedy impending. As a child her mother had terrified her with stories of wickedness being punished by the spawning of monsters, creatures born with tails or scales. The monsters became real, even infecting her dreams. Sometimes Ceruduc woke to hear her crying out or tossing from side to side as she slept. She would cling to him until dawn brought relief, her wild startled eyes staring up into the darkness.

*

The wind had entered with Atius, then swept on ahead of him; buckling the walls of the hut and scattering the pelts on the floor. It growled in the thatch, routed the tallows and flattened the smoke, making it swirl round Morrigen when she rose to greet him. For a moment it seemed to her that he was its creator and to blame for its onslaught, for angry grunts and the stamping of mud from boots partnered the gusts as they laid siege to the carp and Caedor in his cage overhead.

Then Hyra closed the entrance hurdle and a deep resonant boom ended the sudden hush:

'Henge! I'd hoped to never see it again! So much for your rainmakers. There's a tempest blowing and they're running round outside like a flock of sheep in a storm. Pity it can't take them with it. Fresh air is what this place needs. Another month of it and it might blow some sense into you all.'

Morrigen grinned as Atius emerged from the smoke, attacking it with his arms. 'Yet you've come.'

'For better or worse. I promised Hyra I'd be with you by the Spring Rites, and so I am.' The merchant paused, his anger giving way to a chuckle as he noticed Morrigen's shape. 'So what Hyra told me is true. You look better for it. Skin and bones didn't suit you. Nothing to grip.'

Morrigen laughed, thrown off-balance by Atius's candour. 'According to the shamans I'll be a mother by the night of the full moon.'

'In that case you'll still be carrying it in the autumn. Never believe shamans. What they don't know they invent and what they do know they exaggerate.'

The two of them embraced, then stepped back to survey the changes nine years had fashioned. Morrigen grew uneasy at his scrutiny. Atius had been her first lover. Her cunning had never deceived him and her pleasure at seeing him again was tempered by a sense of threat, the air of self-sufficiency that had always surrounded him. Age had withered him slightly, sharpening his face and hiding the line of his mouth behind his beard. But the hint of fox had increased. His gaze was more direct, more piercing, less visibly sympathetic and willing to suffer her faults.

'So you've agreed to help us?' she said.

'If I can.'

'I didn't think you'd come . . .'

All small talk. The courtesies meant nothing. A second conversation was taking place simultaneously: a probing for weakness, the establishing of a relationship, memories passing to and fro between them with an understanding that made words unnecessary.

Atius ended it. 'I'd save your welcome till you know my terms. I'm a merchant. Demand pork from a pig and you first have to feed it. My services have their price.'

Hyra started to protest, to be interrupted by Morrigen.

'We'll meet it.'

Atius stared at her, smiling wryly. 'I want the sole mining rights to all the lands you won from the Dobuni.'

'That's ridiculous!' cried Hyra. 'The lands have been divided amongst the chieftains. They'd never agree.'

Again Morrigen overrode the interruption. 'Anything else?'

'Yes. Payment in cattle for every month spent at work on the temple. Those are my terms. The rest's up to you.'

There was a moment's silence, then the distant slosh of oxen being driven home through the mud. The fire collapsed, spilling embers across the hearth. Hyra began to protest again, but Morrigen paid him no attention. She was still staring at Atius in an attempt to weigh the advantages of his help against the hazards of his presence. The design of the temple had made little impact on her, but unlike Hyra she had come to realize that specialist skills would be required to mine and work the stones. More importantly, she had also perceived that she stood to gain the most from its completion. It would reflect her authority, enable her to extend her influence over both the seers and the chieftains. Atius would have to be indulged, and for at least two years. By then enough men would have been trained in handling the stones to make him redundant.

She lowered herself to the pelts, the decision made. 'I'll have to summon the chieftains to a meeting in Council before granting you the mining rights. The cattle are yours.'

Hyra was not typical of his age, or perhaps of any. For he harboured notions of equality between men that now openly rebelled. 'No one else is to be rewarded! Why Atius?'

'Because no one else can build it. Stone isn't timber. To build Henge you need masons, men who know how to move and shape stone. Without them it'll remain a circle of planning-pegs and some empty holes.' Morrigen paused, risking a thin smile at Atius. 'I'll speak to the chieftains as soon as possible, the rest you must arrange between yourselves.'

Atius was uncharacteristically subdued when he and Hyra left the hut. He had noted that smile, but he had also detected intrigue and a flicker of invitation that suggested that but for her condition and Hyra's presence . . . No, it was impossible, a mannerism misread. But his doubts remained as he braved the wind sweeping across the Dwellings. They reminded him that in Morrigen's world nothing was permanent, that everything shifted according to her needs. He sighed heavily, and said, 'I'd not be Ceruduc for all the sheep in the land. That's what we all are, all of us – not just the rainmakers: sheep. She's as unscrupulous as ever, yet we flock round her without giving a thought to the consequences. I was a fool to come and I'm a fool to stay.'

Hyra was still too indignant at the merchant's greed to sympathize. 'When can you start?' he demanded.

'Are you defending her?'

'She's changed. Nine years is a long time.'

'Not long enough. She'll never change. No one does. The same person lies on the racks as who once slept in the cradle. Morrigen's a shrew; half witch, half bitch. As to you and your temple, the day it's finished she'll tell the tribesfolk that it couldn't have been built without her.'

'How can you say that when we've yet to start it?'

'Because I know Morrigen, and I know you. You'd see it yourself if you weren't so obsessed by Henge. It means too much to you.'

'Is it wrong to want to praise the Gods?'

'Wrong or right, it's also vanity. I want wealth whilst I live, you want a Henge that'll win you life after death. We build temples for ourselves, not the Gods.' Atius laughed as he saw the anger on Hyra's face. 'We used to be friends, good friends. Let's be so again and stop hiding behind cant. Tomorrow I'm yours. But today I need food, a woman and sleep.'

Hyra grinned. 'In that order?'

'Can you better it?'

Hyra moved to one side as a line of pack-goats laden with horn and leather rounded the Council Dwelling. 'You should take a wife.'

'And do as you did or end up a drunk like Ceruduc?'

'He hasn't touched mead since the day he learnt he was to be a father.'

'It won't last. To Morrigen he's like a mine that's been worked until it's empty. She'll have no time for him once the baby has been born.' Atius frowned. Hyra's reply had been too glib, too quick and evasive. 'And what about Lyla? Have you seen her yet?'

He was right. Hyra turned abruptly away from him to wave at a passing seer.

'You don't want to answer?'

Hyra coloured. 'There's nothing to say.'

'But you haven't seen her?'

'No.'

'That's a mistake, Hyra. She's a good woman, wiser and stronger than you think. You'll need her support if you're not to be wounded by Morrigen.'

'Morrigen means nothing to me.'

'That's a lie. She means something to both of us. That's why we're here. If I was you I'd send a courier to Lyla tomorrow.'

Hyra deflected the advice as best he could. Atius had touched a nerve. The domestic peace between Morrigen and Ceruduc had prompted memories of his own marriage, the pleasures shared that had preceded discord. After four years apart he was beginning to miss both Lyla and the children, and more so than he cared to admit. Morrigen's presence had made it harder to endure. For if pregnancy had softened her it had also evoked their brief snow bound affair. Eleven years had passed since Leoid's death, nine since Hyra's discovery of the cause. He had not forgiven her, or forgotten, but there had been moments during the past few months when he had found himself wishing that he had left Ceruduc to his drunkenness.

The two men had climbed the ramparts and turned to look down on the encampment. 'I thought this place had been destroyed,' said Atius.

'It was. Morrigen rebuilt all the huts. You may mock her, but she's done a lot for the tribesfolk. Trading routes have been opened. New strains of grain have been introduced, better breeding stock added to the herds. There's more land under the plough, less shortage of food. It's hard to define, but I sometimes feel that the Cunei are creating an empire like that of the

Two Lands. The defeat of the Dobuni gave us confidence, Morrigen has been able to channel it.'

Atius surveyed his surroundings. Amongst the traders mingling with the villagers who had gathered for the Rites he noticed prospectors and travelling miners, their tools in bag rolls on their backs. Merchants from Karnos were peddling amber in exchange for skins. But despite the bustle of commerce his sceptical eye was quick to realize that the business of worship still dominated the life of the Dwellings. Many of the villagers carried bones and cult offerings to the dead. White-robed priestesses intoned the evening chant as they awaited the sunset and their first glimpse of Serapha. A bed of hot coals was being raked smooth for some shamans to walk on and cleanse their souls. There was only one sight he did not remember, the cluster of tents in the lee of the ramparts.

'So the Dobuni are still here?'

'They're harmless. Most of them are women.'

'Who ply women's trades,' said Atius, indicating the pots drying in the wind and the single carved post that signified the presence of a brothel. Unlike most Cunei, for whom the sexual act was as much ritual as pleasure, it was to Atius no more than an appetite that required occasional indulgence. Later that day he returned to the tents, satisfying that appetite in the company of a young and sturdily built Dobuni whose athleticism was equalled by her stamina. Only once did his enjoyment cloy, and that was when she freed the braids in her hair and it tumbled to her waist, echoing Morrigen.

*

A spring morning. Lapwings wheeled, bow-legged lambs grazed the scrub, the first gangs were already at work.

Yet it was not what Hyra saw that so intoxicated him, but what he could not see except in the arrrangement of pegs and ropes that criss-crossed Henge. As a seer, as a husband, even as a father, he had felt that he was squandering his life away, engaging too little of himself. His travels had been routed by chance, for he had taken Tuah's advice and allowed the wind to be his guide. But a contradiction he could not quite fathom had finally shaped his journey, and his work on the Temple of the Heavens and now Henge itself had added purpose to direction. Again he tried to explain himself.

'Nothing else matters to me,' he said, continuing his circuit of the bank with Atius and Ceruduc. 'It may take a lifetime to build, but if it survives us it'll have been worth the effort.'

Atius smiled. Hyra's enthusiasm was self-evident. Why then did he have the feeling that in this cautious, middle-aged sage even the enthusiasm was a form of escape; from Lyla, from Morrigen, from some inability to cope without being propped by a sense of mission? He looked round. Many of the stones brought to the temple during the Toil lay heaped near the entrance in readiness to be sledged and dragged away.

'We're hoping to use them to build a tomb to the dead near the Funeral Way,' explained Hyra. 'It's proving harder to move them than I thought. The holes have had to be widened, the stones levered on to their sides before we could haul them to the surface.'

'Are you leaving any?'

'No. The Toil's left too sour a taste. But the Serapha Stone stays, so do the Element Stones.' Hyra paused to indicate the four stones that stood in each corner of the temple, forming a rectangle. 'They were brought here by the Cunei. Anyway, they're too important to go.'

'Why?'

'Used together or with the posts put up by Leoid they align with most motions of the moon, as well as sunrise and sunset on the days of both Midsummer and Midwinter Rites. There's something quite extraordinary about their placing. They form a perfect rectangle, the short sides record the positions of the sun and the long sides those of the moon. Yet if Henge had been built anywhere else the rectangle wouldn't have worked. The entire temple would be useless.'

The three men fell silent as they scanned its precincts. To each it posed different problems. Hyra saw alignments, the precision with which each new stone would have to be placed if they were to be accurately recorded. Ceruduc viewed it as the chieftain responsible for providing and feeding the work force. Atius saw the difficulties created by the handling and raising of the stones.

'Are you sure you need nearly eighty stones?' he asked.

Hyra nodded. 'Thirty for the uprights in the circle, thirty for their lintels. Two to flank the entrance and fifteen for the five arches in the centre.'

'And their size?'

Hyra did not answer for a moment. A reply meant defining his vision of what it would look like when completed. It meant explanation, an attempt to clarify the link between its purpose and physical shape, as well as the symbolic shape commemorated in each of its component parts. But the attempt had to be made. 'You've been to Abury?'

'Of course.'

'Even now it's still the most sacred temple in the land. Yet somehow it's unfinished. The stones are unshaped, they lack unity. The stones that stand here must be worked and dressed so that each resembles the next. If they're to be ringed with lintels they've got to be exactly the same height. The lintels will provide balance, make the final temple complete. The same applies to the arches. We build to honour the Gods. It's easy to forget that.'

'You're evading the question,' growled Atius.

Hyra had paused to reflect, not invite comment. He was staring at the ground as he walked and when he continued he spoke slowly, spacing his words. It was as if he was thinking out loud and had forgotten the merchant's presence.

'The temple must appease both Bala and Serapha. The thirty circle stones will record the number of days between one full moon and the next. The five arches are to be shaped like a set of horns.'

'I don't see the connection,' said Atius.

'The shamans regard horn as an extension of the soul of a bull. Both Gods will have been placated. The horn's are Bala's, yet they'll sit inside a circle, the womb of the Goddess Serapha. The entrance will also share two purposes. Face away from it and you'll look towards sunset at the Midsummer Rites, look outwards at the Sacred Way and it aligns on the Serapha Stone and Midsummer sunrise: winter death, summer birth. The stones are to be placed so that if we raise posts outside the temple and look through the arches we'll see both sun and moon in certain positions, further uniting the Gods. Henge won't merely praise them, it'll also record their motions and shape.'

Sudden squalls of nervousness betrayed Hyra's excitement; the hands slapping together in emphasis, a finger worrying an insect bite on his neck. But there was also a diffidence to him, the rare modesty that goes with great learning made simple. To Ceruduc it was proof of genius.

'It comes back to what I told you yesterday about forging an empire. The buildings a tribe constructs are a summary of its talent. Once finished Henge will be unique. Its fame will spread. It'll attract merchants and settlers, new ideas and new discoveries. If the Gods permit it, one day it'll stand at the centre of a culture that embraces trade as well as worship, learning as well as power . . .'

Atius had begun scowling, obviously impatient. Hyra halted, suddenly wary, then went on to answer the merchant's original question as casually as he could.

'The stones are to be individually dressed, but like the posts in the Temple of the Heavens they'll also need tenons at the top to prevent the lintels shifting. The lintels themselves will have to be mortised underneath, and perhaps dished slightly to make them that much firmer. I also want to cut them to the shape of the circle and link them together with tongue and groove joints. That should be straightforward, carpentry applied to stone. Now their size. This is very important. The Plain's so large that if it's not to dwarf them they've got to be as big as possible. The uprights ought to be as tall as three men, a pace thick and two paces wide. The lintels can be slightly smaller, but the arch stones will have to be the biggest of all – otherwise it'll be hard to see them behind the lintels – perhaps as tall as four men and . . .'

Hyra broke off again as Atius started striding from the temple. 'What is it? Where are you going?'

The merchant halted. Ceruduc had never seen him so angry, or so incredulous. A hand jerked upward, then stabbed at the Plain. 'Home! And if Ceruduc has the sense he'll leave for the Great Marsh tomorrow. You're mad, Hyra. And dangerous. There's no one I fear more than those who demand the impossible and then persuade others it can be done. It can't be. Have you considered how long it's going to take to build, the number of men you'll need? And what of the timber for the sledges and lifting cribs, the thousands of cattle that'll have to be slaughtered to provide hide for the ropes? You'll need antler picks, flints, mauls, enough scaffolding to mean felling a small forest. Oh yes, I know you've plotted it all and made plans of the design. But you can't plot the weight of a stone that's the height of four men. Where are you going to find them? Who's going to bring them here? Or do you think those precious Gods you keep talking about are going to spirit them through the air whilst you stand idly by? You're a fool, Hyra, a blind sanctimonious fool!'

'We'll sledge the stones from the hills near Abury,' said Hyra, genuinely bewildered by Atius's attack.

'How delightful! It's a two day journey from Abury, over hills, through forest and a marsh. Even with four hundred men at the ropes and perfect weather it'll take most of the summer to get one stone to Henge. Just one! And you calmly decide on seventy-seven. Why not double it? It's all the same. Apart from those hauling you'll need huntsmen to supply them with fresh meat, tents, baggage-oxen, women to gather oak-galls and tan the hide for the ropes. More flint mines will have to be opened. You'll need a hundred men doing nothing but felling timber, another hundred cutting a path through the forest and finding a route through the marsh, laying a track where it's deepest. In autumn the ground will turn to a quagmire, in winter it'll vanish beneath snow. In summer you'll have to travel from one water-hole to the next. Stones will break loose, maiming and crushing those hauling them. And having reached Henge – if you reach it at all – you'll need another four hundred men to dress the stones, pounding them with mauls until they're the shape you want. The mortises will all have to be hollowed, the tenons cut, the post holes all dug to exact but varying depths if the stones are to stand level. You'll have to kill forty cattle to plait one hawser strong enough to pull the stones; you'll need at least two hundred. And with a thousand men at work, plus women and children, who's going to gather in the harvest and farm the land? And then there are the lintels. A masterstroke! Hyra's gift to posterity and the Gods. You say you want them shaped, smoothed, lifted into place. That's no problem. We'll just empty the villages of every man who can walk and tell them that the Lord of the Rites has a task for them that'll keep them occupied until they're fit for the racks. It'll be a charnel house not a temple by the time you've finished with them.'

Atius halted to stand staring at Hyra; and only then, in the strained silence that followed, did Hyra comprehend what he was intending to set in motion. Until now the concept had blinded him to the means by which it was to be translated into fact. He had judged the number and size of the stones until they fitted his plan, heedless of what it entailed. The task of construction had receded into abstraction, a distant irritation best left unconsidered lest the method mar the result. Yet now he could see it for what it was; a ripple in water that would reach out and touch every village in the land until it had mobilized an entire tribe, taxing its resources, its wealth and its patience. No one would be immune, no one spared. Even without a drought or a failed harvest it would take at least five years to build. The sheer magnitude of the labour ahead left him humbled and slightly afraid. For a moment he doubted his nerve, his ability to see it through. He looked round, but as always now the new temple superimposed itself on the old. It had become part of him. There could be no absolution until it was finished. He turned to Atius.

'I'm going to see it built. With or without you.'

Atius glanced at Ceruduc. 'And you?'

Ceruduc lowered his head, his conscience at war with common sense. Hyra was his childhood friend, the man who had put an end to his drunkenness. Atius the skilled craftsman who knew what was possible. Such wars are rarely won. He straightened, nodded. 'So am I.'

Atius shook his head in dismay. 'It can't be done!'

'Then think how foolish you'll look on the day we finish it,' said Hyra.

'I'll be dead. So will you.'

'But I thought you were the taker of risks, the merchant who'd stop at nothing to add to his wealth. You're being rewarded. You've nothing to lose by staying.'

. . . and Morrigen to gain, thought Atius. No, that was wrong. He didn't love her, her attraction was no longer sexual. More a curiosity to satisfy. Seeing her again had reminded him of her potential, the conflicts inside her still unresolved. He had met no woman like her, and knew he never would. Her emancipation was not just that of the woman who had acquired power, but of someone who had freed herself from all the moral laws that order the lives of men. And then there were the mining rights and the cattle, the change of course in the voyage into old age, a voyage that until now had seemed fixed and already mapped. He turned towards Hyra, smiling at his own stupidity. 'I want a thousand men and enough food to keep them fed until winter.'

*

As Lord of the Rites and architect of the proposed temple it was Hyra who had to persuade the chieftains to pledge their support. Ceruduc assisted him. Arguments and facts were marshalled, the case presented at a meeting in Council. Afterwards, each of those present had to be flattered and cajoled into parting with men and supplies. The shamans insisted in having a voice in the temple's design. Groups of elders arrived demanding an explanation once the news reached the outlying villages. The Rites came and went – but still the work went on. The two men spent their days conferring with the shamans, their nights feasting the chieftains, snatching sleep when they could. An unhealthy pallor robbed Hyra's face of its colour. Ceruduc grew irritable as the need to dispense hospitality revived his taste for mead. Impatient to begin, exhausted by the lack of progress, each new obstacle seemed to spawn another.

Finally they had to admit defeat.

To rebuild Henge, so the argument ran, was an extravagance the fledgling nation could ill afford. The men were needed to finish the sowing and drive the herds to the summer grazing grounds. To slaughter cattle merely to provide ropes broke all the rules of good farming. The Temple of the Heavens was more than adequate for the needs of the tribe. The defeat of the Dobuni had ended the Toil of the Stones, to begin it again would smack of a return to enslavement.

Morrigen took over.

The birth was imminent and the stimulus of exercising her authority acted as an antidote to the controlled tension of the waiting. Her methods were made obvious from the start. 'It's no use flattering them,' she said. 'They need to be threatened, given no choice.'

Couriers were sent out, the chieftains summoned. One morning she spoke to them in Council. Ceruduc and Atius awaited their verdict in Hyra's dwelling whilst its owner paced the bracken. Suddenly Morrigen swept triumphantly through the entrance, black lines zigzagging her cheeks and her robes of office billowing round her. She glanced curtly at Atius. 'You've seven hundred men. They're yours until the Harvest Rites.'

Hyra ran forward, intending to embrace her, only to be halted by Atius. 'That's not long enough.'

'Could you do better?' retorted Morrigen.

'Who's to feed the men?'

'You are. I asked for swine and cattle but they refused to part with them until we prove it's possible.'

'So that's fifty men wasted on hunting. Flour?'

'Some will be provided. The balance depends on the harvest.'

'Ropes and timber?'

'They wouldn't give them. You'll have to make the ropes out of nettle and deer-hide and cut the timber where you find it.'

'Tools?'

'The flints from the mine nearest the river are to be divided between you and the chieftains. But I couldn't get any oxen or picks. It's the men or nothing.' Some trace of Morrigen's methods still lingered in her voice. It sounded harsh and intolerant.

Hyra was too elated to notice. 'What did you say to them? Last time I spoke to them they wouldn't even part with a cutting flint. They might have been deaf.'

'Even deafness can be cured.' Morrigen smiled. 'I told them that the portents had warned of the coming of a contagion if Henge wasn't built.'

'But that's a lie!'

'It's a means to an end, my dear Hyra. You want Henge rebuilt, so do I.'

Atius had started chuckling to himself. 'There are some fruits, Morrigen, that aren't ripe till they're rotten. You're one of them.'

'And there are some that never ripen at all. You three share their faults . . .' Morrigen's strength had failed her. Even when in the Council Dwelling she had felt the first tremors inside her. She collapsed slightly, tipping forward and pressing her hands to her belly.

Ceruduc ran forward to prop her. 'What is it?'

'I don't know . . .' Again she could not speak. A second wave of pain began its slow roll through her stomach. A pause. Time for Ceruduc to realize what was happening. Then a sudden cry as the pain sharpened, bringing the months of waiting to a close.

*

There was a brief pause, the lull between contractions, then the next one would commence and the pain would begin again, spreading outward from her belly until her whole body had been engulfed.

'Use the wedge.'

She did so, clamping it between her teeth to stifle the scream that brought the only release she could endure. The pain reached crescendo then gradually subsided. 'How much longer?' she gasped.

'It'll be soon enough now.'

'You've said that before.'

'I'm saying it again.'

Always the same answer, the same unruffled flicker in the eyes staring down at her. The wise woman's eyes; part shaman, part sorceress, the afterbirth of countless deliveries dried into a sepia patina down the front of her robes. Lank hair framing plump plum-coloured cheeks, chipped teeth stained livid by sloes, scrubbed inquisitive hands pressing against the entrance to her womb. All else was mist. Disembodied voices. The crowd waiting for news. The low chant of the priestesses in attendance. Then the pain would begin again and she was alone with her suffering and the unborn child inside her.

It had seemed so natural at first, an instinct she could control unaided. Exchanging Hyra's dwelling for her own, its central post her support, she had squatted and waited, certain it would soon be over. Ceruduc's panic and utter uselessness had made her smile fondly. The first contractions had been gentle, rhythmic, curiously sensual. The crowds had gathered and their offerings of milk and seed still lay heaped round about her. The wise woman arrived, briskly efficient and prophesying that it would be as 'easy as shelling a nut' as water was warmed and the swaddling robes held in the sunlight to be purified by Bala.

And now time and her fears meant nothing. Even the birth of the most misshapen of offspring was preferable to prolonging the pain. She could feel sweat dripping in runnels from her hair, its salt on her face. Her legs were weak. Her robes hung sodden and heavy, their knots untied so that the baby's passage wouldn't be hindered by the links that had kept it in the womb as it grew. She began to speak, but the muscles contracted again and she could feel it inside her, squeezing, straining, forcing itself towards the floor of her pelvis. She cried out, spitting the wedge from her mouth. 'Why won't it come?'

'Calm yourself.' Teina had knelt at her side and was sponging the sweat from her face.

'It's dead, I know it! Have them pull it from me now.'

'Don't say things like that! It's as alive as you.'

'I've done wrong, Teina. The Gods are punishing me.'

'Nonsense!'

But the words came tumbling forth, confession and the dread of her own death muddling with the conviction that the child would be stillborn. Teina listened mystified, even slightly scared by so private and alien a glimpse into the soul of another. The name Leoid meant nothing, the admission of murder she mistook for delirium. Even so, she sensed that Morrigen's compulsion to speak echoed more than imaginings. 'What are you trying to tell me?' she asked.

She had left it too late. The next contraction had made Morrigen reach forward and clamp her teeth to the post. An animal gesture, almost primaeval: the pelt of matted red hair, the teeth parted white against the grain of the wood, the numbness and sudden inertia that came over her when the pain finally faded.

The sound of celebration from beyond the walls of the hut timed the silence that followed. Ceruduc tried to enter, to be imperiously turned back by Teina lest his presence encourage demons to aggravate the birth. The wise woman emerged out of the mist. 'You must lie down. The child is bound in the womb and won't be delivered until it's free.'

Morrigen protested, panicking. 'But the knots are loose!'

'Do as I say.'

Aided by Teina, she forced herself upright, only to collapse to the ground as vertigo tilted the thatch overhead and her legs weakened beneath her. She straightened as best she could, braving a smile as Teina began combing her hair with long, even strokes.

'I feel so helpless.'

'It'll be over soon.'

Morrigen tried to relax, breathing deeply. Never before had she felt so vulnerable, so dependent on others. A shaman approached her. He had a moist wrinkled face and was carrying a length of ivy.

'Serapha has called on me to free the child,' he said.

Morrigen vaguely remembered being instructed in the Rite he was about to perform, and so lay silent as he wrapped the ivy round her wrists and ankles, binding it in place with knots. He raised a knife, then asked her to tell him her name.

'You know who I am.'

'It'll fail if you don't answer him,' explained the wise woman.

Morrigen stared round. News of the complications affecting her labour must have reached the crowd, for they too had begun chanting. The priestesses had removed their robes and formed a spiral, a group of seers checked slates and tally staffs for the astrological portents. She repeated her name and the full title of her office.

'And now I cut through your bonds and your child's bonds,' added the shaman. 'For once your limbs are free, the Goddess will release the child from the knots that have impeded its birth.'

He knelt and began hacking at the ivy, chopping it into small pieces and tipping it into a cooking pot. Water was added and heated. The shaman filled a beaker with the infusion, lifted his High Priestess's robes and began sprinkling it over the swollen hump of her belly. When he had left, she returned to the squatting position and braced herself against the post.

'Remember, the more you fight the harder it'll be for the babe,' advised Teina, again combing her hair in an attempt to calm her and remove any knots that might invalidate the work of the shaman.

Morrigen drew breath. Her labour intensified. Occasionally, in the lull between contractions, fragments of another world managed to permeate her pain: the priestesses uncoiling into the Serpent Dance, Teina fussing round her, the concern on the wise woman's face. Birth and the first moments of childhood were fraught with peril. Demons could snatch both mother and child, or take one and spare the other. Teina, like many an old spinster without children, the possessor of an unquenchable appetite for doom and all forms of catastrophe, had once told her that for every two babies who reached adulthood another eight lay on the racks. A runner was sent out to place an offering at Henge. The crowd grew tense, an expectant hush descending over the Dwellings as dusk drew nearer.

For Morrigen there was only the pain, the spasms that swept her body as the pauses shortened. There was a sudden flurry of activity. 'Is it coming?' she blurted.

The wise woman nodded, again stretching her hands between Morrigen's thighs. 'Push,' she commanded.

'I can't.'

'It'll be there at dawn if you don't . . . again . . . that's better.'

Morrigen began panting, dizzy and exhausted, blood surging into her head as she gathered breath and tried to force it free.

The wise woman took control of her breathing, telling her when to bear down and when to rest. 'I can feel it now,' she said finally. 'Two more pushes and you'll be rid of it.'

'Is it alive?'

'We'll know soon enough. Push –'

So again Morrigen sucked in air and stiffened the muscles in her stomach. The priestesses stopped dancing. Teina whispered encouragement. The wise woman splayed her hands to catch the baby as it dropped: she could feel its head, the hair pressed damp to the skull. 'Once more –'

'I haven't the strength . . .'

'Try.'

Morrigen did so. A blood vessel burst in one eye, starring it scarlet. But still she kept thrusting. Suddenly her whole body was lapped by an intense searing pain that took the blood from her face. She cried out. Gripped the post. Saw the wise woman's lips urging her on as like a backcloth to the pain she felt something shapeless and wet slide slowly between her thighs . . .

And then it was over.

A slap, a distant mewl of sound. A blue but bloody shape was held in front of her, still connected to her by a cord. She began weeping, pain mingling with joy and her fear that though living it might be flawed. Gradually she became aware that the priestesses had linked hands and were circling in the same way as the sun: the evidence she had been waiting for.

'I told you I'd have a son,' she murmured, gazing up at Teina.

The old woman grinned and held out a bundle. 'He's perfect.'

He seemed so frail and delicate that for a moment Morrigen did not trust herself to hold him. Her arms lifted, then fell.

'Take him. He's yours,' prompted Teina.

This time she did so – and as his weight came to rest she felt as if all other weights had been borne away by his touch. There was no tiredness now, no pain. It was both the most complex and the most simple moment of her life; too profound for analysis, too obvious to need it. She tightened her grip on him, smiling contentedly. His brow had been daubed with ochre to give him strength. His face was still puckered and spotted with blood. But his blue eyes were wide open and they stared up at her with a wisdom and clarity that seemed to pierce her to the core. She opened the swaddling robes, instinctively counting fingers and toes before wiping the last of the mucus from his nose. He whimpered slightly, unclenching a fist, then his throat gaped open and the whimper gave way to a bellow.

*

Later, when the afterbirth had been delivered and buried beneath the floor of her hut to nourish the soil, Morrigen placed her son to her breast and lay at peace on her bed. The crowds had dispersed to celebrate and the drums were broadcasting news of the birth to the villages on the Plain. The wise woman and priestesses had gone, only Teina remained. Despite the old woman's happiness, she appeared troubled and ill-at-ease. Suddenly she sat beside Morrigen.

'You tried to tell me something before the baby was born. Do you remember?'

'No.' Morrigen had been alerted by the abruptness in Teina's voice. She shrugged, feigning indifference. 'What did I say?'

'I couldn't make sense of it all. You were rambling. But it concerned the Darkness and the killing of a healer and a seer called Leoid.'

'Nothing else?' It was important she knew.

Teina remembered the description of hemlock being pounded. Morrigen was smiling at her in an attempt to persuade her to deny what she'd heard. She hesitated, aware that she had trespassed on a past that was best forgotten. Then chose retreat. 'No.'

Morrigen relaxed. 'I was delirious. I'd have said anything to ease the pain.' She closed her eyes. The joy had left her. She had intended the birth of her son to mark a new beginning, an end to duplicity. But already she was lying, and the lies were as practised and fluent as any that had preceded them.

*

Ceruduc came to see her in the evening. She was alone and half asleep, and for a moment neither of them spoke. Compared to her son, so perfect and untouched by the world, Ceruduc appeared worn and battered. His beard was stubbled, his cheeks mapped by an intricate network of veins. He was also slightly drunk. Morrigen forced herself to welcome him, then lifted the baby from her breast, holding it towards him. 'Look at what I've made.'

Ceruduc held out his hands to take it. For an instant it hovered midway between them. Suddenly Morrigen lowered her arms, withdrawing her son from his reach. 'He's mine,' she said simply.

Ceruduc stared at her in disbelief. 'But I'm his father.'

'I don't care. I suffered to bear him.'

'He's my son, Morrigen.'

'And does that give you the right to claim him as your heir? As son of a High Priestess he belongs to the Gods, not you.'

'Do you know what you're saying?'

'Yes. The child is mine, and always will be. Better that he have no father at all than be heir to a drunkard.'

Ceruduc sought for excuses: protectiveness, exhaustion, some passing foolishness sleep would banish. It was no use. 'I'm leaving at dawn with Atius to begin searching for the stones,' he said firmly. 'I intend holding my son before I go.'

Morrigen was clinging so tightly to the baby that her breast had flattened beneath it. There was a long silence, then she relented and handed Ceruduc his son. 'I've named him Tyrus, after my father,' she said.

'You can't do that!' protested Ceruduc. 'The choice is as much mine as yours.'

'It's too late. The name offering has already been given.'

Ceruduc deliberated arguing with her, then turned away, gazing at his son. Instead of pleasure he felt embittered and helpless. Since entering the hut Morrigen had robbed him of his self-respect and given warning of what lay ahead. Even at his drunkest the longing for a son had remained constant. Until now he had hoped that the birth of that son would close all the gaps still outstanding between himself and Morrigen. They would become a family, other children would follow. She would relent and swop her office for a future as his wife, a home in the marshes. But he now realized that he was to be excluded from the future, treated as an encumbrance to be temporarily humoured then ignored, dismissed, forgotten. There would be the occasional summons to her hut. His son would be handed to him then snatched away, a stranger he did not know. When they met there would be awkwardness, when they parted only loneliness and the next summons to look forward to . . .

There are two formal embraces traditional to the Cunei: a kiss on the brow in greeting, and on the cheek when saying goodbye. Ceruduc opened the swaddling robes and scanned his son, memorizing his every feature in an effort to store away a portrait of him that would remain a momento for ever. His body was warm and soft and his fingers squirrelled through his beard when he reached forward to kiss his cheek. He returned him to Morrigen, then backed away and walked quickly from the hut.

*

By nightfall Ceruduc was drunk. He did not appear at the feast held to celebrate Tyrus's birth, nor could anyone find him when his absence was noticed. At dawn, when Atius roused the men and headed north across the Plain, he lay asleep near the river, his robes torn, mud in his hair and his cheek in a puddle. When he woke he gave orders for his tent to be moved to a wooded knoll outside the encampment. By noon he was drunk again. Hyra went to see him. He refused to be shifted, finally becoming threatening and violent. During the days that followed the dogs gathered round him, the strays, the lame, the unwanted, all of them drawn to his tent by the tenderness he had reserved for his son and now did not need. Within a month the first puppies had been born and the dogs rose as a pack when anyone approached, yapping and snapping and driving them back. For a while the children used to creep up behind his tent to laugh and throw stones at him. Repetition and fear of the dogs soon ended their game. Ceruduc was rarely seen, and when he was he was drunk. To the villagers, as to himself, he had all but ceased to exist.

# CHAPTER XVIII

'I've never known such a rumpus. It's not natural. Nor's it right for Tyrus to be humped up and down dale like another of them stones.' Teina snorted, hitched up her robes, then scuttled through the mud with all the belligerence of the timid.

'Either stop fussing or wait for me in my tent,' said Morrigen.

'Where he'll be kept awake by the din. Poor mite. All that bellowing and hammering and he'll end up deaf, that's if the stench doesn't bring on a fever. Eight days we've been here, and that's eight too many. It's a wonder I'm not flat on the racks.'

'Much more complaining and I'll ask Atius to find you work with the other women.'

'And who'd take care of Tyrus? You? You'd lose us both and that's the fact of it.' The cataract in Teina's right eye had become more pronounced as she grew older, but in compensation the left eye had evolved a method of rolling from side to side in its socket so as to maintain the same field of vision. And what she saw did not please her: the men splashing through the mud towards the ridge behind her, the cold autumnal wind tugging at the surrounding scrub. 'What a place! Take me for a fool if there aren't monsters in the forest and sprites in the hills. We should never have come.' A second snort, then she tightened the sling round her waist and marched off in the direction of the camp, mumbling to herself in disgust, Tyrus's circular face peering owl-like over one shoulder.

Morrigen waved at her son, affection holding her gaze until he had bobbed beneath the slope of the hill and she was distracted by Atius's approach. She inspected his face, checking it for the truculence with which he had treated her since her arrival, then smiled gratefully at its absence as he joined her.

'The second stone's on its sledge,' said the merchant. 'Four others are waiting to be lifted.'

'And the third stone?'

'Still buried in the chalk, but we'll have it cut by dusk.'

'What about the Tan?'

'Peaceful enough. I don't blame them for wanting us gone. We're felling their timber and hunting their deer. Let's hope they're consoled by the livestock you sent them.' Atius frowned. 'I could have used the extra cattle. We're short of rope again. Boar-skin stretches when it's wet and the deer have moved deeper into the forest. Send too many men out hunting and I'll be short for sledging the stones.'

Always setbacks and obstacles, thought Morrigen – difficulties to be overcome. She turned and stared out over the river in the valley below, momentarily exchanging the present for the past. She had washed in that same river when a novice at Abury, a day's journey to the west; forded it when departing as a priestess for Henge, Atius her guide. Two nights later he had come to her hut, his body still damp with its waters . . . Old ghosts: better forgotten.

Beyond the river lay the forest, steaming in the sunlight after a sudden downpour in the night. Elms towered upwards, their branches spread open like parasols to shelter the stunted oaks beneath. The faint thud of axes, men cutting timber for rollers. Beyond the forest's crown the hills lifted steeply in folds, outcrops of chalk rising sheer as cliffs along the crests. Behind her the downs sloped emptily to the skyline, only the trading route that linked Abury to the Eastern Seas cutting its swathe through the scrub. An eagle patrolled overhead, rust against blue. A raw and untamed world, she decided, a fitting landscape for the stones it was being forced to yield. They lay all round her, their weathered surfaces half-hidden by the march of the gorse. Even now two masons were searching for those that might prove suitable for Henge, first tapping them with hammers to test for internal flaws and then branding them with chalk if the tap rang true.

Atius noticed her gaze. 'That's only the beginning. They may be the right shape, but start digging and you can be sure that four out of five are split underneath or break along the wrong line when we fire them.'

'It'll soon be autumn,' reminded Morrigen. 'In six months' work you've not sledged one stone to Henge. The chieftains are impatient. Without results they'll remove their men.'

'That's your affair, not mine. I'm a merchant who has some knowledge of stone. It's you and Hyra who want Henge built, not me. I need flour, more oxen, winter clothing for the women and children. You're trying to hurry me. That's when mistakes get made and men end up maimed.'

Morrigen smiled. 'We pay you well enough.'

'Not well enough to work miracles.' Atius faltered, regretting the arguments that marred their every encounter. But her smile was so contrived and supercilious it made him still angrier. 'Don't judge others as you judge yourself. Not everything has its price. We've no guide but trial and error. No one alive has shifted stones as heavy as these. I've seven hundred men in camp, plus their wives and children. They all have to be fed, kept at peace, told what to do and when it's to be done. In six months we've had a dozen rest days. I'm doing Ceruduc's work as well as my own. Yet since you've arrived you've done nothing but find fault. Take Teina's advice. Return to the Dwellings and leave us alone.'

'As High Priestess of the Cunei I have every right to be here.'

'Damn who you are. You're flesh and blood like the rest of us. Cut you and you bleed. I'm not fooled by cant, Morrigen. Nor can I be bewitched like Hyra or turned into a self-piteous drunkard like Ceruduc. I've been employed by the Council to build a temple. And I'll do it. But don't you start telling me how.' Atius paused, then reached out and twisted her chin, forcing her to look at him. 'Let's understand each other. Perhaps then we can be friends instead of foes.'

Morrigen coloured as she saw the contempt in the merchant's gaze. As always she felt an imposter stripped of all disguises by his frankness. She freed her head, turning it away. 'I'm sorry. I don't want to argue with you. It's just that it's always I who have to calm the chieftains and placate the Tan. I had to come. How could I explain the delay without knowing its cause?'

Child-birth had not touched her. Her body appeared to have shrugged it aside as a passing aberration that left her beauty untouched. And when she spoke the truth – as she had done then – a mixture of innocence and utter defencelessness took the hardness from her face. Atius was not deceived. Morrigen at her most irresistible was Morrigen at her most dangerous. He walked on across the scrub, forcing her to break into a run to draw level.

The ground fell away, revealing some seventy circular tents clustered in lines against the hillside. Pigs rooted through the mud. Goats brought in to be milked added their bleats to the din. Near the edge of the encampment the small herd of cattle Morrigen had brought with her was being slaughtered to provide fresh meat and hide for the ropes. The scent of blood had panicked and terrified them, and they bellowed incessantly as the slaughterers in their crimson aprons moved through the pens, hammers raised.

Morrigen shivered, hooking an arm through Atius's as she saw the women squatting near the pens flay and scrape the fat from the still bloody hides with thin slivers of flint. It was a task she knew well: the stench, torn hands, the gristle and warm blood that glued clothes to bodies as it clotted. Once scraped, the hides had to be sliced into strips and soaked in buckets of urine to free the remaining hairs. The younger women moved to and fro between a line of trenches and the buckets, picking up armfuls of prepared strips and then trampling them beneath the dung in the trenches to make them swell and ready for tanning. Others trudged up the hill with goatskins of water. The children were stirring the pulped acorns and oak-galls in the tanning pits to help accelerate the extraction of the tannin. Some pits were already in use, others were being emptied and the raw leather that had been taken from them was being rubbed with cattle brains to help soften it. As a child, Morrigen had found no labour more unpleasant, and she abruptly turned away as another basket of heads was upended and the women split open the skulls and deftly scooped out the brains.

'Day after day, that's all they do,' said Atius quietly. 'And that's not the end of it. The thongs have to be woven, tightened, plaited into ropes capable of pulling the sledges. I've nearly a hundred women at work, and all you can do is look the other way.'

'You forget, I wasn't always a priestess, nor was I born a chieftain's daughter. I don't need to be told how to weave a rope. I wish I did.'

Atius realized that such admissions betrayed more about Morrigen and the reasons for what she had become than any number of attempts at analysis.

'The men's work varies,' he said, leading her away from the pits. 'Some cut timber and carve pegs for the sledges. They are rollers to be trimmed, earth to be dug from round the stones. Yesterday I sent out a search party to look for antlers for picks. Flint has to be knapped, firewood gathered. There's never enough food to call back the huntsmen. We need more wedges for splitting the stones, more arrows and nets. We've fallen behind on rendering down the animal fat to provide grease for waterproofing the ropes. I'm not complaining. As you said, I'm being paid. But what sustains the men?'

'Pride? The wish to make an offering to the Gods?'

'They could do that in their villages, well-fed and dressed in dry clothes.'

'You tell me.'

'Very well. In their innocence they believe that Henge will so please the Gods that all suffering will cease. That there'll be no more contagion, no tempests or failed harvests or babies snatched for no reason from their cradles.'

'No one can promise them that.'

'But do you agree with them? That's what matters. Or do you believe only in yourself and the power Henge will give you when it's finished?'

'Of course not. You seem to think that the Gods mean nothing to me. You're wrong. At times they torment me.'

Again Atius sensed that she was speaking the truth, that some secret terror of retribution prompted even the most ruthless of her actions. He smiled uneasily, baffled by the contradiction, then said, 'Come and see the third stone. It's the largest we've found.'

They walked uphill to where the down flattened on to a windswept ridge. The stone lay close to its rim, surrounded by the chalk and earth excavated from round it. Morrigen stared at it in amazement. 'It must be ten paces long. Even a thousand men couldn't haul it!'

Atius grinned. 'We'll move it.' He paused, his grin fading as he explained the problems posed by its size. 'Most of the stones split quite easily. They're the right shape and lie parallel to the chalk. This one won't budge. We've forced wedges into the crack, soaked them in water to make them swell and then tried hammering them. Nothing happened. Now we're using fire, using fat and bellows to build up the heat. You can see the scorch marks along the line of the crack.'

The ashes were raked from the stone. The men strapped bark on to their feet as protection against the heat, then scrambled on to the stone and formed a line either side of the fault, each holding two buckets of water. At a given signal, the water was poured into the fault, engulfing them in steam.

There was a sharp muffled crack. The stone shifted on its bed, widening the fault.

'Now they'll use the mauls,' explained Atius. 'They're smaller stones of the same type, for the stone is so hard you can only work it with itself. Bronze blunts, flint splinters. Watch.'

Atius examined the line of the fault and took up position at one end of the stone. The men waited, arms stretched overhead, mauls poised to strike. 'Now!' he cried. The mauls swung downwards in unision, ricocheting into the air after slamming against the crack. The stone moved again, its fracture widening still further. And so the work went on: more fires were lit, more water fetched, more mauls pounded into fragments by the force of impact. By dusk the stone had been freed from its parent block and lay ready to be sledged.

That evening, as the men celebrated their progress over a rare meal of beef, Morrigen breast-fed Tyrus in the privacy of her tent. The act of feeding him no longer drained her, for since her arrival she had felt as if an invisible energy had swept her up and was carrying her headlong in its flow. At first she had assumed that she owed it to the change of surroundings, not realizing that the stones themselves were the cause. They were delicate yet massive, living creatures that both symbolized the Gods and had been in growth since the conception of matter. The camp existed because of them, making them obsessive to all those involved in the work. Over the last few days she had come to share their enthusiasm, finding in the problems that confronted them the chance to escape from herself. On the following morning, robed as High Priestess and watched by the entire encampment, it was she who washed the stone with spring-water and gave back part of it to the earth as seed to be reborn.

Atius ignored her. Too much a cynic to be concerned by the resurrection of stone, he instead checked the dowels on the sledge, the position of the rollers beneath it, the lines of cables that fanned outwards from the draw bar at the front – all the minor details so easily overlooked. Finally he grew impatient. He glanced round to see her standing on the stone waiting for Bala's light to strike it, arms raised so that the fall of her robes suggested a bird preparing for flight. When the sun rose, her hair filled with colour, haloing her in sunlight and somehow implying that she also was a source of light. Those nearest to her began prostrating themselves in homage, and the sudden vanity that crossed her face so angered the merchant that he instantly gave orders for the work to commence.

'The Rites weren't over!' cried Morrigen, jumping to the ground.

'We're here to move a stone, not praise you.'

Atius turned, silencing further protest by lifting a long timber wedge and knocking it into place beneath the stone. More wedges were tapped alongside it. The men took up station and began thrusting down on them, heaving, pushing, straining to shift the stone. Suddenly it moved, kicking free of its bed, and the slow task of levering it sideways on to the sledge could begin. Once completed, and lashed securely in place, its corners were blunted with bundles of reed and the men smashed beakers of tassine against its prow before hurrying forward to take their place at the poles.

Morrigen paced nervously, tense and on edge, still angry with Atius. The stone dwarfed those round it: the men preparing to retrieve the rollers and return them to the front of the sledge when it started moving; those gathered with levers at its rear; the four hundred or so men hunched over the poles that had been threaded at intervals through the ropes. Atius stalked to and fro, bellowing instructions, checking that everyone was in position. The shamans chanted, waving the skulls they had brought from the tombs nearest Henge to watch over the work. Atius robbed one of his drum and moved well clear of the sledge, eyes sweeping the length of the ropes. The men watched him, fidgeted, punched holes in the turf to provide purchase . . .

The drum had been struck. For a moment nothing happened. The men were thrusting forward, backs arching, sinew swelling their shoulders as they slipped and straightened and the ropes tightened behind them. The strain on the ropes orchestrated a shrill whining sound as the pressure built up. One snapped, scattering those holding it. A sudden splintering, a roller giving way . . . The sledge jerked forward.

'Don't slacken!' cried Atius, as the men started cheering. 'Increase the speed to a slow walk.'

With the dead-weight broken, the haul grew easier and the pace quickened. Ahead of the sledge a secondary gang had started clearing away the stones and gorse that impeded the route. The first lines of men crested the top of the hill. More ropes were uncoiled at the rear to slow the descent. The front of the sledge reared into the air, turf and mud dropping from the runners. It tilted, then the balance suddenly shifted and it toppled forward, slamming on to the rollers and skewing sideways to the slope. The ropes tightened and the sledge lurched into motion again.

'We've done it!' cried Morrigen as Atius sped past her.

The merchant halted and stabbed a finger at the far side of the valley. 'There are four rivers to cross, two ranges of hills to climb, and a month long journey ahead. I'd save the rejoicing until it's upright at Henge.'

But if Atius was too much a realist to surrender to self-congratulation, Morrigen's euphoria was echoed elsewhere as the cumbersome downhill progress continued. In combination, stone, sledge and those hauling them made an awesome spectacle. The stone towered grey and massive into the sky. Four hundred men manned the poles, another hundred were steadying the sledge and shifting the rollers. The shamans were chanting the Song of the Dead. Wives and children crowded round, urging them on. Most had discarded their clothes and daubed one side of their body with ochre and the other with chalk to give them strength and prevent accidents. Half red, half white, their backcloth the washed-out blue of an early autumn sky, no speculative fiction could have prepared Morrigen for what she was watching become fact.

But the euphoria was premature. At the bottom of the hill the ground levelled and softened. The pace slowed, then slowed still further as the rollers sank deeper into the mud. The ground humped into a series of hillocks that caused the sledge to tilt and slip on the rollers.

'We'll have to call a halt,' announced Atius, as he and his men struggled to lever the sledge back into position.

'We've only just started!' protested Morrigen.

'I've no choice. If someone gets crushed or loses a limb the men will think that the Gods are against them. One mishap now and the temple will never be built.'

So the haulers lowered their poles and squatted exhausted amongst the ropes until the sledge was secure. To Morrigen's dismay it was to be the first of many such halts. All the women who could be spared from the tanning pits were brought in to help flatten the ground. The work went on without pause, the sledge jolting over the rollers, the men heaving and chanting as their burden lumbered forward, often merely a pace at a time, the women slipping in the mud as they hacked at the earth with their picks and trampled it flat. The task of keeping the sledge square on the rollers was proving harder than Atius had anticipated. Many snapped, others vanished into the mud. Only when the ground was firm did they function properly. By dusk the stone stood no more than four hundred paces from its hill-top home.

Atius was in despair. 'Go on like this and it'll be midwinter before we reach Henge. It's the rollers. They reduce the friction but the weight of the stone prevents them rolling as they should. The men have been overworked. The delays break their rhythm.' He paused, glancing sideways at Morrigen. 'It can't be done. Not unless you use smaller stones.'

'If the Tan could drag stones this size to Abury, so can we.'

'It's a two day journey to Abury. We've a swamp to cross, half the breadth of the Plain.'

Morrigen stared down at the stone, now boxed by shadow against the darkening sky. Reason insisted she relent, but instinct made her think of Hyra and all she owed him. In her mind Henge became the debt she must now repay. The temple Hyra had conceived must be the temple he saw built. She smiled, amused but also exhilarated by so uncharacteristic a lapse. 'We'll rebuild the sledges, use thicker rollers,' she said finally. 'The size of the stones mustn't be changed.'

'So you can be venerated for achieving the impossible,' snapped Atius. 'The men aren't oxen who can be whipped back into place when they're too exhausted to move.'

Morrigen looked round at the encampment. The lights from the cooking fires lit the men as they lay sprawled outside their tents, silently greasing their hands against blisters, too tired to joke or lift themselves from the mud. Atius was right, she thought: *men aren't oxen* . . . she hesitated, holding the words in her head. It was so obvious, so simple – but like all ideas whose novelty makes them suspect she forced herself to stifle it. It faded, returned. Then she said, 'Why don't we use oxen?'

'Because . . .' Atius sought vainly for reasons. 'It's never been done. No tribe in the land has used cattle to haul stones.'

'Does that mean it's impossible? We're using four hundred men to move one stone. Reach the hills and the number will have to be doubled. You've only seven hundred people altogether. Who's to hunt and move the rollers? But fifty teams of oxen could move this stone. We'd need trained drovers, a gang to clear the route and another to stay with the sledge: perhaps two hundred men in all. Discard the rollers and we'd have men available to carry on building the sledges and prepare the stones for the journey.'

'Even if it worked, where would you find the oxen? We've six teams in camp.'

'Can you get more?'

'No. Not unless you can persuade the chieftains to each supply a dozen.'

'They wouldn't listen.'

Silence. Morrigen gazed out over the valley. Intuition told her that she was close to the answer. The more she searched for it, the more muddled grew her thoughts. There was a pause during which Atius must have said something, for then she heard the splash of a beaver. She rested her chin against her knees, awaiting guidance. A distant bellow, a bull auroch calling to its mate –

'Did you hear it?' she whispered.

'The auroch? Of course.'

'It's the one beast that could pull the stones.'

Atius frowned, momentarily baffled, then stared at her in amazement. At such moments his doubts surrendered to the notion that she really did possess some mysterious affinity with the Gods. No other portent could have reprieved her, no other suggested a solution. She was still speaking, urgently, cautiously weighing her words.

'It'll mean a delay. We'll have to set up camp in the forest. Pits will have to be dug, nettle gathered for nets. Everyone will be needed for the hunt. Work on the stones will have to stop. Once snared, the aurochs will have to be penned, fed, broken, taught to stand in the yoke and answer to the drovers.'

'What about the chieftains? The men are due to return to their villages to help with the harvest.'

Morrigen grinned. 'If they want them back, they'll have to come and fetch them.'

'Will they come?'

'One or two. Most are too far away.'

Atius probed for further flaws. Aurochs were wild black cattle, renowned for their ferocity but instinctively shy. Their numbers had dwindled with the increase of cultivation on the Plain. Deprived of territory, accustomed to moving in large herds that left them exposed to the huntsman, they had retreated into marsh and woodland, only venturing on to their traditional grazing grounds when food was scarce. And yet they were the only animal capable of both dragging the stones and ending his dependence on the chieftains. 'The delay doesn't matter,' he said finally, forced into agreement by the portent's timing and the logic of her argument. 'If we can break them to the yoke it'll transform the moving of the stones. Tame enough and we could sledge four a time, doubling the teams when we reach the hills. 'We'll abandon the rollers. It's the sledge runners that need altering. I'll have the carpenters rebuild them. Each sledge needs only a pair, not too broad and curved at the front to avoid snagging – similar to snow shoes but solid timber. We'll grease them daily and use water to reduce the friction.'

Morrigen stared up into the blackness of the hills when Atius left her to give instructions to the men. The portent had offered further proof of her powers; why then was she shivering? why then her fear? Power won by subterfuge left her mistress of her fate, but the precision of so improbable an omen suggested that some external force had possessed her, that the Gods truly had chosen her to serve them. Then her shivering ceased as a second supposition amended the first and she suddenly imagined herself as absolute ruler of the Cunei; chieftain, Goddess, founder of a dynasty that would one day pass to Tyrus and her grandchildren.

A seed had been sown, and she did not neglect it when the tents were dismantled and moved to a clearing in the forest. A small herd of aurochs was tracked to its grazing grounds, surrounded, driven cautiously towards the line of pits that had been tucked amongst the trees. The aurochs proved a dangerous adversary. They had curved horns and squat powerful bodies: men were gored, two died beneath a flurry of hooves.

Once helpless in the pits they were given water diluted with a poison that made them sluggish and easier to handle. One by one they were slung in a harness and hoisted into pens. Cold winds stripped the leaves from the trees as their horns were blunted, the testicles sliced from the younger bulls. The herdsmen began taming them, a slow painstaking task that went on almost continuously. At night, the pens bathed in the yellow light of the torches, Morrigen would leave her tent to watch them being hobbled and yoked into teams. They bellowed and struggled and their eyes shone in the light, awaking in her some curious reciprocal longing to be untrammelled and free herself. When this mood touched her, she could not sleep, but would roam the darkness of the forest, pretending to herself that she was a wild cat stalking its prey.

A second herd of aurochs was sighted. Once again the routine of trapping and training took its toll of the men. But their efforts were rewarded. Forty days after abandoning the stones Atius could call on nearly a hundred and fifty teams that had been broken and taught to stand in the yoke.

Morrigen felt cheated. Atius's popularity was as great as her own. The men respected his competence and good humour. Always the first to rise and the last to bed, he drove them by example. They found his bluntness refreshing, his energy contagious. His irreverence seemed a virtue when measured against the ritual surrounding their High Priestess. One day he jokingly said, 'You'd better be careful. I'll be as powerful as you before long.'

With only Tyrus and a disgruntled Teina to occupy her time, the joke nagged at her thoughts, acquiring a meaning it did not have. Certain that his wealth could purchase the loyalty of the chieftains if he decided to plot her downfall, she decided to take action to tame him. One evening, the clearing echoing to the preparations for the departure, she invited him to join her for a meal in her tent.

The merchant scanned the food spread out on the pelts.

'Boar broiled in herbs, stuffed quail, heart of hind – I'm too suspicious to be won by being feasted. Everything you do has a reason, even this.'

'Isn't friendship enough?'

'In anyone but you.'

'Then think of it as a reward, a tribute for all you've done.'

Atius laughed and filled two beakers with tassine. 'Payment suffices. My men have struck six seams of copper since I came here.' He handed her one of the beakers. She was wearing woven robes that hung loose to the floor and sat lightly on bare shoulders. By chance – or was it intended? debated Atius – the tallows behind her shaped the outline of the body beneath. His gaze tipped quizzically to hers. 'Where's Teina?'

'She won't disturb us.'

'That's not what I asked.'

Morrigen shrugged.

'You don't answer.'

'It's not important.'

Atius sat and began discussing the journey ahead. The pelts were soon strewn with the remains of the meal. The ewer of tassine stood empty. But the merchant had stayed on his guard, matching beaker for beaker. He congratulated her on the meal.

'You may taste it again.'

'Once is enough. Surfeit is as damaging as hunger.'

Morrigen should have noted the warning. But the tassine had lulled her, and in her mind the evening had evolved into a test of wits fed by nuance and gesture. Her eyes shifted to the cradle in the corner. 'He won't wake.'

'And Teina?'

'With friends.'

'So you and I are alone?'

'Yes.'

A single word, but in it Atius read flirtation and a sudden shift in mood. He rose and walked towards her. She smiled, tentatively, as if she might back away or was uncertain how to react to his approach. But Atius had recognized that smile for what it was – something counterfeit and deliberate. 'I stumbled once,' he said. 'I swore I'd never do so again.'

'And if I caught you?'

'You'd let me drop when it suited you.' Atius paused, searching her face. 'And what of Ceruduc? As the men have broken the aurochs, so you broke him.'

'It could not last.'

'Because you wouldn't let it.'

Morrigen did not answer.

'And Hyra?'

'He's not here.'

'But if he was?'

'It would make no difference.' Morrigen lowered her head as the merchant reached up and smoothed the hair from her neck. Her body brushed his, its length stretching and curling as it moulded itself to his shape. Static rustled in the warp of her robes as he slid them from her shoulders. His hands encircled her. She stood motionless, pressing against him, certain of victory. Suddenly he spoke.

'Some risks have to be won. For I've the feeling that it might prove as dangerous for me to leave as it would be to stay.'

'And which do you intend?' Morrigen let the question trail

into silence. They were dealing in riddles, delays, the awakening of senses left dormant too long. Then his hands fastened on her robes, jerking them back into place . . .

'Leaving.'

For a moment Morrigen could not move. Then she swung round, hair whipping across her face. 'Get out!'

Atius chuckled, unconcerned by her anger. 'Ah, that's better. I think I prefer the serpent to the temptress. It's what you are, not a means to an end. I wasn't fooled. You forget, guile is common currency amongst merchants. You may have tempted me once, but I know you too well to let it happen again.' He paused, deflecting a blow flung ineffectually at his chest. 'Don't be so childish. Why is it that a woman's vanity is her own worst enemy? I'm not trying to offend you. You'll see it more clearly in the morning. Don't threaten. You need me too much. The hand that feeds is always the last to be bitten. I feel pity for you. Disappointed. You've so much strength. But the goodness in you lies so deeply buried that not even you can reach down and touch it. Tonight you've proved that you're no more than an ageing woman chasing fool's gold.'

Morrigen had begun crying as Atius spoke. During the course of the evening all her old affection for him had resurfaced. Since Tyrus's birth she had made love to no one; but the need had not left her, and there had been moments tonight when the need alone had made nonsense of her motives for seducing him. Atius knew her for what she was, could mock her faults and respect her virtues without letting praise spill over into adulation. Yet once again he had misunderstood her, seen only evil when none was intended. She slumped to the floor as the night air dimmed the tallows and his footsteps faded. Teina returned to find her asleep beside her son, one arm wrapped tightly round him as if terrified of losing him.

*

Merchant and priestess made no mention of that evening when next they met. But its legacy was self-evident in Morrigen's face. She had been rejected, abused, reminded of her age – the list lengthened as the aurochs were herded and the encampment returned to the Hill of the Stones.

'If we're to reach Henge by winter you must stop brooding,' advised Atius. 'Words may wound but they'll never draw blood.'

Morrigen refused to listen, deliberately avoiding his company as new runners were fitted to the sledges and three more stones were lashed into place. It was Atius who had told her to be what she was and not what others wished her to be. She had obeyed him, and in the wake of their quarrel there were moments when it seemed to her that he was to blame for her faults.

Mutual self-interest signalled the final truce. A first trial with the aurochs proved more successful than either had hoped. One afternoon fifty teams hauled the largest stone to within sight of the river without a single halt. With extra men available to clear the ground of obstacles the efficiency of the runners made the rollers superfluous. The following morning all three hundred aurochs were released from their pens and led in pairs to the yokes.

'The sledges are travelling in single-file,' explained Atius, as the men made ready. 'I want to cut a permanent track we can use again.'

'What about the river?' asked Morrigen.

'The banks have been sloped. We've dammed it upstream to reduce the flow.'

'And the hunting parties?'

'Sent out at dawn. The women have gone with them to gather forage.'

The need to discuss the next stage of the journey cleared the air, left both regretting their conflict. To make amends, they walked together amongst the men as tents were folded and fires doused. Finally Morrigen joined Teina as Atius took up position beside the leading sledge. The sky was overcast, threatening rain, and a gusting wind swept the reeds on the river-bank. The drovers stood waiting, whips raised. The aurochs, their black winter coats beginning to thicken, snorted and shook their yokes, hooves trampling the mud. Atius glanced at the four stones, garlanded, daubed, each painted with an eye, then cupped his hands and gave the orders for the start.

Whips cracked. Men shouted. The aurochs lumbered forward, the hawsers tightening as the sledges jerked into motion and the men sluiced water in front of the runners.

Reaching the river, the aurochs stopped to drink and had to be forced on with sticks. The leading sledge accelerated into the water, churning it up and drenching those round it. The far bank marked the first uphill slope the aurochs had encountered, but they took it easily, pushing on through the marsh ahead as if somehow possessed of a collective instinct that told them that there would be no rest until shed of their burden.

For the next two days they moved slowly southwards, a noisy sprawling caravan of huntsmen returning from wildfowling, children, drovers, women and baggage-oxen. Marsh gave way to the woods that climbed the hills ahead. Drizzle slopped in chains from the trees as their lower branches were cut back to allow the stones to pass. At night, too weary to pitch tents, the men huddled in the lee of the sledges. The aurochs were unyoked, hobbled, set free to graze. At first light the ropes were greased to keep them supple, a meal of bread and cold meat was hastily swallowed, then the trek continued, the lead sledge following the route blazed by the clearing gangs. The climb steepened. The teams were doubled, four days spent dragging each pair of stones up the long escarpment that cut into the hills. Ropes frayed and sledges slipped. Limbs were crushed, fingers sliced by the runners as neatly as with a knife. The drovers struggled to keep the aurochs moving and the tension even on the ropes. On the final day they worked in darkness, the stones stark in the moonlight, the Goddess they were to be raised to praise.

Beyond the hills lay a broad tract of swamp, thick with bog-oak and sedge. The descent proved as hazardous as the climb. The sledges skewed and careered out of control. One somersaulted, shedding its stone, its timbers shattering as it tore its way through the aurochs and bounced amongst the rocks. Five men died that day, and three more lives were lost before half the aurochs were moved to the rear of the sledges to act as brakes and help slow the pace.

Then came the swamp itself. Even as they approached it, and Atius breathed the stench of decay, he sensed the trouble ahead. 'Slow down!' he bellowed.

'What's wrong?' demanded Morringen, pushing her way through the reeds.

'Take another fifty paces and you'll be up to your knees in mud. It'll be worse for the aurochs, worse still for the sledges. We'll have to call a halt and lay a timber track where the ground's softest.'

Morrigen peered ahead of her as the clearing gangs hacked

at the sedge. There was a thick scum on the water and marsh gas bubbled up in their wake. 'Can't we go round it?'

'And add another month to the trek? No. We'll send the children and oldest women through first. The rest of us will have to stay with the aurochs and sleep where we can.'

And so the passage through the marsh began. Normally crossed in a morning, it took six days to negotiate. Leeches weakened the men, water sloshed round them as they carried in the timbers for the track and bound them in place. By the end of the second day those who had remained with the sledges were too exhausted to note their hunger or filth. At dusk, swarms of mosquitos thickened the air, adding to their discomfort and so panicking the aurochs that many foundered to their deaths in search of escape. Forage had to be brought in for them in baskets, the water caused swelling and sickness. One afternoon all fifty teams on the third sledge sank up to their bellies in the mire when the track suddenly collapsed, many struggling so violently that to avoid drowning the others they had to be slaughtered still yoked.

For Morrigen the swamp meant incessant anxiety lest Tyrus develop a fever. She insisted on carrying him herself in a sling on her waist. To help banish her fears she spent her days with the men, herself taking a whip and sharing the work of the drovers, her robes sodden, mud smearing her face. Atius was awed by her single-mindedness. It was the first time he had observed her when confronted by failure, and he saw in her now the qualities that had won the rising. It was she who sought out the injured and comforted the women, she who inspired the gangs and kept the sledges moving.

Once the swamp lay behind them, the pace quickened. They skirted a line of hills and began the climb on to the Plain. Wounds healed, the aurochs regained strength as they grazed, high scudding cloud watched over the stones as village succeeded village and Henge drew nearer. Fourteen days after clearing the swamp they reached the site of the final battle against the Dobuni.

'And about time!' declared Teina, when Morrigen told her the news.

'Two more days and we'll be there. Hyra's sent a courier. He's going to meet us.'

'Good riddance to him,' retorted Teina, chomping busily on her teeth. 'First he decides on a temple that means enough toing and froing to wear out my feet, then he skulks in the Dwellings and lets others build it for him.'

'Henge is mine,' said Morrigen angrily. 'Without me there'd be no men to build it and no aurochs to haul the stones.'

Sensing her mistress's mood, Teina humoured her conceit. It was a mistake, for the lines between fact and fiction had become so blurred in Morrigen's mind that she interpreted the flattery as proof that it was she who had conceived the rebuilding. The possibility of founding a dynasty was resurrected, returning to her thoughts when the caravan finally reached Henge.

It was a dank, misty morning. But by noon the mist had dispersed to reveal plumes of coloured smoke rising in greeting from the villages. The wind had arched the smoke, merging the colours and shaping rainbows overhead. The crowds that had gathered in welcome pressed forward, waving, cheering, holding up the bones of their forefathers. The warriors lining the Sacred Way tipped their axes in salute as the sledges swung through a gap in its banks and began the approach to the temple. The priestesses laid branches of wych-elm in the path of the aurochs and tossed garlands over their horns. The shamans' drums carried them into the Rite of Delirium. Hyra and the seers began intoning the Song of the Dead as the sledges came to rest.

And Morrigen saw little of this, heard even less. Through it all she was quietly reviewing her life, withdrawing into herself, her mind a clutter of dreams, hopes, the son she cherished. She sallied backwards – through murder and triumph and men she had discarded without ever learning to love – then switched to the future, the appetite for power she had yet to sate. Once again it was the portents that had steered her thoughts, for the morning's first sound had been the cry of a fox; omen of stealth and duplicity.

# CHAPTER XIX

Two years passed. But still Morrigen held back, content to wait upon chance rather than force an error. Yet gradually her influence increased. Like a spider stitching its web, the strands of her power multiplied and tightened as she slowly extended her authority. One spring, to avenge the rape of some women gathering forage by a party of Tan, she ordered Abury to be sacked. Two of its stones were removed to Henge to stand astride the entrance and the Tan made to swear homage to their new mistress. It was a victory that gave resonance to all she had achieved. At Abury she had been a handmaiden and novice. At Abury she had first used guile to serve her needs and had embarked on her journey to power.

After the Tan it was the turn of the Juba. Like a whirlwind, she swept north and east at the head of her warriors; subjugating, colonizing, forcing the vanquished to pledge fealty to the Cunei. If the presence of Tyrus and Teina and some of her priestesses lent a hint of femininity to the tents from which she planned the campaign, the campaign itself was often brutal and hard fought. But exposure to battle during the rising had numbed her to its effects. She shirked no dangers, suffered the hardships of the men. As hill-forts fell to the advancing Cunei and envoys sued for peace, it seemed to her that the Gods were protecting her, checking her madness and supporting her ambition.

Both Hyra and Atius were critical of the campaign and played no part in it. But her absence allowed them to continue Henge unhindered. The work force was doubled. The aurochs moved endlessly between the temple and the Hill of the Stones. By the date of her return, a start had been made on the outer circle and the inner stones stood upright in readiness for the lintels to be added.

Morrigen's arrival filled the Dwellings with warriors and her retinue. Hardened veterans of the war mingled with the tribesfolk and merchants. Gradually its occupants grew immune to the confusion, even the seers becoming adept at deflecting the constant requests for an audience with their master.

But one afternoon in late summer, shortly before the harvest, the seer on duty outside Hyra's dwelling finally met his match. The boy was about ten, with a square serious face. The girl was younger, the woman obviously her mother; for both shared a slenderness, the same quick smile and patrician gracefulness.

'I'm not moving,' repeated the woman. 'We've come a long way. My daughter's tired. A man more courteous would let us wait for him inside.'

The seer sympathized, but his master's instructions were explicit: no strangers were to enter his quarters. Yet the girl's exhaustion was visible beneath the dust on her face. When she smiled at him he found himself looking round to make certain that no one was watching, then quickly waving them on. 'He'll be back from Henge before dusk.'

The dwelling was cool and spacious after the crowds outside. Fresh bracken lay green and still smelling of sap on the floor. Sunlight picked holes in the thatch. A pile of tally staffs and measuring lines lay abandoned in one corner. The children were tense and on edge. Their mother encouraged them to play, then paced apprehensively; tidying clothes, re-arranging, occasionally smiling as an old beaker or a familiar cloak caught her eye.

The complications dogging the rebuilding were still circling through Hyra's thoughts when he entered the Dwellings. Dressing the stones was taking longer than expected. The importance of placing them at an equal distance apart and to the same height from the ground had meant constant adjustment to the depth of the holes. The width of the stones varied considerably. Their bases had had to be bevelled to make it easier to turn them once upright. Some had begun tilting, others were sinking into the ground. The slight uphill slope on which the temple had been built had added to his problems. He tried to dismiss them, too tired to concentrate. Tonight he intended forgetting Henge for a while and going fishing with Atius . . . He frowned, halted by children's laughter coming from inside his hut. Reaching its entrance, he bellowed for a servant and demanded a reason for the intrusion.

'The woman told us to leave them be.'

'What woman?'

The servant took shelter behind a stammer.

'Never mind,' barked Hyra. 'I'll get rid of them myself.'

The woman had her back to him when he entered. He glimpsed a boy and girl shinning up one of the posts that supported the roof. He was hot, his feet ached. The day had been long and its problems intractable. Anger gathered a shout in his throat. Suddenly the boy cried 'Father!' and dropped to the bracken. The woman's head swung into profile . . .

Hyra stared at her, the shout spilling unspoken from his lungs. 'Lyla,' he whispered.

She carefully smoothed the creases from her robes, unable to answer. And then his arms lifted to greet her and she ran forward, lithe, smiling, light on her feet.

Their embrace was awkward and drawn out. Even when they parted the wariness remained. Emotions were suppressed, clues sought in physical changes, the children employed as an excuse for small talk. Cronus and Kirsten came forward to greet their father. After that the conversation flagged and they were compelled to fall back on each other. Lyla ended an uneasy silence.

'The children wanted to see you.'

Hyra watched them as they played. Kirsten turned and grinned shyly at him: she would be easy to win back. But Cronus seemed distant, even hostile – as if the years without a father had bred loneliness and resentment. 'And you?' he said, evading her gaze.

'I'm not sure. Even now we're here I think it may have been a mistake. Perhaps that's why I came. Either to be rid of you and take a second husband or try and begin again.'

'It's six years, Lyla. You could have come sooner.'

'Or you to me.' A pause. 'We're both in the wrong. Don't let's begin with a fight. I wanted to see you here, in the Dwellings, in your own world, with Morrigen beside you.'

'She's been away since early spring. I hardly see her. Only Tyrus seems to matter to her.' Now it was Hyra who hesitated. 'You know about Ceruduc?'

Lyla nodded, glad of the backwater. 'I saw his tent. I couldn't face him. I wanted to speak to you first.'

'Morrigen asked him to lead the campaign against the Juba. He refused. We've all tried to help him. He's growing worse. He's never sober, never washes, and won't leave his tent. I disagree, but Atius thinks that Morrigen could still save him if she chose to.'

'But she won't.'

'Can you blame her? He's not just a drunkard any more. Mead is an addiction. A day without and he becomes violent. A month ago he nearly killed Teina trying to take Tyrus from her. He's filled his tent with stray dogs and their pups. Go down wind and you can smell the stench.'

'He's still my brother. Morrigen deliberately destroyed him. She must share the blame for what he is. Yet you sound as if you're defending her.'

'I'm trying to warn you of what you'll find when you visit him. Besides, I haven't the time to worry about Ceruduc and Morrigen.'

'Because of Henge?'

'Partly, but the temple isn't a panacea, a means of forgetting her.'

'I've heard a lot about it.'

'I was grateful for the men you sent, and the flour.'

'I'm looking forward to seeing it for myself.' Lyla had thawed slightly, her voice was less abrupt. 'I want you to show it to me.'

'Haven't you been there yet?' retorted Hyra, offended.

'I came to see you, not what you're building.'

Hyra averted his eyes from the lancing look that accompanied the rebuke. After so long a separation she was almost a stranger, for in his mind he had carried only one image of her when apart, that of the pregnant whining woman who had made his life so wretched. But the portrait was no longer accurate, and he now realized that he had been clinging on to it as a justification for leaving her. She was stronger, calmer, even prettier than he remembered. She was also being honest, a rare virtue when measured against the sense of intrigue that went with Morrigen like a shadow. He tried to imitate her.

'Atius told me that he gave you an account of my travels when he stayed with you last year. There's more I want to tell you. But for now all that's important is that you know how little I thought of you. I'd banished you from my life. To forgive would have been impossible, forgetting was easy. But after I'd returned and Tyrus was born I began to think of you again. It was partly loneliness, partly the baby you'd lost, partly missing the children.'

'And women?' Lyla was standing motionless in front of him, a vagrant tress of hair falling unnoticed over one eye.

'A merchant's widow I met on Epius. No one else. I'd been shipwrecked. I was alone on a strange island. I suppose it was inevitable. But since I came back there's been no time for anything but Henge.'

'Is there now?'

Silence. Both knew that everything said so far had been a prologue to this one question. Lyla waited, too proud to plead but willing his surrender and an end to her loneliness. Hyra scanned his hut in the hope that its emptiness might provide an answer. But it was empty no longer. Cronus was swinging from a rafter, grubby-kneed and laughing. Kirsten stood beneath him, clapping excitedly at her brother's daring. Their noise filled the hut, giving it gaiety and life. His eyes shifted to Lyla.

'Yes.'

'And what you told me about Morrigen is the truth?'

'Yes.'

'I need to be sure. You've wounded me once, next time I may not mend so easily.'

'There'll be no next time.'

Lyla hesitated, remembering the way the villagers had mocked her when it first became known that Hyra had deserted her, the long struggle to win their respect. Until now she had thought that only she had suffered, that Hyra had been spared the scars. But watching him as he stared round the hut she had realized that despite having Henge to occupy him his life had been as empty as hers. She smiled, then finally relented and placed her head to his chest.

Next morning she was the first to wake. Hyra lay beside her, his body still warm and rank after making love to her at dawn. The children lay curled beneath their pelts. It was all so new and unexpected that her first instinct was to fight her happiness. Almost fearful of disturbing her husband, as if perhaps it would prove to be a dream which his waking would dispel, she moved closer to his shoulder and went back to sleep. That day, for the first time since the start of the rebuilding, Hyra was the last of the men to reach Henge.

*

Lyla was killed shortly before noon. The men were raising one of the stones in the outer circle when it toppled sideways, crushing her beneath it. It happened so suddenly that no one had time to pluck her from its path and only Morrigen shouted a warning. Death was instantaneous. Of those who witnessed the accident, only Atius was troubled by Morrigen's reaction to it, and it was to be many months before he finally decided that it might not have been an accident at all.

At the time it was impossible to apportion blame. The two women had not met since Lyla's return and they were picking their way amongst the picks, mauls and discarded flints that littered the site, discussing Tyrus as they went.

'I took him on campaign,' Morrigen was saying. 'I'd have worried about him if I'd left him behind. He can talk now, just a few words.'

'He means a lot to you,' said Lyla.

'Everything.'

'But his father means nothing?' The question marked a change in the character of a conversation that both had been careful to restrict to the progress of their children; the safe common ground that allows women to forget their differences.

'You haven't seen him yet. He's a drunkard. What would be said if I took him back?'

'That you've learnt charity, that you still respect him for what he did during the rising.' Lyla paused. 'I want you to come with me to see him.'

Morrigen did not reply. Lyla's ability to accuse by probing for faults had not deserted her, and the years alone in the High Vales had added a dignity and poise that made Morrigen feel threatened.

'Will you come?'

'Is it so important?'

'Not to me, but it may be to Ceruduc.'

'Then of course I'll come,' said Morrigen, glancing across the temple to where Atius and some of the men were preparing to haul a stone into place. The shear-legs used to reduce the angle of pull stood upright beside it. The stone had been dragged down the ramp cut into the side of the hole and ropes were being lashed round its summit. Men were shouting, dust filled the air. Masons perched amidst the scaffolding enclosing the inner arches, hammers endlessly tapping as they carved out the protruding tenons on which the lintels were to rest.

The two women climbed the bank. Beyond it, food was being cooked and ropes plaited outside the rows of tents and turf huts that spilled untidily across the scrub in an effort to house the work force. The shifts had just changed. One gang was levering a stone from its sledge on to rollers so that the aurochs could return to the Hill of the Stones. A second gang had begun the preliminary shaping of another, pounding long parallel grooves down its face with their mauls. It was a taxing, monotonous task. Chippings took the skin from their faces, accidents were common. Once finished, the ridges between the grooves had to be carefully chipped away, inch by inch, day after day, until the surface was even. A third gang, watched by Hyra, was giving one of the uprights its final grinding by dragging a smaller stone to and fro across it, using water and chopped flints as an abrasive.

Lyla smiled fondly at her husband's forgetfulness. He had promised to explain what was happening, but since their arrival had been too absorbed in the dressing of the stones even to glance at her. 'Can I watch the stone being raised?' she asked Morrigen, seeing the men begin hauling at the ropes that fanned down from the shear-legs.

'Of course.'

'Is it safe?'

'I think so.'

Morrigen remained where she was as Lyla moved closer to the stone and craned forward to watch it shudder and rasp against the stakes lining the hole as it reared upwards and began its ponderous climb into the vertical.

Drums were beating. Nearly three hundred men bent backwards, muscles straining as they tugged at the ropes and Atius called the time. The masons lowered their hammers, enjoying the break from routine. Lyla turned once, to grin excitedly at Morrigen. Morrigen waved, then glanced round to see Hyra walking towards his wife. As her gaze shifted, she suddenly noticed that the cross-piece linking the shear-legs was beginning to work loose. Her eyes switched to the stone. It was still rising, but at a slight angle, so that if it fell it would fall upon Lyla.

Thoughts accelerate at such moments, slowing time and racing one into the next. Everything that Morrigen now thought was almost instantaneous, her final decision was made within a second of realizing what might happen. In her mind it seemed to her that the Gods themselves had placed Lyla beneath the stone. But if fate had brought her here – to these circumstances, to this precise moment – it was to Morrigen that the Gods had given the choice of taking or sparing her life. For no one had seen what was happening, it was only visible from where she and Lyla were standing. And Lyla was still peering into the stone hole, unaware of the danger. Lyla . . . the one woman she had always feared and never been able to outwit. The stone was still climbing. She could hear the thump of mauls, Atius shouting, her heart quickening against her ribs. And then she knew she could not do it and began running –

'Lyla . . .!'

The shear-legs snapped, splintering so suddenly that the noise brought a scream from her throat as she again repeated her warning.

Lyla twisted sideways, head flung back, to see ropes whipping through the air, timber falling – the stone begin skewing towards her. She lifted her arms, too terrified to move. Then came darkness, a vast weight snapping and breaking her open as it bore down on her body, burying her beneath it.

*

Atius reached her first.

The stone lay across her and all that was visible was a fold of hair sprinkled lightly with dust. He knelt beside it, eyes already turning away in search of Hyra. And then he glimpsed Morrigen, smiling. It was a curious smile, almost triumphant. But it barely had time to lodge before he saw Hyra approaching, hands steepled neatly beneath his chin, feet lifting mechanically over obstructions. The temple was silent. The men were still picking themselves up, but the drumming had stopped and so strained was the atmosphere that the silence seemed louder than the clamour that had preceded it. Hyra moved on, still in shock. He had yet to show symptoms of either grief or reaction, and to Atius his expression appeared remote and absent-minded. He halted, staring down at the hair as the wind tugged at it.

'Why?' he whispered. 'Why Lyla . . . ?'

'It was an accident. She'll have known nothing.' It was pointless trying to console him, but Atius was hoping to prompt him into continuing speaking.

'It was the first time she'd been here. I haven't seen the children since they were babies. Now I've got to tell them that their mother has been killed by the one thing I thought more important than fatherhood, this temple. I'm not sure I can do it.' Hyra spoke quickly, as if the words themselves were a release. In his mind he was remembering lying beside her after they had made love, the languid body that now lay hidden from him. He reached down, smoothing her hair between his fingers. 'There's no chance that . . . ?'

Atius shook his head. 'You know what they weigh.' He looked up to see Morrigen standing behind Hyra. In trying to comfort Hyra he had forgotten her smile.

'I saw it too late,' she said. 'There was nothing I could do.' That was the truth, and the cause of her elation. The split second of indecision would have made no difference. She had finally conquered her evil and attempted to save life instead of take it.

'You shouldn't have let Lyla go so close,' said Atius.

'She wanted to watch. It seemed safe enough.'

'The fault's mine, no one else's . . .' Hyra was still stroking Lyla's hair, but with a tenderness that hinted at the calm before some inward storm that had yet to break. 'The Gods have spoken. The work must be stopped. It was I who thought of the temple.'

'And I who should have checked the shear-legs,' added Atius.

'No. I'm to blame. I started it, and I've the right to end it.' Hyra paused to stare up at the men gathered in silent groups round the stone. 'Send them away. Tell them to return to their homes. There'll be no Henge.'

Atius and Morrigen glanced at each other, one frowning grimly, the other trembling, both of them conspirators drawn together by their determination to rally Hyra. 'It was I who found you the men and thought of the aurochs,' said Morrigen quietly. 'Atius has spent two years teaching the men how to move and dress the stones. Does what we think not matter?'

'It's Lyla that lies dead.'

'But stopping the temple won't resurrect her,' said Atius firmly. 'The work goes on. We've travelled too far to turn back, both of us. If her death is to have any meaning Henge must be completed, for your sake as well as hers. She can't live to see it, but Cronus and Kirsten will. They may blame you now, but when it's finished they'll perhaps realize that you had no choice and that Lyla did not die for nothing.'

'I can't do it,' whispered Hyra.

'And what about the men? Lyla's not the first, nor will she be the last. Nearly a hundred men have died because of you. Are their deaths too trivial to trouble you? Is the work to be halted because of the wife you abandoned? Stop it now and it won't be because you wish to mourn her, but because of guilt, your own cowardice.' Atius spoke gruffly, angrily, purposely taunting Hyra in an attempt to force a response.

For a moment he feared it was wasted effort. Hyra was still clinging to Lyla's hair.

He had begun weeping and his face had the cowed, bewildered look of someone close to defeat. Suddenly he shuddered and released his hold on the hair. 'Have the other shear-legs fixed into place. Ask the men to return to the ropes.' He glanced at Morrigen. 'I'll tell the children later. Make sure that no one else breaks the news to them.' He paused to stare at Atius, a half-smile held lightly by his lips. 'I'll build it, but don't ask me to look at what's left of her when the stone is lifted.'

It was said so courteously that Morrigen knelt at his side and threw her arms round his neck in hope of draining his grief.

Atius could not answer. No language he knew had equipped him to reply to such courage, or a smile so tragic.

*

Morrigen halted to turn and look back when climbing the slope to the Dwellings. Distance made a miniature of the temple, and the lines of men heaving at the ropes resembled ants bearing home a twig. But the scene was still as familiar; the creak of the shear-legs, the slap of the ladders as they were placed against the vertical stone and plumb-lines were lowered to check for a lean, the shouts of the men as chalk and old mauls were packed round it and tamped firm with hammers, the slop of slurry being poured on top so that if the stone shifted during the winter its change of position would be recorded by cracks in the clay . . .

The recital was no help. Not today, with one set of shear-legs snapped and the stone lifting to display Lyla's broken body spread burst open beneath it. She trembled. Her elation had faded, to be replaced by sympathy for Hyra and a sense of foreboding she was unable to explain. For that final glimpse of Lyla, arms held pointlessly overhead, had fuelled a reaction now inexorably gathering momentum. She tried to check it, eyes turning away to pan fields patched white with the ripening corn, the fat cattle grazing the Plain beyond. In the far distance, amongst the tombs and tents, she noticed a courier hurrying towards the Dwellings, the arrows at his waist glinting in the sunlight.

Her gaze shifted – as she knew it would – to the torn weathered tent looking down from the hillside above her. Part of it had collapsed, grass and nettles had rooted in its walls; dogs lounged idly beneath the surrounding elms. Ceruduc would have to be told, she thought, her tremble worsening as his sister's image returned to haunt her. She was still staring at the tent when a flight of crows clattered from the elms; harbingers of strife or calamity.

By the time she had reached the Dwellings so ominous a portent had combined with Lyla's death to carry her close to hysteria. She was tense and apprehensive, and gave orders that she was to be left undisturbed until after the Rites. Teina brought her Tyrus, and mother and son sat playing together in her hut; Tyrus giggling as she smothered him with kisses and flicked her hair over her face so that it hung like a curtain to the ground, a house for him to play in. Such moments were usually her happiest. She became a child again, sharing his pleasure and taking part in his games. But today even Tyrus could not soothe her or rid her of the pressure forcing itself against her brow. Instinct told her that she was marking time, waiting for something.

Suddenly she noticed a sheaf of corn lying on a slate. It was small and battered and had been plaited into the shape of the Moon Goddess; though she recognized it she could not place it, nor could she remember having put it on the slate.

A cackle, a wheezing, the tapping of a stick . . .

'I asked to be left in peace,' said Morrigen, not looking round.

The cackling grew louder.

Morrigen spun. 'Did you hear what I . . . ?'

An old woman was hobbling across the pelts. She was stooped and gnarled. Despite the wens that had sprouted from her scalp her hairless skull shone and glistened like dented well-polished leather. Her face was shrivelled, age having eroded her features into a network of corrugations punctured only by the deeper hollows of eyes, nostrils and mouth. Her palsied hands were as knotted as the staff with which she had propelled herself across the pelts to stand, bent and still wheezing, staring at Morrigen.

Morrigen backed away, an illogical unease making her pull Tyrus into the protection of her robes. 'Who are you?' she demanded.

Tyrus looked up at his mother, confused by the sudden halt in their game.

The old woman pointed at him. The wheezing quickened. 'Would he ask that question of you?'

'Of course not. He's my son.' Morrigen paused, her misgivings increasing. 'How did you get in? Why didn't the guards stop you outside? Who are you . . . ?'

The repetition was unnecessary. Even as she spoke she was scanning the old woman's face: toothless mouth, bloodshot eyes, hooked unmistakable nose. Her own eyes widened in shock and recognition. She tried to pretend it wasn't true, that it was a trick of the mind. Then she heard the querulousness in the voice and saw the high brow duplicated in the son at her side.

'Mother . . . !'

'Is that who you want me to be?'

'It's who you are.'

'Yes.' The old woman nodded, displaying no pleasure as she hobbled closer to her daughter, her stick tapping its melody.

'Speak to me!' cried Morrigen.

Her mother gasped for breath, holding it inside her as if in need of replenishment before being able to talk. 'So you saw the crows,' she said finally. 'Thought you might. Carrion. All of them. Black as night and darker than death. But I'm not dead, child. Still flesh, blood and bones – except I don't bleed any more, too old for that. See.' She lifted a hand and a knuckle-bone showed white and clean where a wound had yet to heal. 'I've cheated death, child. Cheated the crows.' The hand turned towards Tyrus. 'But he won't . . .'

'Please, mother!'

Silence. The pressure against Morrigen's brow had enveloped her entire head, amplifying the chattering sound made by the old woman's stick into a booming, dissonant labyrinth that muddled her thoughts. 'I'm frightened,' she murmured.

Another cackle, harsher than its predecessor. 'Because your own mother's come back to you?'

'Yes. I thought you were dead. It's hard to know what to say. I've sent couriers to the village to find you. No one had seen you or knew what had become of you. Where have you been living? Why wait until now before coming to see me? Why not during the rising or after the defeat of the Dobuni? You must have known I was High Priestess.'

'Did you hear what I said?'

'Yes.'

'Only the boy can spare you and bring back the sun.'

'What do you mean?'

Her mother did not reply. She stepped closer, as if to embrace both her daughter and grandchild.

'No! Stay where you are!' Morrigen backed away, tugging Tyrus with her. Her face had paled and her teeth clicked noisily together when she began begging her mother to go.

The old woman did not move, merely smiling knowingly when she noticed the sheaf of corn on the slate. 'Tuah gave you that on the night I brought you to Henge to stand in the Lines. Sixteen years, yet still you keep it beside you.'

'I thought I'd lost it. Someone else must have put it there.' Morrigen faltered, the green of her irises drowning the pupil as comprehension struck her. 'You did!' she whispered.

'Maybe. Maybe not. That's for you to decide.'

'How did you get past the guards?' Morrigen hesitated, then began trembling when logic demanded that she touch her mother.

'So you're still afraid of me? You always were. Nothing changes.' The old woman chuckled and held out an arm. 'Go on. Touch it.'

Morrigen reached forward, intending to grip her mother's wrist. Her hand hung suspended, began shaking, then fell away, slapping against her thigh.

Her mother smiled. 'I wanted to embrace you. You wouldn't let me. And now you're frightened to lay hold on me lest it's only air you touch, only my spirit you're seeing.'

'Leave me alone!'

'Will that bring you peace?'

A pause, then a thin troubled sobbing that made Tyrus look up at his mother, confused by her behaviour. Suddenly the old woman began speaking of the crows again, chanting the words as if they were a spell or incantation. But Morrigen had stopped listening. She swayed, corrected herself, then fell, hands pressed to her ears. Tyrus began crying.

*

A second voice, calm and courteous and strangely distant.

'The Rites have been celebrated. A courier is waiting to see you . . . Is something wrong?'

Morrigen did not move for a moment. She could not remember why she was lying where she was, or for how long she had been there. The delirium held her in too strong a grip to be easily exorcised. At first she could not control it, and when she finally looked up the guard kneeling at her side was reminded of an animal at bay, so hunted was her expression and so wild were her eyes.

She glanced round, suddenly cautious and fearful of betraying herself. Tyrus was kneeling puzzled beside her, a thumb hooked firmly in the corner of his mouth. Her dwelling was empty. Even before framing the question she knew the answer – but it had to be put. 'Has an old woman just left me.'

'No. You gave orders that you weren't to be disturbed.'

Morrigen stifled a shiver, then forced herself to turn to where she had last seen the sheaf of corn: it had gone, the slate was empty . . .

Her guard was still speaking. 'The courier insists on seeing you. He's waiting outside.'

Again Morrigen had to struggle to appear composed. 'Lyla's death has upset me,' she said. 'We were close friends.'

'The Lord of Rites is with his children now.'

Morrigen turned away. 'You can send in the courier.' Once the guard had departed, she rose to her knees and looked searchingly at Tyrus. 'Who was I talking to?' she said gently.

His small face grew tearful and uncertain. 'No one.'

'Why didn't you stop me?'

'I was frightened.'

Morrigen smiled. 'Go and find Teina. Ask her to take you to the cattle pens. You'd like that. Some more calves may have been born during the night. But I want you to say nothing of what's happened. Do you promise?'

Tyrus nodded, fighting back tears, then hurried away to the kitchen quarters.

Morrigen slumped across her bed. As always after one of her

'lost days' she felt drained and very tired, both physically and mentally exhausted. But there were other symptoms she failed to recognize, for until today no lapse into insanity had been quite so convincing. Yet there was nothing to be gained by trying to persuade herself it was authentic. Inspired by Lyla's death, her mind had invented both the reappearance of the corn and the conversation with her mother. Aware that her madness was again building up inside her, she closed her eyes, determined to bury it and keep it at bay. She had no choice. If anyone suspected its existence the shamans would think that demons had possessed her and demand the right to bore into her skull in hope of releasing them.

But the pieces only finally snapped into place when the courier entered her hut and she read the concern on his face. She had seen him earlier, shortly before the crows. But only now did she realize that the portent predicted by their appearance had come true. The sheaf of corn she had imagined as lying on the slate was intended as a warning. And her hallucination? no more than her mother's spirit come back from the Underworld to invoke a curse on her daughter.

Even before the courier spoke she knew what he was going to say.

'Something's happened to the harvest,' she said.

He stared at her in amazement. 'Aedum sent me,' he replied, naming a chieftain on the western edge of the Plain. He opened the pouch at his waist and withdrew a small bundle of corn. It was not quite ripe, but black spots had mottled the stalks. When he tapped it the husks floated to the ground, revealing ears of corn that were grey with mildew and already withered by disease. He glanced helplessly at Morrigen. 'It's spreading fast. Six more days and it'll have struck every field on the Plain.'

# CHAPTER XX

It was a perfect site from which to view the devastation. The down sloped slightly, then rose in a soft curve to marry the rest of the Plain. From its crest the fields were laid out like a patchwork, each patch trimmed by the stones picked laboriously from the rich, flinty soil. A few of the fields lay fallow, poppies seeding amongst the weeds to lift their scarlet cups to the sun. But where it could be cultivated the Plain was traditionally a granary, making the fields a panorama of whites and golds as the harvest drew nearer and the reapers made ready. But there were no golds today, only a blackened rotting wilderness that stretched almost to the skyline.

Atius lowered his head. 'How much can be saved?'

'A little wheat perhaps,' said one of the grim-faced elders standing between the merchant and Morrigen. 'But no oats and no barley. We began reaping as soon as the courier reached us. Even cut and stooked it went black. The yields are small and the blight's still spreading. By tomorrow night there'll be nothing worth saving.'

Morrigen stared down at the women picking their way through the remnants of the harvest in search of the few ears that had been spared. In the neighbouring field the reapers were moving in line across the one corner not yet stricken, flint sickles flashing as they cut the corn high in the stem to leave the stubble as forage. One piece had purposely been left untouched as an offering to the Gods. She pointed to it. 'Have it cut. You'll need every bushel you can reap.'

'The Gods may be offended.'

'And men may starve if you leave it. It's a risk we must take.' Morrigen paused to watch the line of tribesfolk moving silently towards the nearest village, half-filled baskets balanced on their heads. 'How long will it feed you?'

'If the weather holds, until the Midwinter Rites. But it may rot in the pits, we're having to thresh as we reap.'

'Have it ground as well. Better stale than no flour at all.'

'How can we store it?'

'In the pits. We did the same during the rising. Line them with bark and seal them with clay to keep out the rain.'

'And the seed for next year's planting?'

Morrigen shook her head. Exhaustion made it difficult to think. 'I don't know. For four days now Atius and I have been travelling from village to village, offering advice, silencing rumours, trying to calm and stop panic. I've hardly slept for the last two nights. Use common sense. Don't demand answers I'm unable to give.'

'Set a little aside,' added Atius, coming quickly to her rescue. 'The Council will buy in more on behalf of the tribe once the worst is over. It'll be shared equally, according to the needs of each village.'

The merchant glanced at Morrigen. Her face was puffy and swollen, her lower lip raw where her teeth had worried the skin. Four days in her company had warned him that she was veering dangerously close to some form of mental crisis not entirely explained by the blight. He had yet to define it, but studying her now – staring out over the Plain as she awaited the accusations that had become part of their progress – he also detected the beginnings of desperation or panic.

Finally one of the elders summoned up sufficient courage to speak. 'Some say we've sinned, that we're being punished by Bala.'

'Believe that and you're doomed,' retorted Atius. 'You're elders. The villagers respect you and listen to what you say. If you surrender, so will they. The harvest has failed. It's happened before and it'll do so again. Blame the weather, the wind – anything you like. But don't blame Gods whose existence you've yet to prove.'

The elders could ignore such blasphemy. They turned to Morrigen, forcing her to reply, their dour faces leaving no doubt as to what they thought of her travelling accompanied by a heretic. She hesitated for a moment, then swung round to confront them.

'I know what you're trying to say, that as High Priestess I can be held responsible for both the pestilence and its consequences. But would the Gods destroy what they once created? Have I so offended them that you must suffer? No, demons have caused the blight and you must fight them as best you can.'

'The shamans have tried to banish them. It made no difference.'

'So you've already admitted defeat?'

'What else can we do?'

'Divide the villagers into groups and send them out into the forest. Strip every nut tree and bramble of its fruit. Gather dog nettle and spurrey, anything that'll stave off hunger if the winter brings famine. Gather leaves for forage, mark out any stands of elm so that you know where there's bark fodder for the cattle. Ration the flour. Organize hunting parties. Cut firewood now whilst you've still the strength. Nothing must be left to chance. Hang owls over the cattle pens to bring immunity against tempest. Leave basins of milk in the fields for the Gods to drink from should they turn into beasts. All the livestock that have been given to the temple are being driven to the coast to be bartered for fish. It'll be smoked and shared out amongst the villages. But you're to regard it as a reserve, not to be touched until the pits and cattle pens are empty.'

It was a faultless performance, Morrigen at her most compelling, and a complete contradiction of the elders' assumption that as a woman she would know nothing of the practical problems posed by the failure of the harvest. They crowded round her, one even promising to make an offering to the Gods for sending her to save them.

Morrigen ignored his gratitude. 'I've not saved you yet, Shaedon. Famine is not the rising. Hunger and fear are enemies more dangerous than any number of Dobuni. We've a long winter ahead. Your loyalty will be tested before it's over.'

'You've won a reprieve, that's all,' said Atius, when they left the elders and began the journey to the next village, escorted by Morrigen's retinue. 'Today they praise you, tomorrow they may want you dead.'

'Stop it!'

'It's the truth, Morrigen. And you know it. Already the seers are insisting that you purify yourself by fasting.'

'That's their right. It's a reasonable enough request.'

'It'll achieve nothing. It's piety run amuck. By midwinter you'll all be fasting, whether you want to or not. Things are going to get worse, much worse.'

The air was humid, almost oppressive. Behind her Morrigen could hear the shamans rattling skulls to drive away the demons, her priestesses scattering water in an attempt to cool the winds. She shivered, hiding her fears behind a brittle gaiety. 'I do believe you're worried about me.'

'You need help. Don't let pride make you reject it.'

'I thought you'd promised Hyra to return with him to the Hill of the Stones?'

'I'm offering to stay.'

'To do what?' said Morrigen sharply. 'Play the nursemaid and protect me from harm? You forget, three months ago I was leading the Cunei into battle against the Juba. I don't need you, Atius. I'm not the innocent priestess you once made love to. I can fend for myself.'

'By slaughtering all those who stand in your way? How can you speak of innocence? You were as ruthless then as you are today. The only difference is that you're now so steeped in blood you think only bloodshed can save you.'

'And with you beside me I'd be forced not to spill it, to act what I'm not. I'm reliant on no one. Famine is certain. I don't want you acting as my conscience and hindering me in what has to be done.'

'And what will have to be done?' demanded Atius.

Morrigen turned away, refusing to answer. At moments such as this she despised all men; for the arrogance that halted any attempt to understand the intricacies of women, for their belief that it was they who ruled and what they surrendered to women was given merely to humour and keep to heel. Suddenly she was calm again. The threat of danger was oddly reassuring, even exhilarating. If disaster struck, she would survive it. It meant a challenge, a test of her sanity, the chance to prove that she was her own mistress not a cripple who could not walk without men to prop her.

*

If Morrigen believed herself free of the influence of men, she knew better than to make a similar claim against her own sex. Lyla and her mother might both be dead, but in the wake of the death of one and the imagined reappearance of the other they had fused into a third abstracted woman that continued to haunt her. By the date of her return to the Dwellings she was permanently nervous and on edge. Two days later she was forced to accompany Lyla's funeral cortège to a tomb on the edge of the Plain.

The day had been cold and blustery, and dusk was already

falling when they reached its stone façade and began the descent into the darkness. To appease Serapha, Hyra had decided that his wife's remains should be laid to rest in an earth covered long tomb. The wind funnelled through the entrance, driving the light from the torches against the low stone roof overhead, the darkened side chambers, the discarded incomplete skeletons that crumbled underfoot as they moved along the central gallery, crouching as they went.

Morrigen's resolve slowly weakened. Her absence would have been unthinkable, but the tomb was so crowded she could barely move and the seers blocking her retreat added to her claustrophobia. Water dripped from the stones. Skulls stared up at her. Bats' eyes glinted in the torchlight; when one flew past her, brushing her face, panic made her turn and throw herself against Atius. 'Let me out!' she cried.

'I thought you could fend for yourself?'

'Please, Atius! Not now . . .' There was an urgency in Morrigen's voice that cut sharply through the chant of the seers, making them falter and stare at her. 'Please,' she whispered.

'Go further forward. There's more room.'

'But . . .' Morrigen turned. Ahead of her, where the gallery widened, Hyra stood with his children. In his arms he held a basket bearing Lyla's bones. She shook her head. 'I can't.'

'Why not?'

'Isn't it obvious?'

Hyra was removing each bone from the basket, holding it up into the light, touching it to his cheek in farewell, then lowering it to the ground. Many were splintered, scraps of flesh still clung to them. The torches caught them in silhouette, shaping their shadows on the far wall of the gallery. To Morrigen these shadows had become Lyla herself. Even the glimpse of a broken rib was sufficient to make her shudder. Sweat began dripping from her face. Despite the wind, she found it difficult to breathe. When she looked round it seemed that the walls were pressing in on her, slowly smothering her – as the falling stone had smothered Lyla.

Hyra turned, beckoning her forward. Grief had pinched his face, making it drawn and wan and suddenly old. Kirsten was crying at his side. Cronus stared at his mother's bones, his face expressionless. Morrigen made herself approach the basket. As High Priestess it was she who had to place the skull on the ground, eyes turned to where Serapha would rise on the eve of the Midwinter Rites, the year's shortest day. She lifted it out, cradling it in her fingers.

The seers began chanting again. The torches flared, bending and distorting the shadows. The skull was smooth. So tight was her grip on it she feared she might break it. It fell without warning, shattering and spilling teeth as it hit the ground. She panicked, turned – pushing her way past Atius and the seers. A cheek grazed the wall. She did not notice the pain. Those who impeded her escape were thrust aside, her screams deafening their protests. No obstacle could halt her, and she did not stop until the tomb lay behind her and the first stars reared up overhead.

Atius found her lying in the grass, whimpering softly. Her body was bent, like that of a foetus, her legs hunched against her breasts. He stared down at her for a moment, then knelt. 'Your mind isn't well. You need help,' he said gently.

'No.'

'It's nothing to be ashamed of. I've seen it before. In men who've been too long in my mines, in women who've lost their children. The healers could help you.'

Morrigen lifted her face, gazing up at him. 'And if they fail? Have you seen those who survive the Rite but are not mended? They become demented. Some take their own lives. Still more wander from village to village begging food as they go. You can see the madness in them; in their eyes, in the way they walk without looking where they're going.'

Morrigen's own eyes were lit by starlight and all Atius could glimpse in them was the emptiness she had just described. 'Then you admit that something's wrong with you?'

'No!'

'You need help. I'm offering to give it to you and do what I can to see you mended. If you won't listen, there's no point in my staying.' Atius turned to go.

'Don't leave me!'

'Only if you admit that you're unwell and allow the healers to open your skull.'

'I can't do that!'

'Then I'm going. Hyra can be cured. You can't. We leave for the Hill of the Stones tomorrow.'

Morrigen plucked at Atius's sleeve, searching for excuses to make him stay. 'What about the famine?'

'I've twice offered you my help, twice you've refused it. "I don't need you to act as my conscience." Your own words. Or have you chosen to forget them?'

'I was angry. I didn't mean it.'

'And tonight you need sympathy but not advice? And what of tomorrow? No, Morrigen. I'm not staying.'

Nothing Morrigen said could alter the merchant's decision. Later that evening she went to Hyra and asked him to halt work on Henge until winter was over. Once again her pleas were wasted. 'I can't,' he said. 'I need to forget what's happened, so do the children. I can only atone for her death by finishing the temple.'

'I'm frightened.'

'Is that why you ran from the tomb?'

'Yes.' Morrigen paused. 'I can fight the famine, but I can't fight myself. Not alone.'

Hyra hesitated. The glow from the tallows had softened her face, removing all trace of the hysteria he had detected in it when lit by the harsher light of the torches. Even grief-stricken and still stunned he had sensed her desperation. But Cronus was listening to what they were saying, and his expression was so openly contemptous that he found himself refusing Morrigen to placate his son. 'You'll be all right,' he insisted. 'If you want help, send us a courier and we'll return at once.'

Morrigen's despair grew worse when she returned to her hut. Even Teina could not cushion her loneliness. She slept fitfully, waking in the middle of the night to find her bedding wet with tears and her body seized by the sudden irrational sensuality that marks the approaches to middle-age. Unable to contain it, she rose and crept in silence through the deserted encampment, imagining herself to be a lynx on the prowl. The dogs began yapping as she climbed toward Ceruduc's tent. She had not spoken to him for nearly a year, and when he appeared in the entrance, cursing the dogs and carrying the stench of soured mead, the moonlight framed a massive bloated body that she at first did not recognize. The mead had split his cheeks into blotched angular planes. Rotting bracken filled the tent. A litter of mange-patched puppies lay sprawled in one corner. But still she could not check herself.

No words were spoken, no reasons sought. The act was silent, brutal, grotesque. Ceruduc was too drunk to be aware of much of what took place, but Morrigen's imitation of a lynx had become so real that she could not bring herself to end it. She took off her robes, parading herself before him then falling to her hands and knees and moving towards him in a series of feline undulations that rippled her body and dragged her breasts through the filth. So convincing was her performance, and so bewildering the violence of its climax, that when Ceruduc woke from his drunkenness in the morning to find her gone, it seemed to him for a moment that he had not made love to Morrigen at all, but to a wild beast that had come in out of the night to seek temporary refuge from a storm.

*

Winter broke without warning. High winds gusted across the Plain, stripping the trees down to the black bones of their branches. Then came the snow and an overnight blizzard that left drifts banked against the ramparts and roofed the Dwellings in white, isolating the encampment from both Henge and the villages. Wolves gathered in its wake, plundering the flocks and harrying and scattering the cattle. Without food and protection, many of those that survived were so emaciated that they soon fell victim to the cold.

For Morrigen, now alone, her strength sapped by a six day fast, the depredations of the wolves meant another enemy to be conquered. It began to seem to her that the nearer she approached her determination to found a dynasty, the further it receded. The coming of the snow had brought the famine she feared. As supplies dwindled and store-huts emptied, the corpses increased. The children and the sick were the first to succumb, but as winter tightened its grip the effects of hunger became daily more visible. The granary pits were soon bare. Hunting was hazardous, the goats dry of milk. Without forage, the pigs began to starve. Without sufficient food to combat the cold, malnutrition led to disease and the first symptoms of panic.

Morrigen was helpless. Hyra and Atius had set up camp at the Hill of the Stones and were now isolated themselves. Ceruduc's only appearance in the Dwellings ended in abuse and an attempt at abducting Tyrus. She tried to cloister herself in her hut and let others contend with the shortages, but as the situation worsened the whispered accusations of blame became harder to ignore.

'What do you expect of me?' she demanded, when yet

another deputation of seers entered her hut with their grievances shortly after the Midwinter Rites.

'Speak to the Gods as they once spoke to you. Beg them to take pity on us.'

The reminder of the lies she had told in order to predict the Darkness made Morrigen tremble. She was trapped, and in a web of her own making. Again and again she had pleaded with the Gods and been answered by silence. She scanned the faces of the seers, her unease growing as she saw their hostility. 'So you think I'm to blame?' she said.

'Who else is at fault? You are our High Priestess.'

'I've been purged. I've given you my hair. My lynxes and hawks have been slaughtered, the carp eaten. I've kept a seven day silence and made an offering to the stones. For two days and two nights I stayed awake in the Temple of the Heavens. I've nothing else to give.'

'But your life . . .'

The words had been spoken from behind her. Morrigen spun to see Naxos staring at her, smiling warily. Nearly three years had elapsed since condemning him to the wolf pit. But time had not dulled his contempt or silenced his criticism, and she at once sensed that if any one seer was capable of inciting the others to turn against her, it was Naxos. She smiled graciously. 'And would my death end the famine and melt the snows?'

Naxos was plain-spoken, but he was also rash – qualities that once combined can be more handicap than advantage. He had not anticipated Morrigen's reply and her smile left him uneasy. He tried to recant. 'I'm warning you, that's all. The tribesfolk are being punished and they don't know why. They need someone to blame.'

'The racks are already full,' added another of the seers. 'And mostly with children.'

'I'll speak to the stewards,' said Morrigen. 'We'll increase the ration for the young.'

'What with? There's no flour, no nuts. We've only the breeding stock and the last of the fish.'

Morrigen turned away: during the last month she had come to perceive that no enemy is more daunting than those that cannot be seen; hunger and cold, the snow flurrying against the walls of her hut. From beyond them she could hear the shamans chanting as they circled the ramparts, the thump of clubs as they beat the ground in an attempt to drive away the demons. 'Tell them to stop. They haven't paused since day-break. They're squandering their strength.'

'And the food for the children?'

The sound of the chanting had filled Morrigen's head, numbing her thoughts. She pressed her hands to her eyes. 'We'll organize a hunt. Every one who can still lift a bow will be instructed to take part. I'll go myself.'

'And if it fails?'

'It won't.'

But it did. A sudden blizzard filled the tracks of the deer and forced the hunting parties to turn back lest they lose their way in the forest.

In the aftermath of so public a censure by the Gods, Morrigen's resilience was tested still further. Though outwardly her authority remained unchallenged, the criticism made by the seers had set a precedent that others were quick to copy. Her powers were failing her, they argued, gaining new recruits to their claim in both the shamans and few chieftains who had been unable to return to their villages.

'They want you dead,' insisted an anxious Teina.

'What can I do?'

The question had no answer. She grew irritable, prone to baseless suspicions that veered close to farce with the belief that her handmaidens were poisoning her food. She dismissed them, replaced them, dismissed their replacements, leaving the hapless Teina responsible for the preparation of her meals.

And whilst Morrigen refused her food, others died for lack of it. Every day the encampment woke to the sound of lamentation and the cries of the starving. The racks buckled beneath the weight of the dead and the carrion come to feed on their corpses. Few dogs remained alive. Thatch from the huts was fed to the breeding stock. Rumours of cannibalism led to an old woman and her son being stoned. The living became a mockery of the dead. They spent their days shivering in their huts, apathetic and gaunt, their robes hanging loose from their bodies, only venturing out at dusk when the ration sledges made their rounds. It was as if, decided Morrigen, the will to live was failing them at the same pace as their strength.

'Send a courier to Hyra,' begged Teina one morning.

'I've already done so.'

'When?'

'Twelve days ago.'
'They've abandoned us.'
'Stop it, Teina!'
Teina fought back her tears. She was stirring a pot of gruel over the fire. Her movements were sluggish, her once plump face now hollow and sickly. Every now and then the effort defeated her and she had to pause to regain her strength. Ladling some of the gruel into a bowl, she began carrying it towards Tyrus. Suddenly she stumbled, collapsing and gasping for breath.

Morrigen hurried to her side and asked what was wrong. Teina attempted a smile. 'Would that I knew, child. Maybe the Gods have come to claim me. I've cheated them often enough.'
'Ssh. Don't say such things. Come, I'll help you to the fire.'
Teina stared up at her mistress. The enforced cropping of her hair had transformed her features, revealing her age and pale skin drawn drum-tight across her cheeks. Fatigue had swollen her eyes and the cold had so cracked her lips that the skin had flaked, leaving open sores in its place. Teina had know her too long to be unaware of her faults. The cunning, the cruelty, even the madness, she had sensed them all, then swept them aside and allowed herself to be deceived for the sake of peace. For Teina also knew that beneath the evil lay the most fragile and complex of women. She had never ceased loving her once, and it almost hurt her to see Morrigen as she was now and compare her to the woman who had so enriched her old age.
'You should eat more,' she said. 'No one's trying to harm you.'
'I've no appetite for it.'
Teina sighed. 'It won't matter soon. We'll be dead. All of us.'
'Don't be silly.' Morrigen paused, uncertain that she had the strength to rally Teina as well as herself, or any faith in what she was saying. 'The snow can't stay here for ever. It's the full moon soon, the weather may change. I've asked the rainmakers to lay out the bones of their forefathers in an attempt to disperse the clouds. We've lit a fire on the ramparts, that should warm the soil and keep the demons at bay. It's a matter of time. Something will happen.'
But what? she thought, walking over to her son. Above him, through a chink in the wattle, she glimpsed a group of women

squabbling over the carcass of a dog, an old man dragging himself through the snow in the direction of the mortuary racks. She shivered, turning away. In the last few days such sights had become commonplace. Many thought it was a sin to take food from the earth during times of hardship, believing that by doing so they were wounding and mutilating the flesh of the Gods. To refuse to eat and lay down one's life meant rebirth, a journey to the Northern Star and the promise of eternal life.

Morrigen lifted her son from his bed. His body felt light, his ribs protruded where they pressed against hers. She touched his face: it was hot and feverish. She turned in horror towards Teina. 'Tyrus isn't well.'

Teina blushed. 'I didn't want to alarm you.'

'You should have told me!'

Teina began sobbing. 'I was trying to help you. You're not well yourself. There's so much else you have to worry about. I hoped he'd get better.'

Morrigen did not linger on passing judgement. The fault was hers. Teina was too weak to tend properly to Tyrus. She turned to her son. 'Are you hungry?'

Tyrus nodded. He would be three in the spring. Infancy lay behind him, and his black hair and lanky frame already suggested the boy.

Morrigen smiled at him, concealing her fears. 'Good. I'll cool some gruel and you can eat as much as you want.' After two mouthfuls he took his fingers from the bowl and began complaining of a pain in his stomach. Morrigen glanced anxiously at Teina. 'He must eat more.'

'It's a dog. He's not used to it.'

'Nor am I. Nor's anyone. But it's all we have unless we cull the breeding stock.' Morrigen paused, stared briefly at her son, then reached a decision. She rose and shouted for the warrior on guard outside her dwelling. When he appeared she ordered him to slaughter one of the sheep.

The warrior shuffled uncomfortably. 'A guard has been placed on the pens. They're in lamb and not to be harmed.'

'And if my son dies, so will you!' barked Morrigen, too concerned to remember that it was she who had given the order. The warrior retreated, later returning with the carcass of a ewe.

'Naxos will use it against you,' warned Teina. 'Why don't

we flee and take shelter in the forest? We'd be safer, we could feed ourselves.'

'We're staying here.' A form of paralysis had afflicted Morrigen with the discovery of her son's ill-health. Fear muddled her thoughts. She could not sleep that night and spent it kneeling beside Tyrus, soothing him and telling him stories to take his mind off the pain.

As Teina had prophecied, the loss of the ewe did not pass unnoticed. When the matter was raised by the seers, Morrigen became threatening, cursing and screaming until they finally departed.

Teina herself was too weak to leave her bed. Even wrapped in additional pelts she continued to complain of the cold. Over the next few days her body grew wasted, the flesh contracting over her skeleton until the joints were visible. Teina's decline was matched by Tyrus's. Instead of playing he lay listless by the fire, vomiting much of his food, his belly swelling, his thin body wracked by fevers that left him drained and wet with sweat.

More hunting parties were sent out as the sky turned a dull purple that the shamans interpreted as proof of conflict between the Gods and the demons. They returned with six deer, a bear and a net laden with small birds that had dropped frozen from their perches. The temporary reprieve brought fresh hope to the living. But with hope came a renewed attack on Morrigen, and so acute was her sense of danger that she was able to detect it the moment she entered the Council Dwelling to attend the morning meeting. The chieftains evaded her greetings, the shamans took refuge in the Song of the Dead, the seers' faces betrayed aloofness and disquiet. Morrigen took her place in silence and the day's business began . . .

Should the racks be emptied and those on them burnt to leave space for others? How was the venison to be distributed? Should the seers walk the embers then be lowered into the river, a priestess coupled with a shaman in a final bid at placating Bala?

Morrigen said little as each of these issues was discussed and resolved. They were preliminaries, a means of underlining the gravity of the crisis and rousing feeling against her. Then came the question she had been waiting for.

'We face disaster,' said Naxos, again speaking on behalf of the seers. 'We can delay no longer. The laws that govern the

Rites state that when the survival of the Cunei is threatened it is the duty of the Council to make an offering to the Gods.' He paused, turning toward Morrigen. 'Do you agree?'

Morrigen hesitated. She was the offering. To agree meant condemning herself to death. To disagree would anger the shamans and provoke accusations of treason. She chose attack.

'My answer doesn't matter. Naxos wants me dead. In Hyra's absence you've decided to make the law your servant and have me offered in sacrifice.' She laughed harshly, pointing at Naxos. 'I spared him once. This is how he repays me. How you all repay me for what I've done for you. I drove out the Dobuni, defeated the Juba and Tan, made the Cunei as wealthy as any tribe in the land. Yet now I stand accused of causing the pestilence, bringing the snow and the famine. Next you'll be telling me that I gave birth to the demons themselves.'

There was an uneasy silence. But as Morrigen scanned those round her she sensed that only cunning could save her. She trembled, momentarily reminded of Ishtar: trapped, condemned, her fate already decided.

'What choice do we have?' replied one of the shamans. 'You may die anyway, of hunger or disease. If that happens your spirit will enter the Underworld and be lost to us for ever. Only if we slay you before your strength fails can we transfer your soul to your successor and purge it of evil.'

A second silence. Murmured agreement. A few of the shamans consulting their chieftains before committing themselves to so momentous a decision. Morrigen deliberated another speech, anger, a direct appeal to the tribesfolk. Then she remembered that the villages were cut off and Teina and Tyrus were too weak to flee. She slumped forward, shock taking the colour from her face.

'You can't do it!' she cried, suddenly panicking.

'Not now, that would be wrong,' answered the shaman. 'The Gods will have heard what has been said here today and we must give them the chance to spare you. But there is still no word from the Hill of the Stones. Conditions will be much worse in the villages than they are here. We cannot delay for long.'

'And what about me? Am I to sit in my hut and do nothing?'

'Only the Gods can save you.'

'And if they don't?'

The shaman lowered his head, evading her gaze. 'The moon is full in eight days. If no sign has been received from the Gods by then your life must end. This is the law.'

*

Morrigen did not return immediately to her hut. She needed time to think, and so tramped through the snow and made her way to the river. Ice had linked its banks, sealing it over with a white membrane thick enough to bear her weight. It was bitterly cold. Icicles hung from the trees and the wind snatched at her robes. Up-stream, some shamans had cut holes in the ice in hope of spearing a fish or reading the portents by watching its motions. But it was the past that had brought her to the river, and it was the past that held her thoughts as she walked alone on the ice, for it was here she had come after murdering the healer.

She tightened her cloak, suddenly angry that she should be forced to risk retribution or surrendering to madness by having to resort to cunning. She had no choice. It had all been so much more clear cut than she expected. She had anticipated threats, a veiled reference to Ishtar. Tyrus's illness had distracted her. She should have realized the mood of the Dwellings, plotted, made plans, prepared her defence. And now she had eight days in which to save herself.

Anger gave way to despair when she returned to her hut. Tyrus was whimpering, Teina too weak to move. In her absence her priestesses had scattered musk and suspended shale amulets from the roof. The fire had been stoked, new tallows lit.

'I told you you'd be all right,' said Teina. 'I knew they wouldn't harm you. Look, they've even left us some meat and tassine.'

And outside in the snow the seers were circling in trance, appealing to the Gods in the voices of animals lest the Gods turn into birds and carry Morrigen away with them.

'You can stop worrying,' said Teina cheerfully, ignorant of the reason for the chant. 'A few more days and all three of us will be well again.'

Morrigen closed her eyes. 'No, Teina,' she whispered. 'I'm to be sacrificed. They're trying to please me, hoping that by giving me everything I need I won't resent them for what they're doing and return from the dead to haunt them.'

Teina stared at her in horror. 'But you're High Priestess! How can they take your life after all you've done for them?'

Morrigen began crying. 'I don't know. I'm cold and frightened. I can't think any more.'

'You mustn't despair. You're not dead yet.'

'It's hard not to. I'm at the mercy of the Gods.'

'Then ask them to help you. If that fails, take Tyrus and flee.' Teina paused, purposely harbouring her strength for a moment in order to try and lift Morrigen's spirits. There was no point in saving it for herself: one day, perhaps two – that was all she had left. 'Atius is right, there's not a seer but Hyra worth wasting a thought on. And that's the fact of it. Good riddance to them. You're worth all of them put together. The people need you, abandon them now and you're no better than they.' Teina added a final snort for good measure.

It was a hint of the Teina of old, the Teina of better days. Some of it reached through to Morrigen, temporarily rallying her. Later she went to the Temple of the Heavens and spent the afternoon begging forgiveness for her sins and imploring the Gods to show mercy.

At dusk it began snowing again. The temperature tumbled, gusting winds driving the drifts against the walls of the hut. Morrigen huddled beside the fire, listening to its spit and the piteous grunts of the boar placed unfed in the cattle pens in order to divert the demons away from the breeding stock. Morning dawned dull and windless, dark snow-laden clouds pressed low over the Plain. Morrigen stared up at them. The weather had worsened: the Gods had not heard her. One day gone, seven left.

It started snowing again in the afternoon, and for the next three days all contact between huts was made almost impossible by the blizzard that swept the Dwellings. Some huts vanished, only the slight humps in the drifts marking the graves of those entombed inside them. Daylight and darkness merged into one. The passing of the days was recorded by the lulls between gales, lulls which offered the living a chance to slaughter the last of the livestock and loot the store-huts.

The silence that followed the blizzard seemed to maroon the encampment in a new and immaculate world, so white was the snow and so perfect the stillness. For a moment it was even possible to forget the suffering it hid. In the evening a pale wintry sun broke briefly through the clouds. But by the time the surviving priestesses had joined their mistress to celebrate the Rites the snow had returned. After they had left, she changed Teina's robes and placed hot stones round her. The extertion weakened her. Banking up the fire, she forced herself to go back to sleep. Once, when it was still dark, she heard Tyrus crying out. When she next woke it was morning and Teina's bedding lay scattered across the floor. Their owner had vanished.

For a moment Morrigen could not bring herself to abandon the warmth of her bed. Then she rose and quickly searched her hut. The entrance hurdle had fallen. Beyond it she glimpsed deep, broken tracks, as of someone dragging themself through the snow, stretching away towards the ramparts. She followed them, suddenly screaming 'Teina!' and breaking into a run when certain where they led.

As always in the mornings a few shamans and mourners were gathered round the racks. They watched her gravely, with the wariness and embarrassment that the reprieved reserve for the condemned. Heads were solemnly shaken when she asked if they had seen Teina. 'They belong to the Gods, and it's the Gods that have buried them,' said one, indicating the racks.

Morrigen followed his gaze, backing away in bewilderment when she realized that none of the corpses were visible. The snow had covered them, leaving only their shape to mark where they lay. Those that had been exposed the longest were encased in tables of ice, leaving a rigid outstretched arm or an arc of blue-tipped fingers to flag their existence.

'Go on. They can't harm you.'

Morrigen hesitated, then brushed the snow from the nearest block, to find herself being inspected by a woman's eye that stared open and opaque from deep in the ice. She shivered, hurrying on to where the most recent arrivals lay hooded by the snow. She began brushing it from their faces, checking, turning away in disgust, continuing her quest. Teina's face was the sixth she uncovered. Her eyes were closed, snow clogged her mouth. Hoar had bleached her hair and the beginnings of an icicle hung like a pendant from the lobe of one ear. Morrigen stared at her for a moment, recalling the plump gentle woman whose laughter and chatter had cheered so much of her life, then bent and kissed her before drawing the snow back over her face.

She retraced her steps, moving blindly through the drifts. The hut seemed forbidding and silent. Beside Teina's bed were her only possessions; a horn comb, needle and thread, a nugget of gold given to her by Morrigen. She carried them to the entrance and threw them high into the air, not watching where they fell.

She remembered little of the rest of that morning. She must have fallen to the floor and begun weeping, for when she next heard a voice if was Tyrus calling her name. She rose and went over to him, kneeling at his side. 'Where's Teina?' he murmured.

'Asleep with the Gods.'

'Is that a good place to be?'

'Yes.'

'And does it mean she won't play with me any more.'

'Yes.' Morrigen began crying again. Fever had heated his skin and when she placed a hand to his heart its beat returned to her as slow and irregular.

For his mother it was the turning point. Panic became rage as she stormed into the Council Dwelling and demanded that the shamans attend to her son. Snails were ranged round his bed. Mistletoe was boiled to pulp and laid over his belly. Morrigen remained at his side; watching him, comforting, wiping the sweat from his face. Once he opened his eyes and gazed up at her. His eyes were very bright and almost colourless, so that for a moment she felt she was looking through them into the spirit beyond. He could not speak, but suddenly she sensed that he was speaking more clearly than at any time in his life, and when she understood what he was trying to say. she screamed and screamed and could not be calmed. By mid-afternoon she could endure her torment no longer and went out into the snow.

She climbed the ramparts, staring out over the Plain. The wind had blown bare the downland, then rearranged the snow into an imitation of that same downland, piling it into fields and coombes and bluffs. She was barely aware of it. Her thoughts were random, disconnected: forgotten incidents, words she had used, people she had met, all fragmenting in her mind – life's clutter and bric-à-brac. The sky was lighter now, a drab grey that hid the sun, the one portent that could save her . . . *I've cheated death, child. Cheated the crows. But he won't*: her mother's words, her own words, the words she had placed in her mother's mouth when imagining her reappearance after Lyla's death. *Only the boy can spare you and bring back the sun*. The cold cleared her head, cutting through the muddle as cleanly as a knife. She trembled. As once her imagination had summoned up the corn that was the clue to the beginnings of the holocaust, so also had she prophecied its end. The Gods had spoken to her and given warning of what lay ahead. The waiting was over. Suddenly she knew what had to be done. But she still unsure of herself and could not bring herself to return to her son, not now, with the decision made. Dusk had fallen when she left the ramparts and began the search for proof.

*

It was dark inside the soothsayer's hut, the mutton-fat dips that lit it waging a losing war against the smoke. Its owner was a doleful unassuming man, his current diffidence masking a failure to cope with all that had taken place since the start of the famine. He needed propping, and Morrigen needed facts. She tried to compromise.

'You're the wisest of all the soothsayers,' she said, drawing closer to the fire. 'For twenty years you've studied the portents and divined the future. And out of those years you say only two haven't seen a change of weather after the second full moon after the Rites. If that's true, what are you frightened of?'

'I could easily be wrong. Hunger, the dead . . . it's difficult to be certain of anything in times such as these.' The soothsayer looked round at the tools of his trade: the bones hanging overhead, the drums used to carry him into trance, his whistles and lime basket, the snake skins that allowed him to leave his body and journey into the future. 'Even if I'm right it'll be too late to save you.'

'That doesn't matter,' countered Morrigen. 'Now let's go through the portents again. You've checked the goat?'

'Yes.' The soothsayer indicated the carcass hanging from one wall. It had now been skinned and cleaned, but prior to that he had opened its uterus and studied the foetus inside to check its growth and size. 'The kid was well-formed. It would have been born in about thirty days.'

'So we know that spring is approaching. Good. What about the Constellations of the Bull and the Ram?'

'How can I observe them? The weather's made it impossible. Apart from the goat, my only guide is experience. It's colder now than at any time since it first snowed, much colder. It can't last. I've also drawn the stones.'

'And they said?'

'That the snow will begin melting within a month.'

'Have you told anyone?'

'Of course. I've spoken in Council, yesterday as well as today. They didn't believe me. They're convinced that the Gods won't spare us until you've been sacrificed.'

'And the other soothsayers, what do they think?'

'Many have died. Some agree with me, the rest have sided with the seers.' The soothsayer paused, his eyes lifting to Morrigen. 'I'm sorry,' he murmured. 'I fought beside you during the rising. I haven't forgotten what you did for us. I've done all I can to try and save you. They wouldn't listen.'

Nor was Morrigen. It was all so vague and tenuous. Like all Cunei, her companion did not believe in the exercise of free-will. Decisions had to be supported by omens and prophecies. Yet still she was not satisfied. From the soothsayer she went to a rainmaker, then on to another soothsayer, then a third and a fourth. More stones were taken from fires and examined for cracks. Bones were studied, trances attempted. To the optimists she paid little attention, to the pessimists she put her questions and voiced her doubts. It was as if she wanted to agree with them, was prepared to allow her own death rather than accept that a passing hallucination could make her endure the alternative.

By the time of her return to her own hut the turmoil was building up inside her. She glanced uneasily at Tyrus. He lay motionless and half-buried by his bedding, and though one arm rested on the floor she at first thought he was still awake. She walked closer, then turned – stifling a scream.

*

The Council was already in session when Morrigen entered in the morning. Her eyes were bloodshot and her face was pale. But she walked steadily, displaying a stoicism and courage that shamed those present into silence. Then every one began talking at once, hurriedly inventing conversations or renewing those that were already over in order to avoid confronting her. She halted, framed by the entrance, grey-robed and stubble-haired, almost becoming a statue she was so still and so lifeless.

Then she broke down, screaming hysterically and calling on the Gods to take pity on her son.

One of the chieftains asked her if Tyrus's condition had worsened.

'He's still alive,' she whispered. 'The fever has left him. He even took food when he woke . . .' She faltered, again surrendering to tears.

'You have two days,' said Naxos sternly. 'Others will take care of Tyrus after that.'

Morrigen swung angrily towards him. 'Don't bury me before I'm dead.'

'There's still no sign from the Gods.' Naxos's voice was without sympathy or regret. 'Three days and two nights, that's all you have.'

'You're wrong, Naxos. All of you are.' Morrigen spoke very faintly. Those listening had to lean forward to hear her words; only a detail perhaps, but it seemed to make her the judge and they the condemned. 'I have ten days, Tyrus has none.' A sudden tic jerked the corner of her mouth. Her fingers tangled through her robes, twisting, coiling, then releasing them. 'At first I could not sleep last night. Teina's death, concern for Tyrus, my own fate . . . some of you will understand. But sleep came, and as I slept the Goddess Serapha appeared before me. You will say I was dreaming, and so I was. But so was I dreaming when I foresaw the Darkness, and if I was trying to save myself I would not tell you what she said. But I must. If I disobey her the famine won't end until no Cunei still lives . . .' She paused. She had closed her eyes, but even that could not check her tears – or Naxos's first premonition of his own fate. She went on. 'Tonight, when darkness rules our lands, I am to sacrifice my son and offer him to Serapha. He is to be slain and buried beneath the Temple of the Heavens. My own death is to be delayed, only taking place if the weather has failed to change within seven days of the full moon. If it doesn't, I'm to follow my son to the grave and be buried beside him. Serapha has spoken to me. Those are her wishes. Those who defy them do so at their peril . . .'

Naxos tried to interrrupt, but she gave him no chance. Her voice had risen slightly and her eyes had opened. But save for the quick fidgets still troubling her fingers she might have been momentarily frozen by the cold. Every one else was completely silent.

'Now you know what it means to carry the burdens of this office. I give you my only son in order that the tribesfolk may live. They will not forget, nor will they forgive you for treating me as you have. The Gods made me with child, and I have loved that child as I have never loved any one. Now he is to die. And if Serapha's pledge proves true there are those amongst you who will live to regret blaming me for our plight. I am High Priestess of the Cunei. You are my servants not my masters. Remember that tonight, and remember it again when the sun next rises and the snow begins to melt . . .'

Morrigen stopped, unable to prolong either her dignity or her eloquence. Her self-control failed her for a moment, a shudder rocking her body when her grief suddenly surfaced.

No one had spoken. Disbelief and horror had gathered on the faces of those round her. Some were open-mouthed, some staring at her; some searching inside themselves for a strength to match hers. The timid pondered the future, the warning in her last words. The guiltless thought of their own children and the ritual ahead. Then it was too late to speak. She was gone, leaving the space she had framed filled with clouds and a sullen, turbulent sky.

*

Later that morning Morrigen moved Tyrus's bed into the corner of her hut so that he could sleep undisturbed. Then she called in the seers and priestesses and issued her final instructions. Many implored her to reconsider: she refused. Once a young woman burst into the hut and threw herself at her feet, offering to sacrifice her own child if Morrigen would spare Tyrus. She was very gentle with the woman, thanking her and making sure that she had food for her family before guiding her to the entrance. All those who saw her that morning were to remember her mood as one of listlessness and calm: 'It was as if she was sleep-walking and couldn't be woken,' said one of her priestesses, perceptively, later trying to explain it.

By noon the crowds had begun congregating outside in the snow. Despite their hunger and all they had suffered her own strength seemed to reach through to them, sustaining and reviving them. They chanted her name, ignoring the cold as they hacked branches from the nearest trees and laid them along the route she would take to the temple.

She spent the afternoon sitting silently with her son. For

much of the time she stared down at him, her face partially hidden in the thin light from the tallows. Every now and then she spoke to him in a whisper or tried to make him more comfortable. If any one approached she leant against him as if to protect him from their stares. Tyrus was very still. He lay in the darkest corner of the hut and it was difficult to see him. Those who succeeded noted pale cheeks and eyes that were sometimes open, sometimes shut.

Dusk was falling when his mother wrapped him tightly in her cloak and began the short uphill walk to the Temple of the Heavens. The villagers wailed as she passed. Drums alerted the Gods to her compliance with their wishes. A light wind drove the snow from the drifts, polishing them to ice. Warriors lined the approach to the temple, twilight darkening their faces.

Inside, the torches blazed, banishing the shadows and lighting the skulls hanging above the crowds packed between the posts. Despite the cold, the priestesses were naked, their bodies alternatively ringed with chalk and ashes. The shamans wore their masks, the seers their amber head-dresses. In the central courtyard, aligned to both midsummer sunrise and its midwinter setting, a small grave dropped squarely into the chalk.

Morrigen took her place beside it. The son in her arms still seemed ignorant of his fate. The light dazzled her at first, half closing her eyes, so that she appeared dazed and in shock as she stared blindly ahead of her and the shamans began their lament. The priestesses joined in, swaying slowly. The smoke thickened, swirling and lifting when the drums found rhythm and the movements of the dancers grew faster. Priestesses and shamans mimicked a ritual coupling. The seers imitated the processes of birth. Many were so weak that they fell to the floor, only to be trampled as the lament grew louder, filling the temple and agitating the skulls overhead. But there was no pause in the Rite. Without the rituals of coition and birth the Gods would not hear them or acknowledge their offering. Its tumult spread outward into the snow, the crowds forgetting the cold and their wretchedness when the noise engulfed them. At its heart, the eye of the storm, stood Morrigen.

The seer conducting the Rite in Hyra's absence approached her out of the smoke. Torch-light played on his face, showing strain and uncertainty. 'The axe has been prepared,' he said.

'The boy is ready.'

'Then show him to the Gods.'

Morrigen opened her cloak and lifted Tyrus high over her head; first turning him towards the invisible sun, then to the winter Moon Goddess now soaring unseen into the heavens. Holding him there, she seemed to weaken and collapse inward on herself, then be reminded of something before quickly returning him to the shelter of her cloak.

'It's still not too late.'

'No.' Morrigen paused, violently shaking her head. 'It has to be done.'

'Someone else could hold him for you.'

Again the offer was declined. 'Just be quick. I . . .'

The seer reached forward when she faltered. She pulled away, straightening. Her self-control was inhuman and he could read no expression on her face. It was as if, he thought, she had so successfully repressed her feelings that they temporarily ceased to exist, and now lay drowned and inert. He turned to Tyrus. His body was rigid, the fingers clawed, the glare so great it bounced back off his face. His eyes were glazed, suggesting that he had been given a draught to numb him to what was happening. His mouth hung slackly open. A wedge of tongue sat pressed between his teeth and his lips were blue and discoloured.

The seer beckoned to a warrior standing anxiously in the smoke. He stepped forward, a bronze axe balanced on outstretched hands. He kissed Tyrus's cheek, then withdrew as the seer began intoning the Song of the Dead:

> 'Between us and the Sacred Gods,
> Between us and the hosts of the wind . . .'

The familiar words echoed into the night.

> 'Between us and the drowning water,
> Between us and the heavy temptations . . .'

Faces loomed out of the smoke, vanished, reappeared; the white of the chalk streaking the priestesses, the shamans' masks turning the temple into a menagerie filled with bears, wolves, stags. Ashes were sprinkled into the base of the grave. The warrior straightened his axe.

> 'Between us and the power of wrath . . .'

Morrigen opened her cloak, holding Tyrus in front of her, his face to hers, as verse succeeded verse and the Song moved to its close. The axe rose through the smoke, its blade glinting in the torch-light. Morrigen closed her eyes.

> 'Between us and the shame of the world,
> Between us and the glory of death –'

Morrigen did not witness it, nor did she hear it. One moment she was still holding Tyrus, the next he was suddenly forced from her grasp, liquid and matter splashing her face. At first she remained perfectly still, hands still held out in front of her as if she was a somnambulist who had strayed from her bed and was being careful not to bump into anything as she walked. And in her mind she was asleep. Some part of her had been torn out and what remained would always be silence. Then she realized that she was screaming and that her hands were clutching at emptiness and that Tyrus lay twisted on the ground like an abandoned child's doll, his skull split open. She fell, dropping on top of him and cradling his broken head until she was lifted from the blood and borne away into the night.

*

She did not want to wake, and so tried to force herself back into sleep. Potions had been given to calm her, but instead of deadening they acted as a filter, remorselessly exposing sudden flashes of memory, building them up, piece by piece, until the full horror enveloped her and she again began writhing amongst the pelts, eyes closed, hands to her ears. The skull might reassemble itself, its shattered fragments becoming petals on some unnatural flower that opened to sprout Tyrus's face, smiling at her, concentrated upon some game that held his attention. Such moments were the worst. She would cry out, beating her head against the ground until the flowers finally wilted and his image dissolved into blackness.

Those attending her watched helplessly. Every now and then an involuntary spasm swept through her body, lifting it clear of the ground. Then oblivion would claim her, her limbs unwind, her head fall still. Some were reminded of a woman giving birth. There were the same periods of calm punctuated by sudden contortions no healer could halt. And in a sense she was giving birth, not to Tyrus, but to his memory, and all she had stifled inside her since returning to her hut after speaking to the rainmaker and soothsayers.

The new day finally reached her: grey light seeping in through the walls, wind plucking at the snow on the roof. She stared up at her priestesses, suddenly alert, her grief hurriedly controlled as she searched for errors and any lapse from caution.

'I want to go to him,' she whispered.

'The grave has been covered.'

'Take me to it.'

'You need rest.'

'I need my son. Rest can wait. Do as I say.'

The priestesses gave way. She was very weak and had to be supported as they escorted her through the snow and began the climb to the temple. Black clouds patched the sky. Snow was imminent. The drifts were compacted where the crowds had gathered. Few people had yet left their huts and those that had prostrated themselves as she passed.

Apart from the warriors outside the entrance, the temple was deserted. Snow hung down over the eaves, anchoring it to the ground and making it seem like an outcrop of pure white rock. 'Please leave me,' said Morrigen. Her attendants retreated. She paused in the entrance, then walked on alone, eyes fixed on the courtyard.

Spears trailing lengths of coloured hide marked the corners of the grave. To the height of her waist it had been heaped with bones placed there by the shamans to guard the child in its earth bound sanctuary. She knelt beside it, then opened her arms and begged the Gods to accept her son into their care. She began weeping, a small hunched figure with the temple all round her. Until now all emotions had been disciplined, trained to answer to her needs. Twice she had verged on defeat, but no one suspected, and now she could speak to him without fear of betrayal.

'You were dead,' she whispered. 'The axe couldn't hurt you. Me, yes – but not you. You were dying when I went out on to the ramparts. I could see it in your eyes. That's why I left you. And when I returned it was too late . . .' She paused, shivering, wrapping her arms round her chest. 'You were so cold that night. I couldn't warm you. I had to keep moving your limbs to stop them stiffening. It was worse in the morning. They wanted to see you. All through the day I had to guard you, open and close your eyes, pretend to be comforting you . . .' After that the words became meaningless, pleas for forgiveness muddling with the prophecy that had inspired her decision to conceal his death and use it to win a reprieve.

Suddenly she stopped herself, giving a long, strident, hysterical laugh that echoed back at her. She started pulling the bones from the grave, then pressed her face to the earth. For a moment she deliberated uncovering him, holding him in her embrace. Then she remembered her final view of him and retraced her steps and went out into the snow.

*

That afternoon she ordered hunting parties to be sent out and her possessions transferred to the Temple of the Heavens. Few dared complain. To those who did she answered, 'Remember, in seven days it may not be my home but my grave.' So composed was her voice that after that they wisely stayed silent. Later she toured the Dwellings, consoling the bereaved, listening, rallying, going from hovel to hovel and even allowing herself to be touched by the dying. The charade ended when she returned to her new home. She ordered water to be warmed and made her handmaidens scrub her until the stench of the hovels had vanished. Her robes were burnt, her hair picked over for lice. At dusk the seers arrived, asking for mercy.

Three days later the first of the hunting parties returned, bringing with it the carcasses of eight horses they had surprised on the Plain. The arrival of fresh meat fuelled the beginnings of hope. Morrigen denounced it. 'Two meals do not make a sign,' she said.

'What other proof could you want?' asked one of her priestesses.

'You'll know it when it comes.'

It came at dawn on the following day. Morrigen was still asleep when one of her handmaidens came running into the temple, laughing gayly and shaking her mistress till she woke. 'The Gods have heard you!' she cried. 'Look!'

Morrigen chose to listen; to the steady dripping of water, the soft thump made by the snow as it slid from the thatch overhead and slapped to the ground. She rose and walked towards the entrance, drums pacing her steps, the distant sound of rejoicing rising up from the encampment below. Finally she halted, content to indulge the unfamiliar warmth on her cheeks.

Away to the east a big perfect sun sat shimmering in the haze of its own heat. There were no clouds. Yellows met golds then ran to blue where the sky swept away to the horizon[1].

[1] Any who may think the event described towards the end of this Chapter unnecessarily grim, or would like to learn more of the facts that inspired such interpretation, should turn to *Woodhenge* (1929), M. E. Cunnington.

# CHAPTER XXI

'Go and wait in my hut. You'll be safe there. Cronus will look after you.' Hyra lowered an arm round Kirsten's shoulders, protecting her from the stares of the warriors swaggering to and fro along the ramparts.

'Can't we stay with you? I'm frightened.' The presence of the warriors and the drunken laughter echoing out from the Temple of the Heavens had left Kirsten apprehensive. She was nine now, but there was no sign on her face of the brave, gay smile that had bewitched the men during the winter.

'You'll be all right, I promise.' Hyra turned to his son. 'Let no one enter until Atius and I return.'

Cronus scowled, his body slouching in defiance. The winter had toughened him; the hardships it had forced on him and the slow grim journey to Henge with the sledges both combining to speed the transition from boy to young man. But the closer he drew to Henge and the scene of his mother's death, the more taciturn he had become. In the last few days Hyra had noted a bitterness that verged on accusation in the shrewd brown eyes he had inherited from Lyla. He met his son's scowl, again trying to explain. 'I had to come back. I'm Lord of the Rites. This is my home.'

'How can this place be your home, any one's home?' demanded Cronus, lifting an arm at the encircling encampment. The snow had given way to mud, the surrounding trees were already in bud, but the line of heads grinning down from the spikes in the causeway still retained some trace of their features.

Hyra stared up at them: Naxos, many of the seers, two chieftains, a sprinkling of warriors and shamans – all her enemies and nearly thirty heads in all. 'Have them taken down and buried!' he shouted at the nearest warrior, evading replying to his son.

'The High Priestess has ordered them to be left untouched.'

'Do as you're told!' growled Atius. 'If they're not buried by dusk I'll remove them myself – and bury you alongside them.'

The warrior hesitated, then called to his companions and began uprooting the spikes. Cronus watched. 'She's an evil woman, father.'

'I know.'

'Then why have we come back? Why can't we return to the hills?' Cronus paused to stare at his father for a moment, then took Kirsten's hand and led her away in the direction of Hyra's dwelling.

Atius watched them. 'A child's questions are always the hardest to answer,' he said quietly. 'Try and understand how he feels. He's right, and you know it. Do you really believe she'd have allowed Tyrus to be sacrificed? He was her only son. Nor were Naxos and the others plotting to overthrow her. They're dead because they blamed her for the famine.'

'Let's at least listen to what she has to say.'

'Oh, yes! And be fooled again. She'll plead panic, win you over with tears and promises. She's as cunning as a cornered wolf.' Atius paused as a group of villagers went by on their way to the fields. Two months had elapsed since the change of weather; only their pinched faces and the absence of children and the old betrayed evidence of all they had endured. The racks were nearly empty, the huts rebuilt, even the cattle pens had begun to fill. 'And don't make the mistake of blaming yourself, he added, seeing the doubt on Hyra's face.

'We should have stayed. The famine was worse than expected. They threatened to kill her.'

'And both Teina and Tyrus are dead. But those aren't reasons for turning the Dwellings into a fort and filling it with sycophants. Nor do they give her the right to set up house in a temple.'

'No one's protested to us.'

'Stop defending her, Hyra. They don't dare. They think she's the voice of the Gods, the gallant mother who martyred her only son in order to melt the snow and end their suffering.'

'Is she really so ruthless?'

'Yes! A thousand times yes! Only you're too much a fool to see it.' Atius glanced angrily at the Temple of the Heavens. 'Come, let's be done with it.'

The laughter grew louder as they began the uphill climb. Reaching the temple entrance, a guard blocked their path and asked them to remove their daggers. Atius smiled wryly as he obeyed. 'All her enemies are dead, yet still she's afraid.'

As Hyra followed him into the gloom, a handmaiden holding out a basin of water stepped from the shadows. 'All those who see her must first purify themselves,' she said.

'It's your mistress who needs purging,' snapped Atius, sidestepping the basin.

Hyra stared round in dismay as they moved between the lines of posts. The temple bore scant resemblance to the vast open space over which he had once so carefully laboured. The skulls had gone, to be replaced by coloured skins that hung down from the rafters, dividing it into rooms. Bear skins covered the ground. Handmaidens glided past carrying ewers and trays of sweetmeats. In one room he saw a group of warriors sprawled lazily against goose-down bolsters. Laughter rolled coarsely from another, bringing with it a glimpse of a drab, naked slave-girl dancing mechanically to the beat of a drum. In a third, a hollowed-out length of wood tipped water into a carp-filled trough; a fourth offered two men training a bear to stand on its hind legs. Once they passed some lynxes pacing their cages. Their spotted coats had lost their sheen and they had the cowed malevolent stare of beasts deprived of their freedom.

Atius's temper worsened as each new room they passed paraded its splendours, its warriors too drunk to stand. 'So this is what we spent the winter dragging your precious stones to Henge for! We buried a hundred men. The Cunei faced starvation. Many still do. But not their saviour Morrigen and these buffoons that surround her.'

For once Hyra was unable to excuse her. Ever since the thaw and the arrival of the first couriers with news of Tyrus's death and the events leading up to it he had done his best to defend her behaviour. Time had lessened his grief over Lyla, but it had also seen a renewal of sympathy for Morrigen. Where once her beauty had blinded him to her faults, now compassion made it hard to condemn them. But the sight of the rotting heads of the seers, many of them friends he had known as novices, had finally swayed him, and he shook his head in disgust as another of the warriors lurched past towing a giggling handmaiden in torn robes in his wake. 'She can't do this,' he said. 'I'll have them thrown out.'

'And be thrown out yourself?' Atius laughed. 'They'll only

go when Morrigen tells them to. Even then they'll try flattery to dissuade her.'

A priestess was escorting them. Suddenly she asked them to wait, turned and ducked under the hangings.

'They'll be gathered round her like carrion picking over a corpse,' predicted Atius.

The priestess reappeared, drawing the hangings to one side.

Morrigen was alone.

She lay in silence on her back, one leg draped over the other. It was a small room, divided from the noise by the surrounding hangings and a view of the grave in the courtyard. She rolled on to her side and stared up at her visitors. The trinkets and amulets hanging from her limbs tinkled emptily. No one spoke. The two men looked down at her, appalled at how she had aged. Her hair was still docked, but her once lean face now showed swollen cheeks and a ring of fat round her throat.

'You look grumpy, Hyra. It doesn't suit you.' Her voice was soft, almost a purr. She clapped. A serving-girl appeared, bringing beakers and additional bolsters.

'I prefer to stand,' said Atius. 'I've little to say and less wish to remain.'

Morrigen pouted, offended. 'You're cross with me, Atius. Why?'

'Get rid of that rabble and I'll tell you.'

'They keep me company.' Morrigen's manner was like that of a child. 'We're creatures of the night. I won't let them sleep. They can do what they like as long as they keep awake to amuse me.' She paused, her gaze shifting to a slab in a corner of the room. 'The nights are always the worst . . always have been. All that silence and blackness just waiting to swallow you.' She halted, suddenly pulling herself together. On the slab were her son's possessions – even his clothes – all laid out and neatly folded as if waiting for him to walk in and claim them.

'He's dead,' said Atius harshly. 'Like those whose heads you had mounted on spikes.'

'They were conspiring to murder me. Many confessed.'

'Then why not banish them to their villages?'

'They were guilty of treason.'

'You're lying.'

'Prove it!'

'I can't, not yet. But I will, and when I do you'll have cause to regret asking me to help build you your temple.'

The merchant had drawn blood. Morrigen rose and walked towards him, breasts pressing forward against her robes, bare feet silent on the skins. 'Are you threatening me?'

'Telling you the truth. But of course, I forget, you're so used to lies that the truth means nothing to you any more.' Atius had hoped to avoid cynicism. It was too impoverished an ally, but what other weapon could he use when confronted with Morrigen sitting in this room, day after day, staring at Tyrus's grave whilst others slaked their appetites at the expense of the tribesfolk?

'Do you know why Tyrus is dead?' she demanded.

'No. But I do know that you'd have fled before letting him be killed.'

'I had no choice. The Gods had spoken to me.'

'They've done that before, remember?' said Hyra. 'Then it was Leoid, who was it this time?'

'Serapha spoke to me, I promise!' cried Morrigen. 'The people worship me. Some think I'm a Goddess. I saved their lives and ended their hunger.'

'You're no Goddess,' replied Atius quietly. 'Gods live for ever. If I thought you'd do the same I'd happily take my own life. You, an immortal! That's one pleasure we'll all be spared.'

Morrigen spun round, whimpering softly. For days now, ever since the sledges had first been sighted, the prospect of Atius's and Hyra's return had nourished her hopes. They would heal her and take pity on her. For two months now she had remained in this room, eating in it, sleeping in it, rarely venturing beyond the temple walls. At night she prowled its rooms, searching for consolation amongst drunkards and flattery, men whose names she did not know and women whose youth she despised. To some of those men she had given herself; in darkness, lit by torches, naked, still clothed. But in their embrace or alone in her room, Tyrus's face continued to haunt her. Only with her lynxes had she found peace. They were imprisoned, just as she was. To them she could speak without fear of betrayal and in their eyes she had seen the understanding she sought. She turned toward Hyra.

'Don't leave me again.'

'Don't listen to her,' growled Atius.

Hyra wavered. His gaze slipped away, then met hers. 'Why did you slaughter my seers?'

'I've told you. Naxos wanted me dead. They all did. I sent

couriers to you. You never came. I had to punish them. The famine was terrible. There was no food. Once Teina died I couldn't think.'

'What about Ceruduc?'

'He's vanished. We're not even certain whether he's dead or alive.'

'Yet you knew he was alone, a drunkard without food and only a tent to keep out the cold.'

'Yes.'

'And you never sent someone to make certain he was all right?'

Morrigen shook her head.

'He was Tyrus's father!'

'Stop it!' Morrigen banged her fists against her head, then moved closer to Hyra. 'Why didn't you come?'

'The couriers never reached us. Even if they had we couldn't have helped you. We had our own war to fight. We were stranded by the snow in the hills. Four stones, six hundred men, without fire-wood or winter clothing.'

'I needed you!'

Atius had remained silent during this exchange; watching Morrigen for any change of expression, ears straining for the discrepancies in what she said – the minute chinks in her defences. But her plea to Hyra came to him as a shock; not merely because he knew she was telling the truth, but because he realized, perhaps for the first time, that Hyra had an influence over her that he and Ceruduc would never have. She might turn to others for physical love, but in the end she would seek shelter in Hyra's gentleness when bruised and in need of refuge. And Hyra would never refuse her.

Suddenly it was Atius who felt bruised. 'I'm going,' he announced.

Hyra turned to him, surprised and confused. 'I thought we'd agreed not to leave until she'd emptied the temple and returned to her hut?'

'You can't do that!' cried Morrigen.

'And even if we could they'd come back.' Atius shrugged, apologizing to Hyra. He glanced at Morrigen. 'Don't forget, we may have buried a hundred men but the rest are in camp at Henge. They're loyal to Hyra and me, not you. If you want a fight, say so. The mines are mine, so are the furnaces and breeding cattle you need to rebuild the herds. You've won a hollow victory.' . . . And so have I, he thought, as he walked back through the laughter and out into the sunlight.

*

Something was nagging at Atius, and it continued to trouble him as he and Hyra began supervising the dressing of the four stones they had sledged to Henge during the winter. Hyra did not notice the change in the merchant. Henge had swamped him and sucked him under. In its stones he could forget both Lyla and Morrigen. People, emotions, even his own needs – all were subjugated in order to complete it.

That spring, as Morrigen mourned and cattle and seed were exchanged for land and distributed to the villages, the gangs reassembled and the work gathered momentum. For Morrigen and Hyra it was tempting to think that the world they ruled was a little of all worlds contained in one, that nothing could exist outside its orbit. But that was far from the truth.

'It's a sixty day journey from one end of these lands to the other,' said Atius once. 'There are villagers who've never heard of you, men who'll never see Henge. They hunt the same forests and reap the same fields without ever leaving them. You preach progress, they want peace. You may mock them as ignorant, but there's no peace here.'

That was self-evident. By midsummer there were nearly a thousand men at work on the temple. The tents rose from the scrub, hot winds cracking the earth and sending the dust swirling across the Plain. A jargon evolved, the gangs acquired names and Henge its legends: the stone that kept falling, the white stag found dead in its precincts, the barren woman who came to it to conceive and gave birth to six-month triplets.

One day Morrigen appeared, led, as always, by a pair of lynxes and mounted on the white bull that now carried her whenever she strayed from the Dwellings. Atius ignored her. The shifts had just changed: one gang was preparing for the erection of the last of the lintels in the inner arches, another was about to raise a stone in the outer circle. Men hurried to and fro with picks, ropes and timbers for the crib. The merchant let them pass, then went to where Hyra was measuring the distance between stone holes to check their accuracy. He pointed towards Morrigen.

'She won't stay long,' said Hyra, quickly dismissing her. 'We need more flint for the grinders.'

'Can't we take some from the men digging the holes?'

'And face another delay? The last hole we sunk was two paces high and solid chalk to its base.'

Like all such problems it was eventually overcome. But it served to remind Hyra of the slowness with which the temple was rising, the endless set-backs that daily confronted them. He smiled to himself. The fault was his; sometimes he wondered if he owed his insistence on perfection to a fear of finishing it, of being stranded again, without purpose or reason for living.

After the first stone had been raised he had studied it from the Funeral Way. It appeared wider towards the summit. He went south and looked it at again. The effect was still more pronounced. That day he had it removed from its socket and carefully tapered so as to correct the perspective, leaving a slight bulge in the centre. The result was an optical illusion that suggested perfect straightness when viewed from a distance. Since then every stone had received similar treatment: a detail, a minor subtlety, but eight days work for a gang of twenty masons.

Joined by Cronus, he walked over to the lintel lying on its side at the base of its uprights. 'Are you ready?' he asked, glancing at the men.

They laughed, their gang-leader winking at Cronus. 'As ready as we'll ever be.'

Hyra paused to check that the mortise holes had been scooped clean to take the tenons, then moved on: the men knew what to do. 'Can we watch?' said Cronus.

Hyra smiled. 'Of course.' It was rare for Cronus to show any interest in the temple's construction; the request hinted at an end to the months of estrangement.

Father and son stood side by side as the men levered first one end of the stone and then the other on to timbers. Once they had raised it waist-high and the packing was becoming unstable, a large timber platform was built alongside it, boxing the uprights and forming a layered crib on to which the stone was slowly shifted. The packing was placed on the crib. Using levers and ropes, the stone was jacked back on to it again. The crib was heightened, the lintel raised, the packing replaced; each stage being repeated as the lintel climbed the face of the uprights. By mid-afternoon it lay parallel to the tenons on their summit.

Hyra smiled as he followed its ascent. It all seemed so easy, yet it had taken him and Atius months of trial and error with earth and timber ramps before stumbling on the notion of a crib.

Atius was on the far side of the temple guiding the erection of the upright for the outer circle. Morrigen's presence had left him uneasy, but it had also reminded him of Lyla's death, of some forgotten expression he had seen on Morrigen's face when the shear-legs splintered. Again and again he had searched his memory in hope of tracing it. So far it had eluded him, but it did not prevent him observing her as she watched the men take their places at the ropes.

The drums began beating. The stone rose slowly from the ground, the shear-legs creaking as the ropes tightened and took up the strain. Morrigen stood close, her retinue discreetly behind her. The men began chanting. The stone continued its climb. Suddenly Atius saw Morrigen glance up the shear-legs, then smile . . .

The merchant closed his eyes, holding that one image in his head. Morrigen smiling . . . *I saw it too late, there was nothing I could do.* Lyla dead beneath the stone. And Morrigen smiling, triumphant, guilty of murder by default and purposely giving her warning too late.

For a moment he did not move. He opened his eyes, seeing for the first time the torment and cruelty that the years of ambition had gathered on her face. Then all the rage contained since his return finally insisted on outlet. He bellowed her name.

She approached, watching him uncertainly and already on her guard. His fist lifted as she stepped within reach, then fell, sweeping back and forth across her face until it was a crimson blur and she was screaming at the pain and her bodyguard had dragged him clear, pinioning his arms to his side.

Hyra began running across the temple. The men hauling at the ropes were unable to pause and the stone was still rising. Priestesses were screaming, men shouting, Atius trying to shake off his captors. Morrigen had collapsed, the fine powdery waste on the ground sticking to the blood when she lifted her face and looked up at Atius.

'Kill him,' she whispered.

'No!' Hyra halted beside her as her guards drew their daggers. 'Kill Atius and Henge will never be finished. The men will leave and refuse to come back.'

'It's your temple. Use slaves. Look what he's done to me. No one strikes me and lives.'

'Listen to her!' roared Atius. 'She murdered Lyla and yet still she demands blood for blood.' Hyra had swung round as he spoke and was now staring at him, eyes wide, mouth hanging open. 'Yes, Hyra. Believe me for once. She knew that the shear-legs were about to break. After the stone fell I saw her smile. It was no accident.'

'That's not true!' cried Morrigen.

'She was your wife,' said Atius quietly.

Hyra looked at the stone rearing upwards above him, too stunned to speak. Cronus had pushed through the crowd and was now gazing at Morrigen, the tears shining wetly on his face. Hyra glanced at him, then at Atius, then Morrigen – the trinity pulling him different ways. His eyes stayed fixed on Morrigen. 'Did you know what was happening?'

'No!'

'Then why smile?'

Morrigen fumbled for words. She was trapped. The truth meant confessing how close she had come to allowing Lyla to die; to deny the smile meant invention, concealing her innocence behind lies. Whatever she said would not be believed. She did not reply. Her skin was torn, one eye hooded. Her nose was bleeding and both lips were cut. The pain was immense. Finally she hauled herself to her feet.

'Your silence condemns you,' said Hyra.

'Do you really believe I'd stand aside and watch Lyla die?'

'I believe nothing you say.' Hyra stood very close to her. Both were unaware of Atius's curses and the men jeering at the guards.

'Atius is wrong, I promise.'

'You've made promises before.'

Morrigen began crying. To stand accused by Hyra of a crime she had not committed cut deeper than any blow. 'Sometimes I think I was cursed at birth by the Gods. Whatever I do is always wrong. Take life, save life – it never seems to matter.'

'Then release Atius. Without him we'd both be dead. The rising would have failed.'

'And if I do will you stay?'

'To finish Henge, not for your sake. You may deny it and I can't prove it, but Lyla lies dead because of you.'

'No!'

And suddenly Hyra knew that she was telling the truth. Now it was he who was trapped. To side with Morrigen could only widen the rift between himself and Cronus. To deny the truth to appease his son was cowardice. In the end he stayed silent. Morrigen was watching him, poised on surrender. For a moment it seemed to her that to give way would be an acknowledgement of guilt. Then she saw the sorrow and understanding on Hyra's face and sensed his predicament. She turned, pointing at Atius. 'Let him go.'

Hyra had also turned, to see his son sneering at him, despising him for what he had condoned.

*

'I'm tired of fighting her,' said Atius. 'Tired of being pulled apart by hating her and having to pretend that she means something to me. Tired of trying to make you see sense. Tired of temples and hauling stones and watching men die when they don't need to. Just tired.' He waved a hand at the darkness. 'I loathe this place. I don't belong here. I'm leaving, Hyra. Leaving and not coming back.'

A stray shard of light from the tallows lit Atius's face, allowing Hyra a view of the ruts and lines that fatigue had placed on his cheeks. His beard was grey, his hair thinning, the fires that had once burnt in his eyes had dimmed and lost their strength. I could be looking at myself, he thought: arteries hardening, reactions slowing; the body mapping the journey into old age, safe haven and sleep. Atius was still speaking.

'Come with me. This is no world for the children to grow up in. Did you see Cronus's tears this afternoon? Morrigen had murdered his mother and you wouldn't even condemn her.'

'She didn't do it! Please . . . we've spent most of the night arguing about it. Lyla's dead, Morrigen smiled. That's all we know.' Hyra paused to glance at Cronus and Kirsten lying asleep in the shadows. 'And if I had condemned her?'

'I'd be dead. Perhaps you would as well. But at least Cronus would know that you had the courage to stand up to her. And what about Kirsten? There's not a man in the camp who wouldn't lay down his life for her. Never once during the winter did I hear her complain. Does she deserve a father who's seen one wife be killed and tried to forget by taking Henge as a second? Leave with me tomorrow. Return to the High Vales whilst you've still the chance.'

. . . early summer, thought Hÿra: the scent of hay and the first hinds dropping their fawns. He shook his head, fighting the dream. 'I can't.'

'And I'll tell you why. Because Morrigen owns you and you can't step free of her. That's why you forgive when you should condemn, find excuses for her where none exist. She won't change. And you won't change her. You're a great man, Hyra, greater than you know. Sometimes when I look at Henge and see what you've started I think that there really are Gods, Gods who've chosen you to build it, touching you with their genius or whatever it is that orders our lives. But you have one terrible weakness, Morrigen. And one day she'll destroy you as she would have done me today.'

Hyra rose from the fire and slowly circled his hut. The Dwellings were silent. Even the wind had fallen, as if it too needed rest. It had been a long day and a longer night and it was becoming hard to think and find the words he wanted.

'I can't leave until Henge is finished,' he said finally. 'If Morrigen destroys me then, so be it. The temple will be built. I'll have done what I set out to do; built a temple that will still be here on the Plain when all our names have been forgotten, that the rain won't rot or the winds tear down. And what will be remembered then? That the Cunei once lived here? That Morrigen murdered to gain power? No, Henge will speak for us: of the Gods we worshipped, of our knowledge and strength and what we must have suffered to see it completed. In a thousand years from now it will still be standing. And if the sun and moon are still in the sky those who come to it will know that our Gods are the true Gods and have not failed us. Isn't that worth staying for?'

'We'll all be dead. We live now, here in this hut, not the future.'

'And what if we're reborn?' Hyra smiled. 'I have a faith to support me, you don't. That's the difference between us, why I can stay and you're going.'

Suddenly Atius knew that Hyra was right. The thought saddened him, but it wounded too deeply to be shared, so he smiled and said, 'It was I who made you carry on with the temple when Lyla was killed, yet now we know that Morrigen may have caused her death it's you who insist on staying. Don't you find that strange?'

Sensing the evasion, Hyra turned and looked at the merchant. His smile had faded and he was sitting beside the fire, gazing glumly into its embers. He knew then that Morrigen had broken him, that he was running away from her and didn't want to be told that there was nowhere to run to . . .

'No,' he said simply: and for Hyra that was the truth, just as for Atius the truth lay in tiredness and the need for peace.

At dawn the two of them walked out across the encampment and climbed the ramparts. No one had stirred and the rising sun offered its warmth as if to them alone. Rooks cawed round their rookery in the elms, one occasionally launching himself from the branches to survey the scrub below in solitary patrol.

Yes, thought Hyra, that's us; we launch ourselves into our lives and guard ourselves as best we can without really knowing why or where we're going.

*

Atius left that morning, watched by the entire encampment. Drums tolled in farewell and the crowds chased after him as he crossed the causeway, a single baggage-ox plodding in his wake. Those who had worked with him begged him to stay and openly wept.

Hyra and Morrigen remained on the ramparts. Morrigen's face was still discoloured and bruised and she did not speak as he turned on to the track leading to Henge. Hyra fought back tears. Atius: merchant, alchemist, builder, rogue – no definition seemed able to capture him; this man he had loved and now lost until death reunited them. He turned once to wave, then was gone. The last they knew of him was the roar that rose from the tents when he reached Henge. And with that farewell, perhaps the one that most pleased him, Atius passes from this story.

He touches it again only in the rumours, none of them substantiated, that reached Hyra in later years. He was drowned in the Western Seas with a cargo of gold. He was consumed by lightning for striking Morrigen and vanished without trace. A merchant bound for the Two Lands shared a tent with him in a sand storm and found him dressed in lion skins and chieftain of the tribes of the desert . . .

There are others, equally picturesque and improbable. But

the truth is less fanciful, for he returned to his mines and wealth, and with the passing of the years even his memories of Morrigen faded into the past. At first he felt lonely and would question traders as to what had become of her and Hyra and Ceruduc. He never saw Henge again. But he was to outlive most of his contemporaries. A slave girl whose freedom he had bought on the first day he saw her was even to bear him children. It is said that old men who met her felt they had stepped into the past, so much were they reminded of Morrigen. But even that remains rumour.

*

Four days later Morrigen and Hyra were alone in the Council Dwelling when the stranger entered and the final act of that season of holocaust could at last be played out.

He was a tall man, supple and muscular, and there were traces of Dobuni blood in his dark skin and curved fleshy nose. But there the similarities ended. For he seemed to pad rather than walk as he crossed the bracken, escorted by two members of Morrigen's bodyguard. He also, noted Hyra, had a curiously lopsided look that suggested a grafting of differing bones. Then there were his eyes. They stared through him, not at him; and though he was ṣoon to preceive that the loss of one sense had in some way been compensated by the distortion of another, they at first struck him as merely being globular and outsize, like those of a fish.

The two warriors appeared apologetic and slightly embarrassed by the intruder. 'We couldn't stop him,' said one. 'He insisted on seeing you.'

'Who are you?' demanded Morrigen, as the stranger halted in front of her, a large bundle gripped tightly in his hands. 'What do you want?'

There was silence. The stranger struggled to end it, just as he had done when driven from his father's hut with stones as a boy to roam the forest and teach himself the tricks on which survival depended. But now, as always, the result of his labours was a single incomprehensible grunt. He blushed, hanging his head.

'Show them, Shallon,' said one of the warriors.

He shuffled glumly for a moment, fighting shame, then lifted his head and opened his mouth. Morrigen backed away in disgust as she saw the swollen stump of his tongue. 'Take him away!' she cried.

'No! Wait,' said Hyra. The stranger was a mute, cursed at birth by the Gods for staying too long in the womb. All shelter would be denied him, no woman make space for him in her bed. But the years of persecution had branded him with a sorrow and humility that Hyra found impossible to dismiss. 'I've seen you before,' he added.

'That's right,' volunteered one of the warriors. 'He wanders the villages doing tricks to earn his keep. Someone once called him Shallon after the demon of Silence. The name stuck.'

'How long has he been here?'

'Since last night. We've moved him on but he kept coming back. He slept outside the High Priestess's dwelling.'

Hyra turned to him, smiling gently. 'You're here for a reason, aren't you?'

Shallon nodded.

'Try and explain. No one will harm you.'

Shallon hesitated for a moment, then lowered the bundle, his eyes shifting to Morrigen as he opened it.

Morrigen did not move as she stared down at the bronze axe and single boar tusk and let them bear her back into the past; the tusk to that first glimpse of him when she stood in the Maiden Lines, the axe to the rising and the war he had waged with it.

'They're Ceruduc's . . . !' whispered Hyra. He turned to Shallon. 'Where did you find them? Is he alive?'

Shallon shook his head.

'Where is he?'

Shallon lifted his arms and fluttered the tips of his fingers, then wrapped round them round his chest and began shivering.

'It was winter. There was snow,' said Hyra.

The mute nodded, miming a drift and himself digging into it. Then he stopped and pointed at the bundle.

'You found his corpse?'

Again Shallon nodded, this time glancing anxiously at Morrigen as if afraid of being disbelieved.

But Morrigen was oblivious to his presence. She had knelt and picked up the tusk and was pressing it to her face, now damp with tears. Nostalgia and sentiment had swept the arguments aside. All she remembered were the few moments of peace, his tenderness and laughter, the poor pleasures they had shared.

Hyra stared down at her, bewildered and angry as he recalled her indifference to Ceruduc's drunkenness and the way she had treated him. He frowned sadly. Leoid, Lyla, Atius – now Ceruduc; the ghosts measuring the years that had brought him and Morrigen to the present. A sudden sense of loss, and loneliness, made him kneel at her side.

'I loved him,' she murmured.

'You wronged him.'

'Yes. But it isn't too late to put that right.' Morrigen paused, tipping her head to one side. 'Is it?'

'He's dead, Morrigen. The wolves will have eaten him by now. Even if Shallon could lead us to the place where we found him there'd be nothing left. We can't even bury him.'

Morrigen shuddered, then glanced at the mute. 'Leave us. You'll be rewarded before you go.'

Shallon shook his head, refusing to budge. Before any one could protest he had reached down and brushed the tears from Morrigen's face. He rose, hurriedly finding two beakers and passing them to one of the warriors. A moment later he was walking on his hands across the bracken, arms extended, a beaker balanced on the sole of each foot. Morrigen laughed. Suddenly he flicked the beakers into the air, catching them deftly in his hands as he cart-wheeled back on to his feet.

Hyra smiled at the suddenness of Morrigen's change of mood. 'He's trying to persuade you to let him stay. He's either a wise man pretending to be a fool or a fool pretending to be wise.'

Morrigen clapped happily. 'He's a fool, of course! But he makes me laugh. Look!' she cried, as Shallon rolled himself into a ball and threw himself forward, somersaulting towards the entrance. 'You can stay! I need a fool, don't I, Hyra? Yes, yes. That's all I want. Silent, clever fools.'

Hyra looked at her. She was smiling and clapping and urging Shallon on. Ceruduc was already forgotten. He picked up the axe and retrieved the tusk from her grasp. When he left she was still laughing at Shallon's performance. She didn't even notice his departure. It was all as if nothing had happened.

*

Later that day Hyra ordered one of the unshaped lintel stones to be placed on its sledge and dragged from Henge to the site of Ceruduc's tent. A hole was dug where once it had stood. He placed the axe and tusk at its base and watched in silence as the stone was hauled upright.

It was only much later that he realized that an instinct of which Ceruduc was unaware must have led him to that copse to live out the years of his decline. For the copse marked the mid-point of a line between the end of the Funeral Way and Tyrus's grave. And as if that was insufficient an epitaph, it also acted as a foresight which when seen from the grave recorded the sunset at the equinoxes, the two days in the year when the hours of darkness and light are equal and the heavens are at peace.

*

So the winter had ended. And Morrigen could put the past behind her and make ready to claim her inheritance.

# BOOK III

# GODDESS

# CHAPTER XXII

The wind tugged at Hyra's cloak as he stared forward from the top of the stone. Snow covered the Plain, adding to the glare of the sun. For a moment he thought they had veered off course. Then he glimpsed the faded wind-torn pennant that marked the next stage of the route flapping from its post. He grinned. 'We're nearly there.'

'Today?'

'Easily. The men are in a hurry. They want to make camp and begin celebrating. They'll be too drunk to move by morning.' Hyra jumped down into the snow, slapping it from his boots before embracing Morrigen. 'We've one valley left, that's all.'

'We're not there yet. I'd better send out the hunting party.' Morrigen smiled at the unexpectedness of Hyra's embrace, then released him. She turned and tramped through the drifts to where some men squatted in the lee of a sledge, pointing westward across the snow-bound Plain. 'I saw deer there earlier. And this time don't leave them to the wolves.'

The men laughed. The excitement was contagious. Earlier in the winter, on the second journey from the Hill of the Stones, a blizzard had forced them to abandon their kill and take shelter. By the time the weather had cleared only the hooves and antlers remained.

Morrigen joined in their laughter. Once such an incident would have irritated and angered her. But if ever she had been happy, then the last three years were the years of that happiness. And now, in a single winter, they had sledged the last dozen stones to within a morning's haul from Henge. She smiled at the thought, then watched the men as they set out on the long semicircular trek that would carry them down wind of the herd. 'Shallon!' she shouted. A moment later the mute swung overhead, pole-vaulting the gap between two of the sledges, to land on his feet on the stone behind her. 'Have the shamans sound the drums.'

Shallon grinned, then vanished. The drums began beating,

the Plain coming suddenly to life as nearly a thousand men and women emerged from the temporary wind-breaks they had dug in the snow. The baggage-oxen were whipped into reluctant motion. The cables lifted from the wooden frames built over the fires to prevent them freezing. The clearing gangs picked up their ox-bone spades and started digging a track through the drifts, following the line of the marker posts. If was easy now, this was the third time they had retraced their steps along the same route, and the surface of the ice underneath was still firm and easily exposed.

Hyra took his place beside the leading sledge as the men checked the ropes linking stone to sledge. 'Remember!' he bellowed. 'Keep the slip-knots greased and be ready to run when you hear the whistles.'

The men grinned at the reminder: to forget meant being crushed alive when the sledge picked up speed. They strapped on their snow shoes, each being careful to make certain that the flints wedged into the bottoms to provide grip were still secure. The cables rose from the snow when the men spread out along their length and stamped their snow shoes into the ice.

Hyra looked round, again checking that the women sluicing hot water against the sledge runners to unfreeze them after the halt were clear of its path. Then he gave the order. The men jerked forward in unison, breaking the inertia, quickly settling into a rhythm as the sledge jolted forward and the runners slid crisply over the ice. As the pace quickened, more men went to the rear of the stone and took up the strain on the brake ropes. The ground began to slope. Ahead now it fell sharply away for nearly six hundred paces to the base of the valley.

Morrigen glanced anxiously at Hyra, unwilling to interfere but convinced he had left it too late. 'The whistles.'

'Wait!' Hyra's gaze swept to and fro between the runners and the angle of the slope. In his mind he was calibrating speed, distance, the optimum moment for release. Suddenly he cried 'Now!' Whistles shrilled. The slip-knots on the cables were freed. The hauling gang divided, dragging the cables with them as they broke into a run and hurriedly cleared the track. The sledge sailed silently past . . .

Morrigen grinned, instinctively nibbling a lip, as stone and sledge gathered speed; timbers creaking, runners tossing up a surf of splintered ice in their wake. The sledge lurched as it hit a dip in the ground, then straightened, accelerating and skewing from side to side as it hugged the contours of the slope. Soon it had reached full speed and she could hear the rasp of the runners, the bounce of the sledge as it tilted and swayed and slapped at the ice. The men watched in silence lest it veer off course, then began cheering as it gradually slowed pace, ploughing its way through the drifts in the valley until it finally came to a halt.

Three more stones still waited to follow the first, but now a second tradition took precedence as the men removed their snow shoes and raced each other to the bottom of the hill, brawling and throwing snow as they went. The sledge was moved to safety, another dragged into place and dispatched on its journey.

Even now, after a winter spent perfecting it, the sight of the sledges careering downhill had an excitement that never dulled. There were four such slopes on the route that had been chosen when the first snow-fall made the aurochs redundant. In combination they turned six days hauling into a morning's pleasure, the absence of all risk to the men more than compensating for having to repair and drag the sledges from the drifts if they left the track. And, as Hyra reminded himself, it was Morrigen who had thought of it, Morrigen who had selected the route, Morrigen who had inspired the men and brought them without loss of life to within months of Henge's completion.

He turned to watch her as she walked amongst them, returning their banter with the gaiety with which it had been given. It was becoming hard to remember the Morrigen of three years ago. At the time, as any Cunei might, he had seen the events of that winter as being bites on the same rotten apple: each was part of the whole. If Shallon's arrival with news of Ceruduc's death had reduced that apple to its core, it had taken time for Morrigen to recover from all she had suffered. At first she had isolated herself in her dwelling, then, at Hyra's suggestion, exchanged it for tents pitched on the Hill of the Stones. What Shallon's skills had started, Henge itself had completed. Together with Hyra, she had thrown herself into finishing the temple, finding in the problems it posed neither time nor inclination for brooding. Her spirits rose, her hair regained its length, the dewlap round her neck slowly vanished.

And now the advent of another spring had yet again seen a change in her beauty. For if in middle-age she lacked the bloom of their first encounter, she was still striking, still the gauge by which women much younger than her measured their beauty.

Hyra smiled fondly as he followed her progress amongst the men. The approach of old age has its side-effects, of which nostalgia is the most common. A year ago they had made love; loneliness and a wish to recapture the past making it impossible for Hyra to resist. The act had not been repeated, but like the one tree on an otherwise empty moor its isolation had exaggerated its significance. Even now Hyra's sudden blush of remembrance still proved he had yet to forget.

'We did nothing to be ashamed of,' she had said recently, snow bound in their tents whilst crossing the Plain.

'It wasn't the reason I stayed.'

'There's no point in trying to pretend I don't exist. We need each other. You calm me and still the evil in me. I give you something to fight against. You'd like to think that you stayed to finish Henge, that I mean nothing to you. But the truth is that we've been together so long that we'd be lost if we were parted.'

She was right, Hyra knew that. Living alongside her since her arrival at the Hill of the Stones he had realized that she had a hold over him he might never be able to break. Alone and childless, the truth might have been easier to accept. But Cronus's presence had bred guilt, left him feeling that he had been examined and found wanting. His son was fifteen now and had been initiated into manhood. He was still taciturn, still sullen, but the passage from adolescence to young man had fostered a rebelliousness and anger that made father and son seem like strangers.

'Why can't we be friends?' Hyra had asked him once, after another of the arguments that shaped their relationship.

'You know why,' Cronus had retorted. 'She murdered mother, yet you treat her better than you ever did mother. You've betrayed those she killed. Better that Henge be destroyed than Morrigen be forgiven.'

In essence, all their conflicts stemmed from that single root: Lyla's death and Morrigen's part in it. But Cronus's contempt had wounded Hyra, and he remembered it again as the last of the sledges was released to career into the valley and the men set up camp in the snow. After six years, Henge was approaching completion. Each day now brought nearer his promise to the children to return to the High Vales once the last lintel had been raised.

He glanced at Morrigen, laughing happily as Shallon juggled with balls of snow to amuse her. He had grown fond of the mute, sensing in him another and welcome ally in the struggle to help Morrigen control the turmoil still buried inside her. The men clapped and whistled as she attempted some juggling herself. Hyra turned away as he heard her laughter. To see her so cheerful could only make it harder to keep his promise.

A few days later the weather broke and the snow began to melt. The aurochs were driven across the Plain from Henge and the work of dragging the stones to the temple was able to start. And as tracks reappeared from beneath the snow and travel became easier, the first chieftains and emissaries again gathered round Morrigen.

For nearly three years she had been in permanent motion between Henge and the Hill of the Stones, governing the Cunei and their subject tribes from wherever each day's trek saw her tent be pitched. Thanks to her the Cunei's dominion extended from the Eastern Seas to the Forest of Souls. To the men she had become a mistress who bestrode the forests and downland like a mystic colossus. To the women she was living proof that someone of their own sex could give birth to an empire. Her energy and ingenuity were the hall-mark of every venture she initiated. It was she who proposed that groups of merchants be sent north, south, east and west – not turning for home until new lands had been reached and new oceans charted. Their eventual return added to the trading routes and introduced new skills. Cattlehide sails replaced the oars on the boats; woven fabrics became as common as skins; the first ploughs to be pulled by an ox cut furrows across the downs; Cunei craftsmen mastered smelting and the forging of bronze; new tracks boxed the compass as the lines of baggage-oxen bearing the wealth of the Cunei moved to and fro across the land. Seers and merchants collected round Morrigen as if at the court of a monarch. The chieftains respected her. Pampered, fêted, adored, her every gesture was interpreted as a portent from the Gods. The shamans had successfully proved – to their satisfaction at least – that she was the child of a union between Bala and Serapha: again and again she heard herself referred to as a Goddess. And still she was not satisfied: *only one thing is immortal, the reputation we leave behind after our deaths.* Hyra did not know it yet, but Kai's words when she first saw Henge were now driving her on. If Tyrus's death had ended all hope of founding a dynasty, there could be no such ending in the quest for immortality.

'Slow down. You've done enough,' advised Hyra, as spring became summer and the last stone finally reached the temple.

'I can't.'

They were alone in her tent. The shamans were chanting outside. A group of merchants awaited an audience. Other noises – the tap of hammers, the steady thump of the mauls shaping the lintels – were barely noticed they had grown so familiar.

'At least return to the Dwellings.'

'I need to keep moving.'

'You've no reason to any more.'

'Oh yes I have.' Morrigen swung round towards Hyra, trembling slightly. 'What happens to us when we die?'

Hyra frowned at the urgency in the question. 'You know that as well as I do.'

'Tell me.'

'Those who have sinned are consumed by the Seven Fires of the Underworld. The rest of us are taken to the Northern Star and later reborn.'

'I want to live forever. Here, on this earth.'

'You can't do that. None of us can.'

'Goddesses can. Goddesses can do as they please. I'd be all right if I was divine, it's being human that's so hard.'

Such was the intensity with which she spoke that Hyra suddenly realized that all she had achieved in the last three years had fed, not exhausted, her madness; that when she finally slowed down and returned to the Dwellings it would resurface, wilder and more uncontrollable than ever. He shivered, finally aware that those years had been no more than a marking time, the lull that precedes the storm.

*

Morrigen stared forward as her white ox carried her between the stones flanking the temple entrance. Whistles shrilled, rising octave upon octave until their sound became a screech capable of driving away any demons mingling with the crowds now cheering her arrival. Beyond the temple the Plain was awash with tents, livestock and smoke. Pennants lifted their colours against the blue of the sky, the neat milky clouds drifting in packs overhead.

In front of her stood the runners chosen to carry the news to the villages, the shamans holding aloft the tools with which Henge had been built. Beside the seers in their ceremonial cloaks lay the stone itself, the single lintel that once raised into place would end six years' toil.

She dismounted, grinning triumphantly at Hyra before taking a basket of bone-ash from the priestess at her side and scattering it against each of the stones. The inner arches, now a perfect set of horns, soared up round her as she walked amongst them, robed in white deerskin and the black feathers of the raven. The outer stones had been daubed red with ochre, then painted with vast green and yellow eyes that stared out at the crowds. Above them, resting on the circle made by the lintels, sat antlers and tusks, woodpeckers' beaks and the dried gills of salmon, ammonites and shells and the carapaces of sea turtles. The one space yet to be filled was bridged by the jawbone of a whale that had been brought from the Dwelling of Mysteries.

Morrigen halted beneath it as the Rites began, her red hair framed by the eyes on the uprights. Her priestesses moved into the Bear Dance, falling naked and dead when approached by a shaman wearing the mask of a bear, then rising reborn and liberated from its belly when touched by the bones that had been brought from the tombs. Drums began beating, summoning up the ancestral guardians of the Cunei to witness what was about to take place. Morrigen remained still, content to listen to the chants and the noise of the crowd. In her imagination her body had become weightless, so that for an instant it seemed to her that the Gods had lifted her from the earth and imbued her with their divinity, making her the Goddess she so yearned to become.

In honour of those who had died building the temple the chieftains were to lever the lintel onto its crib and lift it into place. They stepped forward and began the work; some old and all but infirm, some sons of friends who had fought beside Morrigen and Hyra during the final campaign against the Dobuni. Hyra watched them, silently mourning Ceruduc.

Once the lintel reached the summit of the uprights they began shifting it sideways, carefully levering the tongued joints protruding from either end over the lip of the neighbouring lintels until they were in line with the grooves into which they would finally slot. The crib was removed. One end was rocked into place. A minor adjustment – one last tap with a post – then the entire stone dropped on its bed, the joints locking as its weight forced it downwards . . .

The silence was brief. But for a moment it seemed to Hyra that the entire tribe had been struck dumb by what it had achieved. Then the noise became deafening as the crowds tumbled forward down the bank to begin the celebrations. The shamans scaled the stones and ran along the lintels, beating their drums as they went. The priestesses began dancing, their naked bodies wet with sweat, their feet kicking up the dust as they looped the stones and wove under the arches to press their bodies against the uprights forming the horns, symbolically coupling with them and in reward being enriched by Bala's fertility.

'We've done it!'

Hyra turned to see Morrigen grinning at him, hands held out to take his. He smiled uncertainly. 'Yes. Yes, I suppose we have.'

'You're crying!'

'Am I?' Hyra touched a cheek, staring intently at the moisture that had washed off on to his fingers. He gazed up at the stones, a slight unassuming figure with his windburned cheeks and greying hair. His shoulders slumped with tiredness. 'It's been a long time, too long. Now we can rest.'

'Henge isn't an end, only a beginning. There are other lands to be won, new skills to be learnt.'

'I've learnt enough, Morrigen. More than enough.' Hyra looked at her for a moment, then turned and slipped unnoticed through the crowds.

That afternoon he went fishing with Kirsten. In the distance they could hear the noise of the celebrations; but the river was silent, a black ribbon unwinding beneath the trees, its far bank bleached white where the spring floods had ripped at the turf and cast aside their flotsam. Birds sang from the forest. 'Listen to them,' said Kirsten, glancing at her father, then smiling and taking his spear from his fingers when she saw that he was asleep.

*

The celebrations continued for five days. At night, the moon bathing the Plain, cattle were slaughtered and goatskins broached. By day there were games, running races and wrestling. Only in Morrigen's dwelling was there no distinction between darkness and daylight. Torches banished the night and the gloom made night out of day. Chieftains and warriors filled its rooms. Sides of venison and beef moved endlessly between the kitchen quarters and the feasting chamber, ending up as bones to be picked over by the dogs who had gathered to scavenge.

With Henge finished there was now no reason for Morrigen to remain in her tent. She returned to her dwelling and her room with its view of Tyrus's grave. For a while she was content and glad of the comforts it offered. After a few days, in response to repeated requests that her dreams be made public, she decided to give way and allow their repetition as revelations from the Gods. Until now she had carried the tribesfolk with her by force of character alone. She could not see that the dreams meant pretending an alliance that did not exist. They marked a return to lies and the need for invention. She devised them when preparing for bed, adding or amending when she woke; the weather, farming needs, the various cults all suggesting ideas she could translate into a portent.

But despite the dreams and the bustle surrounding her, the years in motion had come to a halt. She grew restless and troubled. Hyra had taken refuge in solitary walks through the forest. Not even Shallon could amuse her. As the days passed and the tribesfolk dispersed to prepare for the harvest, the private Morrigen grew very different to the High Priestess who held court in the mornings.

The chieftains departed and the dogs moved elsewhere. Dust settled in the shadows. Soon cobwebs filled them and she would feel them breaking against her face as she prowled the empty chambers, a single torch lighting her nocturnal journeys into the darkness inside her. At first she was so dismayed by her change of mood and the speed at which her turmoil had gained control of her that she let habit dictate her actions. When certain that Shallon and her handmaidens were asleep, she would go to her lynxes, talking to them and entering their cage to lie her head against the soft warmth of their flanks. They never turned on her. If they snarled, she stared back at them until they finally blinked and lowered their heads. Whatever the reason for their acceptance of her presence, Morrigen preferred to think that she was partly an animal herself, that they had sensed in her some echo of the wildness they had lost and welcomed her company.

But the nights spent caged with her lynxes were only one halt on the ominous itinerary that ruled her sleeplessness. The ramparts saw her often, so too did Henge and the packed chalk that marked Tyrus's grave. The conversations with her dead son were one-sided and divided by silences. Soon the silences became hard to endure and she began answering on Tyrus's behalf, fleshing out the pitfalls and pleasures of a boyhood she could not accept as having ended. And then reality would claim her with the abruptness with which she had abandoned it, leaving her temporarily rudderless and unable to reach even the simplest decisions.

There was still another side to her insomnia. It was the breeding ground for her dreams and, as the crowds that gathered to hear them grew larger, so also did the portents themselves become exaggerated and extravagant. In Serapha's name she spoke of comets and monsters. She invented a giant who had remained motionless for so long that a tree had sprouted from his shoulder and birds built their nests in his beard. So fluent had these lies become that she began to believe them herself, and then could not remember what she had said. There was no retreat. The tribesfolk might think she was cursed or that her powers had deserted her. What at first had seemed a means of adding to her authority had, by a device of her own choosing, become essential to its continuation.

Scenting danger, she began speaking of herself, gradually investing herself with a sanctity that many interpreted as proof that she was Goddess. This notion gained credence. Wherever she went there was always someone who mentioned the celestial union that had created her. Soon she became convinced of their claims. To strengthen her case she adopted a pose and costume redolent of divinity. She wore only white and black. Her features grew serene and composed. She slowed her movements until it seemed to many that she was in permanent trance and enjoyed only transitory contact with the ground beneath her.

Hyra rarely saw her during the months that followed Henge's completion. The walks were an attempt to gain breathing-space, time in which to reach a decision. Cronus made it difficult. Impatient to be gone, already showing signs of the warrior, he brooked no excuses and permitted no lee-way. One day the children went with Hyra on his walk.

'I need rest,' said Hyra, as the familiar arguments flared. 'Yet you want me to leave at once and begin a twelve day journey to the hills.'

'You promised we could go as soon as Henge was finished,' retorted Cronus. 'But every day you find another reason for staying. Anyway, you've done nothing but walk for nearly a month. We could have reached the hills long ago.'

Hyra smiled. It was late afternoon and the sun had deserted the glades for the branches reaching up to it overhead. Cronus was right. Even now his children were struggling to keep pace with him as he hurried on through the forest. 'I'm Lord of the Rites,' he said. 'I can't just abandon my duties.'

'That's an excuse. We're still here because of Morrigen, mother's murderess.'

'Cronus!' cried Kirsten, intervening before conflict became accusation.

Hyra took her hand, calming her. 'I don't need my daughter to wage my wars,' he said, smiling at her blushes. If Cronus troubled him, Kirsten gave only pleasure. In the years since Lyla's death she had blossomed into womanhood, administering his household and mastering the rituals that governed it with gaiety and kindness. If she had a fault it was her beauty, for it left her prey to the warriors who mistook her vivacity for flirtation and acted accordingly. Hyra turned to his son. 'You're right. We're still here because of Morrigen. Because I first met her when I wasn't much older than you and I've the arrogance to believe she still needs me.'

'You're not her servant, father.'

'No. But I'm her only friend.' They began moving on through the trees. 'I'm worried by what I've seen of her since Henge was finished. You may mock me for walking alone in the forest like this, day after day, but it's given me time to think. Morrigen's mad, tormented by demons. But is her madness a necessary part of the genius that's achieved so much for the Cunei, or is it merely a sickness that's slowly destroying her?'

Cronus felt uncomfortable. It was the first time he had heard his father speak in this way, and it came to him now that he was treating him as an equal and friend, not just as a son. It also provided insight into the attitudes that had shaped his life, that made him so modest of his own achievements. 'I don't know,' he said quietly.

'And I hope you never meet a woman who forces you to find out. But if you do I hope you'll have the strength to try and help her. I must stay, just as you must go.' Hyra paused, suddenly at peace. He now knew that these daily ramblings had slowed him down naturally after the years in motion, allowed him to come to terms with himself without guilt, accept his age and his past and the knots that still held him to Morrigen. 'A father's shadow is no place for his son. The hills are yours. If you're old enough to fight me, you're old enough to be sworn in as chieftain and master of our lands.'

And in the excitement that greeted this announcement neither Cronus nor Kirsten noticed the sorrow on their father's face. He had committed himself to Morrigen, yet already he sensed that he might have left it too late, that nothing he did could now save her.

*

That evening he went alone to the Temple of the Heavens – even now he could not think of it as her dwelling. He had intended avoiding her for a little longer. But having decided to stay he felt the need to confront her, prove once and for all that the decision was right.

The temple was silent, only Shallon and a group of elders lingered in its rooms. Outside he could hear the priestesses chanting the evening Rites, the camp servants laying the dust by sprinkling it with water. The smell of lynxes hung foetid amongst the shadows.

Morrigen was alone in her room. Already, in the month and a half since her return, her beauty had begun to fade. A red rash looped her throat, scurf flecked her hair and the lack of fresh air and exercise had dried her skin and robbed it of its colour.

'You look sad,' she said, as Hyra drew the hangings behind him.

'I don't feel it.'

'Tired then.'

'Yes, tired. I was at Henge at dawn for the sunrise. We've start placing the foresights to mark the winter full moons.'

Hyra sat beside her. 'It's strange, even now I can't believe that it's finished.'

'Is it what you wanted?'

'It's what the Gods want that matters.'

'But if you were a God?'

'But I'm not.' Hyra shrugged. 'Sometimes I'm pleased, sometimes disappointed. It's only when you've built something that you can see its faults. There's more that could still be done. I'd like to line the Sacred Way with stones and cut a second line joining it to the Funeral Way. If we dredged the river and levelled the rapids we could float larger stones down it.'

A pause, then Morrigen said, 'You could be a God. You've heard the tribesfolk. If no one prevents it they'll make me a Goddess.'

'You must stop them.'

'Because it isn't true?'

'Yes.'

Morrigen held back. The seed had been planted, but he needed lulling and soothing before she could go further. She reached across to him, then fell back against the bolsters, pulling him with her. 'Do you ever think of the winter we spent in the hut?'

'Of course.' Hyra smiled as memory bore him back through the long troubled years of their lives together. 'We were younger, happier – even though we were being hunted.'

'We were alone, just as we are now.'

'You can't repeat the past.'

Morrigen smiled bleakly. In her world there was no past, only cause and effect, limbo and flux. She changed tack. 'You thought of Henge. Every one respects you. You're a greater man than either Atius and Ceruduc. To the tribesfolk you're a legend. Yet you seem unaware of it.'

'What do you want? You only flatter when you need something.

'How suspicious you are.' A hesitation. She half turned towards him. 'Perhaps only you . . .' It sounded glib and sentimental and not at all how she had planned it. Yet it was the truth. In the last few days she come to realize that all her actions since Tyrus's death had been ruled by the wish to win back Hyra. 'Is that so wrong of me?' she added.

'Please . . .' Hyra closed his eyes. But he could not close his ears: her words beguiled and he wanted to hear them. Nor his senses: the fire was warm and he could feel the press of her body when she rolled on to her side.

'It's the truth,' she whispered.

'Yet you abandoned me for Ceruduc.'

'I couldn't stop myself. He had started the rising. He was a chieftain and warrior. I thought muscle made the man.'

Leave, thought Hyra urgently. Now. Everything she touches she destroys. Every word she speaks has more than one meaning.

His limbs would not obey him. He opened his eyes to see her face close to his. Fire-light caught it, breaking it into flat tables of skin that had the hardness and coldness of stone. He picked out the lines, the wrinkles, the imperfections that swayed him by making her more human, less dangerous. Go, he repeated. But still he stayed. She grinned innocently, playing on his confusion with a confession.

'Sometimes I used to pretend that it was you I was making love to, not Ceruduc at all. Yet now there's no need for pretence you treat me like a temptress who's trying to possess you.'

'I came here to talk to you, for the sake of your company.'

'And what about me? Can't I have needs? Must I always act the High Priestess and mistress of the Cunei?' Morrigen rose as Hyra turned away, evading an answer 'Look at me!'

She was naked, her robes lay heaped at her feet. And such was Hyra's dismay that he could not fight her. What flattery had failed to achieve, her body corrected when she dropped beside him and guided his hands to her skin. She was gentle and calm, and for a moment he allowed himself to be misled into believing that he was draining her madness from her, recapturing the contentment they had shared in the hut.

Her mood and manner did not last. At first their bodies fitted easily together. Gradually Morrigen grew fiercer. Her fingers spread, ploughing his spine. Then her limbs straightened and her hair swirled round her when an instinct she could not curb compelled her body to simulate the motions of her lynxes. Hyra tried to halt her. But she could not be stopped, and so only broke free of him when she had taken what she wanted and saw the bewilderment on his face.

*

Silence.

Hyra lay as if paralysed by what her behaviour had revealed. Morrigen rose, slowly gaining control of herself by pacing the shadows until the energy still trapped inside her had finally dissipated. Dogs barked. The sounds drifting up from the Dwellings reached them as echoes of a world they had momentarily abandoned.

'I've been tricked. It meant nothing to you,' said Hyra sadly.

'Nothing? How can you tell me what I need? All men are Gods when they make love, yet you don't seem to realize that you could be one forever. You're afraid of letting go.'

She's delirious, thought Hyra, watched her glide to and fro through the gloom. 'I'm happy as I am,' he joked, forcing light-heartedness to help calm her.

'That's not true. You've known sorrow and suffering. You left Lyla because you were unhappy.' Now she had lulled him, she wanted to make him question himself, see doubts where none existed. 'Sometimes I think you threw yourself into building Henge in order to escape from yourself.' She paused. 'Become a God and there'd be no need for atonement.'

'You can't believe that! You'd still feel hunger and cold.'

'Did I complain of the cold when we fled in the snow? Did I plead hunger during the famine? They're human faults. The Gods don't acknowledge them. Nor do I.' Shadow concealed Morrigen's face. Her words might have been coming from out of the darkness or from something disembodied and without form. 'Don't be frightened,' she whispered.

'Have I reason to be?'

'No. It's just that . . . I've asked the shamans to make me a Goddess. They've agreed. I'm to be deified as Serapha made flesh on the night of the next full moon. I want you to become Bala. We'll both be Gods. It's what I want, Hyra. What I've always wanted. Gods live forever . . .' Morrigen's voice trailed into silence.

At first Hyra thought she was still delirious and not answerable for what she was saying. Then her eyes broke white from the shadows and he realized his mistake. He stared at her for a moment, too bewildered to know what to say. 'Are you seriously suggesting that we be deified?' he whispered.

'Yes.'

'You're mad.'

'Don't say that!'

'No one's immortal. The shamans can say what they like but it'll make no difference to you. Allow such a ceremony to take place and you and I will be responsible for creating Gods in our image, as man and woman. That's arrogance, a presumption of divinity. The sun is our God, the moon our Goddess. At the Rites we worship earth, water, fire and air – but never ourselves.' Hyra paused, searching for words to convince her. 'Do you really believe that when some shaman pronounces you a Goddess you'll suddenly become one?'

'I don't know.'

'Well you won't.' Hyra turned away, angrily shaking his head. 'I now realized why you seduced me. Why didn't you just ask me? My answer would have been the same if we were still in the forest. Your life's become so complicated that you can't even talk to me without concealing a simple question behind cunning.'

'I wanted to make love to you again.'

'Nonsense. It's a habit. You used cunning to win power and cunning to maintain it. Now you can't stop. But cunning won't make you a Goddess.'

'Please, Hyra. Let me try.' Morrigen lifted a hand, holding it out to him. 'I was so happy when we were building Henge. Now I'm so wretched again. I should have kept moving. Coming back to the Dwellings meant returning to Tyrus, all the souls of the people I've wronged. Maybe if I was a Goddess they'd leave me in peace and let my torment end?'

'It'll end when you're dead, not until . . . Stop it . . . !'

Morrigen had withdrawn her hand and begun biting it as hard as she could.

Hyra threw himself forward, making her lose her balance and release her grip on her hand. She held it up, revolving it and carefully surveying the broken skin that marked the imprint of her teeth. 'There was no pain,' she murmured. 'I could feel nothing. Nor can the Gods.'

Hyra rose and stared down at her, gathering breath. Without warning she suddenly hauled herself onto her haunches and advanced towards him, hissing, teeth snapping, hair veiling her face. He backed away, warding her off with his arms. Her hiss grew sharper, her motions wilder. He tried to calm her, finally aware that his refusal to approve her deification had severed the last links with her sanity, leaving an aged demented woman who could not be healed. She would not listen. He continued his retreat, hurriedly retrieving his clothes as she quickened pace and her teeth plucked at his legs. He looked down at her for a moment, trying to remember the youthful still unscarred priestess he had met beside the river. But the present imposed too strongly, and he saw only the animal she had become when she spun away and began circling her room as if to mark out her territory.

Then he turned and walked back through the emptiness and out into the night.

*

'Are you both ready?'

'Please, father. Can't we watch?' said Kirsten.

'No. We must leave at once. She won't forgive me for not attending the ceremony. I've been hunted before. We'll only be safe once we've reached the forest.'

The sun had nearly set and it was already growing dark inside Hyra's hut. Cronus glanced through the entrance at the bobbing torches moving slowly towards Henge. 'I'm going to fight her, father,' he said. 'I'll find the men, and the arms, and we'll . . .'

'Not now, please . . .'

Cronus turned and examined his father. The last twelve days had suddenly aged him; the threats, the tantrums, the remorseless attempts to break his spirit by first flattering and then threatening him with death all combining to speed the advent of old age: the lined despairing face, the eyes now dark and swollen from lack of sleep and the struggle to defy her. And by dawn she would have become a Goddess. 'We ought to go,' he murmured, hurriedly shouldering his bow and the bundle of food.

'Yes.' Hyra nodded but did not move.

'Come, father.' Kirsten took his arm.

'A little longer, that's all.'

Kirsten waited, aware that he needed this pause to mourn what he was leaving. She looked round, trying to see it through his eyes. Shadows filled the hut, but it was cold and gloomy and even the possessions they were unable to take did nothing to warm it. 'You may come back,' she whispered.

'No. She was a good woman, once.'

'Three nights ago she tried to poison us.'

'I know.' Hyra trembled, then tightened his cloak and stepped out into the twilight.

The sun had now set and a full moon sat balanced on the curve of the downs. It was bright and very close. Bats sliced the air in quest of food. The Dwellings were already deserted. The sole signs of life were the pigs rooting in the midden and the goats rolling in the dust to seek sanctuary from the gnats.

'Do you think she'll have missed you yet?' asked Kirsten, betraying her nervousness.

'I don't think so. I told her I'd join her at Henge for the ceremony.' Hyra looked up to where the domed roof of the Temple of the Heavens rose in silhouette against the sky. I should have told her. I've lied. We're sneaking away like thieves in the night.'

'There was no choice. Either you led the ceremony and made her a Goddess, or fled. If you'd told her the truth she'd have refused to let us leave.'

But even Kirsten's common sense could not console her father. Three years earlier it had been Atius who had run away from Morrigen. Hyra had watched him. Now he was doing the same.

They crossed the ramparts. In the distance, a squat pillar against the dusk, Hyra saw the stone marking his memorial to Ceruduc. They walked on across the scrub towards a group of tombs that lay clustered round the end of the Funeral Way. At one they halted to mourn the wife and mother that lay at peace inside it. They moved on again.

'We're going the wrong way, father,' said Cronus.

Hyra smiled, avoiding his son's gaze. 'I may not see her again. It won't take long.'

Brother and sister glanced at each other, then submitted, following their father on to the track leading to Henge. Soon they had company: the tribesfolk with the furthest to travel, the baggage-oxen and children, the herdsmen delayed by having to water their stock. Many were chanting Morrigen's name, and Hyra had to draw his cloak up round his chin to hide his face from the torches. Fires arched the sky, lighting the darkness ahead. There was a noise of wailing and drums.

Henge rose slowly above the sky-line. The tops of the stones glittered wetly in the light. From a distance they might have been rocks breaking surface in an inland sea. Gradually it drew closer. Hyra's emotions were held so firmly in check that for a moment he was able to study it as a stranger would have done when confronting it for the first time. The stones massed one against the next. The continuous circle of lintels holding it in place whilst weaving height and space into its massive skeleton. The glare from the torches lit some of the stones and left others in shadow, breaking its symmetry yet somehow suggesting that the temple itself was a source of light. Hyra smiled contentedly. Its ability to mirror moonlight and sun was one of the qualities he had most strived to capture. Then emotion intervened and so detached a scrutiny was no longer possible. Kirsten sensed his change of mood.

'Let's leave,' she suggested.

'Not yet.'

Hyra took his daughter's hand and let the crowd carry him closer to the temple. Not since his youth had he come to it as an anonymous spectator who had no part to play in the Rites. Determined not to let his self-control slip or his gaze return to the stones, he forced himself to look round and feed on its sights and sounds. Pedlars touted sticks of meat. A group of old men were gathered round some frogs being prodded with sticks in an attempt to make them race. Smoke drifted on the breeze. Women gossiped and calmed their babies, the men discussed the prospects for the harvest.

He smiled as he listened to their conversations. He found the continuity and outward normality reassuring, for they seemed to lend a purpose to Henge that not even Morrigen would be able to banish. His ears listened, but his eyes moved on – irrevocably drawn towards her . . .

'We ought to go, father. Someone may recognize you.' Cronus tugged at his arm.

Yet he had to watch, and now waited in silence as the crowd thickened, surging round him. There was a sudden awe-struck hush. The procession had been sighted. There were cheers. The tribesfolk began shouting her name. Then the procession loomed out of the darkness and entered the halo of light that ringed the temple.

Her lynxes led it, blinking against the glare. Then came the bears and wolves and domestic livestock. Behind them were the boars, wild cats, deer and other creatures of the forest. Ravens strutted in their wake. Naked men dragged cages filled with lizards and birds. Her priestesses carried shallow baskets bearing snails, spiders and hedgehogs. There were water troughs brimming with fish, snakes that hung wrapped round the arms of their bearers. Frogs, lambs and ruby-red foxes. Squirrels, beaver and wild-eyed hares. And behind them walked Morrigen, their mistress, the Goddess who had tamed them and in whose name they had been captured and brought to Henge as proof of her dominion.

Crab-apples and acorns hung from her hair. Sheaves of corn hemmed the white of her robes. Chalk coloured one cheek, ashes the other. Gold and silver dressed her throat and bare arms. And now her own name echoed through the temple as she took her place beneath the arch in its centre and scanned the faces of the seers, searching for Hyra.

'Where is he?' she demanded.

They pretended not to have heard, each shifting responsibility for an answer on to his neighbour. But Morrigen had no need of an answer. She knew instantly that he had failed her and finally abandoned her. For a moment her disappointment showed on her face. Her head slumped. All round her she heard cries of adulation and praise, the squawk of birds and the baying of wolves.

'He may yet come,' ventured one of the seers.

'He will never come.' Morrigen shivered, then straightened. 'We'll begin without him.' She stepped forward. Moonlight struck her face, intensifying the black and white of her cheeks.

There was no precedent for what was to take place. She had devised it herself, conceiving the passage from woman to Goddess as a sudden inward change that would emanate mystery and the knowledge of her immortality. It needed no props, no offering, no invocation. It would happen because Serapha willed it.

She waited, arms uplifted to the moon and her eyes staring out into the darkness.

The drumming quickened pace, growing louder, harsher. The wait lengthened. The seers shuffled uncertainly. Animals were whipped into place. Morrigen closed her eyes, her body tensing as she willed the proof she was waiting for. The air was close, almost oppressive. The sky was cloudless and the stars glittered brightly overhead –

One shifted, trailing a cone of light in its wake as it plunged closer to the moon. A second followed it, to glow yet brighter when it took up station again –

To the tribesfolk no omen of Morrigen's divinity could have

been more fantastical or convincing than so sudden a displacement of stars in the direction of Serapha. They threw themselves to the ground. The seers and shamans dropped prostrate in front of her. She shuddered, still waiting . . . then opened her eyes to see nothing but heads, bent like stepping-stones, stretching away into the darkness. Only the animals she had brought to witness this moment were ignorant of what had happened. They were watching her, bewildered, silent now, their confusion showing as a quizzical stare on many of their faces. She spun, but their eyes followed her, trapping and holding her in place. The noise was immense. Whistles had merged with the drums. She pressed her knuckles to her brow. Henge! As once it had seemed the place that might nourish her dreams, it now rebuked her for her vanity and punished her blasphemy. Suddenly she could bear it no longer. She screamed, then screamed again . . . as away in the darkness Hyra and his children moved unnoticed into the night.

# CHAPTER XXIII

'Ask her to come out. No one's seen her for nearly a year. What use is a Goddess if we can't see her for ourselves?'

'How do we know whether she's dead or alive? It's not right that she should shut herself away like this.'

'What's happened to Hyra . . . ?'

'What does she look like . . . ?'

'Why won't she speak to us . . . ?'

Questions, always questions and faces pressing in on him. And all Shallon could do was show the crowds the stump of his tongue and push his way into the Temple of the Heavens.

Once inside, he moved quickly through the rooms filled with priestesses and chieftains hoping for a glimpse of her; the warriors and lynxes who guarded her; the hangings and screens that hid her from view. A final post to avoid, a last curtain to push aside –

Her thin withered face would look up at him for a moment, then she would collapse back to the bolsters, content to lie there as he washed her face, changed her robes and prepared her morning meal.

Some days his presence seemed to revive her and she might exchange the bolsters for Tyrus's grave, solemnly talking to him until something snapped inside her and the charade ended. Unable to make a distinction between the real and the imagined, so also she made none between the living and the dead. Her son's heart still beat in her mind, his voice still spoke to her. Even Teina, Ceruduc and her mother peopled these conversations. By noon she might be asleep, tossing unhappily until the noise from the Dwellings woke her and it was time to return to the bolsters and sit waiting for nightfall in silence.

At first she had feared she might not survive the year now drawing to a close, that the combination of Hyra's inexplicable disappearance and the failure of the Gods to make her a Goddess might prove impossible to endure. In the end she had taken refuge in seclusion, becoming invisible as she had done as a child and allowing only Shallon to minister to her needs. In contradiction to her isolation, her reputation had continued to flourish, the mild winter and growing wealth of the Cunei adding yet further to the aura surrounding her. To the people she was a Goddess, to herself the most wretched of women.

The worst days were those closest to the full moon. As once they had provoked her to evil, they now cut the restraints on her sanity. Initially she tried controlling her behaviour by drinking potions to make her sleep, but the resulting nightmares were so much more terrifying than anything she did when awake that she finally admitted defeat. One night, when the temple was silent and the encampment deserted, she freed her lynxes from their cages and went with them on to the Plain. It became a habit. Her legs grew muscular and callused from imitating their lope. Her teeth sharpened. Her eyes grew accustomed to the darkness. She learnt to stalk a hind and distinguish the scents of the prey that gave her lynxes their diet. She was reverting to the wild, living by instinct, and in doing so had discovered that by allowing her madness free rein at night she could at least check it by day.

Her confidence grew, and when Shallon entered her room one morning shortly before the Harvest Rites she felt certain enough of herself to risk a public appearance. 'I'm getting better,' she told him. 'The people have the right to see me.'

Shallon could say nothing, but his eyes betrayed his doubts.

Morrigen swept them aside. 'I'm their Goddess. The sun and moon don't hide themselves from those who worship them, nor can I.'

Shallon did his best to dissuade her. She ignored him, dressing in the white robes of her divinity before abandoning her room and walking unannounced into the feasting chamber.

Silence. Those gathered there stared at her as if at a ghost. No one greeted her or pledged their loyalty.

'What's wrong?' she cried. 'You act as if I'd returned from the dead. Anyway, I ordered you to find Hyra, not idle and take advantage of my absence.'

Still no one spoke. Old age comes gracefully to the Cunei, the gentle weathered beauty of the women making the process barely perceptible. But Morrigen's beauty had been so immense, so much a part of the mythology that surrounded her, that few had ever considered that it might eventually desert her. But the Goddess who stood in front of them was as ugly as any woman they'd seen. The year of self-imposed exile had plundered her features and plucked her hair, leaving a wrinkled face and a red stubble that ran to grey where it hung lank over her ears. And the only person present who was unaware of it, was Morrigen herself.

Shallon drew closer, certain that their stares would end her ignorance, leaving her hysterical and in need of comforting.

'Where's Hyra?' she repeated.

'We cannot find him,' admitted one of the chieftains.

'And Cronus?'

This was more dangerous ground. The chieftain hesitated. Even after a year alone nothing seemed to have escaped her attention. 'He's still alive,' he said finally. 'He has about eighty men. They've attacked a village near the sea and taken shelter with the Eastern tribes. But he can't fight you for long. The Gods won't permit it.'

'Of course they won't. But I want him dead.'

The chieftain frowned unhappily. 'He's Hyra's son. You risk angering the villagers.'

'I don't care. He's guilty of treason and defying a Goddess. Arm enough men to hunt him down and bring me his head when you've done so. Go! All of you!'

Morrigen followed him into the mud. News of her reappearance had assembled the crowds. They fell silent, dismay at her loss of beauty fighting their devotion. She sensed their bewilderment, but failed to recognize its cause as she had herself lifted on to her bull and taken to Henge to celebrate the Rites. It was the first time she had entered the temple since the night of her deification. Old memories soured her mood when her priestesses began their dance. The day was dull and overcast. She could not concentrate. The stones appeared to be fragmenting and pressing in on her, becoming the souls of those she had wronged. She could feel the drums pounding in her ribs and filling her head with their boom. She shuddered, searching for Hyra. But Hyra was not there and so suddenly she began dancing, pirouetting and strutting and shouting at her priestesses when they failed to follow her steps. Those watching started whispering, embarrassed and alarmed by her performance. There was no rhythm in her movements. Her robes fell from her shoulders, revealing withered breasts and skin that was beginning to flake.

'She must be halted,' said the seer who had been appointed Lord of the Rites after Hyra's disappearance.

'And risk retribution for angering a Goddess?'

Morrigen was in a world of her own making. She pumped her arms, arching her spine and bending backwards to offer herself to the shamans. Her motions had become flagrantly sexual, but instead of suggesting supplication they were merely pathetic, the shameless posturings of an ageing woman.

The drums stopped without warning, stranding her in the centre of the temple.

'Who said you could stop?' she cried, turning on the shamans. None of them answered, nor did they lift their drums. She looked down at herself, following their stares. For a moment she tried to deny what she had seen. Then she backed away, clumsily covering herself from those watching.

There was silence. Then Shallon stepped from her retinue and led her away, unresisting and softly whimpering. She started to collapse. He picked her up, cradling her in his arms as he carried her through the silent crowd and began the journey back to the Dwellings.

*

That evening she went to her lynxes, calling to them the way a mother calls to her children as she approached. They growled in welcome, licking at her face when she entered their cage and pressed her cheek to their muzzles. She began talking to them; of the nights spent together out hunting on the Plain, of her wish that she was one of them, of her behaviour at Henge.

Suddenly intuition told her that she was not alone. She turned to see Shallon standing quietly in the shadows, his lopsided face striped by the bars of the cage. Curiously, she was neither angry nor ashamed. In his eyes she saw the understanding she had failed to find in the shamans and seers.

'How long have you been listening?' she asked. During the five years since Shallon's arrival they had evolved a language of signs and gestures that minimized speech. 'Since I entered the cage . . . ? He nodded. 'But you can tell no one.' He angrily shook his head, placing a hand to his mouth. 'I've upset you. I'm sorry. You wouldn't betray me even if you could.'

Shallon's eyes lit up with pleasure as he moved into the dim net of light cast by the tallows on the wall, his steps as silent as his tongue. Morrigen smiled as she saw the compassion on his face. 'It's strange, isn't it? The only man alive who shares my pain is a mute who acts the fool to amuse me.'

Shallon joined Morrigen in the cage. To her amazement her lynxes remained as docile and untroubled by his presence as when she had entered their cage. 'You've done this before,' she said, watching their long pink tongues rasping wetly across his cheeks. She smiled sadly. 'So both of us are in need of friends.'

Shallon grinned, gently embracing the lynxes before managing to explain by mime that he had seen her sharing their food and leaving the dwelling with them at night.

'I can't help it. You can't speak, but I can't be what I am. You saw what happened this afternoon. They were shocked, disgusted. If it happens too often they'll think that the Gods have failed me. Some of the chieftains may begin plotting to overthrow me.' Morrigen paused, holding out a hand. 'I'm frightened, Shallon. Hold me.'

He did so, clasping her so tightly he could feel the trembling in her body. She looked up at him. His cheeks were still damp and deep in his mouth she glimpsed the livid plug of his tongue. 'We speak but no one hears us,' she whispered. 'Sometimes I think we'd be better if we were all mutes like you, if the whole world was silent. We say things that wound and we do not mean. Our lives become lies we're unable to put right . . .'

Shallon put a hand to her lips, halting her flow. She was rambling and barely aware of what she was saying. And anyway he did not agree. He'd suffered silence too long to think it a blessing. Silence was the curse he had borne since childhood, the cause of the years spent an outcast.

*

Morrigen woke next morning to see Shallon standing beside her bed. Instead of lowering a basin of water, he tried to pull her to her feet, gesturing urgently towards the entrance.

'No!' cried Morrigen, resisting. 'They'll mock me and laugh at me. I refuse to let them see me.'

But Shallon persisted. He forced her upright, dragging her behind him through the crowded rooms. Rumours of her behaviour during the Rites had already reached many of the villages, adding to the numbers gathered round the entrance. There was the same shocked silence as she stepped outside. But although she now knew the reason for it, she did not flinch or evade their stares as Shallon led her downhill and into the encampment, the crowds following behind her.

'Where are you taking me?' she demanded.

Shallon pointed to the large circular dwelling in the lee of the ramparts.

'That's the Dwelling of Mysteries!' cried Morrigen, trying to halt. The dwelling was where the Rites of puberty and initiation were celebrated. Many thought of it as a place of magic. Even now Morrigen recalled averting her eyes from it as a young priestess lest the sorcery that went on inside it add to her barrenness. Antlers broke the cone of the thatch. When the wind gusted from the north it acquired the resonance of an instrument and the tribesfolk closed their doors, certain that the spirits of the dead were dancing in its emptiness.

'Why have we come here? asked Morrigen, puzzled by what the mute intended.

Shallon pretended to be unwell, then touched his skull and pointed at the dwelling.

'Are you trying to help me?'

Shallon nodded, leading Morrigen towards the shamans grouped in the entrance. She asked one of them if any special Rite was about to be celebrated.

The shaman glanced into the dwelling. 'A herdsman has been possessed by demons. The healers are going to exorcize him.'

Morrigen spun, to stare horrified at Shallon. Suddenly she understood. He had purposely brought her to watch in the hope that she would consent to being exorcized herself. She shuddered, unable to speak without being overheard. Again and again she had debated admitting her torment and allowing her skull to be opened, but always the dread of what might happen if the Rite went wrong had made her stay silent.

The shamans assumed she had come to witness the exorcism. Bone amulets were hung round her neck. A tress of her hair was carried as an offering into the gloom. A moment later she found herself being escorted between the posts that ringed the darkened interior.

Shamans chanted softly in the shadows. Soothsayers stood motionless, awaiting the manifestation of prophecy. There was an odour of must and decay, for all round her lay the skulls, bones and masks that were stored in the dwelling when not in use. A hoarse cry ended her inspection.

Ahead of her she glimpsed a young herdsman bound to a carved post in the central courtyard. Healers surrounded him. On the ground lay a triangular arrangement of snake-skins on which they had laid out their tools: lancets and flint flakes for trimming lacerations, oyster shells, a shark's tooth, some hafted fragments of obsidian. All of them wore rondels of bone taken from earlier trephinations, some still edged by part of the healed cicatrix. Ashes of human skull had been plastered over their heads to steady and guide their hands.

Morrigen turned to Shallon. 'It won't save me,' she whispered. He nodded vehemently, mimicking the release of the demons from her skull.

She shivered, switching her gaze to the herdsman. Fleece stuffed his ears and his body hung slumped against the post. Its grain was smooth, burnished by sweat and the motions of those who had stood roped to it before him.

His head swayed listlessly into the light, illuminating the portion of scalp that had been peeled from the bone. One of the healers lifted a flint-tipped bow-drill and placed it carefully against the herdsman's skull. His companions began circling the post, treading in the blood that had fallen from the wound until it had been absorbed into the dust, returned to Serapha. The bow-drill began turning, the gut that powered it twisting to and fro round its central shaft. Fragments of powdered bone began flecking the herdsman's hair. Every now and then the healer working the drill dipped it into water to cool the flint, then wiped clean the wound, leaving it a raw, glistening white.

The drill jumped slightly. The healer quickly withdrew it to avoid bruising the membrane beneath, leaving a ragged hole in the herdsman's skull. A second hole was started. Soon a dozen holes stitched a neat suppurating cluster round the segment of exposed bone. The drill was removed and replaced by a serrated flint, two of the healers taking it in turns to carry out the tedious, protracted task of linking the holes so that the complete rondel of bone could be removed. The chant softened, gradually fading into hush as the healers prepared for the release of the demons.

Morrigen had watched spellbound as the work went on. The drill's rhythm was almost hypnotic. The chant had been a monotonous dirge that rose and fell as each finished hole brought the moment of release ever closer. The herdsman appeared unaware of the pain. For a moment she even thought she could endure it herself if it ended her suffering. Many had survived the Rite. Free of the demons, she might finally enjoy the peace that had so long eluded her.

A young novice priestess was led forward in the hope that the sight of her virgin body would tempt the demons from their sanctuary. Her black hair had been drenched with musk. There was panic in her eyes, but somehow she compelled her limbs into a fluid suggestive walk as she approached the herdsman. The healers waited, then examined their patient. The novice was led away. They gathered in conference, finally ordering a caged swallow to be placed against the hole in the herdsman's skull. The bird was lifted from its cage. Its throat gaped open and its wings began beating when one of the healers raised it above his head. Suddenly he released it and ordered it to carry away the demons.

The noise returned the herdsman to consciousness. He began straining at the ropes, hurling himself from side to side. Morrigen turned away, appalled by what was happening. He started screaming. The clot had broken from the wound and a thin trickle of blood was seeping from his skull. The shamans nodded contentedly. The tantrum had ended his torment, the demons had left him. If he was to die now his soul would travel to the Northern Star to await the joy of resurrection.

Morrigen glanced at Shallon. 'Is that what you wanted? By nightfall he'll be dead. And so would I if I did as you want.'

Shallon despaired. In the world of the Cunei such words were blasphemous, final proof of the demons inside her.

But although Morrigen refused to submit to his wishes, the events of that morning lingered on in her thoughts during the days that followed. They served as a shock, a reminder of what might happen if her behaviour betrayed her or her decline continued. Her seclusion came to an end. Throughout that winter and the spring that followed she gave audiences, visited Henge, instructed her priestesses, discussed trade and tribal rivalries with the merchants and chieftains.

No one could explain the change. But once those who saw her grew used to her petulance and age it was hard to resist being bewitched by her presence. Her energy was undimmed. She missed nothing, no detail affecting the far-flung reaches of the empire she had created was too small to merit her attention. Thanks to her, an expedition was raised to prove that the lands of the Cunei were part of an island surrounded by water.

Thanks to her, contact was established with the tribes beyond the Dark Seas and the trading routes secured with a line of hill-forts. Although Hyra was not found, and Cronus not captured, she chose to ignore it, forgetting both father and son in the constant demands on her time. She ruled as if she was a monarch, holding court in the Temple of the Heavens and filling it with luxury and the advisors who helped her govern.

If the temple was her palace and Henge the spiritual heart of her kingdom, the Sacred Dwellings were its secular pulse. To house the endless visitors who thronged through its entrance, more dwellings lifted their thatch above the ramparts. Outside it, livestock pens and merchants' huts mingled with the hovels of the villagers who supplied it with food. Lines of tents ran north to the edge of the forest. Rafts and dug-outs plied the river laden with goods. Every month added another tongue to the babble of differing languages that echoed through the encampment.

Surrounded by evidence of all she had achieved, there were moments when it seemed to her impossible that the two Morrigens could continue to co-exist. By night she was still acting the savage and roaming the Plain with her lynxes, by day administering her lands and preaching the need for progress. Finally, after a series of incidents in which she was nearly discovered, she succeeded in breaking this pattern by carrying on with her work until long after dark and exhaustion gave way to sleep.

'But it can't last,' she told Shallon once. 'When the time comes I won't waste my life by trying to prolong it. Let them remember me as I am now, not as I was or might yet become.'

By late spring she had come to terms with the realization that her past was catching up with her again. Outwardly, she appeared unchanged. But inwardly the struggle to maintain her self-control had drained much of her strength. One morning she asked the soothsayers to predict the cause of her death. When they returned with their answer she knew at once that they were lying.

'You flatter me,' she replied. 'Yet you've told me nothing. You prophecy that neither sickness nor the hand of another will end my life. That's not enough. I want more. And this time I want the truth.'

'The portents are unclear. It isn't easy for us.'

'Then I shall make it easy. You either tell me by noon tomorrow how I am to die or risk death yourselves.'

The soothsayers filed anxiously from her room, plucking knowledgeably at their beards as if to suggest by a mannerism the powers they had been accused of lacking.

'I need to know,' said Morrigen, turning to Shallon. 'Is that so wrong of me? I've hardly slept for days. I can't eat. I'm becoming afraid to leave this room again. I look at myself in the waters and see an old woman who's the image of the mother she hated. Yet I'm a Goddess.' She gave a thin, troubled laugh; her thoughts running random and confused. '"Where's Hyra?" I ask. "Find him for me." They know but they will not tell me. So instead I have you. You, Tyrus and two beasts in a cage. A mute, a dead son and a pair of lynxes. And not one of them can speak to me . . .'

She was out of control. Nothing Shallon did could now halt her. Her breath reached her in gasps and her fingers were pulling at her cheeks.

'They're watching me. All they want is a reason to get rid of me. They plot and they whisper, just as I did when Ishtar was High Priestess. Even when I sleep I hear their voices. They're evil, Shallon, evil . . . !

Suddenly she was screaming and there was blood on her tongue from where she had bitten it to stop herself speaking.

Shallon calmed her, holding her close and locking her arms to her side so that she could not damage herself. Her body was shaking, her bottom lip raw, her eyes hollowed from lack of sleep.

'I'm all right now,' she whispered. 'You can let go of me.'

Shallon released her, watching carefully for any sign of a relapse. But instead she slumped to the pelts, still trembling and weak.

The mute opened his mouth. He twisted it, made a circle of it. He narrowed it, widened it – all in an attempt to form a word.

Morrigen sensed his struggle. 'Try!' she implored.

In all Shallon's life he had never attacked his silence with as much desperation as he was now employing. And in the end, as always, he could only grunt and hang his head.

'It's not your fault,' said Morrigen, determined to make amends. 'Nor am I to blame for what I am. The healers think we're cursed, but one day they'll realize that such things are an illness.'

Shallon smiled, not believing her, then resorted to mime in an effort to explain that most of what she had said was imagined. She had never asked after Hyra. No one was spying on her or plotting her murder. They were the product of her mind, fantasies it had invented.

She didn't understand. For when he finished she smiled and said, 'I'm tired. I must sleep,' just as if nothing unusual had happened and it was reality itself that was the illusion.

That afternoon she made herself perform her duties. But although those she spoke to appeared as courteous and attentive as ever, she knew that as soon as they left her they would begin ridiculing her. Again Shallon tried to make her aware of her error, again he failed. Eventually, in a moment of insight so sudden it frightened him, he realized that she did not want to understand him, that for some reason she actually enjoyed her wretchedness and had allowed it to become an addiction.

*

There was some truth in Shallon's diagnosis. For on the following morning, whilst waiting for the soothsayers to speak, her misery seemed to her to be a form of penance for her wickedness which no prophecy could lift.

'Well, have you done as I asked?' she demanded.

'We were wrong, just as you said,' answered one, a bow-legged and flustered man whose joy was quite obviously forced. 'At dawn we stirred the ashes and scattered them over the river.'

'And did they sink?'

The soothsayer attempted an obsequious smile. 'No. The wind carried them against the current.'

'You're lying!'

The soothsayer shook his head, taking refuge in allegory. 'It's the truth. As the ashes vanquished the water, so will you defeat death and the laws of nature.'

'Then you can prove it to me tomorrow. We'll meet at dawn by the river.'

The soothsayers tried to persuade her to accept the portents, but she refused to listen. 'I've lied too often to be fooled by others,' she told Shallon. 'This time I want the truth.'

And the truth was as she had expected.

Morrigen and the soothsayers assembled on the river-bank next morning. The dawn was chill and the sun lay hidden behind cloud. A silt-stained salmon broke the surface of a pool, idly slapping the water when it flopped on to its belly. A line of ducklings bobbed astern of their mother. Morrigen watched impassively as the ashes were scattered over the water – to be washed down stream by the current, sinking as they went.

The soothsayers protested. 'The Gods spoke differently yesterday,' said one, remembering her threat.

But Morrigen appeared not to hear him, nor did she carry out her threat. To Shallon she said, 'The Gods have spoken, but do I have the courage to obey them?' But apart from that one enigmatic acknowledgement of what had happened she never mentioned the incident.

Her mood veered from despondency to sudden outbursts of laughter as the day drew to its close. Both extremes were as illusory as the other. Yet her mind stayed alert, the proximity of death giving it a clarity that had long been absent. Her thoughts trawled the past, catching memories in their nets and then holding on to them in an attempt to find the answer she was searching for. At one point she recalled the loneliness she had felt on arrival at Henge when uncertain whether or not she was pregnant. Nineteen years had elapsed since then, exactly half her life. The equation had a neatness and logic that made her ponder it more. Then the answer suddenly lodged, making her shiver and cry out.

That evening she and Shallon sat alone in her room. Dusk had fallen. Outside in the twilight the seers and priestesses were welcoming the rising of the full moon. Another full moon, tugging at her as it tugged at the tides and compelled her to actions she could not halt. Its light found chinks in the thatch, streaking her face. She sat very still, her body occasionally stiffening as if a war was being waged inside her.

Shallon tried to amuse her by juggling with clay balls.

'Not tonight,' she said. 'I'm in no mood for tricks.' She rose and began circling the shadows. She poured a beaker of tassine and set it down untasted. Her motions were wayward, jerky, irregular. She kept touching things, shifting them and then moving on. Shallon watched her anxiously. The silence lengthened. Suddenly he felt her hands on his shoulders and turned to see her staring down at him.

'I want you to leave here, tonight. Go and not come back.'

He gazed at her in amazement, shaking his head.

'You've got to. There's no other way.'

Bewilderment became defiance as Shallon gripped the hangings behind him, refusing to move.

'Please, Shallon. I've never demanded anything of you before. I'll give you food. Go into the forest and stay there. You'll know when to return.'

The mute attempted to answer, but even mime failed him. Without thinking, Morrigen picked up a lump of chalk and walked over to the slate slab near the fire. She held up the chalk. 'Let this be your tongue.' Shallon hesitated, torn between relinquishing his hold on the hangings and risking being forcibly thrown out if he disobeyed her. Finally he joined her, uncertain of what was expected of him. She handed him the chalk. He placed it between his fingers, looked down at the slate, then scratched a single tentative line on it. 'Now place another line beside it . . . Try shaping a roof . . . There, you've drawn a hut.'

Shallon grinned, momentarily forgetting her request as he stared down at his handiwork. It was rough, it was crude, the strokes did not match, but it was nonetheless a hut. In his excitement he began covering the slate, attempting a spear and a bow, a distended ox with horns and legs.

Suddenly Morrigen realized that by accident she had stumbled on the one discovery that had eluded Leoid, a means of communicating by shaping images, a language that could be written instead of spoken. So lucid were her thoughts that she understood at once that with time and practise and in more gifted hands than Shallon's she had touched upon an invention that would one day change her world and make Henge and the tally staff redundant. Cut smaller slates, she thought, use common symbols that can be taught to every one, and we'll have found a way of recording knowledge, even passing it on to those who live after us.

She turned to Shallon. 'Now draw what you wanted to say.'

But the chalk would not do what Shallon asked of it. The skill was too novel. All his life he had known silence, and this tongue he had suddenly acquired refused to shape the pictures he wanted. More frustrated by his disability than he had ever been as a mute, he struggled in vain to explain that only since meeting her had he known human company and what it meant to have a home and a purpose.

Morrigen sensed what he was trying to say. She shuddered, taking the chalk from his fingers. 'I could call in the guards. But I won't. Nor am I trying to wound you or sending you away for no reason. I want you to embrace me, then go.'

Shallon stared at her, afraid and still confused. Her voice had the tone of a farewell. Her face was pale and her eyes would not look at him. Suddenly he realized that there could only be one motive for her request. He began crying, then walked forward and placed his arms round her. Her body felt thin and frail, almost brittle. He could feel the beat of her heart and the tears on her face. Then he understood that only by going and leaving her to her loneliness would she find the courage she needed.

When he released her she fell slackly against him, then straightened and backed away. He turned and walked quietly from her room.

*

Afterwards, with benefit of hindsight, a few of those who observed Morrigen closely in the aftermath of Shallon's departure were to compare her to a candle that flares before it gutters.

At the time the analogy went unnoticed. But flare she did, drawing from the reservoir of her strength an energy and vitality that made old men reminisce and remember her as she had been during the rising and when building Henge. On a white bull, propped by wattle, her retinue struggling to keep up with her, she toured the downs and forests of the lands she ruled. She visited villages, mines, grazing grounds, the Hill of the Stones. She ventured into the Great Marsh and the overgrown ruins of the fortress where she had met Ceruduc. She returned to the village of her birth, caves where she once had hidden, the site of the last battle against the Dobuni, the empty clearing where she had nursed Hyra back to health. For her, this progress had the quality of an inventory, an inexplicable need to revisit all the places she had touched during the long years of her climb. Those who saw her later recalled a stooped withered old woman with a scrap of bright red hair and green hawk-like eyes. She remained in motion for sixty days. And then, with as perfunctory a warning as she had given when announcing her departure, she came to a halt, returning to the Sacred Dwellings and refusing to budge from the Temple of the Heavens.

For three more days she endured her loneliness and the memories she had rekindled whilst travelling. Then she was ready.

On the evening of the fourth day she ordered her handmaidens to dress her in the white deerskin of a High Priestess of the Cunei. She put on her amber necklace and her head-dress of ravens' feathers. Alone again, she took the dagger that Atius had given her and placed it beside the fire, then went to her lynxes and opened the door to their cage.

They followed her into the night, padding silently in her wake as she climbed the ramparts. Reaching the summit, she removed their collars, pointed to the distant shroud of the forest, and said, 'Go.' They would not leave her side. She began pleading, telling them that she had given them their freedom and hoped they would hide deep in the forest where no net could end their liberty. When they still did not move, she descended on to the Plain and began the journey to Henge.

The night was warm. A thin seam of cloud veiled the moon and the stars burnt weakly behind it. She walked slowly, breathing deeply and savouring the scents that came to her on the breeze. She could hear sheep plucking at the grass, feel the spring in the turf, see the spread outline of the oaks clinging precariously to the slopes of the downs. Yet it was only when she heard a soft growl and looked back to see her lynxes slipping quietly into the darkness that she was finally content.

Henge broke the sky-line, a brooding inanimate ghost staring out over the Plain. For she saw it now not as a temple, not even as something she had helped create, but as the legacy she would leave behind her; the immortality in stone that had eluded her in the flesh. She smiled and went forward into its embrace. The stones rose round her, cradling her, at last supplying the peace she had feared she might never find. But the knowledge of what still had to be done abbreviated her solace. She turned, hurrying back to the Dwellings lest her resolve weaken.

And there only the empty rooms of her dwelling waited to

greet her. They offered nothing but echoes and the light filling the skulls overhead as she walked beneath them, dagger in one hand, torch in the other. Moths came flapping towards her to die in its flames. Her body felt decrepit and uncomfortable, as if it was borrowed and not hers at all. Occasionally she rehearsed what lay ahead by guiding the dagger towards her robes, pinking the skin beneath. She knelt beside Tyrus's grave, then stared up at the moon. Its face was still hidden but she could see the perimeter of the cloud and knew that when Serapha broke free the moment would have come. She began crying, the tears finding the creases in her cheeks. She tried to speak, but no words came. She smiled contentedly. Then moonlight bathed the courtyard and she raised the dagger and there was a sudden dazzle of light before the darkness sent her falling, falling, falling into a long lazy somersault that flung her backwards into the shadows.

# CHAPTER XXIV

It was nearly noon, but the mist had not yet lifted. It still muffled the sounds of the forest and hung tiered round the trees, reducing their shape to the dark line of the trunks and the outline of the branches overhead.

A stag loomed from the shadows, adding to the courier's unease. It shook its antlers, bounded noisily over a fallen oak, then disappeared into the murk. The courier quickened pace. The mist thickened, rolling dankly round him and reinforcing the fear of all forests drummed into him as a child of the open Plain. He was young and callow and lost. The villagers with whom he had stayed overnight had provided detailed instructions on how to reach the clearing. He frowned unhappily. Even after a month of searching he was uncertain how to break the news. The nearer his destination, the greater his misgivings. So when he glimpsed the bones floating above him in the mist his initial reaction was panic, the conviction that he had stumbled into the lair of wood sprites or monsters. Then he remembered his instructions and pushed on through the undergrowth. The breeze lifted, briefly scattering the mist and revealing the branches from which the bones were hanging. Beyond them, blackened and wrapped in ivy, a single oak rose from the centre of the clearing.

'Who's there?' A woman's voice, calm but alert.

That must be his daughter, thought the courier. He halted, then shouted. 'I've come from the Dwellings. The Council sent me. I'm looking for Hyra, son of Cronus and Lord of the Rites.'

A pause, some whispering. A moment later an old man appeared out of the mist, leaning heavily on a stick.

The courier tried to hide his dismay. Instead of the legend who had served in the rising and conceived both Henge and the Temple of the Heavens, the man who confronted him was dressed as a shaman in moleskin. He appeared older than his years. His beard was full and grey, lined cheeks betrayed his age. The courier fell at his feet, nervously rehearsing what he had to say. They had once been close friends, he recalled, perhaps lovers as well. He anxiously cleared his throat.

Hyra smiled at his visitor's hesitation. 'Please stand,' he said quietly. 'I'm a rainmaker now, not Lord of the Rites.' He paused as Kirsten rose from the fire and hurried to join him, taking his arm.

'So she's found us,' she murmured.

'She's . . .' The courier broke off, unable to say it.

Hyra lifted him to his feet. 'It's all right. You needn't be frightened. We won't resist. Even when we first came here I knew she'd finally catch up with us. And my son, has he been betrayed as well?'

'She's dead . . .' whispered the courier.

The breeze had strengthened, tugging at the leaves and rocking the smaller branches. No one spoke. Hyra collapsed slightly, his body trembling. He tried to straighten, but his muscles ignored his command, forcing Kirsten to steady him.

'She was found a month ago, in her room,' went on the courier. 'We've been looking for you ever since. Her handmaidens went into her in the morning. She was already dead. There was nothing the healers could do to save her.'

'Did no one know she was unwell?' murmured Hyra.

The courier hesitated. Then said, 'She killed herself. With a dagger . . .'

Another silence. The mist was beginning to disperse. Steam rose from the trees as the first shafts of sunlight cut their way through the shadows.

'No one betrayed you,' added the courier. 'Cronus has returned to the Dwellings and taken his place on the Council. It was he who told us where to find you.'

Hyra was no longer listening. It was all too sudden and finite to take in. Cronus was safe, Morrigen dead. He knew that the shock had yet to come, but that when it did his emotions would switch from joy at his son's return to a grief that would be hard to control. He touched his face to find it damp and cold. Already he was travelling backwards through the past towards the young woman he had seen in the Lines, naked, embittered, already scarred. He turned to his daughter.

'I must prepare an offering for her soul.'

Kirsten stared at him in amazement. 'No, father! She'd have shown you no mercy if she'd found you. She never stopped hunting us since the night we fled. I'm grateful she's dead. She killed others, it's right she should kill herself. Don't become a party to her sins by mourning her now she's dead.'

'She was a great woman, the greatest of her age. Others will build on the foundations she laid. Don't forget that when Tuah first came to this oak the Dobuni still ruled us.'

'She was a murderess!'

'And we murdered her. We expect too much of those who lead us. We ask them to be virtuous, and in doing so shape their vices. We court them, flatter them, make them believe that they can achieve what can't be done. If Morrigen was evil, it's because the Cunei demanded the impossible of her and forced her to try and give it to them. We all share her guilt, and all of us are poorer for her dying.'

There were tears in Hyra's eyes and his voice had cracked as he spoke. But watching him, the courier began to understand the dignity and strength that had won him his fame. His mother and sisters had died at the hands of the Dobuni, his father had fallen in battle. He had seen his wife crushed by a stone, his son hunted and his friends precede him to the grave. Yet there was no bitterness to him. He seemed to have shrugged his suffering aside, leaving his humanity untouched.

'Was it one blow?' he said suddenly.

The courier nodded. 'Yes.'

Hyra sighed, smiling for the first time since the news had been broken. 'So her courage didn't fail her. I'm glad.' He paused, then lifted his arms and began chanting the Song of the Dead.

Kirsten stayed silent as she waited for him to finish. As the only witness to the two years of his exile, she had seen him age as he fretted about Cronus and tried to accustom himself to the unfamiliar hardships of forest life. She had comforted him when dispirited, shared his pleasure at the way the local villagers had accepted him as their rainmaker and misled the warriors who were searching for him. Unhappy herself, she had done her best to hide it. But she now realized that her own exile was drawing to a close; and smiled to herself as the courier's glances told her that at seventeen her beauty had not suffered during the years of seclusion. Life lay ahead of her, and she longed to reach out and grasp it . . . Her father had fallen silent, the courier was speaking again.

'I've other news. Cronus is waiting for you at Henge. He and the Council hope you'll return with me to the Dwellings and take office as Lord of the Rites.'

Hyra surveyed the clearing, purposely evading Kirsten. 'I'm staying,' he said finally. 'This is my home. As once I built Henge, now I make rain and turn back the wind for the villagers. It would be wrong to abandon them.'

'Don't be silly, father!' cried Kirsten. 'The villagers won't mind. Of course you must leave.'

Hyra smiled. 'Must I? I'm an old man. I've nothing else to give. You need company, I want solitude.'

The courier intervened. 'With Morrigen dead, the chieftains are beginning to quarrel. Only you have the authority to keep the peace.'

'And risk losing it for myself? No, I'm staying. Let Cronus finish what I started.' Hyra paused to indicate the skull perched on the summit of the oak overhead. 'My father. My son brought him here. He may have cursed me for taking him from the hills, but I swore I'd never move him again.'

Suddenly Kirsten knew that there was no point in arguing. On the day of their arrival she had sensed that he might always remain here, that somewhere in his past he had touched a dream in this clearing and had come back to search for it.

The following morning Kirsten and the courier left for the Dwellings, leaving Hyra alone. When the forest had swallowed them, he picked up his fishing spear and set off for the stream. As he walked, he thought of the evenings he had spent with Morrigen by the river, of the sudden openness of her smile. Of Lyla and Atius and Ceruduc, those she had bruised or destroyed. Of Henge and a snow bound hut, her limbs lacing his. All memories now, healed over without trace or seam.

The stream was silent. The rain he had smelt in the morning was no longer in evidence. Drowsy high summer and the sun on his face. He hesitated for a moment, as if still held by the past, then walked down the bank and into the water.

# AUTHOR'S NOTE

Stonehenge's history is so complex, the questions it poses so many, its purpose so open to speculation and so easily incorrectly interpreted, that at times it may seem like a riddle intended to baffle or provoke. What follows are merely clues.

Stonehenge's construction roughly spans 1,500 years, beginning in about 2,800 B.C. with the digging of the bank and the erection of the Heel Stone, and ending in about 1,300 B.C. with the re-erection of the bluestones in their present setting. *The Priestess of Henge* is set in about 2,100 B.C., a moment of much significance, and continued archaeological debate, for it marks the removal of an unfinished double circle of bluestones – originally brought from the Prescelly Mountains in Wales – and their replacement by the existing sarsen circle and the inner trilithons, and their lintels. The use of stone in this way, some weighing 50 tons, remains unique in neolithic architecture: it has no precedent, no parallels, and no imitators.

But Stonehenge cannot be isolated. Within a few miles lie thousands of burial barrows. Sites such as Avebury and Woodhenge are as relevant to the way of life that spawned Stonehenge as Stonehenge itself. To some of these sites modern man has assigned a complex geometry and the most sophisticated of astronomical purposes. Many regard them as testimonials to a primitive Eden. But if anyone should doubt the hardships of the early Bronze Age, or think that fact and my fiction share no common ground, let me remind them that excavations at Woodhenge have unearthed the remains of a young child whose skull had been deliberately cleft before burial.

Such evidence, though often exaggerated, is hard to dismiss. In the fate of that three-year-old child can be seen the fears and superstitions that shaped the lives of its contemporaries. If my fiction does them less than justice, if the authors whose scholarship I have plundered disagree with the use I have made of it, the fault is mine alone. I can but hope that the reputations of all of them, both the living and the dead, will continue to flourish.